MURDER
at the
Portland Variety

FORTHCOMING BY M. J. ZELLNIK

Murder at the Rose Paperworks

MURDER

at the

Portland Variety

A Libby Seale Mystery

M. J. Zellnik

Midnight Ink
Woodbury, Minnesota

First Edition
First Printing, 2005

Book design by Donna Burch
Cover design by Ellen Dahl
Cover image © 2005 by PhotoDisc

Midnight Ink, an imprint of Llewellyn Publications

Library of Congress Cataloging-in-Publication Data
[To come.]

Midnight Ink
Llewellyn Publications
2143 Wooddale Drive, Dept. 0-7387-0786-4
Woodbury, MN 55125-2989, U.S.A.
www.midnightinkbooks.com

Printed in the United States of America

For Grandma

ONE

From the moment she entered the lobby of Crowther's Portland Variety, Libby Seale could tell something was amiss. The first clue was the quiet. Normally the building was abuzz with voices, running through a song or dance number on the stage, sometimes accompanied by the piano in the pit. Even if no acts were rehearsing, there should have been the inevitable hammering as stagehands assembled the scenery for incoming acts. And it was dark in the lobby, as if no one had turned on the electricity yet, or even lit any of the gas lamps used to conserve energy when the electric lights—still a novelty in 1894—were off. The only light came through the dull windows of the box office, making the theatre entranceway look grey, despite its bright red carpeting.

Slipping through a side door that led backstage, Libby hung her coat on the peg in the hallway and gathered up her purchases. She was later than usual in getting to the theater and needed to get the fabric and notions she had bought on her way into work into their proper cubbyholes before starting to sort out the mending. Her job as assistant in the costume department at Crowther's meant she helped the wardrobe mistress with any and all of the varied costuming needs of a busy vaudeville theatre, even if that entailed running errands in the hours before work officially began. Today this had included several stops on her way into work to buy the material and trimmings for the new set of dancers' costumes, and she had gotten lost twice trying to find her way around an unfamiliar part of town. But she was in no position to complain, since her status at the Variety was only temporary. She was very much hoping that, when the time came, they would offer her a permanent job. She had arrived in Portland only six months before. In that time, she had still failed to find a secure means of earning her way in the world.

Where on earth *was* everybody? The backstage area was never this quiet the afternoon before a show, especially when new performers were arriving and settling into their small dressing rooms with varying degrees of audible discomfort. Crossing the stage on her way to the costume shop, she saw May hurrying toward the stage from the aisle. May was one of the youngest members of the resident ensemble, "The Dancing Whirlwinds," and Libby had taken a liking to the quiet, sweet girl who tried to act so worldly. In fact, right now, with her fearful eyes and tear-stained cheeks, she looked more like the thirteen-year-old Libby suspected she was than the sixteen-year-old she had claimed to be when Mr. Crowther hired her.

"Miss Seale! Isn't it terrible?"

"What is it, May?"

May looked up at Libby with her big blue eyes. "Didn't you hear about Vera? I mean, Miss Carabella?"

"What is it about Vera, May? Is she still here?" Vera Carabella had been a performer in one of the featured acts, "The Electrical Magic of Signor Carlo," but their run had ended the previous Saturday night.

"She's . . . she's dead!"

With that, May's eyes started welling up, and she grasped Libby's arm to steady herself. "I have to go. The other girls are waiting for me out front, but I left my bag in the dressing room. Mr. Crowther cancelled the show and sent everybody home."

A thousand thoughts ran like lightning through Libby's mind. It felt like she had just seen Vera only moments ago! "What happened?" she asked the girl as gently as she could. "An accident?"

May shook her head. "The white slavers got her! Just like they got some other chorus dancer a few months back." Libby heard the words, but they sounded so far-fetched that her mind refused to make sense of them. Her face must have registered this incomprehension, for May went on, eyes bright and feverish, without any prompting from Libby.

"That's how I got my job here. They found one of the Dancing Whirlwinds in the tunnel beneath the theater, dead! And everyone said that it was white slavers that got her, too! They say they take girls through the tunnels and put them onto ships headed for . . . well, I'm not sure where . . . All the other dancers were so upset that, for a while, no one in the city would come in and audition for the Variety. And they lost some of the other dancers who worked here because they quit." Now that the topic had shifted to matters theatrical, May had lost her fearful look, and burbled like a child. "So, when Mr. Crowther put out the word that there were positions in the chorus open, I . . ."

Libby had to break in, "But what about Vera, May? What happened today?" She tried hard not to sound exasperated.

"The police were here when I arrived. They said some workmen in the tunnels found Vera's . . . body this morning, right in the same spot where they found Polly . . . that was the other dancer, Polly. And then one of them—a policeman—said to watch my back. Then, when they thought I was gone, I heard him say to the other one that girls like dancers and actresses had to expect this sort of thing." She looked indignant.

Before Libby could frame the multitude of questions that popped into her mind, the girl started off toward the Whirlwinds' dressing room. "I have to go! I'll see you tomorrow, Miss Seale."

Mechanically, Libby made her way to the wardrobe room, released her armful of packages in a heap on the table, and sank into a chair.

She couldn't quite believe Vera was dead. While they hadn't been close friends, she had gotten to know Vera well over the magic act's four-week engagement at the Variety. Libby was too busy to become friendly with most of the featured performers, but circumstances, in the form of a backstage accident, had brought Libby and Vera together. The very first week that "The Electrical Magic of Signor Carlo" was playing the Variety, Mr. Maynard, the theater's bookkeeper and office manager, had spilled a brand new bottle of India ink all over the front of Vera's costume, ruining it beyond repair. Vera had been frantic at the loss of the gown, which was only a year old. It had been made for her at great expense in San Francisco, and she had been enthusiastically grateful when Libby (until six months before a seamstress for a large and fashionable New York dressmaker), had managed to whip up a stylish and sophisticated new dress overnight.

Libby would have been the first to admit that the gown itself could never have been called high fashion, since the front of the peacock blue skirt was cut away in a wide swag to reveal Vera's shapely legs. Even so, it had an air of elegance that lifted it (and presumably Vera as well) out of the realm of the vulgar. Vera had been delighted by it, and she and Libby had been fast friends from that moment on. Libby now found some small measure of comfort at the thought that the dress she'd made had brought the doomed performer some happiness, for perhaps one of the last times in her life.

At that moment Hatty Matthews, wardrobe mistress, came through the door carrying a load of costumes that was every color of the rainbow and almost as tall as she was. Hatty was in her early fifties, with jet black hair (enlivened by a few strands of silver just above her forehead) and classically Asian features. Though she was tiny, she had the strength of an ox, as well as a no-nonsense but motherly disposition that endeared her to Libby and everyone at the Variety. Her husband, now deceased, had been a British soldier stationed in Hatty's native Hong Kong, but when exactly she had come to these shores, Libby didn't know.

"Oh, good, Libby, you're here." Hatty said, putting down the mending with a sigh and flopping down on a chair. Her English was nearly flawless, but since she had learned it as a British colonial, one could hear traces of middle-class British pronunciation nestled alongside the Eastern coloration of her l's and r's.

"Hatty! Did you hear about what happened to Miss Carabella?"

The older woman gave a sad sigh and pushed her spectacles up on her nose. "Oh, yes, it's tragic. The police were here all morning, talking to Mr. Crowther in his office." She looked at Libby with concern. "You were friendly with her, weren't you?" Libby nodded. "I was going to ask you to stay and help me with the mending, but if you would like to go home, that's certainly all right."

"The mending!" Libby blurted out. "How can you think about mending now?"

"Life goes on," Hatty said quietly. "Best not to let the bad things keep you from doing what needs to be done."

"May told me it was white slavers. It . . . that . . . sounds like something out of a penny dreadful! Surely there aren't really white slavers right here in Portland?" She had read about all the crime and mayhem here in America's "wild frontier," but with all the worries and fears she had about being on her own in a new city, it had not occurred to her to worry about an illegal trade in kidnapped women.

"Ah, sit down, my dear, and I'll tell you what I know. You have heard of the Shanghai tunnels running under the city, I assume?"

"I think so." When she had first arrived in Portland and was doing piece-work for local tailors, one of them had regularly received deliveries of imported silks and other materials via a basement entrance to his shop. He had explained to Libby that many of the cargo ships delivered their packages via the tunnels that came up from the harbor. "They're those tunnels that go down to the waterfront, aren't they?"

"Exactly." She added dryly, "I'm sure you have noticed that it rains a bit in the Pacific Northwest. The tunnels were built to make it easier to deliver cargo in inclement weather. Or so they say. I wouldn't be surprised if they were really built to make it easier for smugglers and thieves to navigate the city underground."

Hatty went on to tell Libby of the criminal gangs that preyed on both men and women, drugging them and spiriting them down to the waterfront for nefarious purposes. In the case of the men, they would wake up on a strange ship at sea, only to find they had been sold to the captain of a vessel in need of a crew. Since many of the boats were headed for China, the term "Shanghai" became common parlance for the crime ("to Shanghai") as well as the tunnels. If Hatty had any personal feelings about the fact that it was the land of her birth that was being slandered by this slang, she kept them well hidden.

The fate of the women abducted was murkier, and all Hatty knew were the rumors . . . that attractive girls were sometimes abducted from the seedier bars in the area, taken on ships far away from their homes, and from anyone who might rescue them, then stranded in remote parts of the world, unable to return home. The saddest part was that, once a girl had been ruined in this way, she was effectively unable to ever return home, even if she could find the passage, since her reputation and virtue would be in shreds.

"So our theater basement has an entrance to these tunnels?" asked Libby, fascinated. "May said something about another body being found under the theater a while back. A dancer here . . . ?"

Hatty cut her off, anticipating the rest of her question. "My, my, no wonder you're so upset. Please, don't go thinking this sort of thing happens all the time at the Variety. But yes, it's true enough. I suppose it would have been a little over two months before you started working here. There was an unpleasant incident involving one of the showgirls here, but it was something she brought upon herself. Her name was . . . well, she called herself Polly Pink. She was . . ." She squeezed her eyes closed, apparently trying to come up with a delicate euphemism, "a gay girl from the streets trying to move up in the world, and people here thought that's why she was killed. They say she must have let a man into the theater after hours, someone she knew from her previous line of work, and he drugged her, then dragged her into the tunnels through the basement, intending to sell her to the white slavers. They found her dead down there with the drugged rag still over her face. Apparently, her killer had used too high a concentration of chloroform in his attempt to subdue her, and she died."

The more Hatty told her, the more apparent it became to Libby that there was a whole world of unsavory characters and criminal activity that she never read about in the papers. It made her wonder whom one could trust to get an honest assessment of any city or town. As she looked out the small grimy window at the city street, Portland seemed newly menacing, as if she had never really seen it before.

Lost in her reflections, it was a few minutes before she realized that Hatty was no longer speaking. Instead, the costumer was looking at her with a mixture of pity and exasperation. But when she spoke her voice was kind. "There isn't any point dwelling on the crime, Libby. Let's get to work; these aren't going to mend themselves." With that, she looked meaningfully at the pile of costumes.

Hatty was right, of course. Best to move forward and throw herself into her job, rather than endlessly analyze the circumstances that led to Vera's death. With difficulty, Libby turned her thoughts to the tasks at hand.

A few moments later, as she was diligently darning a torn stocking, Hatty asked her if she had gotten the new buttons and ribbons. With a start, she remembered her purchases, though it seemed like days ago that she had bought them. "Oh, Hatty, I got the loveliest yellow brocade for the new Rickshaw Ballet costumes, and I found some dear little pearl buttons reduced for quick sale at Prager Brothers, which might work on those spats . . ." For the first time since she had arrived at the theater that day, a sense of normalcy returned.

The rest of the day passed slowly, the theater almost empty without any of the performers. The one loud interlude in the day occurred when Signor Carlo, the magician whose assistant Vera had been, flounced into the theater and proceeded to mourn her melodramatically. Ostensibly, he was at the theater to supervise the moving of his trunks to the railroad depot, but having waved the bored and taciturn movers towards the dressing rooms, he flopped down in the middle of the stage, practically begging for attention. He spotted Libby, who had been drawn out of the wardrobe room by all the noise, hovering in the wings.

"Oh, Miss Libby! My Vera, *la mia bella,* she is gone!" He jumped up and grabbed Libby to his chest in an expansive Mediterranean hug. "You have heard what those monsters, those animals, did to her!" Theatrically, he bowed his head for a moment of silent reverence. But just a moment.

Then he commenced a tirade espousing the theory that whoever had done this awful deed was obviously trying to sabotage him. The rant encompassed everything from the horrible backstage conditions at this theater to the fact that Portland had always shown too little respect for the great talents of Signor Carlo. Libby, who had seen him perform, found the word "great" a bit of an overstatement. In her opinion, Carlo (who called himself "Signor" although Vera had confided to Libby that the closest he had ever been to Europe was New Jersey) had almost no talent whatsoever. The fact that he put on a likable-enough act was primarily because he was canny enough to make Vera's blatant sensuality the center of attention.

It was common knowledge among the types of men who frequented theaters that a magic act was a good chance to see a beautiful, scantily-clad woman contorting herself into boxes or behind nearly-transparent screens as the magician worked his illusions. All Signor Carlo's tricks had required Vera to wriggle her body to and fro: he made doves fly out from beneath her dress and found a shiny gold piece behind first one ear, then the other.

The highlight of the act was the "electric chair" trick, in which Vera supposedly allowed 20 volts of electricity to course through her. With elaborate showmanship, Carlo waved a magic wand, to which an electric light bulb had been attached, up and down over Vera's seated body. Sure enough, as the bulb grazed Vera's arms and shoulders, it lit up seemingly of its own accord. As he raised the wand, her hair rose up with a crackle and her shapely legs, tied to the chair, shuddered slightly. Carlo worked this magic, complete with patter about the awesome danger of electricity when not properly controlled, and the crowd was always silent, fascinated.

The one night she had sat out front to watch the show, Libby had glanced around the audience during this trick and noted with a smile that the men down front seemed particularly enamored of it, or more likely of the cutaway slit up the front of Vera's blue dress. Several of the men were regular stage-door Johnnies, who filled Vera's dressing room after every evening performance. As Carlo waved his electric wand, Vera had aimed a few winks directly at this crew, but Libby suspected this was all for show. Not once in all the weeks Vera had been in Portland had Libby seen her accept any offers for late-night suppers or drinks. Vera knew how to play to the men and accepted their flowers and compliments, but she was wise enough to know that to favor one man in particular would be to lose the adoration of the throng. Libby realized now that, after all of the men had left every night, Vera was left in her tatty dressing room with nothing but a lot of overflowing vases. She wondered sadly if, beneath the glamorous façade, Vera's life had been lonely.

Recalling the magic act's true star, she suspected that Signor Carlo, who was still reciting his litany of woes, was in even worse shape career-wise than perhaps he realized.

"And tell me what I am to do now?" Carlo was saying. "I have to go back to San Francisco and find a new girl, and then take all the time to train her, and—*il Dio mio!*—it is all too horrible to think about. Not that Vera did so very much in the act, you understand. As long as there still is a Signor Carlo, the act will rise again! But yet, she had a certain style, my Vera."

He slumped against the proscenium arch, then glanced surreptitiously at his watch. "Where are those moving men? I must be at my train in five minutes! There are nothing but lazy, no-good people in this city. They must hurry . . . I will stay in this city not a minute longer than I have to! It is a lawless place that would do such a thing to my *carissima*. What sort of a city is it that treats Signor Carlo this way?"

Without waiting for an answer, he rushed through the wings toward the dressing area, yelling about having a train to catch. During his entire speech, Libby had not said a single word, not that Signor Carlo seemed to notice. All the way from backstage and up the stairs, she could hear him instructing the porters how to carry his trunk, yelling about its delicate contents and swearing that he would have their heads if they dropped it. Libby noticed that whenever he got angry or flustered, his Italian accent slipped from thick to nonexistent. With a sigh, she headed back to her sewing.

TWO

MRS. PRATT WAS ALREADY at the breakfast table finishing a piece of lavishly buttered toast when Libby came downstairs the next morning. From the looks of it, it was the tail end of what had been a hearty breakfast, complete with eggs and bacon. Libby, who unsurprisingly had not slept too well, practically recoiled at the sight of the greasy bacon platter. She was also unprepared, in her sleep-deprived state, to cope with Mrs. Pratt's current state of excitement.

"Tsk, what is the world coming to? We'll all be murdered in our sleep one of these days, I'm sure." Mrs. Pratt paused, but only for a moment, to place a cup of coffee in front of Libby. "Terrible, terrible." She was pointing to the front page of the newspaper, and before she even looked at it, Libby knew what story Mrs. Pratt must be up in arms about. Sure enough, even from across the table, Libby could see the far-left column of the *Portland Gazette* proclaiming: *Cold-Blooded Murder In The Shanghai Tunnels.*

"Oh, my dear, I'm so glad you came down for breakfast before I left for church." A devout Irish widow, her landlady went to mass daily, praying for her departed husband (and, Libby assumed, for the continued health and well-being of her pampered housecats). She pointed to the headline, as if Libby would have missed it. "I assume you'll be starting to look for a new place of employment first thing this morning?"

Libby didn't answer, but since Mrs. Pratt didn't pause to wait for one, the omission was not noticeable. Mrs. Pratt continuing speaking as she picked up one of the cats and stroked it with increasing vigor.

"Oh, but this town used to be such a safe place, before all these outsiders and foreigners came to town! Back when my dear Brendan was still here, God rest his soul, he would say to me, 'Maggie,' he would say, 'when they bring that railroad all the way to Portland, it's bound to bring trouble along with it.'"

Behind that reference to "outsiders" lay a distrust of almost anyone born outside of the United States (or Ireland). Here on the West Coast, Libby had found, anti-Chinese sentiment was a powerful force. Libby often heard casual slurs against "those wicked Chinamen with their secretive ways," as if they were deliberately stealing jobs from white men. And even as Portland's matrons shopped in the local Chinatown for imported fabrics and porcelain with which to decorate their overstuffed parlors, they never wavered in their belief the Chinese had nothing to offer America. Just yesterday, while shopping for the trim for the Rickshaw Ballet costumes, she had heard a sales clerk refer to all the Chinese as "Yellow Devils." It was this forthrightness, this open display of prejudice in Portland that she found particularly shocking. Back in New York, she had not been exposed to it on such a regular basis.

Sometimes Libby wondered if Mrs. Pratt's distrust of "outsiders" extended to non-Christians—she had never actually mentioned to her landlady that she was Jewish. At first Libby had assumed she must know, but now she was pretty certain the fussy older woman had no idea. There never seemed an appropriate moment to bring the subject up and find out for certain, and so she let the matter slide, from day to day and week to week, telling herself that she was sure it wouldn't make any difference. Now she wondered if she was being naïve. Though she had been shielded from them growing up in an insular Jewish neighborhood in New York, Libby knew there were people in the world who reviled the Jews as much as the locals did the Chinese. She gave a small, sad sigh. Intolerance and violence everywhere, she thought, dark reflections of all the bright and shining marvels this century could offer.

"Aye, he was a wise man, my Brendan." Mrs. Pratt paused, lost in nostalgia, and then gazed intently at Libby, finally noticing she hadn't spoken at all. "No, I don't suppose you can afford to just quit your job, can you, Dearie? But you will promise me you'll come home straight from the theater every night, won't you?"

Libby actually smiled at the earnestness behind the plea. Mrs. Pratt certainly could talk her ear off, but her heart was in the right place. She appeared to genuinely care about Libby, and the slightly hectoring tone she used actually endeared her even more to her, as it reminded Libby of happy mornings at home with her mother. The thought prompted a pang in Libby's heart. When, if ever, would she sit across the breakfast table from her mother again? Libby spoke for the first time that day, her voice slightly scratchy, "I promise, Mrs. Pratt, I will be careful."

"You're not getting sick, are you?" Mrs. Pratt reached over and felt Libby's forehead, gazing at her intently as if trying to diagnose the problem. "You didn't actually know this . . . showgirl, did you? At the theater, I mean?" Her landlady's tone grew sympathetic. "She was a friend?"

"No, I didn't know her very well at all," Libby lied, a forced lightness in her voice. It was simpler to lie, and she really didn't feel like discussing Vera right now.

Mrs. Pratt looked unconvinced. "I'm sorry, Miss Seale. I should have seen you were upset. Father Callahan will understand if I miss mass today. I'll stay here and sit with you."

"No, please. I'm really quite fine. Please don't change your plans for me." All Libby wanted was a chance to drink her coffee in peace, and perhaps see what the paper had to say about Vera.

"Well then, I'll be off to mass, but you eat your breakfast and don't give the cats any of that milk!" She pushed herself up from the table and left, cats mewing at the door after her.

To quiet them, Libby placed her saucer of milk down, as she did nearly every morning, and lifted up the newspaper. To her surprise, she found she couldn't bear to read the story about the discovery in the Shanghai tunnel after all. Somehow seeing the news of Vera's death printed in black and white would make it so much more difficult to bear. Putting the paper down, she sliced herself two thick pieces of Mrs. Pratt's excellent, homemade oat bread, topped them liberally with butter and cheese and placed them in the warming oven. While she waited for them to toast, she scanned the front page for anything other than the story about Vera to occupy her thoughts.

There was little in the paper that would qualify as good news. The most prominent story on the front page was devoted to the ragtag collection of unemployed men and drunkards in California who had banded together, calling themselves "Coxey's Army" after the Midwestern folk hero who'd sworn to march on Washington and demand jobs from the US government. It wasn't just California either; the whole country was in the grip of a depression, and all across the West, drifters and unemployed men swore to reclaim their jobs back from the foreigners and unfair bosses.

She moved on to a story about the continuing Pullman strike. President Cleveland was once again threatening serious action if the striking railroad workers didn't get back to work. Somewhat mitigating the harsh tone of that particular piece was a small article next to it, which suggested that Congress was about to make the first Monday in September a legal holiday in honor of all laborers. She skimmed both articles, munching absentmindedly but contentedly on her toasted cheese bread, without really absorbing any of their content. It took all of her concentration not to glance at the story jumping out from the left side of the page. Finally, buoyed up by a full meal, she felt she could face reading it.

She needn't have bothered. Despite the eye-catching headline, the story was little more than filler, and contained no more information than she had herself, and in some cases not even that much. Most of the text was devoted to the mayor's statement to the effect that this horrible crime was indicative of the general decline of morals in the city. Clearly, an increase in law enforcement downtown was sorely needed, and if reelected, he would address that very issue in his second term. The mayoral election was only a few months away now, and to Libby's eye it looked as if the mayor was using Vera's death merely as an opportunity to grandstand. The article didn't mention Vera's name until the last paragraph, and they couldn't even get that right, referring to her as "Vera Carbello, a dancer employed by the Portland Variety." With a sense of disgust, Libby tossed the paper aside and went back upstairs to prepare herself for work.

The boy came out of nowhere, barreling directly towards her as she turned the corner from Third onto Taylor. He clutched a large sack to his chest, dripping what looked like it might be blood, but before Libby could take a closer look, the boy sprinted past her. A block or so behind him she spied a commotion, as several men chased after him. A ruddy-faced, overweight man in a bloodied apron stopped to catch his breath, shaking his fist at the retreating figure, shouting, "Catch him! That's over three dollars' worth!"

She had been walking from her tram stop slower than usual, almost dawdling, since she was not looking forward to another long day fending off memories of Vera, but abruptly all sluggishness vanished. Dropping her bag where she stood, Libby sprinted off after the boy. She had a commanding lead over the crowd of men down the street, and she could see the boy breathing hard as he ran only about thirty feet in front of her.

She reacted completely without conscious thought, with a reflex born of her childhood experience watching over her father's fruit stand on Rivington Street. As a young girl, she had often chased after some youth who had pilfered an apple or pear, aiming to hold the thief by the collar until her father could catch up. Back then, there were few boys she couldn't outrun, and she was almost always successful in catching them. But as she ran down Taylor, beginning to gasp for air, the thought entered her mind that perhaps this particular race had not been a good idea. Even at ten, her father had disapproved of his daughter running through the streets, and (losing steam now) Libby was forced to admit she was no longer the runner she had been at ten. Her overworked lungs felt trapped inside her constricting bodice, and her skirts felt incredibly heavy.

But it did feel good to be using her body, to be pushing herself to her limits. Despite her hammering heart, the thrill and excitement of her exertions were helping to dissipate the heaviness she had been carrying around all morning over her friend's murder. Even as it became clear Libby had no real hope of outrunning the young thief, the attempt was helping dispel the sense of impotence she had felt ever since hearing about Vera's death.

The boy turned onto Front Street and headed for the docks, and Libby finally came to a ragged stop. She knew she would never catch him now. The waterfront, with its big ships and piles of cargo and supplies, would provide an endless array of hiding places. Of all the areas in the city, the blocks along the Willamette River were universally considered to be the most dangerous and lawless. She reckoned the boy would have no trouble finding a safe place to hide in exchange for part—or all—of his loot.

A crowd was gathering around Libby. The men who had been running behind her had also given up on the chase and were catching their breath and straightening their clothes. One of the men who had been most actively chasing the child, a big disheveled fellow in workingman's clothes, weighed in. "Little devil headed for the docks. No way to get him now."

She heard the murmur of high-pitched voices and snatches of conversation on all sides, evenly divided between comments about the thief ahead and her own inexplicable and unseemly behavior. "Did you see that?" "He was trying to bunco the butcher!" "Who on earth is that girl?" "Well, I never!" But Libby ignored them, or tried to, suddenly very self-conscious about her impromptu, and very public, sprint. A burly police officer, distinguished by his dark blue serge jacket and official-looking badge, joined the excited mass of people and, noting only one breathless woman in the center of a crowd of men, made his way towards Libby with a scowl.

As his large hand tapped her shoulder, she flinched reflexively. "Would you like to tell me what's been going on, Miss? Exactly why were you running down Taylor Street like some madwoman?" The policeman towered over her, and Libby felt like a little girl again. It was almost as if her father were suddenly there, reprimanding her as he used to. *What were you thinking, Libbeleh! You bring shame to our family!* But this time she had no reason to feel guilty, did she? And yet when she spoke she sounded nervous. "I was trying to catch that boy. I assumed he must have stolen something, and when he ran past me . . ."

"You mean you had no idea what, if any, crime had been committed and yet you took it upon yourself to chase this alleged criminal?" Libby realized the murmuring crowd had quieted down, and she felt very exposed, as if everyone around her could tell she didn't belong here. This wasn't her father's fruit stand on the Lower East Side, and she certainly wasn't a young girl anymore, free to run in the streets like a child.

By now, the fat man in the bloody apron, who turned out to be a butcher, had caught up to where the crowd was loitering and marched up to the officer. "Same boy got ten dollars' worth of prime steak from Allan and Lewis last week. And nobody puts a stop to it! I don't know what this city is coming to." The butcher shook his head in disgust, though whether at the crime itself or police incompetence it wasn't clear. "I heard about Allan and Lewis, and Sym's Wholesalers the week before that, and I was sure I was ready if the boy set his sights on my store. I instructed my apprentice not to let anyone sign for credit unless that person was known to us by sight. But before we could ask him to sign for it, the boy just took the load of steaks I had wrapped up and started running away. I didn't even realize what was happening until he was halfway down the block."

"Yes, I see." The officer gave a great sigh, indicating his displeasure at the thought of having to write up a report on this sort of thing. Libby took the opportunity to turn away and quietly leave, but the policeman raised his hand, motioning her to wait while he finished with the butcher. "I suppose you'll have to come down to the station. Not that I suppose there's much hope of getting the boy now." He turned to Libby, "And you . . . I have half a mind to take you downtown as well. Creating a public spectacle that way." He suddenly realized that the crowd around them was watching eagerly, waiting to see if the law would really go so far as to take a young woman into custody for chasing a thief. As if sensing this would not be a popular move, he grumbled after a long moment, "Very well, go along. But I trust this is the last time I'll see your face at one of these disturbances."

Libby's face was burning, and she kept her head down and headed off in the direction of the Variety. She was mortified, wanting only to disappear. What *had* she been thinking, running down the street like a banshee? Why did she constantly do exactly the opposite of what she ought to do? *To come home in such a state, Libbeleh! Always with you it is something.* Why couldn't she respond to life's struggles with the calm strength of her mother? Her mother, who had always gently (or sometimes not so gently) tried to keep her from making the mistakes that would inevitably bring down the wrath of her iron-willed father.

All her life, Libby's mother had cautioned her against being so impulsive, and all her life, it seemed, Libby's father had been disappointed in her. She recalled a steady stream of grim lectures from him that ran right up to the terrible night, just days before she had run away from New York. *Whatever you have done, you must somehow try to make it right. It is your duty, no matter how painful. Your behavior dishonors our entire family . . .*

She had to go back home sometime. She knew that. But she was still not ready. Every fiber of her being told her that if she went back now, nothing would have changed. If she went back now, she would only run away again. Running away from New York had been just as instinctual, if just as wrong, as her behavior today, when she dropped her bag and sprinted after that thief.

The thought of her bag made her realize she had left it lying in the middle of the street. She had to retrieve it before she continued to the theatre, even if it meant that (once again) she would be late. And what if it were gone? Oh, that would be the last straw! Nervous, she turned to head back and found herself face to face with a man, quite a good looking young man, regarding her with a crooked half smile. In his arms he carried the large carpet bag she had just remembered.

"Yours, I believe, Miss? You seem to have forgotten all about it in . . . your haste," he said, rather formally, but his eyes still smiled.

Libby blushed slightly and reached for the bag with a subdued "Thank you." He held on to the bag and gave her an appraising look. She steeled herself for the inevitable lecture about her unladylike behavior which would come next, but he surprised her.

"It's a pleasure to see such . . . civic mindedness in a woman," he deadpanned.

She wished he would just give her the bag and let her go. "It was probably foolish of me to have reacted that way when the boy ran past me. I don't know what I was thinking."

He seemed to realize she thought he'd been making fun of her. "No disrespect intended, I assure you. I was being sincere." To be fair, Libby recognized there was no disapproval in his voice, which carried discernible traces of the East Coast. He bowed his head sheepishly, "And, I must add, I would have been no help. I can make no claims to athletic prowess. While you . . ." he paused. "Well, if they ever get around to holding that modern Olympics they've been arguing about over in Europe, you for one will be all ready to go."

So he *was* making fun of her, but lightly. She surprised herself meeting his eyes with a smile. "I fear the modern Athenians are no more liberal in their views than their forbears, and I suspect they won't allow women to compete." His crooked smile reemerged. "At any rate, I really must be going," she added. "May I have my bag, Mr. . . . ?"

His smile became a full-fledged grin, as he swept his hat off his head with his free hand, "Peter Eberle, Miss . . . ?"

"Libby Seale."

"You're from New York?" It appeared he had noticed her accent, too.

"Yes." She smiled.

"Well, Miss Seale, I'm glad to see the New York schools provide a solid grounding in Ancient History. And I insist upon walking you to your destination, in case you are tired from your Olympian labors and need a helping arm."

At that, she actually blushed. What an odd conversation this was to be having, thought Libby, with a complete stranger at the intersection of First and Taylor. This Mr. Eberle was flirting with her in a most outrageous fashion, and what surprised her more was that she was tempted to flirt right back. Almost as if she was Vera and flirting came naturally to her. At the remembrance of Vera, she suddenly felt ashamed of herself, for no other reason than that she was standing in the warm sun, smiling and being happy, while poor Vera was not yet in her grave. But she couldn't simply walk away from this kind young man. That would be more than impolite, so she hurried to change the topic to something safe and ordinary as they walked slowly down the street towards Crowther's. "Tell me, are you from New York as well?"

"New Haven, Connecticut . . ." He held up his hand to forestall her next comment, "No. No, I didn't go to Yale. My father is a groundskeeper there. But I did used to tag along with him to the campus and sneak into whatever lecture was going on in the main hall that day. I suppose you might say that I have a Yale education without the all-important Yale diploma. And of course, as a result of my haphazard course of study, I only know a little bit about a great many topics. But it's a type of education which serves me well in my present line of work." Once again, he answered the question before she could get it out. "I'm a reporter for the *Portland Gazette*, covering everything from farming implements to international affairs. And street crime as well, which I suppose brings me to you. I was up at Third when I heard a commotion, saw a boy racing past clutching something bloody, smelled a story and . . ."

Well, thought Libby as he went on and on. He's sweet, but he does like the sound of his own voice. As Peter continued talking, she took stock of him. He was on the slim side, not that much taller than she was herself, with green eyes and straight brown hair that refused to stay off his face.

". . . imagine my surprise when I saw this pretty, well-dressed young lady take off after him. That made it a rarer, and much more interesting story." He pretended to sigh sadly. "If only you had caught him, I could've put you on the front page: *Gallant Maiden Comes to Aid of Butcher in Distress.*" Despite her avowal to be no more than polite, Libby couldn't suppress a laugh. "Still, give me an exclusive interview and I'll put you on page two." Finally, he stopped.

Libby decided she had better extricate herself, as gracefully as possible, while she still could. "Oh, I'm sure there must be many things going on in Portland far worthier of paper and ink." She reached out her hand for the bag, which he had continued to hold. "I'd better hurry to work before I become even later than I already am. I really am grateful to you for seeing after my bag, but there is no need for you to carry it any longer. I'm almost there, at any rate."

He gave a little mock bow. "Seeing as you won't give me an interview, you might at least do me the honor of allowing me to escort you door to door." He popped his bowler back onto his head. "I'll be happy to carry this to wherever it is you work."

"I'm quite capable of carrying it myself."

"I'm sure you are. I'm sure you're capable of many, many things." There was that disarming smile again. They began to walk again. "What is it that you do, Miss Seale? Something tells me there's very little call for lady runners in Portland."

She shot him a look, but decided not to be baited back into a discussion about her earlier antics. "I'm a seamstress . . ." it was out of her mouth before she realized, "at Crowther's Portland Variety."

Peter's reaction was exactly what she feared. His eyes glinted at the name of the theater. "Where they found the body of that showgirl yesterday."

She had no doubt a barrage of questions was about to follow that simple statement of fact, and so she cut him off with, "But I'd really rather not discuss it."

He hastened to assure her, "No, no . . . of course not. I understand." But she could tell he was disappointed.

Libby couldn't help herself. "And it wasn't 'a body' . . . I mean, it wasn't just some body." She heard her own voice thicken. "She was a lovely woman, a true friend. Miss Carabella. And she wasn't a showgirl . . . she was a magician's assistant."

Now he looked abashed, and she was sorry for her outburst. He hadn't meant to be insensitive, she knew that. Very likely he hadn't been the one to get Vera's name wrong in that morning's article. She wished she could think of a way to ask him without making it sound like an accusation, but there wasn't. Or she couldn't think of one.

Both were silent for a bit, but they continued walking together side by side. The theater was only a short block away now. It was Peter who broke the silence. "Almost there. Need someone to vouch for your tardiness?"

"No, really, I'm not that late. But thank you." They were at the stage door now, and Libby gathered her belongings from Peter's outstretched arm. "You've been very kind, carrying this for me."

"It was a pleasure running into you," Peter said, tipping his hat. Libby didn't smile. "I'm sorry. I promise—no more jokes."

Libby started to open the stage door.

"Wait . . . Miss Seale. The Choral Society at St. James Church is having a musical evening this Friday. Would you be interested in joining me?" There was a puppy dog eagerness in him that was at odds with his jaunty and cocky sense of humor.

She couldn't. It was too risky. Already she liked this young man far more than their brief acquaintance should have allowed. The word "yes" lingered on the tip of Libby's tongue, but instead she said, "Oh, I'm so sorry. Right now . . ." she half cocked her head towards the inside of the theater, as if to remind him about what had just happened there, "I just don't feel I can think about socializing. I'm afraid the answer must be 'no.'"

Peter's face fell, but before he could say anything more, she said goodbye and slipped through the stage door.

Today the theater was alive with activity. The arrival of some new acts, a troupe of Scandinavian gymnasts as well as "Little Anita, Child Contortionist," seemed to be the cause for more frivolity and laughter than usually attended a change in the bill. Libby guessed it had more to do with a need to put the unhappy news of the day before as far from their minds as possible. No one talked openly about the murder, although there did seem to be more hushed conversations in corners than usual. Libby felt very alone.

Late in the afternoon, a very stout lady strode imperially into the wardrobe room, holding in front of her small straw valise and an oversize hatbox from which protruded—Libby couldn't quite believe her eyes—two curved horns. Her presence, if not her bulk, overwhelmed the small space, as she announced in a thick German accent and Wagnerian tones that could probably be heard throughout the theater, "This is the costume room, yes? I am Frau Blumentraum, singer of opera and light musical interludes, direct from Bavaria, Germany!" The woman sounded like she was reciting from a program note, then Libby realized that she most likely was.

"You must be the new first act closer! I'm Lillian Seale, the assistant wardrobe mistress, but please call me Libby."

"*Ja.*" Frau Blumentraum accepted the invitation regally. "Libby, my Viking helmet needs a good polishing." She handed the hatbox to Libby. "And a good polishing, lots of polish, you understand. Not just to wipe it over." Libby nodded and tried to hide a sigh. "And this," she went on, referring to the little straw suitcase in tones of pure disgust, "is not my bag."

Libby was sure there must be a reason the soprano felt it necessary to impart this information to her, but after a long and tiring day she couldn't make it out, nor was she particularly in the mood to try. Perhaps the blank look on her face telegraphed this to the large German woman, for after a moment, Frau Blumentraum went on.

"I moved aside the screen in my dressing room because I needed more space for my makeup," she paused significantly, and Libby had time to reflect that however much makeup Frau Blumentraum had it wasn't going to be enough, "and there, in the corner of the room, was this!" She once again held forth the offending bag, making it clear she expected Libby to take it and, judging by her tone, preferably burn it.

Libby took it. "Thank you, Frau Blumentraum, I will have your helmet back to you before this evening's performance."

The singer stood her ground. Libby had no idea what she was waiting to hear, but the claustrophobic nature of the room with her scowling figure in it caused Libby to add, "I'm sorry you've been inconvenienced."

Frau Blumentraum didn't look exactly happy with this meager apology, but nonetheless she pivoted on her heel and swept out of the room.

Alone, Libby took a closer look at the straw valise and realized, with a catch in her throat, that she did recognize it after all. Like a photograph, an image came into her head of Vera packing trinkets and tubes of makeup into it her last Saturday night. It was the very last time she had seen the performer alive.

She had gone up to Vera's dressing room during intermission that night to give her a mended petticoat, so it could be packed away with the rest of the costumes for the magic act. Reaching the upper corridor where the dressing rooms were located, she heard giggles, and peering ahead down the dimly lit corridor, she saw a crowd of Dancing Whirlwinds hovering around the door to Vera's dressing room. This was hardly unusual, since to these local girls Vera represented a glamour and worldliness that was totally new and fascinating. Libby wondered what was causing the excitement this time.

Entering the dressing room, she discovered it was Vera's new underwear (trimmed with swirls of lace and woven through with yards of lavender ribbon) that had occasioned the fuss. Vera turned this way and that in front of her mirror, modeling the dainties to the delight of the girls. She hadn't yet noticed Libby's entrance, so Libby had a good long moment to watch how intently Vera stared at her own reflection. Libby's first thought was that Vera was just showing off, but then she noted how genuinely happy Vera looked and how unconscious she was of the crowd watching her every move. There was a certain radiance emanating from her which Libby almost hated to interrupt, but intermission was drawing to a close, and from the state of the dressing room, it looked like Vera hadn't even begun to pack.

"All right, girls," Libby smiled, "back to your own dressing room." The throng of girls, still sighing and whispering, began to withdraw. Vera looked up at Libby and smiled, then glanced at the folded petticoat she proffered.

"Oh, Libby, thank you." Vera started to unbutton her costume. "Now I can start packing."

"Would you like some help, Vera?" Libby asked, not yet ready to leave the warmth and friendliness of Vera's small dressing room. She realized with a start that she would miss her new friend, miss her amusing anecdotes about life on tour and her ready smile. Before starting work at the Variety, Libby had never been exposed to free spirits like show folk, and though sometimes their odd behaviors were inexplicable to her, she enjoyed their refreshing lack of constraints and their easy way with friendships.

"Oh, you are a treasure, Libby." Vera stepped behind a folding screen to dress.

Libby placed the petticoat in the waiting steamer trunk and began to fold Vera's other clothes. "That's a lovely new ensemble, Vera. Though I would say that corset is a little more Paris than Portland."

"Oh, well, it is closing night," Vera's voiced was muffled a bit by the covered screen, "and I'm feeling special." Vera emerged, dressed. "Besides, I think you underestimate Portland. I've performed here dozens of times, but I only recently realized what a lovely, lovely city it is." Vera was beaming as she sat down at her mirror to do her makeup and switched on the row of naked electric bulbs mounted above it. "Why, you know, if I ever decided to give up the theater, Portland is just the sort of town I would like to settle down in."

Something in Vera's tone caused Libby to look up from her packing. "Are you planning to give up the theater anytime soon?"

Vera continued to smile enigmatically. "Well, one can't go on as a magician's assistant forever. I've been on the road since I was . . . well, perhaps it's time to look for a more permanent booking."

Libby watched as Vera carefully plucked a pot of rouge from the numerous pots, jars, and tubes packed neatly in the straw valise which lay open on her dressing table and proceeded to touch up her makeup. In the bright glare of the electric lights Libby could see fine lines at the corners of Vera's eyes, and the thin, papery skin beneath them. Why, she's older than I thought, thought Libby. Probably closer to thirty-five than thirty. It occurred to Libby that Vera's departure from the stage, whenever it occurred, might not be a matter of mere choice.

Her heart suddenly bled a little for Vera, who was through with her makeup now and was writing in the little locked diary she kept on her makeup table, humming slightly to herself with the sweet unselfconsciousness of a little girl. She had never realized how dependent Vera must be upon those commodities no amount of skill or charm could gain her more of: youth and beauty. What did women like Vera do, she wondered, when their looks could no longer command flowers and compliments? Had Carlo indicated to Vera that he would be looking for a new assistant? But Libby dismissed the thought, for if that was true, she couldn't imagine that Vera would look so composed and even joyous this evening.

Vera had finished her diary entry, tucked it into the valise with her makeup, and shut the case with a snap. "Why, Libby, you've finished almost all the packing! Thank you!" She rose from her seat and clasped Libby's hands. "I want to tell you how much it's meant to me, becoming friends with you. I'm sure that's one of the reasons Portland has been such a happy place for me this time. Please say we'll stay friends, even though tonight is closing."

"Or course, Vera! I look forward to seeing you again too, the next time you're in Portland! Do you think that will be sometime soon?"

By way of response, Vera grabbed Libby in an expansive hug, crying, "Oh, before you know it! I am sure of it." A polite knock at the door interrupted the moment, and much to Libby's relief, Vera broke the hug. "Come in!" she called out gaily.

A tall young man holding a bouquet of roses entered through the doorway, "I . . ." He noticed Libby. "Oh, hello." Vera stepped in to make introductions, her eyes shining as she took the flowers.

"Gerald Williams, this is Libby Seale. She's the wardrobe mistress here and one of my dearest new friends in Portland! She made me that lovely dress I wear onstage." Gerald made appropriately complimentary noises, but he looked a little uncomfortable. Libby suspected he wanted to be alone with Vera, especially since he had come back to see her while the second act was still in progress. Most of the men waited until after the show was over.

Libby decided to take pity on him and made a hasty exit on the pretext of checking on the chorines. She didn't even stop to say goodbye to Vera, not wanting to interrupt her while she had a gentleman caller, and assuming she would have a chance later to say a proper goodbye.

Of course, that chance had never come, and thinking about it now, Libby wanted to cry.

She dragged her mind back to the straw bag in her hands. Even closed, she could picture its interior, lined with cornflower blue silk and filled up with neat rows of everything that had been dear to Vera. But when she undid the clasp, the top of the valise popped open on its own. The contents had been shoved in so haphazardly that they had been pressing on the lid. Either Libby was misremembering the methodical way in which Vera had packed it, or Vera must have reopened it sometime later and searched through it in a hurry.

Libby started to look through the bag—there were the tubes and pots of makeup she'd remembered, plus a soiled towel, a small wooden jewelry box, and some old theater programs. Then she realized that even though Vera was dead, she still had no right to paw through her private things. It ought to go to Vera's next of kin, whoever they were.

Libby decided to turn it over to Mr. Crowther right away. She made her way to his office and knocked firmly.

As heavy footfalls headed for the door, she heard Crowther's distinctive growl, "I thought I told you there's no way we can do it right now. We'll have to wait until . . ." The door was pulled inward and stopped as he saw her standing there. "Miss Seale . . . I'm sorry, I thought you were someone else. What is it you want?" He remained standing in the doorway, making no effort to invite her into his office.

Crowther scared Libby a little, although if asked, she couldn't have said exactly what she was afraid of. But there was an undercurrent of violence in him, a sort of violence that reminded her all to well of someone she'd rather not be reminded of. She brushed aside her memories and managed to speak without letting the tremor appear in her voice. "Mr. Crowther, Frau Blumentraum found some of Miss Carabella's belongings that had been left in the star dressing room. I wondered what to do with them."

There was a pause, then he asked carefully, "What exactly did you find?"

With a question in her voice, she replied, "It's a small straw suitcase. It has some makeup in it, plus some theatrical memorabilia and the like. I don't believe any of it is valuable," she added, in case that was what he had wanted to know.

His look of interest faded. "Do whatever you like with it. I don't care." And he shut the door.

Libby was relieved. Crowther's presence was always unpleasant. Of course, she now had no idea what to do next. She still felt she should make some effort to deliver the valise to Vera's next of kin or heir, or someone who would cherish these mementos, but she didn't know how. Who would know something like that? It suddenly occurred to her . . . the police. They were probably digging around looking into Vera's past and would be sure to know what family Vera had, if indeed she had any. Perhaps, too, the contents of the bag might provide some clues.

She decided that first thing tomorrow morning on her way into work, she would deliver the bag to the man in charge of the investigation.

She was just gathering up her coat and preparing to leave for the day, when Jack Reilly came into the costume shop. "Miss Seale, I —" Libby jumped, her pulse racing. She hadn't heard him come in. "I'm sorry. I didn't mean to frighten you. I guess we're all a little on edge today. Thought I'd let you know there's going to be a funeral service for Miss Carabella tomorrow at three, up at Lone Fir cemetery. Can you go there before you come into work?"

"Of course, Mr. Reilly." She was surprised he would even ask.

"Oh, good." He seemed relieved. "You'll have to be the official representative from the theater, since all the performers and crew have to be here before three for afternoon call. Mr. Crowther insisted, since he had to cancel Monday's shows, we can't cancel another. Say, are you all right? You look a little pale."

She nodded dimly. She didn't really think Jack meant to sound heartless, but she supposed that to him Vera was just one in a never-ending stream of guest artists, not really a person at all. His job as stage manager was to deal efficiently when any problem arose and then move on quickly.

"Well, thank you. Enjoy your evening." He walked off to cope with the next item on his list.

She left the Variety with a heavy heart and began her journey home.

THREE

THE SKY OVERHEAD WAS gray and rainy, a cliché for weather at a funeral, but all too common for January in Portland. Libby pulled her cloth coat around her shoulders and listened as the minister intoned a few phrases she couldn't quite make out. Lone Fir Cemetery was larger than she had expected, and walking to the gravesite, she had been surprised to see tombstones in several languages: a cluster of German graves, followed by some that looked like Japanese or Chinese, and even one in Hebrew. So at least she wasn't the only Jew who had ever lived in Portland, even if she felt as if she was the only one in the city now.

There was just one funeral taking place, and Libby threaded her way among the statues and gravestones and settled in toward the back of the crowd. Not that one could really call the attending mourners a "crowd," since there were so few of them. Despite what Jack Reilly had told her, there was another person there from the Variety. Mr. Maynard stood to one side alone, hat in hands. Libby looked around, hoping that perhaps Carlo had changed his mind and stayed on for the burial, but it only took a moment to ascertain that the bombastic showman was nowhere in the vicinity. In fact, there seemed to be few, if any, mourners who might have known Vera before her stay in Portland. There was a tall blond man standing to one side, whom she didn't recognize. For a moment, she considered the possibility that he might be a relative of Vera's, but his pale hair and complexion, so unlike Vera's dark beauty, made that a remote chance. Additionally, he hung to the back of the crowd and left as soon as the minister had finished his droning speech without waiting for the burial. Rounding out the sparse crowd, the few additional mourners were mostly older, and appeared to be retired locals, the type of parishioners who attend all funerals for lack of anything better to do.

A couple of workmen moved forward to lower the coffin into the ground, and the crowd began to disperse. Vera—bright, ebullient Vera—would be traveling no more. The sky was pale, and everything around Libby looked gray: the stones, the gravel walkways, just another gray day in this wet, depressing city. She supposed it was worth something that Carlo had grudgingly laid out the money so that his assistant would not have to lie in a pauper's grave, but still Libby couldn't help judging him for not staying to see her laid to rest.

As the first shovelfuls of dirt thudded against the coffin, Libby saw that Mr. Maynard was already walking briskly toward the exit. Turning back to the gravesite, she bowed her head and under her breath whispered the *yit-gadal*, the Jewish prayer for the dead. She knew it would have meant nothing to Vera in life, but it seemed only fitting that Libby should recognize her death in the only way she knew how.

After a few more moments of reflection, she followed the path back to the street and stood waiting for the streetcar, huddling under a large tree to avoid the drizzle. It occurred to her that the man Libby had met that last night in Vera's dressing room hadn't been among the mourners at Vera's funeral. It appeared his infatuation with the magician's assistant hadn't extended past her closing night. In fact, none of the men who filled Vera's dressing room night after night had shown up to pay their last respects. Vera deserved better.

As she rode the tram and walked to the theater, her mind turned to work. It was laundry day at Crowther's, which meant extra long hours and lots of exhausting lifting and folding. She didn't have time now to go round to the police station to drop off the straw valise Frau Blumentraum had found. Besides, the sky was darkening, and she hoped to get to the Variety before the drizzle turned to full-fledged rain. Holding the small case tightly in her hand, Libby also realized some small part of her didn't want to part with those last remaining traces of the vibrant, colorful woman whose body now lay in the wet ground.

It was after 10 PM by the time she got home, and Libby felt she had never been so happy to see her now-familiar bedroom, to sink down onto her small bed and pull off the uncomfortable shoes. For some reason it had seemed important to wear them to the funeral when she had dressed that morning, but a busy day at the theater wearing her fancy boots had been a trial.

Sighing, she rubbed at her sore feet, then swung around to regard herself in the small vanity mirror. The day's rain had not been kind to her pinned-up hair, and as she removed each pin, the effect was almost comical. Reaching for her brush, she thought of Vera sitting at her own makeup mirror just a few short days before, glowing with anticipation as she waited for her beau with the flowers.

It was sad, really. Why hadn't any of Vera's gentlemen callers had the decency to show up at her funeral? Wasn't there at least one stage door Johnny whose affection had extended beyond the grave? As she brushed her hair with increasingly fervent strokes, she pursed her lips at the perfidy of men. Men were attentive only until they had taken what they wanted. Once their own desires were satisfied, they no longer even pretended to pay heed to the gentler needs of women. She had learned this the hard way in her own life, but today's funeral made it clear that male insensitivity continued after death. To think Libby had always been a little jealous of all the masculine attention Vera had received—now she saw how little it had been worth.

The thought of Vera's erstwhile paramours made her think of Peter Eberle. She had, of course, not seen him since their conversation ended so disappointingly the day before, but she had been half hoping that he would show up at the funeral that afternoon or arrive at the theater to investigate a follow-up article. Perhaps another reporter had been assigned to cover the crime for the *Gazette*. Although, as she considered it, she realized that no reporters had been by the Variety, and there had been no follow-up articles. It appeared Portland wanted, as much as possible, to forget the death in the tunnels.

She finally set down her brush and turned off the light, falling asleep almost instantly. But her sleep was troubled, and she awoke the next morning unable to shake the visions of an underground nightmare, the details of which she couldn't recall.

Skipping breakfast, Libby let herself out of the house quietly, before Mrs. Pratt could ask her why she was leaving so early. The day was raw, and there was a stiff breeze, but Libby hardly noticed it as her mind was twenty feet underground, trying to remember her nightmare. She shuddered thinking how awful it would be to die underground, without light and with practically no air. She couldn't stop her imagination from picturing Vera's fear and disorientation as she was pushed down into the dank blackness.

She was glad her mother couldn't see her now. Surely she would be appalled at the violence of the city where her daughter had taken up residence. That thought almost cancelled out the guilt Libby felt for not writing to inform her family where she was. Every week she would tell herself that the time had come to contact them . . . but every week she found another reason to put it off writing a letter. Sometimes she would compose almost an entire letter in her head, but when she sat at her writing desk, the words wouldn't come. She knew her mother must be half-mad with grief and worry, but she also knew her mother would never understand or condone why Libby had left, no matter how the letter was phrased. Eventually, she promised herself, she would do it. At least write and say that she was alive, healthy and . . . well, she was happy, wasn't she? At least some of the time.

Perhaps it would be best just to wait to explain herself until she went home. Eventually she would have to head back . . . she couldn't stay in Portland, Oregon forever, could she? In light of what she had recently learned about the city, she wasn't even sure she wanted to. Libby was still shocked by the complex and far-reaching web of violence and criminal activity apparently centered in the Shanghai tunnels. It felt, quite literally, as if the ground under her feet was no longer solid or secure. Beneath Portland's placid exterior, it seemed, was the lawless West her mother had always warned her about.

The officer behind the desk looked disapprovingly at her. He was as tall and solid as an Oregon pine, one of the hulking men that seemed to grow like weeds in this part of the world. "What can I do for you, Miss?" The way he accentuated the word "Miss" told Libby all she needed to know about his attitude towards women in a police station.

She wilted a little in the face of his condescension. "I have some information. Well, actually, I have some items which belonged to the victim of a crime. Vera Carabella? Her body was discovered in the Shanghai tunnels near Crowther's Portland Variety last Monday morning? I work at the theater, and we've discovered some of her belongings which were left there and thought they might be of use to you . . . to the police. Or, at the very least, that they should be passed along to Miss Carabella's next of kin."

The policeman's face showed a complete lack of interest. Finally he said, "Body in the tunnels? Yes, I remember that."

Libby persisted, "Is there someone I can leave this with?" She held up the valise, then thought better of handing it over to this dull-witted officer. "Or, possibly, speak to regarding the case?"

"Let's see, I believe Sergeant Branson was the one called out on that. But he's not here now."

Libby waited, but he was done talking. "Is he in charge of the investigation? Is there anyone else I could talk to?"

"Investigation? Oh, no, that's all done." He saw the disbelief in Libby's eyes. "There's a lot of crimes in Portland these days, little lady. Can't expect us to spend forever on every body that turns up in the tunnels."

To the contrary, Libby expected just that, and was just about to tell him so when a florid-faced officer came through the front doors of the station. With a cheerful "howdy," the two struck up a friendly conversation. It was as if Libby had disappeared. Clearly the desk clerk considered the matter at an end.

Her first reaction was to simply walk out of the station, but she knew she owed Vera more than that. Summoning her courage, she forced herself to say, "Excuse me. I would still like to speak with someone regarding Miss Carabella's death."

At this interruption, the two men turned to her, boredom on the desk clerk's face, but a vague interest on the other's. "Carabella . . ." he said. "Wasn't she the actress over at the burlesque house got herself abducted last weekend?"

Libby chose to ignore the fact that he placed the blame for the crime squarely on Vera's shoulders and decided to try a little feminine charm. "Oh, yes," she said sweetly, "she was a great friend of mine, and I was hoping you could help me, Officer . . . ?"

"Sergeant. Sergeant Branson." So this was the officer who had been called to the scene of the crime! "Why, this kind officer was just speaking to me about you. He said you were in charge of the investigation." He started to speak, but she pretended not to notice. "I've just found a clue and rushed right over here to give it to you. You see we . . . I mean at the theater . . . just located some of Miss Carabella's personal belongings, and I thought they might help you search for her killer. May I show you?"

Sergeant Branson saw Libby wasn't going to leave unless he humored her a little, and he said with a sigh, "Why don't you come this way, Miss, and have a seat." She pretended not to notice the two officers roll their eyes at each other as Branson showed her into the next room, which was filled with desks.

Quickly she ran through the way the little suitcase had come to light and her reasons for bringing it to him. He listened patiently for a few moments and then held up a hand for her to stop.

"Miss Seale, I'm very sorry you've lost a friend, but I have to tell you this sort of crime is not unusual, 'specially not in the area of the city where you work. She was a looker, your Miss Carabella, and those are the types these criminals go for. From what we could tell, she must have gone for a drink or to meet someone after she left the theater Saturday night and was just unlucky in her choice of companion." He smiled condescendingly, "If it's any consolation to you, it looks like she fought back hard as she could. She was pretty banged up. You should have seen the gash across her forehead . . ."

He stopped suddenly, realizing that this was probably not the best way to make Libby feel better, and when he went on he was more kind. "Perhaps she was luckier than those girls who go peacefully all the way to . . . Lord knows what horrible fate's waiting for them over the ocean or wherever."

Why would Vera have been wandering around in seedy barrooms? And certainly she had no need to venture further than her dressing room to find male companionship. Libby was about to point this out to Sergeant Branson when a better question occurred to her. "If Miss Carabella was abducted in a bar, or even on the street, why was her valise up in her dressing room? She had it all packed and ready to take away from the theater."

Branson waved the question away. "She just forgot it, I'm sure." His tone implied that flighty women were apt to forget any number of things. "Or perhaps she was planning to go back for it later."

"Isn't it possible," persisted Libby, "she might have been abducted *inside* the theater?"

He couldn't keep a slight tone of exasperation from creeping into his voice as he answered. "We spoke to the doorman, and we know she definitely left the theater that night. A little after midnight, according to him."

"But I understand there was another girl a few months back, Polly I think her name was, who was also found . . ."

He cut her off. "You mean Fanny Watson." He looked pleased to have been able to trump Libby's knowledge. His smug look seemed to imply that a silly female couldn't be expected to get anything right. "Oh, she went by the name Polly Pink at the theater. But, if you'll excuse the vulgarity, Miss, she was just a dockside whore pretending to be a dancer. She probably knew whoever abducted her . . . probably let him into the theater herself, if the truth be known. It was only a matter of time before a girl like her came to grief."

She tried again. "Isn't it possible Miss Carabella also knew her abductor? Maybe the things in the valise would provide some clue as to who. Perhaps it was the same person who abducted Fanny Watson . . ."

"This was just an ordinary waterfront crime, and there's no reason to go poking around in Miss Carabella's personal effects looking for an answer when the answer's as plain as the nose on my face. Look, Miss, I'm sorry for your loss, but there's nothing more we can do."

Out on the street she seethed with indignation, not only at the way the police had treated her, but because it appeared Vera's death was being swept under the rug. Libby found it difficult to accept that her friend's killer was walking the streets of Portland without any risk of detection, since the police were not even looking for him. Surely there was some way to make the police pay attention.

Unbidden, the image of Peter Eberle popped into her mind's eye for the second time in twenty-four hours. She didn't know why, but she felt he would understand her frustration and have a perfect solution. Perhaps he could write an article denouncing the police for not capturing the killer, and then they would have to reopen the investigation. She rejected the thought as soon as it entered her mind. Vera's death had not attracted much attention in the press, so the fact that the case was unsolved was unlikely to arouse any controversy. Besides, she didn't see what right she had to ask Peter for a favor.

Still, she somehow felt that she was letting Vera down. She knew there was no basis for feeling this way, but her soul ached to be able to do something, to show Vera one last measure of friendship. The straw valise in her hand suddenly seemed like a heavy burden, a visible sign of her inability to set matters right. It had belonged to Vera, and now it should be with all her other things, go wherever all her other belongings were going. She had forgotten even to ask that horrid inspector if he knew Vera's next of kin, but immediately she knew his answer would have been no.

Vera must have had a number of personal items other than this little case. Where were they? The costumes, props, and anything related to the act had been in the trunk Carlo had taken back to San Francisco, but what about Vera's street clothes? Libby realized she had no idea where Vera had lived while she was in Portland, but undoubtedly the hotel or rooming-house must still have her effects. Presumably, they also had a permanent address for her, perhaps even the name of her next of kin. Her spirit lifted at this thought. She could turn over the valise to Vera's landlord, and then she would have done everything it was in her power to do.

Now all she had to do was get Vera's last address. Mr. Maynard kept information of this sort for everyone who worked at the theater, so it would be the matter of a moment to get it from him sometime today.

Libby headed off to work in a much better frame of mind, hardly even noticing that she was, once again, late.

FOUR

THROUGHOUT THE DAY FRIDAY, Libby kept an eye out for Mr. Maynard. She reflected wryly that on a normal day, she seemed to trip over him practically every hour, as he was always underfoot in the corridor that housed the dressing rooms, hoping for a glimpse of a half-clothed chorine. But today, it was nearly four in the afternoon before she caught sight of him, deep in conversation with one of the dancers. Not wanting to interrupt, she hovered nearby, pretending to count costumes hanging on a rack in the hallway until she saw out of the corner of her eye that the woman was gone, and Maynard was walking away. She ran to catch up with him. "Mr. Maynard, do you have a moment?"

"For a beautiful woman, Miss Seale, a moment can always be found," he said unctuously. As was always the case when she was forced to interact with him, Libby had to fight the urge to recoil. But as repulsive as she found him, he was not a physically imposing presence. Libby did not feel threatened by him the way she did with Mr. Crowther. "What can I do for you?"

"I understand you have the home addresses on file for all the performers. I needed to return some lost property to the boardinghouse where Miss Carabella was staying."

"Ah yes, Miss Carabella . . . Vera." He managed to make even the name sound salacious. "What a terrible, terrible tragedy. You say you found some property of the late Miss Carabella?"

He looked down at her curiously and, for a moment, Libby was afraid he would just offer to return whatever it was himself. She wasn't quite sure why she felt it so strongly, but she knew that under no circumstances would she surrender the valise to him. She hated the thought of this man pawing through Vera's things, leering over the lip rouge and lace handkerchiefs that had meant so much to their owner.

"Yes, just a small case with makeup and . . ." Libby realized that if she mentioned anything lacy and feminine, it would only whet the man's desire to see the case. "And some old theater programs and press clippings."

"Did you tell Mr. Crowther about it?" he asked, suddenly suspicious.

Libby replied sweetly that of course, that was the very first thing she had done. "He wasn't interested in it, so I thought it would be best to send it along with the rest of her personal effects." With great effort, she forced herself to smile winningly at him. "So you see, all I need is her address."

He paused, then sighed. "Well, if Crowther says it's all right. Let's see, I think she was staying in a boardinghouse on the east side of the river. Come with me, and I'll get the address."

The house where Vera had lived turned out to be less than a mile from Libby's own home, and she set out on foot to find it next morning, valise in hand. It was an unusually sunny day for January, and though it was chilly, she went slightly out of her way to walk along the riverfront. To her left, the sun reflected on the water and made the day feel warmer than it actually was. She stopped once to watch the ships navigating their way in and out of the port, busy even on a Sunday.

In the last several years, Portland had become increasingly significant as a trade center in the Pacific region, and while Seattle, the younger upstart to the north, had its own bustling port, Portland remained the far more important of the rival cities. The twin industries of lumber and wheat kept the harbor crowded with ships bound for all over the globe, and to let the many oversize cargo ships make their way through the narrow stretch of river dividing the city, all the bridges over the Willamette were made with swing spans or drawbridge centers. It was a common excuse that one was late because "the bridge was up." Libby was thankful that both her home and Vera's were on the east side of the river because, judging from the boat traffic in the river, she might well have been held up by bridge traffic had she needed to cross over today.

Mrs. Pratt had been filled with interest at the unusual errand of her boarder. Once she found out Libby had known Vera rather better than she had at first let on, she became quite insatiable in her quest for details about Vera's abduction and murder, taking the opportunity to return to her favorite subject: the shameful moral downfall of Portland. To this, she added the her oft-expressed view that those theater people Libby worked with were bound to be trouble, and why didn't she find a nice job working for one of the reputable tailors in town?

Libby turned away from the Willamette and began walking towards the East Portland neighborhood where Vera had lived. If she was being honest with herself, she had to confess to a certain foreboding about her mission. She had no idea what Vera's life outside the theater had been like, and she wondered if she really wanted to know. What sort of lives *did* actresses and showgirls lead when they were not at the theater? She feared she might find herself embarrassed.

So with some trepidation she knocked on the door of 18 Washington Street. The house looked quiet enough, downright ordinary in fact, as did the man who opened the door. He was tall and pale, with a face that seemed open, friendly, and somehow familiar. He eyed her with interest. "You looking for a room?"

"No, I'm . . . My name is Libby Seale. I worked at the Portland Variety with your tenant, that is, your late tenant . . . Vera Carabella."

"Ah, Miss Carabella." He stopped, lost in thought, and Libby recognized the signs immediately. Here was one more man who had been smitten by the Carabella charm. "She was a beautiful woman. It wasn't right her life should have ended like that. You know, when the police came and told us, I hoped at first they had the wrong woman, that it wasn't our Vera. When they gave us her evening bag and the hat she had been wearing, there could be no doubt." He looked at Libby again, "I saw you at the funeral, didn't I? You must be . . . must have been a friend of Miss Carabella's from the theater?"

Suddenly, Libby remembered the blond man at Vera's graveside, the one who had spoken to no one and left early. So that was why this man's face had looked familiar. "Yes. I worked with Vera, as I said . . ."

The man cut her off nervously. "I'm sorry, I shouldn't make you stand in the cold. Please, come in. Are you here for her things?" he asked, suddenly.

She stood in the small vestibule. The house was not lavishly appointed, but it looked clean and was obviously well-kept. Through a doorway, she could see a front parlor, crowded with overstuffed chairs sporting ornate lace antimacassars.

"Well, I had assumed her effects would be going to her family. In fact, that's why I came. I have something that belonged to her, Mr. . . . ?"

"Englund. Where are my manners today? Lars Englund, pleased to make your acquaintance. Come in, Miss Seale, have a seat." As he spoke, he led her into the parlor, where he hovered a moment uncomfortably. "You should probably talk to my wife. I'll go get her." With that, he disappeared up the staircase, leaving Libby to examine her surroundings with interest.

So this had been Vera's home during her brief stay in Portland. The carpet in front of the fireplace was worn through in several places, but an attempt had been made to divert the eye with two large brass vases on either side of the grate. A large basket of mending sat beside the most comfortable-looking chair, and her practiced eye noticed immediately the attention to detail evident in the perfectly turned seams visible in the shirts spilling out the top of the basket.

She heard footsteps and voices on the stairs, and two young women put on their coats and left by the front door amid a burst of congenial chatter, not having noticed a visitor in the sitting room. A few moments later, a middle-aged woman with a flat, Midwestern face (obviously Mrs. Englund) came down the stairs and approached Libby. Wiping her hands on her apron, she appeared to have been interrupted at some household task. Her face was lined, making her look older than her husband, and her chapped hands spoke of a lifetime of washing and heavy cleaning. Libby guessed there must be ten or twelve bedrooms in a house this large, and no doubt keeping up with the household tasks required for so many people was not easy.

"I am Anna Englund. My husband tells me you were a friend of Miss Carabella." While perfectly polite, a certain animosity shone through when the woman mentioned Vera's name.

"Yes, I brought her valise." Libby motioned to the small case at her feet. "I thought it should go to her family along with the rest of her things."

"Her family? She had no family, at least none that she ever spoke of." Mrs. Englund crossed to the fireplace and began straightening the various bric-a-brac and bibelots along the mantel top. She was obviously uncomfortable being still for too long, thought Libby, who had seen her own mother do the same sort of mindless tidying up without even realizing it. "When she was first here—last June, I suppose it was—I asked her for an address for her people, you know, like I do for all our boarders. You can't be too careful, I always say. Sometimes, some of these short-term tenants think they can skip out owing us rent, and Mr. Englund and I like to have some way to get in touch with them after."

"Vera was here in June? I hadn't realized."

"That's right, she was here doing that magic show at the theater. She'd stayed with us before. We have several theater folk staying here. We run a clean home at reasonable rates."

"I'm sure you do," replied Libby. "It looks like a fine house. But you were saying, you never got a forwarding or permanent address for Miss Carabella?"

"Like I said, we always try to get that. But she said she didn't have any people we could reach, and the room was empty, so Lars—Mr. Englund—said that would be fine. I will say this about her, she always paid her rent on time. And when she came this time, she even paid for the whole four weeks in advance and in cash." Finishing her ministrations with the china figurines, she turned back to Libby. "I have someone waiting for that room, you see, and there's no one else who has come about her things at all. You will take them, won't you?"

"But . . ."

"Otherwise, we may just have to dispose of them somehow. I would just put them out with the rubbish myself, but Lars talked about maybe selling some of her things. Really, Miss, I don't care what you do with them. I just need them out of here."

Libby was suffused with a sudden wash of pity. It had become apparent in death that Vera had forged few truly close bonds. And this landlady was so transparently jealous of her husband's attentions to Vera, that was obvious. It made Libby realize what a common scenario that must have been in the life of the vivacious and pretty performer. Before she could think it through anymore, Libby made up her mind. "Are the things already packed?" she asked resignedly, envisioning an afternoon of yet more packing on Vera's behalf. To her surprise, Mrs. Englund replied in the affirmative, and said she would go upstairs and get them.

Before she could do so, the front door slammed with a burst of cold air, and Libby looked up to see a greasy looking man with an unkempt moustache unbuttoning his large overcoat and hanging it by the door. "Missus Englund, we got a new boarder here?" he asked, seeing the parlor occupied. To Libby he said, "I can show you all around the area if you're new in town, honey."

"Mr. Slade, this is a friend of Vera's come to get her things."

"A friend of Vera's, you say?" He regarded Libby lasciviously. "You one of them dancers at the burlesque?"

"No, I'm a seamstress," she replied. Mrs. Englund excused herself to see to Vera's things, and Libby found herself alone with the rather disconcerting Mr. Slade.

"So, you worked at the theater with Vera then? She was a mighty good-looking lady, that Vera." Libby agreed that indeed, she was quite attractive. He went on, "Of course, girls like that will put on airs, you know. They act all uppity, just 'cause a feller can't help but notice their charms."

He sat down heavily on the settee next to Libby and looked at her meaningfully. "She wasn't like that when I first met her, you know. She was real nice to me at first, the first time she stayed here . . ." He paused and, rubbing his hands together, repeated himself. "She was real nice to old Albert."

Libby edged away from him on the sofa, willing Mrs. Englund to return. In a vain attempt to change the topic, she sat up straighter and asked him if he had lived here long. He told her proudly he had lived in the Englunds' boarding house for seven years, long enough to see most of the theater folk come and go several times over.

"They're an odd lot, those dancers and actresses," he confided. "But then, I guess you know that already, working with them and all. Queer people in those variety shows. Vera Carabella was just a perfect example."

Libby realized she wasn't going to be able to escape the topic and let him go on.

"When she got here last spring, her and me got to be, well, I'll just say we was close. You see, I work as a salesman, and my business takes me out of town during the week, but we got to be friendly chatting here at the house, me and Vera. She would tell me all about her magic show and that poof she worked with—oh, she had some stories—and I would tell her all about the countryside here and my work selling farm implements up and down the Willamette. She was always real interested in my work." At this, Libby hid a smile, and she gave her friend credit for greater acting ability than she had heretofore supposed.

Mr. Slade was still lost in his reminiscences. "On her day off, we would go for walks around the city, or take my buggy, pack a picnic maybe, and go out riding to see some of the gorges round these parts. Sometimes we didn't get back here until very late . . . Ah, she was a great one for driving." His face grew dark. "Of course, this time, things were different. She never had time for me, acted like we weren't even friends at all. I hardly saw her; she was never here at the house when I was home. Come to think of it, seems like she was spending an awful lot of time away from here lately!" His jealousy was palpable.

"Did Vera ever tell you anything about her family or even where she was from?"

He thought for a moment, then shook his head. "Nah, we didn't talk about that kind of stuff. Hey, listen, enough about Vera. You want to go for a walk with me sometime? You're real nice."

Libby was relieved to see Mr. Englund lugging a large suitcase down the staircase and used the distraction to turn her attention away from the greasy lodger. Unlike the invitation she had received from Peter Eberle, there was no question about whether she wanted to accept the date. "Thank you very much for the offer, Mr. Slade, but I'm afraid I have to decline, as my affections are otherwise engaged."

"Oh, it's like that, is it?" He stood facing her, his moustache quivering. "Fine, I was just trying to be nice to a friend of Vera's anyway." Without waiting to hear her reply, he disappeared through the hallway toward the back of the house, where Libby presumed the kitchen was.

Back in her room at Mrs. Pratt's, Libby surveyed Vera's large suitcase and straw valise sitting beside each other on the floor by her bed. They took up most of the small room, and she wondered what on earth she was going to do with them. Luckily, Mr. Englund had insisted on hiring a hansom cab for her, for she could hardly imagine how she might have carried them all the way home on foot.

She supposed she should see if she could find any hint about where to send these things. Thinking there might be an address or family name or something on one of the items inside, she opened the suitcase and began sorting. Aside from a few creased photographs, most of the space was taken up with brightly colored evening dresses and fashionable afternoon clothes in gay colors, just a little bit brighter and more extravagant than most women could pull off. Setting aside the clothes, Libby scrutinized the photographs, but none of the people in them looked familiar, and unfortunately, there was no address book or passport or other identifying information.

She turned her attention to the smaller bag and began methodically sorting through the jumble of crumpled items, setting them out beside her on the bed. She was sure she remembered Vera folding the handkerchiefs carefully and fitting the tubes of makeup into the corners ...

she had noted it at the time because it was the only packing Vera herself had actually done. What had Vera been looking for so hurriedly as to leave the valise in this state of disarray? Of course, it was also just possible that Frau Blumentraum might have opened it up when she found it, just to see if there was anything worth taking.

Libby discarded that theory once she saw the full contents laid out before her. It was unlikely any woman intent on pilfering would have left behind some of the lovely trifles. There were three silk handkerchiefs, all with fine lace borders, and several half-used pots of lip rouge, along with a patterned gold-plated compact filled with pressed powder. A small stack of theater bills and newspaper reviews were tied with a narrow purple ribbon. As she leafed through these papers, a flat, faded white rose fell out from between two pages. She hadn't realized Vera was quite so sentimental and wondered what occasion the rose was a memento of.

The case was nearly empty now. At the bottom of the bag was a smeared makeup towel, which had obviously been used to clean her face. Half wrapped inside it was a small wooden jewelry box, ornately carved with leaves and flowers. Libby opened it, but save for a few broken beads and an empty silver key ring, there was nothing in the box. Taking them out, she held the box up to examine it more closely. It was a beautiful piece of handwork, and she felt a silent admiration for the craftsman who had so delicately carved each small petal and leaf.

As she turned it over in her hands, she noticed a small clasp cleverly carved to blend into the other designs, and when she pushed it, the base inside slid out to reveal a small hidden compartment. In it were several pieces of jewelry that looked valuable and a small envelope. There were two rings, both gold bands, possibly wedding rings? One was a simple flat band, the other more ornate and made of a brighter gold. Libby picked it up, noticing that it was inscribed in a flowing script: "1893 F. W. and H. M. Eternal Love." Curious, thought Libby, but she went on examining the rest of the items. There were two perfect glossy pearl earrings, and another ring, in silver, with what looked like a large garnet in the center. She had never seen Vera wear any of these things that she could recall, but that wasn't all that surprising, given that they looked too valuable to be worn casually around the theater.

What she had guessed would be love letters inside the small envelope turned out to be cash, quite a thick bundle. That was a surprise, at least at first. Then she recalled that Vera spent her life on the road, moving from place to place every few weeks, and realized that would have made it difficult to have a bank account. Or perhaps Vera, like many, just didn't trust banks with her money, which meant Libby was looking at Vera's life savings here. Immediately she wondered how much it was. She counted out $758 and stared at it. That was more than Libby made in a year! What was she supposed to do with it? Surely it would be wrong to keep it for herself, but there appeared to be no one else laying claim to Vera's belongings. She put the bills back in the envelope and brooded.

Vera would never have "just forgotten" her straw case the way that maddening policeman had insisted—not with $758 in it. Maybe Libby had not known Vera for a long time or as a close intimate friend, but over the past four weeks working together at the Variety, she had observed that Vera was not the sort of a woman who would accidentally forget to take her life savings, as well as her most sentimental possessions, when leaving the theater at the end of a run.

She looked at the small pile of jewelry on her bed and felt uneasy. The only way it made sense was that Vera had been abducted *before she left the theater*. Why else would her personal effects still be in the dressing room? But if that was true, what did that mean? Was there really a white slave ring operating from inside Crowther's Portland Variety? If so, it was imperative that there be an investigation before other women were hurt!

She briefly considered returning to the police station with this new evidence, but quickly rejected that idea. The police had closed the book on Vera's death, and they would doubtless be unwilling to reopen it based only on Libby's firm belief that Vera had not left the valise behind accidentally, and therefore must have never left the theater the night she was killed. She needed some firm evidence—then the police would have to pay attention!

She wanted badly to talk this through with someone to see if there was anything she was missing. She quickly disregarded Mrs. Pratt as far too excitable and flighty. She thought about Hatty, but as much as she hated to admit it, no one at the theater should be discounted as a suspect until she had more information. She knew so few people in Portland, which made her feel suddenly lonely. There was one person she could think of who might help her gather enough hard evidence to present to the police, but she was a bit embarrassed to call upon him after refusing his offer of an evening out.

Swallowing her pride, she resolved to find him as soon as possible. It might be awkward, but if it was true that someone in the theater was responsible for Vera Carabella's murder, now was no time to let social discomfort stand in her way of finding the truth.

FIVE

LIBBY WAS STILL UNSURE what she was going to say as she approached the offices of the *Portland Gazette* during her lunch break on Monday, but she knew that she had to find somebody to speak with about her growing suspicions. And if she was truly honest with herself, she knew that seeing Peter Eberle again was something she had wanted to do anyway. At least this errand provided her the opportunity to approach him in a way that didn't concern personal matters. Perhaps once the police had been persuaded to reopen the investigation into Vera's murder, she and Peter could become real friends, her first real friend in this strange city.

The building that housed the *Gazette* was unprepossessing and looked far smaller than Libby had imagined it. Entering, she found herself in a plain front room with a counter running across its width, undecorated except for clippings pasted on the walls. Through an archway, she could see a larger, cluttered room dominated by a fierce looking printing press, which was currently still. Every inch of wall space in this back room appeared to be covered with type cases filled with tens of thousands of individual letter forms of different fonts and sizes. But Libby had only a moment to glance around for, at the sound of the bell on the front door, a friendly looking face peered out from the arched doorway and said, "Be with you in a second."

The friendly looking face soon proved to be attached to the solid body of a man who, at something over six feet, towered over Libby as he regarded her from behind the counter. Despite his size, however, there was something gentle in his demeanor that immediately put Libby at ease. "What can I do for you, Miss?"

"I . . ." Libby was unsure exactly how to answer. Somehow she had assumed Peter would be there as soon as she entered the building. Now she realized that it might be considered forward of a young lady to go about asking after a young man. Would this man look at her the same way that police officer had on Tuesday? Hesitantly, she said, "I was wondering if I might see Mr. Eberle. I'm a friend of his . . . or, rather, I met him the other day and . . ." She hit upon an idea that would make her visit seem more respectable. "I have some more information for him regarding a story he is working on." There—surely that was socially acceptable? And it was just a white lie, since soon enough he might actually be working on the story.

"A story? Well now, we can always use the help of the public," the man said, smiling.

"Can I possibly see Mr. Eberle just for a moment? I promise not to take too much of his time."

"Now there's the problem. I'm afraid Mr. Eberle isn't around the office, and I haven't the faintest clue where's he nosing around today. Would you like to tell me what you were going to tell him? I'm very trustworthy." He gave her a rakish smile. "John Mayhew, editor and founder of the *Portland Gazette*." He held out an inky hand. "Best newspaper this side of the Rockies."

Libby was surprised. Why, he couldn't be more than thirty-five or so and, ink-stained and disheveled as he was, he didn't fit any image she had of a newspaper editor. But she just smiled and shook his hand, saying, "Pleased to meet you."

He must have seen the surprise in her eyes, for he said, "You're from back East, right? Out here the newspaper business is a mite less polished than back where you come from. I pitch in, setting the type and manning the press, same as any employee of the *Gazette*. I'd be happy to pass along whatever you wanted to tell Mr. Eberle."

It wasn't that Libby didn't trust John Mayhew, but now that she was here, she realized that sharing her suspicions with a newspaperman might not be a good idea after all. What if her suspicions were wrong? She stalled for time while trying to decide whether to confide in this soft-spoken giant of a man. "I just can't believe the founder of anything could be so young. How long have you published the *Gazette*? I've been in Portland less than a year, but I got the feeling the paper had been here forever."

He looked proud. "Twelve years now. Founded it when I was twenty-seven, and it was actually the second paper I started. Newspapering's a young man's game on the frontier. Had a paper I put out all by myself up there in the Washington Territory when I was only twenty-four, but the locale was just a little too rough and tumble for me. Truth to tell, I missed some of the comforts of civilization."

Libby was fascinated. "All by yourself?"

"Ah, that sort of rag's just a matter of letting folks tell you what's going on and then putting it down on paper. Not like the setup I got now: four reporters plus a boy to help set the type. Built it all up from nothing." He looked suddenly bashful, "I only got an eighth grade education myself . . . that's why I'm glad to have Petey . . . your friend Mr. Eberle . . . around. Good man with all that book learning, but not above getting his hands dirty, too. Now, you were going to give me a message for him?"

Despite his easygoing charm, Libby decided she'd really better not speak to John Mayhew about Vera's death and the possible white slaver connection at the theater. He'd said it himself—his job was to 'put it all down on paper', and doing that could start rumors about the Portland Variety. She needed a job, and if she embroiled theater in a scandal, Mr. Crowther would never offer her a permanent position there. Rumors might even ruin the lives and reputations of totally blameless people, and she would be responsible. No, she'd just have to wait and try to find Peter at some later date.

"No, I'm afraid I'll just have to try him another time." Libby wondered if she would have the nerve to come back again. "It's been nice chatting with you. And please know, I read your paper every morning and enjoy it very much." She turned to go.

"Can I leave Mr. Eberle your name and let him know how to find you?"

"No, really, the information I had wasn't that important."

He shrugged, smiled, and turned toward the back room, then stopped and addressed one more question to her. "Give a curious editor a little hint. This story Mr. Eberle's working on . . . what's it about?"

"The Olympics," she said lightly and left him looking befuddled as she closed the door behind her.

There were no new acts to put in that Monday and, for once, there were no torn costumes or laundry emergencies. Hatty wasn't at the theater, so Libby was alone with her thoughts as she reorganized the spools of thread by color and went through the big box of buttons, trying to find matched sets that might prove useful at some point in the future.

Mostly her thoughts circled around Vera and followed the same patterns as her musings the night before. How could she prove Vera had never left the building the night of her death? Suddenly, an obvious starting place jumped into her mind: Sam the doorman. He was the one who saw Vera leaving the theater, or so he'd said. She could ask him about it right now.

She leapt to her feet, spilling the buttons in her lap and leaving them on the floor. In the hallway, though, she paused. If Sam was lying about Vera leaving the theater, then that meant he was involved somehow. Libby found the idea of timid Sam as a white slaver highly unlikely. Still, she supposed she should be careful in how she questioned him just in case, not to arouse his suspicions. After all, it might be as simple as he had just been mistaken about Vera's departure, or he was confusing it with another night.

She found Sam at his usual post just inside the stage door, sitting on his stool and reading the small leather-covered Bible he carried with him at all times. When he heard her approach, he put it in his pocket and smiled at her. "Good afternoon, Miss."

Oh dear, how on earth was she going to find a natural way to bring the topic around to Vera? As she hesitated, inspiration struck. "Sam, I was wondering about. Well, I can't stop thinking about poor Miss Carabella. I wanted to ask you if you thought it might be a good idea for me to take up a small collection from people at the theater for some flowers for her grave. But I'm just not sure if that would be forward of me . . ." She felt a lump in her throat, and suddenly she was no longer simply prying for information. "She had become a real friend to me, and I can't stop thinking about the horrible way she died."

He nodded, obviously upset as well. Libby didn't think he was pretending when he answered, "I know some of the folks here might not want to talk about it with you, but you shouldn't fret, Miss. She's gone on to a better, happier place than we can ever know on earth. She was just a poor sinner like the rest of us, but now she's in heaven, and all of her sins have been washed away. She had a good heart . . . I'm sure she's sitting by the right hand of the Lord. I'll tell you what. If you want to take up a collection, you let me know, Miss. Maybe I could set up a tin box here by the door for people to drop coins in when they come through."

Libby was a little discomfited by the turn Sam's speech had taken, and she was relieved he had finally returned to the subject of flowers. "Thank you, Sam, but I think I'll wait and see what a few more people think first. I don't want to upset Mr. Crowther, and I get the feeling he'd prefer we just continue business as usual. I just wanted to ask you especially what you thought, I know you see everything that goes on around here." She started to turn away, then stopped, as if a thought had just occurred to her.

"You know . . . I suppose you might have been the last person to see her alive, that is, before her abductor. You were still here when she left the theater that night, I would imagine."

"Yep, she was the last one to leave. All by herself, she was too—not like some of the others here a man would blush to call a 'lady.'"

"I was helping her pack earlier than night. If . . . if only I had stayed and left with her, maybe none of this would have happened!"

"Now, now, don't blame yourself, Miss. She must have left here and gone somewhere dangerous. Nothing you or anyone else could have done to change that."

"She didn't say anything about where she was going? If she was meeting someone?"

He shook his head. "Nothing at all. She said to me, 'Well, Sam, it's been a fine run in Portland for me this time.' She always remembered my name, was always real sweet. Seems like often we were the last two folks to leave the Variety at night, and we'd gotten friendly. I asked her if she wanted a cab—like I do for you, Miss—but she said it was such a fine night and she wasn't going far, so she'd walk. Had on her blue cloak with the hood, in case it started raining. Mighty fine she looked in it too, glowing as if she somehow knew she was headed for her heavenly reward. Yes, she was in high sprits that night, big smile on her face when she left."

Libby recalled the smile on Vera's face as she gazed at her reflection in her new ribbon-trimmed underwear. "Yes, she did seem especially happy to me too, that night." Libby thanked Sam, and told him she would let him know about the flowers.

Back in the sewing room, as she picked up the spilled buttons, her head was spinning. Either Vera had left the theater, as the police insisted was the case, or Sam was lying, which she didn't believe. She didn't think he had the imagination to spin a lie with so many details. But could Vera have left and then returned later? If so, how would she have gotten into the locked theater? Either way, something didn't add up.

As she left by the stage door, lost in thought, Libby was surprised to see Peter Eberle, leaning against a lamppost with his trademark crooked grin.

"I understand you have some late-breaking news for me. Has the Olympic Committee contacted you about heading up the Ladies' Sports Division?" His tone was breezy, as before. She was glad to see that he didn't appear to be holding a grudge about the fact she had turned him down about attending the concert.

"I see you deciphered my clue. However, I must confess, I'm surprised you came here to find me. I figured you were hot on the trail of something truly newsworthy."

"On the contrary, you made quite a positive impression on my editor, Mr. Mayhew. He seems to think you have a scoop about some new international sporting event."

She grew more serious. "I'm sorry; that was silly. But I wasn't sure quite what to tell him. He seemed eager to know what story I was looking for you in connection with, and, well, there isn't really any story . . . yet." He raised his eyebrows. "Mr. Eberle, I came to your newspaper office to ask for your help."

"I'm intrigued. You strike me as a woman more than capable of navigating almost any situation, so it must be something quite unusual that has you calling on newspaper reporters you hardly know."

Libby was silent, wondering how to begin. As they'd talked, they had been walking toward the Morrison Bridge streetcar stop, Libby out of force of habit and Peter simply following alongside her. Now, noting her hesitation, Peter motioned to a small bakery half a block ahead, its large sign proudly proclaiming: Portland's Finest German Bakery and Coffee House. "Perhaps we should sit down to discuss it. We'll have some coffee, and you can tell me what this is about."

While Libby took a seat at one of the small tables in the back of the shop, Peter went to the counter and purchased two steaming mugs, plus a warm apple fritter to share. She told herself she would just have a polite taste, but the crisp crust and tender fruit were so delicious, she found that she had eaten almost the whole thing without realizing it. Peter just smiled at her, however, and bought a second pastry. When they had finally settled themselves, he resumed the conversation.

"Now, what is it you need my help investigating?"

Libby took a sip of coffee and started thoughtfully. "It's about the death of Vera Carabella. That was the name, you remember, of the woman found in the tunnels beneath the theater last week?" At Peter's almost imperceptible nod, she went on, "As I told you, she was a friend of mine . . . though this isn't just because she was my friend. I know the police believe her death was a botched abduction attempt in one of the waterfront saloons, but it just doesn't seem to fit the facts as I know them."

Quickly, she outlined her reasons for suspecting that Vera never left the Variety on the last night of her life, that she had been abducted from inside the theater. Peter listened intently and didn't interrupt once. Well, thought Libby as she spoke, he listens as well as he talks. When she had finished, she waited over a minute for him to make some comment. Finally, when he did, it was with a question—a question which indicated that, for the moment at least, he was accepting all her theories as fact.

"How many people have keys to the theater?"

"Why . . . I don't know," she replied, unsure where he was going.

"It may be possible that Sam is telling the truth: Vera did leave the theater that night without her case, because she knew she was coming right back. And if she was coming back with someone—after getting a drink, let's say—it means that person has a key, since the theater would be locked up."

"Some sort of romantic assignation, I guess you're presuming."

Peter nodded slowly. He sounded as if he wasn't sure exactly what he meant, but was thinking it up as he went along. "I do have to say the whole situation seems a little out of the ordinary . . . I mean, Miss Carabella is not the usual type of white slavery victim. From what I know about how these gangs operate, they like to prey on younger girls, often new to the area, who have no friends or family likely to notice they've gone missing."

"Like Polly Pink!"

He looked a little put out at being interrupted. "Polly Pink?"

"She was a dancer at the Variety whose body was found in exactly the same place in the tunnels as Vera's. Only it was months ago . . . last spring, I think." She told him what Hatty had told her. "The police treated her death the same way they're treating Vera's."

"So then. . . ." Peter looked confused, and sat silent a moment. "It stands to reason that the same person must be responsible for both deaths, right?" He waited for Libby to nod. "And you theorize that this person is a white slaver working from inside the Portland Variety?"

Libby nodded again. "Vera might not have been a common sort of white slavery victim, but she was very attractive."

"Very, that's true." Peter concurred wholeheartedly. Libby gave him a look. "Well, I did catch the show at the Variety a few weeks back, and Miss Carabella was a decided highlight of the evening."

Libby shouldn't have been surprised that Peter had seen the show or found Vera attractive, but she found that she felt a twinge of jealousy at the thought of him sitting in the audience and ogling Vera. She brushed it aside and returned to her previous train of thought.

"Vera did tell Sam she was only going somewhere close by, which supports your hypothesis that she was meeting a person she knew . . . someone she didn't want to be seen leaving the theater with, but who was waiting nearby."

Peter jumped in, "Of course, once again there's only Sam's word for what she said, although if Sam is lying, then he must be involved in her death."

"I really didn't get the feeling Sam was lying."

Peter gave her a slightly patronizing smile. "With all due respect, Miss Seale, the fact that you find Sam trustworthy doesn't clear him of suspicion."

"I know that," said Libby a little peevishly, "I wasn't taking him off the list, just saying that . . ."

Peter cut in, "Are you making a list? Really?" He cocked his head. "Are you seriously considering trying to investigate the white slave trade and catch a murderer all by yourself?"

"I . . . I guess so," she stammered. Up until this moment, it had seemed like a logic puzzle in a game book. She hadn't really thought about the fact that, if she wanted to bring Vera's killer to justice, and more importantly, stop whoever was procuring for the slave trade at the Portland Variety, she was going to have to do more than sit at a table and spin possible scenarios. She lifted her chin and said firmly. "If the police won't do it, then yes."

"I wouldn't expect help from the police," he said ruefully. "I'm afraid it's fairly well-known, or highly suspected, that whoever is the money and power behind the waterfront crime in Portland has the police in their pocket."

"That's monstrous! Their job is to protect innocent citizens, not collaborate in their downfall!"

"Surely, police corruption is not unheard of in New York. Why, just last year, I believe we ran a story from the national wires that implicated no less than seventeen of New York's finest in a political scandal."

"But we're talking about human lives, Mr. Eberle!"

"And we're also talking about a relatively young city whose entire police department is formed by political commissions and personal connections!" He had raised his voice as he spoke, obviously reiterating already-formed opinions that angered him greatly. Somewhat abashed, he continued in a more pleasant tone. "Of course, I'm not suggesting the entire police force is composed of liars and thieves. However, I highly doubt that those in a position of power would condone a full-scale investigation into the white slave trade. If nothing else, consider the lack of enough trained policemen for a city this size, not to mention the rising crime rate. Surely, your first-hand experience last week, or should I say first-foot . . ." She gave him a look, and he sheepishly acknowledged the feebleness of the jest before going on, ". . . is anecdotal evidence of the rise in street crime, the proliferation of which occupies most of our crime-fighting manpower."

Libby considered this. "Fair enough. We will simply have to investigate this as civilians and present incontrovertible evidence to the police once we have uncovered it."

"We . . . ?"

"You're going to help me, aren't you?"

Peter was silent, and her last statement hung in the air between them. For a moment, Libby was sure he was going to tell her that he couldn't or wouldn't be a party to this . . . she had to admit it . . . rather far-fetched and possibly dangerous undertaking. He stared at her, an unreadable look in his eyes, and she wondered what he was seeing. Then he gave a half-laugh, half-sigh, and resumed speaking as before.

"So, the question is, who has keys to the theater besides Sam?"

"Well, I'm sure Mr. Crowther has one. And I remember hearing him arguing with Vera once. I just caught the tail end of their conversation, but I think they were arguing about money. Certainly Crowther was hopping mad when he came out of Vera's dressing room; he barreled right into me as if he didn't even see me there. I'm glad he wasn't yelling at me . . ."

Peter's voice took on a note of genuine concern, "Miss Seale, if you're right, then one of the men at this theater is a ruthless criminal. If you start asking questions, you'll be putting yourself at a horrible risk."

She was touched by his gentle sobriety. "There doesn't appear to be any other way. I will be careful, and I believe I can find out information without it being obvious why I want to know." She laughed halfheartedly, partly in an attempt to dispel the sudden seriousness that had come over them and partly because she was unprepared to face what the tenderness in Peter's voice might mean. "If there's one thing I have learned about theatrical folk, it's that it's much more difficult to get them to stop talking than to start. Now that I think about it, there must be more people with keys, and I know where to start to find out who."

"All right, then." He assumed a more businesslike tone. "We need a plan of attack. You can investigate at the theater, ascertaining who holds keys and, if possible, what those people were doing that Saturday night." Another thought occurred to him. "Also, the person responsible for both botched abductions has presumably perpetrated some successful ones as well, which we don't even know about."

Libby was horrified. She hadn't thought that this might have been going on for a long time, years even. Who knows how many unfortunate girls might have been dispatched to lives of shame and degradation in far-off ports?

Peter was still talking, ". . . find out if there have been other girls or performers who have vanished under mysterious circumstances."

"Yes. Yes, I will do that."

"Please be especially careful. This is not some melodrama with a villain twirling his moustache. If someone at the theater is involved in the white slave trade, your own life may be in danger."

"I said I would be careful, and I will," Libby replied, unsure of whether she was touched at his repeated warnings or insulted by them.

Peter either did not notice or chose to ignore the tart tone in her voice. He went on, "Now, I believe you said this Polly Pink, before she was at the Variety, was a . . ." He hesitated, clearly uncomfortable.

"A prostitute." She completed the sentence for him. "I know the word, Mr. Eberle."

Peter stared, and Libby wondered if she had gone too far, as usual. A proper lady would never use such a bald word, not when there were so many delicate euphemisms available to her. But although she could swear he was blushing, he recovered his composure and seemed almost amused.

"A prostitute, yes," he agreed. "I think we should also be investigating the other side of this puzzle. How did Polly Pink come to be at the Variety in the first place? If we find the person who offered her a job there, likely we have found our criminal."

She thought. "I know Hatty mentioned Polly Pink and her past to me. But I doubt she would know where exactly the girl had worked before starting at the theater."

"I believe I can discreetly do a bit of investigating and find out where she was working. Once we know that, maybe I can find out who it was that offered her the dancing job that led her to Crowther's Variety." He paused only slightly, but Libby could have sworn he almost blushed again, "My work for the paper brings me into contact with most of the well-known brothels in the city."

Now it was Libby's turn to blush, as she was unable to stop herself from wondering just how familiar he would have to be to "discreetly investigate" the local houses of ill repute.

He went on, "And, I'll be honest with you, I would like nothing better than to uncover a web of corruption centering around Crowther's Portland Variety and to write a story that will force the city politicians to take notice. This could be quite a coup for the *Gazette*."

"So it's settled, then!" For the first time since Vera's murder, Libby found herself looking forward to going into work. The tasks ahead were difficult, but they would certainly be more useful than darning stockings and sewing on beads. "Shall we meet again on Thursday to compare notes on what we've discovered?"

He laughed. "You run a tight ship, Miss Seale. No sooner have I agreed to help you investigate than you are presenting me with a deadline. Have you considered a career as a newspaper editor?"

She answered him with a smile only, but the lack of words as they left the bakery was the easy silence of friends and comrades.

SIX

PETER WAS TWO BLOCKS past his tram stop before he even noticed he'd missed it, so he decided he might as well just walk the rest of the way home. He supposed he should be organizing his thoughts about the investigation, deciding where to begin and how he was going to pursue it while still turning in his regular stories for the *Gazette*, but instead all he could think about was Libby.

She was completely unlike any woman he had known before, and Peter Eberle fancied he'd known more than a few in his twenty-eight years. He found most women predictable and uninteresting, at least as far as anything other than romance was concerned, but with Libby Seale he was never sure what she would say or do next. Consequently, he was fascinated by her.

He had tried to be nonchalant tonight when she stepped out of Crowther's and saw him waiting. In reality, his heart had been thumping and he was as close as he ever got to being nervous. At the last second, he had found his voice, though, and once the conversation had begun, he found himself remarkably at ease. With Libby, he never had to search for words, and she seemed to understand what he was going to say before he said it. There were moments in their conversation when they had almost finished each other's sentences.

All of this was not to say that he hadn't noticed the few, pale freckles on her nose or the way her soft, brown eyes flashed with delight when she was amused. And her thick hair, which she wore pulled back and tied up in some complicated knot he couldn't understand . . . why, he bet that when it was down and she was brushing it out before bed, it reached past her waist. He would like to see Libby Seale preparing for bed. For a good half block, he simply luxuriated in imagining the scene—wondering when, and if, it might become a reality.

As of this morning, Peter hadn't thought he would ever see Libby again, given the polite but definite way she had demurred when he asked her to join him for that choir concert. So when John Mayhew had told him that a very pretty young brunette had stopped by the paper, wishing to speak to him about a story regarding the Olympics, he had been surprised and delighted. He had assumed that she had come to tell him she had reconsidered her refusal, and while that wasn't a usual thing for a woman to do, well, nothing Libby did was exactly commonplace. He had been prepared for the evening to take a turn for the romantic—certainly he hadn't expected that she wanted to see him about abduction and murder—and at first he had experienced a profound sense of disappointment. But then, even as she outlined the sordid and depressing situation that had brought her to him, he found he couldn't help but admire her for her passionate commitment to finding the truth and her intelligent, well-reasoned analysis of the facts. He hated to admit it, even to himself, but he could almost view Vera Carabella's death as a good thing if it meant that now he had a reason to see more of Libby.

So now he was committed to investigating a crime that, if he was honest, he didn't believe there was a chance of solving. Peter hadn't told Libby, probably wouldn't tell her, but he wasn't completely convinced there was more to this than there appeared to be. Very often, the simplest explanation was the right one, and likely Vera Carabella's abduction happened pretty much the way the police thought it did. Perhaps Vera really had just forgotten her bag. Or maybe she had let someone she knew, the criminal, into the theater herself while Sam the doorman wasn't looking. Even if the villain was someone who worked at the theater, the gangs that controlled the white slave trade were clever enough and had long enough practice to avoid detection by a couple of amateurs.

Not that what he had said to Libby about the corruption that allowed crimes like these to flourish had been disingenuous. It really did anger him greatly to see money and influence win out over justice and morality. It was only that he doubted his and Libby's ability to make any difference with their crusade. He wondered if John Mayhew, stalwart and upstanding man that he was, would even print an article if Peter wrote one. He supposed it would have to contain unassailable proof.

He had reached Park House, the residential hotel where he had a small, nearly empty room. Entering it now, he tried to see it as Libby might, were she ever to cross its threshold. Though he had been in Portland for three years now, he had acquired little in the way of furnishings. There were a few small framed photographs of his family back in New Haven and a stack of books on the bedside chair he never used. All the clothes he had in the world—three suits, six shirts and two collars—fit without effort in the wardrobe. Beyond the half-empty bottle of Macassar oil for his hair, the silver-handled hairbrush, which was a present from his mother, and the pool of loose change which littered the top of the hotel bureau, that was everything.

He spent relatively little time awake in this room and had never cared what it looked like, but now he wondered what Libby would

71

think of someone who had never bothered to make a home for himself. A careless bounder, she would probably conclude, and maybe that wasn't far off. Suddenly, it wasn't what he wanted to be.

Well, he thought, getting undressed and ready for bed, nothing to do about it now. If he had been too busy to think about his room before, he was going to be doubly so now. Tomorrow morning he had to meet with a delegation of editors from California making a visit to Portland—Mayhew always gave these assignments to Peter, since of all the *Gazette* staff, he had the most polish. Then he had to interview the new head of the City Transport Commission over lunch before he could even think about attempting to find out where Polly Pink had been employed before the Variety. Given the high caliber of the dancing girls at the theater, he decided he might as well start at the top end of the city's numerous bordellos and bawdy houses.

Well, at least that job might not be so onerous. He fell asleep with pleasant visions in his head.

Libby started off investigating as soon as she arrived at the theater in the morning. She found Jack Reilly, the stage manager, in the back-stage workshop, pasting patches on the colorful paper parasols for the upcoming Rickshaw Ballet.

"Those must be getting quite a lot of wear and tear," she said to him, noticing the many small rips in the crepe paper.

Jack looked up from his work and tried to brush back the lock of dark red hair that habitually fell over his eyes using his wrist, since strips of glue-covered paper were dangling from his fingers. "You could say that," he agreed. "This Chinese number is keeping me busy, all right. I can only hope once it goes in the show, the amount of repair work will taper off. They're rehearsing it over and over at the moment, and I'm spending half my day fixing the props." He motioned toward the back wall, where several two-wheeled carts decorated with red and yellow sequins leaned against a flat. "I keep waiting for one of those rickshaw wheels to fall off during the dance number. They're not very sturdy to begin with, and some of those girls push them around the stage like they're really trying to get to Peking." He smiled, and she knew he didn't really mind.

Libby hadn't really gotten a chance to get to know Jack well, but from what she did know, there wasn't a mean bone in his lanky body. He was quiet, mostly kept to himself, and didn't seem happy unless he was busy with something backstage.

She picked up one of the parasols and twirled it around, admiring the blur of color. "Do you build all the set pieces and props yourself, Mr. Reilly? That must be quite a lot of work for one person."

"Oh, no. I design 'em all and build the smaller pieces. Then the stagehands help me with the construction of the rest of them." He continued to patch parasols as he spoke.

"You do a very good job. The settings really are lovely," Libby said, impressed. "I imagine you work very long hours."

"Oh, it's not so hard when you've been around the stage as long as I have." He paused and looked up at her curiously. "But surely you didn't come back here to talk to me about rickshaws. What can I do for you, Miss Seale?"

"Well, I actually came to ask if you knew when our shipment of laundry supplies was to be delivered today. Hatty asked me to press some shirts, and we seem to be out of starch. I was afraid the new shipment might not come until after I'd left for the day."

He thought for a moment. "I believe we have a large dry goods shipment coming from Meier and Frank Wholesalers sometime this afternoon, but they may not be here until after four or so."

Her face fell. "Oh, dear, I was afraid it might be that late." In fact she'd been sure of it, but she needed to bring the subject 'round to getting into the theater after business hours. "You see, Hatty's still out with that cold today, and I promised her I'd get all the ironing out of the way before she comes in tomorrow. Now I don't see how I'll possibly be able to do that . . ." She trailed off, then leaned in toward him conspiratorially. "Actually, I was thinking about working very early tomorrow, and I wondered if you could tell me whether that's common around the Variety. I certainly don't want to ask about it if it's not something other people habitually do. And I know at some of my past jobs, the company often doesn't want to deal with the expense of paying overtime wages. Tell me, do many people have keys to the theater so they can come in and work early or on Sundays?"

"Not really. I suppose if you needed to come in for a special reason, you could borrow the key from Hatty. I know she has one."

Oddly, she hadn't known Hatty had a key. But somehow she didn't feel that was going to prove crucial to her investigation. "I'm sure you have a key as well. Your work must keep you here late many nights. After all, rickshaws don't build themselves!"

He smiled ruefully. "To be honest, some nights I would love to stay late and work. Going home means dealing with six children, including the new baby—my wife would have my head if I stayed at work too late. We just had a baby, like I said . . ." He waved off Libby's congratulations and continued, ". . . and my wife counts on me to get home at a reasonable hour so she can take a short rest. The baby's a fussy one, not like her older brothers. Name's Ruby, after my grandma . . . finally got a girl on our sixth try. Three months old next week . . ." Despite Libby's continuing smile, he seemed a little embarrassed by having revealed this much personal information and quickly resumed his businesslike tone. "No, indeed, most nights I leave here right after the last show ends. In fact, I can't recall the last time I had to stay later."

This was a bonus. Lying in bed the night before, she had decided that, despite what she and Peter had discussed, there wasn't much hope of getting people to account for their whereabouts on the Saturday night Vera was killed. Now Jack had just unintentionally given himself an alibi—although she could hear Peter's voice ringing in her ears reminding her just because someone said something it was not proof that he was telling the truth. She made a note to try to find someone who would corroborate Jack's assertion that he rushed home to his family every night directly after the show. She returned to the subject at hand.

"So, are you and Hatty the only ones with keys? Oh, and I suppose Mr. Crowther has one as well." He looked at her quizzically, and she was sure he was going to ask her why she was pressing the issue, but instead he counted off on his fingers. She realized happily that for the most part, people would simply answer any questions she asked just because they were always willing to talk about themselves and their work.

"Of course, Mr. Crowther," he agreed. "And Sam—he locks up most nights after everyone else is gone. Oh, and Mr. Maynard has a key. He's the first one in most mornings to deal with business matters like paying the local tradesmen and so forth." He paused. "You know, if you wanted to come in early some morning, I think you could probably just have Mr. Maynard let you in the back way."

"That's a fine idea," said Libby. "I'll have to ask him about that. Thanks so much for all your help, Mr. Reilly!" Putting down the parasol, she smiled at him and left the way she had come, feeling quite pleased with her first foray into detection. Only five minutes and not only did she now know who had keys to the theater, she also could, pending confirmation, cross Jack off her list of suspects in Vera's abduction and murder.

When the stage doorman saw Libby, he smiled gravely, but with obvious pleasure.

"Miss Seale, made up your mind about those flowers?"

Libby had completely forgotten. "Uh, no, Sam. It didn't seem like there was much support." As she said it, she realized the words were probably true. "I think people around the theater just want to forget about the whole incident."

"Terrible." Sam looked genuinely saddened.

She couldn't believe how lucky she was. She hadn't had to broach the subject of Vera's death, since Sam mentioned it first. He went on, "We may not know why it happened, but surely the Lord had a reason for calling Miss Carabella to him when he did. There's no reason for folks to pretend it didn't happen." He hung his head. "I told her to take a hansom cab, but she knew what she wanted to do, Miss Carabella did, and devil take the consequences. She wouldn't listen to me, no . . . but there must have been a higher power guiding her that night."

Sam looked so forlorn, almost as if he harbored some guilt for her death. Suddenly a new scenario entered her mind which might explain why Sam could feel responsible. What if he had left his post earlier than usual that night, before the last person, Vera, had actually left the building? If so, he might have felt he had to lie to the police when they asked if Vera had passed by him that night, not wanting to admit to Crowther that he had not done his job. She wondered how she could test this hypothesis without breaking her vow to Peter not to ask direct questions that might arouse suspicion.

"Sam, you look tired. Are you getting enough sleep?" He nodded, though wearily, and pulled out his Bible, but before he could launch into a sermon, Libby continued. "You must work horribly long hours, since you get here in the mornings and then stay here until the last person leaves. You're probably here, what, twelve hours a day? Fourteen?" She looked at him sympathetically.

"Oh, I don't mind the long hours. Ever since my Missus passed on, I don't have any reason to rush home." He cast his eyes heavenward, and whispered something under his breath. "She was a God-fearing Christian and the light of my life," he added, looking intently at Libby.

Vastly uncomfortable, she pressed on. "Still . . . that must be a long day for you to sit here watching the door. It must get lonely."

"Oh, no, Miss. I have the Lord by my side, keeping me company," he said reverently, patting the Bible. "Better company than the lot of these theater folk, if you don't mind me saying. Some of them are good people, but between you and me, I can tell that some of those dancers and contortionists are in league with the Devil."

He looked at her for confirmation, but her mind was elsewhere. At this rate, she would never find out whether her new theory was true, and she wasn't sure how much more talk about the Devil she could stomach. Libby decided she would just have to risk asking Sam directly, letting him know she was investigating further into Vera's death.

"Sam, I almost hate to ask you this . . ." The doorman looked at her expectantly. "It's about the night Miss Carabella died." She took a breath, "Just between us—and I want you to know I have no interest in getting you in any trouble—is there any chance you might have left the theater early that night, for some very good reason I'm sure, and never saw Vera leave after all?"

Instead of surprise, his face registered understanding. "I can tell, Miss, you aren't satisfied with the police explanation, are you? I thought so, when you started asking me questions about it the other day." He shook his head. "Believe me, she left here like I said."

Whether or not she believed him, she had no choice but to let the matter drop. "Your word is good enough for me, Sam. I apologize if I you found the question offensive," now she tried to cover her tracks, "and I'd appreciate it if you kept this just between ourselves. I don't need everyone knowing that I can't seem to make peace with Miss Carabella's passing. You're so sensitive, I feel it's all right that I told you." At least I hope so, she thought.

"Of course not. Don't you have any fear, child," Sam affirmed. "Now, I don't blame you for wanting to find out what happened. There's something mighty suspicious about that killing. I thought so myself." Getting excited, he spoke more quickly. "You know, if you're trying to find out more, maybe I can help you. I see everything that goes on around here, and I want to get the answers as much as you do."

She nodded. "Thank you, Sam, that would be very helpful." And then she thought, in for a penny in for a pound. "In fact . . ."

Quickly, she outlined her interest in Jack's habitual departure time from the theater, and Sam was able to corroborate everything Jack said, including the new baby's propensity for colic. It was such a relief for Libby to ask direct questions rather than beating around the bush, and she was glad she had decided to take Sam into her confidence.

It was only on his third try that Peter struck pay dirt. Madame Josephine's place of business was an oversize barge, painted scarlet and gold, anchored out in the middle of the Willamette River. It could only be reached by rowboat and was actually one of two houses of ill repute that chose this tactic for ensuring the security of its girls, the prompt payment in full of its customers, and easy access to a change of address when a neighborhood began to prove inhospitable.

Josephine received Peter alone in a small private salon on the lower of the river scow's two levels. On this level, there was also a dance hall and a full size saloon bar, as well as other small meeting rooms which could be booked for private parties. The upper deck was only accessible via a carpeted staircase, always manned by one of the four strongmen who kept order on the boat. This deck had a wraparound covered promenade which contained the girls' bedrooms and Madame Josephine's private quarters. Other than the four hulking bouncers, carefully hand-picked for their strength, continence, and their ability to turn a blind eye, the floating palace was a completely feminine place. Josephine ran a tight ship, and the girls she employed obeyed her every utterance or they were summarily shipped back to shore. This order and discipline had stood them in good stead during the high flooding of 1876, when Josephine and her female employees had manned the unwieldy ship in a thoroughly professional manner, keeping the barge afloat when some experienced sailors on the Willamette had seen their boats founder.

Josephine was now in her early fifties, but as Peter surveyed her lying languorously across a plush divan, he acknowledged to himself that she was still an alluring woman. Without changing her posture she eyed him, but a faint smile played about her rouged lips. Her voice was perfectly friendly as she said, "Peter, darling boy, it's only three in the afternoon. We've never had the pleasure of your company in daytime before." She motioned him to an ornate chair beside her. "You are even handsomer in full light."

Peter forbore from pointing out that the windows were draped with so many yards of lace and tassel-clad plum velvet that the room was, even with the sun high in the sky, a bit on the dim side.

"Josephine," he began somewhat hesitantly. And then, deciding that rather than a question, it would be better to begin with a compliment, he finished, ". . . it appears that the secret to eternal youth must be living on water." She nodded her head graciously, like queen accepting the courtesies due to her. "I'm afraid that it is not pleasure which leads me here this afternoon. I've come seeking a favor from you . . . I need some information."

Madame Josephine didn't exactly sit up, but she shifted her body in such a way that Peter knew that she was now on her guard. "A woman like me . . . I never leave my house . . . what do I know?" Even after nearly thirty years in this country her grammar and her voice carried traces of her native Hungary. She had an almost sing-song quality to her speech that was the conversational equivalent to a shrug.

"A girl by the name of Fanny Watson was killed back in June and her body discovered in the tunnels beneath the Variety downtown. Apparently she died during an abduction by the slavers who prowl the waterfront. I know she was working as a gay girl just prior to her time at the theater. Judging by her reported beauty, I have come to you first—knowing your discerning eye and high standards when it comes to your flock—to see if she was working for you."

He neglected to mention having already inquired unsuccessfully at Miss Dora Lynn's house and again at Liverpool Liz's in Pine Street, figuring the little white lie might flatter Josephine enough to cause her to answer truthfully. Likewise, with all three madams, he had used Polly Pink's real name, figuring that if he saw a flicker of recognition in an eye, then he would know that, even if the answer came back negative, his question had found its mark.

Now he was not disappointed. Josephine's eyes did more than flicker, they rolled. "That terrible name. Was she back to using it at the theater, when she went to go legitimate?" Josephine's tone conveyed more than scorn.

"No. No, she was using the name Polly Pink."

"Well, I will say this for her then: she was not so dull-witted, after all. I gave her that name, you know?" She didn't wait for an answer. "But she was a silly, silly girl to leave me here. None of *my* girls ever end up in the tunnels. It was very, very sad what happened to her, yes, but my other girls, now they see more than ever," her hand waved about the room lazily, and her eyes swept over the opulence around them, "how nice I look after my little ones."

At least until their looks begin to fade, Peter thought but did not say. He had never thought about it before, but he wondered what happened to the girls who "outgrew" life onboard Madame Josephine's barge.

"Can you tell me anything else about Polly? Were there perhaps any gentleman who called on her regularly?"

Madame Josephine's eyes stopped roving and met Peter's with a calculating look. It had cost her nothing, Peter knew, to admit that Polly had worked there, since he already knew she had worked somewhere as a gay girl, and he was already well-acquainted with the services this house provided. No, merely admitting she had employed Polly was not damaging. But what he wanted from her now, that was a different matter. He could imagine her thoughts. Discretion was the foremost quality of a successful madam, and if word reached the ears of her prominent and powerful clients that Josephine was no longer trustworthy . . . it didn't bear thinking on. His question remained unanswered, and he spoke again.

"You can trust me that none of this information will ever be made public, nor my source revealed to anyone." He paused then added meaningfully, "Surely we've been through enough that you can count on my word. It isn't as if I'm going to row back to shore and head straight to the police."

He alluded to an incident on the boat over a year before. A prominent police official had slipped and broken his ankle on the slick deck, and in order to spare him (and his wife) embarrassment, he had been moved by Josephine's flunkies back to his home in town before a doctor had been called. Peter happened to have been on the barge that night and, like everyone onboard, had become aware of this situation in short order, since the police captain was lying on the foredeck screaming in pain loud enough to wake the dead. Josephine, knowing Peter's occupation, had taken him aside and begged him not to report what he had seen. He agreed, and true to his word, no mention of the incident ever appeared in the press. So she owed him a favor, and both of them knew it.

"All right, my darling, I will answer your questions. But you know there are some names I cannot mention . . . but I will tell you what happened."

And so she began, in her own unhurried, Eastern-European way—the runaway farmgirl Fanny appearing in her parlor a year before with nothing to peddle but a fading freshness and an appealing figure, the rechristening and refurbishing of the girl as Polly Pink (an entirely pink wardrobe giving her what passed for a definitive personality among the girls on the boat.) Once she warmed to the tale, Josephine seemed to delight in the smallest details and Peter got a view most men never got of the behind-the-scenes care and craft it took to keep an establishment like Madame Josephine's at the top of the Portland scene. Fascinating as he found it, Peter didn't see that it could possibly help him figure out who was behind Polly's abduction and death.

With trepidation, he interrupted Josephine as she began to re-count the complicated maneuverings surrounding the pre-booking of girls for the New Year's Eve gala held in the ship's dance hall, and the part Polly played in the overall scheme of things on the boat. "I'm sure it takes a lot of preparation . . . But tell me, how did Polly come to be working at the Variety? Did someone from the theater see her here and offer her a job?"

He needn't have worried about interrupting her. Any irritation Josephine felt at being interrupted was wiped away as she heard his question. Her eyes popped. "See her? Well, he certainly didn't see her here! I'd never seen the man before." Her indignation was still fresh after all this time. "One day, in the middle of the afternoon, he shows up—some man saying he is from the theater—and he wishes to speak to one of my girls. Before I know anything, she is packing her bags and is gone."

Even through the sputtering, Peter could make out the gist of her story, and he felt his pulse quicken. "A man from the theater? Do you know his name?"

"No, I never know it . . ." she waved away names as unimportant, ". . . he is burly, you know, unattractive with a big handlebar mustache on his red face and very little hair on the top of his head." Peter assumed Libby would be able to put a name to this rather vivid description.

"But you say he had never been here before?"

"Never," she bristled, "I never forget the faces of my gentlemen."

"Yet he asked for Polly specifically?" Josephine nodded, getting tired of repeating herself.

"Did Polly ever go ashore by herself? Could she have met him . . ."

"No, no," she cut him off, "never by herself. In fact, if I am recollecting it right she had not been in the city for weeks before."

"Before . . . When exactly did he come 'round?"

She sank back petulantly into her cushions, but appeared to be pondering his question. "It was the first Wednesday of the month . . . of June. We had just gotten our delivery of champagne, and so I was allowing them, this man and Polly, to use the green parlor at the other end of the boat, away from the bar where the unpacking was going on."

For a moment, Peter was stymied. Clearly, there must have been a reason this man . . . Peter was willing to bet it was Crowther himself . . . had specifically asked for Polly that day, but he couldn't figure it out. There must be more to the story. He framed his next question as broadly as he could.

"Why do you think he asked for Polly Pink, seeing as he'd never been on the boat?"

Josephine was leaning back, her face turned to the window, one pale hand playing with the lace curtain. She didn't look at him, "Oh, I am just a silly woman. I don't know. I'm sorry."

Peter knew she was lying now. He was willing to bet she had a very clear idea, but this must be what she hadn't wanted to tell him about. Nothing else she had said was incriminating to anyone important. He sighed, "No, I'm sorry. I suppose, after all, the police will have to investigate. I had hoped I might be able to understand on my own without calling them in, since this part of Polly's life may prove incidental to her death. But now . . ."

He trailed off, and Josephine glared at him. But she started talking again.

"A few days, maybe a week before this, Polly had made a . . . new friend. No names, you understand? There had been some sort of tribute in town, and this man, he was the guest of honor that night. All of them, he and the men at this banquet, they all come here to Josephine afterwards to continue the celebration, and this man, he ends up with Polly." She looked straight at Peter, as if to impress on him the oddness of what she said next. "Now, you must understand, these men were already drunk, and most of them disappear up the stair with any girl, doesn't matter who, and are safely home with their wives within the hour. But not this one. First, he insist I must provide him with a blond, and oh, Polly she was very blond. Beautiful white-blond hair, and so lovely with her eyes, which were surprisingly dark hazel color, like river water on a cloudy day. Well he . . . this man, he is very pleased when I introduce him to Polly." Josephine's pride at being able to please even a picky customer was evident. "And then he stays all the night upstairs with her. Not completely talking, she tells me later, but talking a lot and only of Polly." Josephine gave him a superior smile, "Men always talk of themselves. They never want to hear about the girl. But Polly tells him all about herself, where she is from and how she comes here . . . on and on. And in the morning, he asks Polly to go with him."

She looked at him almost triumphantly. "Of course, she tells him no. My girls know better than to go out there in the cold world, where anything can happen to them. Here they are safe."

She had apparently finished. Peter wanted more. "And this man just left?"

"Yes, he left that morning. But a few days later, Polly gets her theatrical visitor, and before I know it, she is a dancing girl. Somebody wanted her off this boat, and within a week, she is off it." And within a month, she is dead was left unsaid, but floated in the air. "So now you know."

Josephine leaned back, satisfied at the effect of her words.

Peter felt confused, but elated as well. His first day detecting, and he felt he had stumbled onto something big. Madame Josephine had left out the name of Polly's conversational partner, but he felt certain he could find it out. He knew just where to start looking. He rose to go.

"Thank you. You've been extraordinarily helpful."

But it appeared Madame Josephine was not finished after all. Her eyes glittered. "Why is it you want to know all about Polly now? It has been almost half a year, and after all, what is she to you? She is just one girl among so many who go missing, except she has the misfortune to die rather than to go where she is told."

Peter was appalled at the callousness in her tone. But she had fulfilled her promise and told him what she knew, and he didn't see that there could be any harm in her knowing why he was asking. "I believe the man who killed Polly was involved in the death of another woman at the theater. A performer there by the name of Vera Carabella. I am hoping to find the connections . . ."

At the mention of Vera's name, Josephine had sat up. Now she broke in. "Yes, the magician's assistant. So that is what you are here about." At Peter's surprised look, she commented wryly, "When it is a girl of the streets who is found in the tunnel, no one asks questions. But this woman had admirers, very high-up admirers."

"Did you know Miss Carabella?" It hadn't occurred to Peter to ask Josephine about Vera, and now he saw clearly that that would have been a mistake.

"You would be surprised what one learns about the goings-on in town even without ever having to leave this room. That magic man she worked with, he is here every week of their run. And many men have mentioned her beauty to me, this Vera. It seems the theater is proving quite the competition to my floating palace while she is there. And it is only last week—" She stopped herself and said solicitously, "It is so sad to hear that she ends up in the tunnel just like our Polly."

Josephine had just opened up so many fresh fields of enquiry, he wasn't sure where to start. "You say Signor Carlo was here every week? Would he have been here last Saturday night?"

"Yes, of course. Every week, right after the last show, he was here by eleven at the latest. Usually he doesn't leave till noon on Sunday. This last week, he was here practically till dinner time. Of course, I make him pay extra, but he only smile and say in that ridiculous accent of his 'Who do I need to see in this backward town?'"

Well, it seemed Carlo, for what it was worth, had an alibi for the evening of Vera's death.

"Did Signor Carlo say anything about Miss Carabella that you recall? Or rather, did any of the men you mentioned having spoken of her say anything about her, other than mentioning her looks?" He realized he was asking too many questions, and too quickly, but words kept coming out of his mouth before he had a chance to figure out the best way to phrase them.

Josephine seemed to enjoy seeing him get a little flustered. "You mean to ask me did anyone say they were planning to abduct or kill her? No, my darling boy, nobody has confessed to any crimes in my hearing."

Her tone suddenly got less jovial. "Peter, Peter, you must be careful what you are digging at. These men who do these things, they are not playing games. Perhaps it would be better to just let Vera and Polly rest in peace." She rose and smoothed her skirts. "Now there is so much I need to do, I'm afraid I must say good afternoon." She held out her hand for him to kiss, which he did and headed for the door. Turning back on the threshold, she gazed inscrutably at him. "So handsome . . . Be wise, my boy, it is better to be handsome than to be smart."

Peter couldn't help feeling he had somehow muffed the last part of his conversation with Madame Josephine. One moment he had been using veiled threats to extract information from her, and the next she had been as firmly in control as she had been at the start, treating him like a child and closing the conversation before he was ready. Part of him wanted to call her right back into the room and continue questioning her, but even as he thought it, he realized that he didn't know what he would ask her. Perhaps he would come back.

Right now, he had to pay a visit to the morgue.

SEVEN

Libby sat alone sewing as morning turned to afternoon, considering the group of people with keys to the Portland Variety. As she mended her way into the afternoon, she envisioned how to approach each of them without arousing suspicion. She found herself wondering what Peter would do in her place, if he had a repertoire of reporter's tricks for bringing conversations casually around to important matters without being obvious.

She decided to tackle Maynard first. As the afternoon deepened, Libby found reasons to loiter in the back hallway near his office, hoping to catch his attention. Given his wolfish proclivities, it shouldn't be too hard to get him to initiate the conversation, since she felt it would look suspicious if, after the numerous times she had dodged him, she were now to suddenly drop by his desk for a chat. Besides, Maynard was at his most malleable in the moments just after you had caught him making an improper advance. Creepy he might be, but not bold—when confronted directly, he tended to get suddenly timid and obsequious.

Libby wasn't certain just how far she was willing to go in encouraging liberties from Mr. Maynard, but she felt it was her duty to use whatever weapons she had at her disposal in her pursuit of the truth. Goodness knows, a female investigator had few enough advantages, besides the obvious one that most men couldn't even conceive of such a thing and therefore paid no attention to anything a woman said or asked.

She had just finished refolding the basket of clean laundry she had 'accidentally' dropped near the theater office, figuring that if Maynard didn't appear soon, she would just have to spill it all over again, when he oiled his way around the corner and spied her crouched on the floor, bent over the basket.

"Well, had a little accident, Miss Seale?" he inquired. His eyes raked over the basket and the frilly feminine underclothes folded neatly inside. Libby had taken no chances when planning to attract his attention. "Do let me help you up."

Without waiting for a word from her, he placed a hand under her elbow and lifted her to her feet. His grasp was firm. He was stronger than he looked, and Libby—automatically seeing the possible implications of this—couldn't suppress a shudder. The hands which had just supported her elbow might be the same ones which had snuffed out the lives of two women. This wasn't a good way to start, thought Libby, shuddering when he touched me! Why don't I just tell him flat out I'm afraid of him?

Luckily, Maynard took her shudder for a shiver. "Drafty back here in these hallways, no? Perhaps you'd care for a nip of brandy? I always keep a little flask in my desk." He winked at her, "Not that anyone needs to know. Just be our little secret."

"No. No thank you, Mr. Maynard, but . . . um . . . thank you." She drew the line at batting her eyes, but she played the helpless, flustered female for all she was worth. Then, as if the thought had just occurred to her, "I owe you thanks anyway for helping me out so graciously the other day." At Maynard's blank look, she added, "With Miss Carabella's address."

"Oh, yes, my pleasure. Anything I can do for a lovely lady." Libby stared at him with wide eyes, so he felt compelled to clarify. "You, I mean, not Miss Carabella." He didn't appear to want to open the topic of Vera, but as Libby remained silent, he tacked on, "Er . . . sad business that. Glad to know it all worked out."

She saw her opening. "Yes. Turns out Vera has a sister back in Topeka and I'm sure she'll be very grateful for her sister's things." If he knew this was a lie, Maynard gave no indication, or he hid his surprise well. Surely if he was a slaver, he would be flustered to think his victim had a family who might pursue the truth about her death.

She tried again, "Oddly, Vera had told me she hadn't any family at all, so I was surprised to learn she had a sister—and six nieces and nephews. I can't think why she lied to me."

He appeared to consider it. "Well, there are so many possible reasons. Perhaps her family didn't approve of her being on the stage."

"Oh, how clever you are." She gave him a big smile. "Still, it hurts me that she lied to me." The smile became a pout.

"I wouldn't take it personally."

"I don't suppose she would have lied to you."

"I can't say as Miss Carabella and I ever discussed her family."

Maynard seemed completely disinterested in the whole topic of Vera's family, and she felt like a fool pouting and playing dumb. He had accepted her lie completely, and unless he was a better actor than Libby thought, it seemed as though he had never thought about the subject before.

She persevered and tried her only other conversational gambit. "She never even mentioned that she performed here at the Variety last June! Of course, I wasn't working here then, so she might have thought it wouldn't matter to me. But I suppose you must have been glad to see her back, though." She gave in and batted her eyes at him, forcing some sort of answer.

"Yes, well, its always nice to see old friends."

She leaped on his words. "I think it's so important to try to get to know the people you work with, don't you? Of course you do . . . If you thought of her as an old friend, you must have gotten to know her well back in June."

From the look on his face, the answer was: not as well as he would have liked. "Unfortunately I'm usually too busy to meet most of the performers. You know, in this business, performers come and go so quickly." It sounded almost threatening the way he said it. He leered at Libby, "But I hope that I'm a good friend, maybe becoming better friends all the time, with those people who work backstage."

Libby realized it was time to retreat. All this talk of making friends and getting to know about people's families had given him, albeit somewhat intentionally, the wrong idea, and it hadn't netted her one concrete piece of information. "I'd better get this laundry back to the wardrobe room."

"Please, don't go so fast. Why, you know, I don't know anything about your family, Miss Seale. Do you have a large family?"

Her family was the last subject she was willing to go into with Mr. Maynard. She didn't even like to think what her father and mother might say if they knew what she was doing and the types of people she worked with. "This laundry really won't wait. Perhaps on another occasion . . ."

She gave a half-smile for propriety's sake and because, much as she dreaded the prospect, she might need to talk to Maynard again, and hurried off down the corridor. At the stair, she glanced back to see if Maynard had gone into his office, but he was still gazing after her and gave her a big grin and a wink.

It took Peter less than two minutes in the morgue to find the edition of the paper he was seeking. The *Portland Gazette* kept an archive room—or in the terminology of the newspaper trade, a "morgue"—with a copy of every single issue that came off the press. Twice a year, all of the individual broadsheets were bound together in leather-clad volumes, but the issue he was looking for was still loose on the shelves in the stack for the month of June.

A banquet or tribute of some kind, Madame Josephine had said, a few days or a week before the first Wednesday in June. In a city the size of Portland, there couldn't be more than one event that fit the bill. He found what he was looking for in the *Gazette* for Saturday, June 2—a Chamber of Commerce banquet on the evening of Friday, June 1, honoring the local businessman of the year. But it was when he glanced down at the paragraph and saw who the guest of honor was that he began to realize that perhaps Madame Josephine had been right to warn him against investigating further. Portland's Businessman of the Year for 1893 was none other than H. Walford McKennock, probably the richest man in the city. Having made his fortune in shipping, he had begun to turn to the railways and trams that were helping Portland grow at such a fantastic pace. If rumor was correct, his was the money behind the new State Street Swing-Span Bridge which, within a few years of opening, was already minting money even as it changed the character of commerce in the city.

For a moment, Peter's mind simply refused to process the information. Why would a man as rich as McKennock have his hand in the white slave trade? He obviously had more to gain than to lose. Of course, that hadn't always been so. Now that he thought about it, Peter vaguely remembered that McKennock didn't come from money; he was a self-made man who had come West back in '49 during the Gold Rush without a penny to his name. Wiser than his contemporaries, McKennock had quickly discerned that panning for gold was much less practical—and less lucrative—than providing supplies and luxuries to the men who had traveled West with him—at a hefty profit, of course.

Peter was distracted by something on one of the *Gazette*'s back pages, which were devoted to "Ladies' Interests and the Cultural Arts." While he had been thinking of McKennock, his hand had been idly turning pages, and all of a sudden, he found he was staring at a familiar name. It wasn't in an article; it was an advertisement for Crowther's Portland Variety, proudly announcing that for the next four weeks they would be presenting, among others, "The Electrical Magic of Signor Carlo," which meant Carlo and Vera had been playing the Variety during exactly the same weeks that Polly Pink had been hired, abducted, and murdered. Peter didn't know what to make of that, if anything. It was probably only a coincidence, he decided. But all the same, it was as if everywhere he looked he found more things to ponder instead of any answers.

He began to feel slightly dizzy. He didn't have any idea how to begin investigating Walford McKennock or what the timing of Vera's first booking—or was it the first?—could mean. He'd had a very full first day as an investigator, but despite having learned quite a bit, he couldn't help feeling he was still groping in the dark.

He decided to leave off playing detective for now. It was proving more difficult than he had at first thought, and it entered his mind to wonder whether Libby was having any more success than he was.

The conversation with Maynard hadn't exactly been a debacle, but some of the bright optimism Libby felt when she talked to Jack this morning had dissipated. By the end of her conversation with the bookkeeper, she felt like she was in over her head.

Part of her wanted to drop the whole investigation right now. Then she thought of Peter and how much she wanted to be able to impress him with her acumen, and of Vera and how much she wanted to not let her death go unpunished. Her natural combativeness and determination returned. And so, barely stopping for a moment in the wardrobe room to drop off the basket of laundry, she headed off to Crowther's office. This was the interview she had been dreading most, and if she let herself have time to get nervous, she feared she'd never be able to muster the courage.

She knocked firmly on Crowther's door. Not waiting for an answer, she swung the door open and poked her head in. "Mr. Crowther. I just wanted to thank you for being so helpful the other day about that valise of Vera Carabella's I found. I thought you might want to know Vera's family was very, very pleased to get all of her personal effects back."

Crowther looked up from his desk. For a moment, he seemed almost at a loss for words, but only for a moment. Then it was back to gruff. "Good to know. Thank you for taking care of it, Miss Seale." He went back to his reading.

She pretended not to notice the implied dismissal and came all the way into the room. Quickly, Crowther swept some papers into his top drawer and shut it with a loud crack. He glared up at her. Her heart was beating hard, but she managed to keep her demeanor confident.

"You know, I had no idea that Vera had worked at the theater before, but her boardinghouse mentioned to me she'd been here in June. You must have really liked her . . ." she paused, as if she'd lost her train of thought, then finished, "act."

His face darkened, and she was afraid he was about to order her out of his office, so she barreled on in as cheerful and submissive a tone as she could muster. "I can't think how you make all the decisions about these things. It must take a lot of work, running a theatre. So many details to attend to, decisions about which acts come and which acts go. To bring the magic act back so soon . . . surely that wasn't standard? What I mean to say is . . . since the Variety seems to be doing so well, you must have good business instincts."

Crowther remained silent briefly, but after a moment, his vanity won out over his reserve. Libby suspected he was not often on the receiving end of a compliment. "Big crowd pleaser, the magician and Vera. All the world loves a woman in peril, don't they?" He laughed in a self-congratulatory way, completely missing the stony look the comment produced on Libby's face. Women in peril, indeed. Crowther went on, "They were part of a rotating bill of featured acts I purchased from an agent . . . Keith, I think. That's right, them and that gypsy woman and, let's see, I think that Frau Sauerkraut or whatever her name is. The contracts I sign specify a number of acts—how many weeks they will be here, and whether or not they headline—and so forth."

Libby nodded. She had seen the occasional theatrical agent come in for meetings with Crowther, but she had never really understood the business side of the Variety, so it was with unfeigned curiosity that she asked him, "You mean you've never even seen some acts—let's say Carlo and Vera Carabella—before they show up here for their first show?"

"It worked out fine, didn't it? She could really fill those seats, and the Shakespearean actors just don't have the same draw. What a pair of legs and a . . ." He caught himself and trailed off. "Yes, yes, as I say, terrible tragedy that she won't be back here again." She suspected that his distress at Vera's killing was motivated more by financial loss than by any real sensitivity, and his next words confirmed it. "Still, acts come, they go, and there's always a newer, bigger headliner to take their place. That magic act was no exception." His indifference, at least, sounded heartfelt.

"But there must be times when a performer is difficult to work with . . ." She wondered if she could get him to tell her what he and Vera had been arguing about that night she had overheard them in

Vera's dressing room, ". . . demanding a bigger dressing room or more money or that sort of thing."

Crowther looked up at her, and the cold appraisal in his eyes sent a shiver through Libby. "You're asking quite a few questions today, Miss Seale. Why is that?"

Caught unprepared, Libby stammered out, "I've never worked in a theatre. I'm just so interested . . ."

He cut her off, "In Miss Carabella, particularly?"

"No, not particularly. It's just that finding her suitcase . . ." she stopped. She had been about to say, *started me thinking,* but that was exactly what she didn't want Crowther to suspect. "That's just why I mentioned her." She decided to try flirting with him as she had with Maynard and said as suggestively as she could, "To tell the truth, I'm just interested in getting to know you better, Mr. Crowther. This job means a lot to me."

Crowther rose from behind his desk, and she was suddenly aware of how his bulk filled up the small room. Dear God, thought Libby, what have I done? He looked even more menacing than usual, as he growled, "Miss Seale, I hope I'm misunderstanding you. I am a happily married man. Now, if you would leave my office." He crossed behind her and opened the door.

She knew she had lost her chance to question him further, but at least she hoped he now thought of her as merely wanton rather than unnaturally curious. "Yes, Mr. Crowther. I'm sorry. Please forgive me for taking . . ."

He cut her off again, practically shoving her out the door. "Yes, I'll try to forget this, Miss Seale." Just before he shut the door on her, he asked snidely, "How many more weeks are you contracted to work at the Variety, Miss Seale? I must check up on that. Managing a theatre, after all . . . it's so important to attend to all the details."

Libby stood facing a closed door, defeated.

The next day Hatty was back. They were busy most of the morning doing the final fittings and alterations for the Rickshaw Ballet costumes, so there was a constant stream of Dancing Whirlwinds in and out of the wardrobe room. While there was no time to speak to her, Libby had plenty of time while dancers changed or fussed to observe Hatty as she worked and consider what she knew about her. Even though Libby spent most of every day with her, it wasn't much. Hatty was brisk, efficient, and kind, but she didn't speak much about her life outside the theater.

Libby knew Hatty had been born in Hong Kong. Her mother had been Chinese and her father an English soldier stationed in the colony shortly after its incorporation into the British Empire at the end of the Opium Wars. Hatty preferred not to talk about her childhood, and Libby had often wondered if it was because Hatty had been illegitimate. Certainly it would have been a common enough story—a soldier a long way from home getting a local girl with child and disappearing soon afterward. Libby wasn't sure if she was correct in her surmises, and she didn't want to ask if Hatty had known her father or not. It seemed far too personal a thing to enquire.

At any rate, Hatty had grown up with her mother in Hong Kong. Apparently, she had moved comfortably between the worlds of the British colonists and the local Chinese, for when she was only sixteen, she had met Private Ralph Matthews, a British soldier who asked her to marry him. According to Hatty, it had been a true love match and, despite the obstacles, they quickly wed. Due to the prejudice regarding such a marriage in their respective homelands, they emigrated to America as soon Private Matthews had been decommissioned from the army. Now Hatty was widowed, and where and with whom she lived—and how she spent her Saturday nights—was a complete mystery to Libby.

Although she had a key to the theater and could conceivably have been involved in Vera's death, Libby still couldn't picture Hatty as a white slaver. Though conceivably she could have returned to the Variety the night Vera was killed, doubling back after Libby saw her leave, the idea of Vera rushing off to some sort of secret assignation with the wardrobe mistress seemed vaguely absurd.

"Did you finish all the ironing? Mr. Fredericks says he hasn't gotten his extra dress shirt back." Libby realized with a start that Hatty was chiding her.

Somewhat embarrassed to have been so transparently thinking of other matters, she answered quickly, "Not yet, Hatty. I had to wait for the new laundry supplies shipment yesterday until late in the afternoon, since we were out of starch. I thought I could finish it this afternoon."

"Do Mr. Fredericks' shirt right now, since he's being as fussy as a rooster about it. I suppose the rest can wait till later," Hatty said crisply. "Your head's in the clouds these days, Libby." Seeing Libby's face fall, she softened a bit. "You're thinking about a newspaper reporter." It wasn't a question the way Hatty said it.

Ever since she had told Hatty the story of her original meeting with Peter, the well-meaning costumer had found a way to work him into almost every conversation. She clearly wanted more information about whether Libby had seen him since, but was above asking direct questions. Because of this eager curiosity, Libby found herself reluctant to reveal that she had met with Peter Tuesday evening, knowing that any mention of it would only lead to inevitable misconceptions she wasn't prepared to deal with. And she couldn't correct them without revealing her investigation into Vera's death. Feeling somewhat guilty at the deception, she shook her head. "I'm sure he's busy with his reporting duties for the *Gazette*. I noticed in this morning's paper that some California newspapermen are traveling through Portland

and Seattle this week to meet with the local press. He's probably busy with that."

Hatty nodded and let the subject drop for now. "Well, you get to ironing that shirt. I'll start hemming all these kimonos. Mr. Crowther decided he wants them a few inches shorter. When you're done, you can help me." As the two women began their tasks, Libby tried to think of a way to bring up the matter of whether any girls had gone missing in the months and years prior to Polly's botched abduction.

"Hatty, it seems like we spend so much time altering costumes. I'm wondering, how often does Crowther hire new Dancing Whirlwinds?"

"Oh, that varies. I think we've hired more girls since you started than we had for a long time before that."

"Do a lot of the dancers leave the show? I'd imagine it must be difficult to keep a well rehearsed troupe of dancers if some of them quit without notice."

Hatty turned the kimono she was working on inside out, and Libby admired the way she way able to do so with one deft flick of her practiced wrist. "Sometimes we go for months with the same group of them. Sometimes two or three leave suddenly. It's hard to say."

"Why is that, I wonder? Why would someone with a regular job in show business quit suddenly? I mean, don't you think that's a little suspicious?"

Hatty pursed her lips. "Libby, these dancers are sweet girls, most of them, but like girls the world over, they are flighty creatures. Sometimes they give their notice, and sometimes they just up and leave. A girls decides to run off and elope or to take a train to a new city and try her luck there." She went back to her work, but looked up again as if something had occurred to her. "Although, now that I think of it, there was one named Marie about a year back who told several of the girls here that she was saving to buy herself a house. Then one Monday, she was gone—just never came in to work, no word to anyone."

"So she was the only one that seemed, well, noticeably odd?" asked Libby.

Hatty considered before answering. "Not the only one, perhaps, but the only one I can think of right this moment. I suppose there may have been one or two other strange disappearances over the years, but that's hardly a crowd." She reached over to lay out the sleeve of the shirt Libby was about to iron. "You need to take special care with the pleats right at the cuffs," she said, signaling that the conversation was over.

Throughout the late morning and early afternoon, as specialty acts brought her their mending and piece work and various Whirlwinds tried on their altered costumes, Libby kept up a steady stream of inquisitive chatter, hoping to hear more gossip about any dancers in the past who had left their jobs suddenly. A few of the older members of the troupe mentioned not only Marie, but also two others who had disappeared without an explanation. Lily Belle had been a promising young dancer new to the area about eighteen months back. She had seemed primed to take over one of the few lead roles in the Whirlwinds, when she abruptly disappeared one weekend.

And no one could remember the name of the quiet girl who had appeared suddenly one week and disappeared just as quietly the next. That was over a year back, according to Tallulah, who confided to Libby that she had thought at the time that the police should have looked into it, but when she asked them, they told her the girl was a suspect in a bank robbery in Salem. "I reckon it's that way with most of the ones who leave in such a hurry," she told Libby. "They're most likely running from an angry husband or just trying to stay one step ahead of the law. Honey, I've seen a lot of people come and go in the three years I've been dancing here, and if there's one thing I've learned, it's not to ask too many questions. No one ever has the answers anyway." Holding up her new kimono and admiring herself in the small mirror, she turned to leave. "I like the trim on this. I think it really suits my eyes, don't you?"

The final fitting of the day was May, whose costumes' hems were forever having to be let down as she was still just a growing girl. As Libby sewed, the grateful chorine prattled on about her plans to become a specialty dancer, and to her surprise, Libby welcomed a chance to take a break from thinking about Vera's death. When May asked Libby if it were true she had come from New York, she admitted that was the case, and May pressed her for details.

"Oh, I'd give anything to be in a fancy theater on Broadway!" May sighed, pushing for stories of life back East. Unexpectedly, Libby found herself enjoying sharing her recollections of life on the Lower East Side and her impressions of the theater culture in Manhattan.

As she took the final pins out of the new seam and handed the costume to the girl, May looked up at her, eyes shining. "I have a feeling someday my big break will come. And instead of this . . ." she waved her costume, "I'll be wearing an expensive silk dress with lace trim! Libby, will you help me sew my costumes when I'm a big star?"

Infected by the enthusiasm, Libby agreed. "So do you have a plan for this act that requires the finest silk dresses?" she asked, smiling.

But instead of answering, May grew uncharacteristically silent and smiled a small secret smile. "I think so," she said shyly. "I can't talk about it yet. I need to make all the arrangements with . . ." May stopped short, as if she'd said too much.

Libby stopped smiling. This sort of talk was new, and she worried that the girl was being led astray by someone whose intentions were less than honorable. She believed firmly that May was far younger than she professed to be and might well wander into a bad situation unknowingly. "May, has someone promised to further your career in return for . . . certain favors?" she asked carefully, not wanting to appear too concerned.

But May shook her head vehemently. "No, no, nobody has promised me a thing. I just meant that I was thinking of finding a theatrical manager, that's all. There is no one, Libby, I swear." She stood up from the edge of the table she had been perched on and neatly folded the petticoat over her shoulder. Libby was sure she was lying. But before she could delve further, the girl was in the doorway. "Thank you for fixing my costume," she said and was gone.

Troubled, Libby made her way back to the back sewing closet to put away her supplies. Hatty sat at the small table, writing in her notebook. She looked up when Libby entered. "I'm making a list of things we need. Did you know we're almost out of bobbins?"

Libby stared at Hatty and her mouth dropped open. All thoughts of May flew out of her head and suddenly a piece of the puzzle that was Vera's death popped into its place. She had been an idiot not to see it before. "What is it? Is something wrong?" asked Hatty, obviously concerned.

"I have to go," replied Libby, quickly putting away her things and reaching for her coat. "No, nothing is wrong. Good night." She practically ran out of the theater with only one thought on her mind. "I must go tell Peter!"

EIGHT

PETER SAT AT HIS desk, trying to force some kind of order on the piles upon piles of press clippings and scrawled notes that made his desktop look like a relief map of the Rockies. He vaguely heard the bell on the front door ring, but had already forgotten that fact when John Mayhew poked his head around the doorway.

"Petey, your . . . lady friend is here." The editor couldn't keep a note of schoolboyish glee out of his voice.

In the years since Peter had worked at the *Gazette*, his colleagues—Mayhew in particular—were fond of teasing him that he needed to find a nice woman and settle down, and as a result of this, he made sure to keep his personal and professional life completely separate. Ever since Libby had barged in here looking for him the last time, she had become the cause of much speculation among the other newsmen.

And what was she doing here, a day early for their planned meeting? Slightly alarmed, he followed Mayhew back to the front counter where, sure enough, Libby stood, peering back at the newspaper press and type cases. Before he could ask her anything, she started to speak.

"I know we said we wouldn't meet again until Thursday, but I just realized something that may be very important." Suddenly aware of Mayhew's quizzical expression, she clamped her mouth shut. Peter came around to the front of the counter and took her elbow.

"Shall we discuss this as we walk?" he said smoothly and guided her out the door, stopping only to grab his hat and coat from a hook by the entrance. As they left the building, she turned to face him.

"Vera had a diary! I feel so silly . . . I had forgotten it completely until I saw Hatty writing in her notebook and . . . Well, in any case, the last night of Vera's life, I watched her sitting at her dressing table writing in it her diary. But when I went through her valise and other items, it was missing!"

"Which means . . ." he left the sentence unfinished, waiting for her to explain further.

"Which means that at last we have definite proof that it wasn't just a random abduction. Don't you see? I thought that her bag had been rifled through, but it's only today that I realized what was missing. Her murderer must have known there was something incriminating him in her diary and taken it out of her bag."

Peter considered this new information. He had to admit, a missing diary would certainly indicate Vera's abduction had not merely been a random one—if it really was missing.

"Is there any chance you missed seeing it in your first look through her things?" he said, "Perhaps it was tucked away under something else in her valise."

"I would have seen it!" Libby replied, slightly miffed that he appeared to be questioning her investigative thoroughness. "After all, I found her jewelry in the false bottom of that wooden box."

They had started walking again, and it was a surprisingly balmy evening for January. The afternoon's drizzle had given way to a cloudy sky, and the park blocks, home of the *Gazette*'s offices, were lined with benches. Peter nodded at one of them, and they sat down as he began to tell his story. He filled her in on what he had learned at Madame Josephine's, chronicling the transformation of the farmgirl Fanny into glamorous Polly Pink with her trademark pink dresses (although he edited out his close relationship with the madam and the reasons for it). He related the details of the mysterious "client" and the offer of a job at the theater which followed his visit. Libby was able, from his description, to confirm that the man from the theater who brought that offer was indeed Mr. Crowther.

Then he told her of going to the newspaper morgue, and her eyes opened wide at his conclusion that Josephine's "mystery man" had been none other than H. Walford McKennock. Finally, he concluded, "Oddly enough, I noticed this all happened the same weeks in June Signor Carlo and Vera were on the bill at the Portland Variety."

"Do you think that's significant?" she asked and then answered her own question. "Perhaps Vera knew Polly!"

The same thought had occurred to Peter when he had seen the advertisement originally, but he hadn't been able to guess what it could possibly mean.

Libby, however, jumped into the breach. "Maybe Vera knew something about Polly's disappearance which was in her diary! Or . . ." She caught her breath, and realized she wasn't sure what else it might mean. "It certainly is an odd coincidence. I wonder if Vera knew any of the other missing girls? I know Vera and Carlo were in town a couple of times before June."

"Other missing girls?" asked Peter quizzically. He was slightly annoyed that she had not mentioned this until now but tried not to show it.

"I meant to tell you," she said apologetically, "but I ran over here thinking about that diary and . . ."

"Perhaps you should start at the beginning and tell me what you've learned these last two days." Quickly, she sketched in the details of her conversations with all the people at the theater.

He listened carefully, then said, "I agree with you. It sounds like Crowther didn't know Vera personally. Still, since he was the one to hire Polly from Madame Josephine's, I think he has to be a prime suspect for the role of white slaver."

Something was nagging at Libby at the very edge of her consciousness and had been ever since she had listened to his description of the Polly's abrupt departure from the boat. As her eye fell on the shiny buttons at the cuffs of her coat, she thought of the small wooden box with its jewels and baubles.

"Fanny Watson!" She broke in on Peter's assessment of Crowther.

Peter looked at her oddly. "Fanny Watson, yes. Of course, that was only Polly's name until Madame Josephine gave her her . . . *nom de guerre*, so to speak."

But before he could go on, she interrupted him. "The wedding ring I found in Vera's jewelry box . . . . It had the initials F.W. on it." She searched her memory, "F. W. and H . . . H something. Oh, I can't recall now. Something about love and eternity . . ." She jumped to her feet. "We should go look, right now! I want to be sure I'm remembering correctly."

She had started walking away so quickly that Peter found himself running a few steps to catch up with her. It occurred to him that Libby was the most active woman he knew, at least if her quick stride now was anything to judge by. He had a sudden vision of the first day they had met, of watching her race through the streets in pursuit of that thief, and involuntarily he grinned. Unaware of this, she was still talking as her large coat flapped behind her in the wind.

"It seems that the more we find out, the stranger and more complicated this whole thing gets. Vera and Carlo's appearance at the Variety several months ago coincided with Polly Pink's abduction and murder. And Vera has a ring that may have belonged to Polly. Perhaps . . ." She trailed off.

"Yes?" Peter prompted.

"Perhaps instead of an innocent victim, Vera was in league with the criminals!" Libby stopped, pondering the ramifications of this, even as she didn't want to entertain the possibility. She went on, "Sam says Vera left the theater, but signs indicate she returned."

"Or she never left at all," he interjected. "We only have Sam's word for that." A thought struck him. "But let's assume Vera did leave the theater briefly. We should have been looking all along at the question: where did she go and who did she meet that night? There could easily be witnesses to a meeting like that." He pulled out a little pad and made a note. "I hope it's not too late! This was nearly two weeks ago, after all. Tomorrow, I'll canvass the saloons and restaurants in the area and see what I can find out. Do you have a publicity photograph of Vera?"

"I can get you one. Oh, you're right, why didn't we think of that?"

The tramcar pulled up, and their conversation ceased for a moment as they climbed aboard, found seats, and paid the conductor. Libby was aware all of a sudden at the folly of rank amateurs undertaking a murder investigation. But she brushed this realization aside and continued her previous train of thought.

"At any rate, at the time Vera was killed, she had a diary which is now missing. She also had in her possession a love token that appears to have belonged to Polly. Oh!" Libby stopped, wide-eyed. "I forgot to mention this to you, but Mrs. Englund —"

"Who?"

"The woman at Vera's boardinghouse. She mentioned to me that this visit, Vera paid her rent for the full time up front, in cash. There was also all that money I told you about in the box with the wedding rings. I didn't think anything of it at the time. I just assumed Vera didn't trust banks, but now I think maybe that's suspicious."

Peter jumped in. "I think so as well. Maybe there was something in the diary that would have explained her sudden windfall." They sat silent for a few moments, each mulling that over. Peter shook his head. "We may be jumping to conclusions here. Perhaps there's a perfectly innocent reason for all the cash. Perhaps Carlo had just paid her in a large lump sum. And you told me she might have been thinking of leaving his act. Maybe it was some sort of bonus Carlo gave her to make her stay."

"Well, she did seem to be considering settling down in Portland. Oh, this is my stop," said Libby, as the tram pulled to a stop at the intersection of Grand and Morrison.

She led the way through the tree-lined streets, past houses whose windows spilled gold into the street. Night had fallen early, and the streetlights had not yet been lit, so the walk was filled with stretches of azure shadows. Peter looked around with interest. This area of town had only recently been incorporated into Portland and was filled with comfortable, newly-built houses, although some were already showing wear and tear. In the distance, he could hear the sound of a dog barking, and farther still, children laughing. The city was growing at an astonishing rate. Soon it would rival some of the smaller cities back East—cities that had taken centuries to reach the size and sophistication Portland had acquired in less than fifty years.

He realized Libby had been asking him a question. "What about Carlo? Where was he the night Vera was killed?"

Peter explained, somewhat embarrassed, what Madame Josephine had told him about the flamboyant magician's whereabouts for the full night after his show. "I suppose he could still be somehow involved with the white slavers. After all, he was in town when Polly was abducted, same as Vera. But we know he can't be directly involved in Vera's death . . ."

"Unless this Madame Josephine was not telling the truth," chided Libby, "After all, we cannot simply trust what people tell us simply because we think they are likable."

Touché, thought Peter, although he couldn't imagine why on earth Josephine would have invented an alibi for Carlo. Nevertheless, he amended his previous statement. "All right. Let us assume for the moment that Carlo was not involved in her death. But you are right, we should talk to him, at any rate. He was closest to Vera, and he may be able to answer some of our other questions about her last weeks."

"But he's down in San Francisco!" she cried, frustrated at all the avenues of investigation she saw closing before them.

"Well, then," said Peter with a grand flourish, "I shall just have to call him on the telephone!" He looked at her as if he expected her to ask what that was.

"There are telephones in New York, you know" she replied tartly, "I have seen one."

"New Haven had them first," he shot back playfully. "First local telephone exchange in the nation."

She conceded gracefully. "In any case, it's a brilliant idea, and it never would have occurred to me. But we don't know that Carlo has a telephone. I would tend to doubt it."

"I'm sure I can arrange a telephone connection with Carlo if I ring my colleague at the *San Francisco Examiner* and ask him to set it up for us. They can ring us here at the *Gazette* offices."

She noticed he was including her in the plan, and she was pleased and touched by his thoughtfulness. Besides, despite what she had said about having seen one, telephones were still a miraculous and thrilling novelty to her. She looked forward to being party to, if not part of, a long-distance call.

Naturally, Mrs. Pratt was fascinated with the young man her lodger brought in. She ushered Peter into the sitting room—a cluttered, lace-bedecked chamber ostensibly for entertaining visitors that was used only rarely.

"I'll go up to my room and bring down those things," Libby told him, with an apologetic look that made it clear she knew she was leaving him in the clutches of the formidable widow bearing down upon him with a tray of tea cakes. As she slipped up the stairs, she heard Mrs. Pratt's distinctive brogue, asking him how he had met Miss Seale, and she wondered what he would answer.

In her room, Libby quickly sorted through the pile of Vera's clothing, turning each piece inside out to make sure there was nothing hidden in the linings. Satisfied the diary was not there after all, she set them to one side and grabbed the small valise, which she had already repacked with Vera's trifles. In the other hand, she picked up the small bundle of creased photographs that had been in the suitcase and hurried back downstairs.

Peter wore his customary amused grin as she entered the parlor. "Your lovely landlady has been doing me the kindness of offering a refreshing critique of the *Gazette*'s editorial policies," he said. Libby smiled, having a very good idea what sort of things had been said in her absence.

She gratefully accepted the hot cup of tea and raisin cookies Mrs. Pratt offered, and for several minutes, she joined in the desultory small talk that convention demanded. After what seemed far too long, however, Peter and Libby managed to convey to the older woman that they had work to do for an article Peter was writing, and the landlady scurried away. They could hear her in the back of the house, clattering in the kitchen and singing to her cats as she washed up the evening dishes.

"I checked again, and there is definitely no diary among her possessions. I brought some things down to look through, in case you can make more of them than I did." Libby said.

Peter scrutinized the small pile of photographs, one by one. Holding up the one of a wedding, he squinted. "Could this bride be Vera?"

Libby had glanced through the pictures earlier, but she had to admit his question took her by surprise. She had assumed by the youthful expression and dated clothing that the photo was of Vera's aunt or perhaps even an older sister. But as she looked again, she remembered the lines she had seen in Vera's face, and she realized that this girl of about twenty could indeed have been Vera herself fifteen years ago.

Libby's trained eye noted the dress's shape. "From the fitted sleeves, and the shape of the waist, I would guess this was about 1882 or '83." She pointed. "Look at the overskirt—Marie Antoinette style. No one has worn that for at least ten years." Peter marveled that she could tell so much from a dress that looked, to him, like every other wedding dress he'd ever seen.

She inspected the man in the picture. His blond hair was almost white, and his pale face looked as if he couldn't have grown a beard if he tried. "I wonder who he was," she said, noting his serious expression as he faced the camera, chin up and eyes staring straight ahead. Neither of them could have been much more than twenty-one, and Libby wondered, not for the first time, who Vera had been before circumstances brought her to show business and Carlo's act.

Peter turned each of the pictures over, hoping to discover some annotations on the back, but there was nothing on any of them. The other photos were obviously older, one a formal family grouping taken in a studio and one of a large group of children in a faded sunlit meadow, where they tentatively picked out Vera at age twelve. There were a few other studio portraits of men and women wearing the resolute gazes of those uneasy before the camera's eye. Peter put them down on the table, sighing. "I don't suppose we'll ever know who any of them were," he said.

Libby opened the valise, and together they examined its meager contents. Peter felt a bit uncomfortable, fingering such lacy and feminine items, and he had to ask Libby what one or two of the cosmetics were, mystified by the inscrutable shiny containers filled with reddish pigments. How sad, he thought, that these few trappings of a showgirl in a blue-lined basket were all that remained of a life. He started to count the cash in the envelope, but stopped when he became aware Libby was taking it as a personal insult to her counting skills.

She showed him the trick that opened the false bottom of the jewelry box, and there lay the inscribed ring, now an ominous symbol of the great mysteries that lay behind Vera's public persona. "1893 F.W. and H.M Eternal Love . . . " read Peter, running his finger along the inscription. "H. M. . . . McKennock!"

"I thought his name is Walford McKennock."

"That's what he goes by, but it's actually H. Walford. His full name is Henry Walford McKennock."

"You don't think . . ." Libby could hardly contain her excitement. "Could he have fallen in love with Polly that night on Madame Josephine's barge and secretly married her?"

Peter considered this for a moment, weighing the possibilities. "Of course, he's a very prominent man and quite wealthy enough to have simply set her up as his mistress. So why would he have married her . . . ?"

"It might not have been a wedding ring, just a token of his affection. Oh, Peter, it all fits!" With a jolt, she realized she had called him by his given name. Reddening, Libby fiddled with the rest of the jewelry in her hands. Peter had noticed as well and was filled with a warm pride

112

that they were now close enough—intimates, really—to dispense with formality and titles. This thought was almost immediately followed by a fear: perhaps she thought of him like a brother! Of course, that was the answer. She had likely used his forename the way one would for a family member, a child, or a pet! Feeling like a confused schoolboy, he hoped it wasn't evident on his face how much it meant to him.

"Well, I suppose we'll just have to investigate the matter further at the McKennock soiree this Saturday night."

She was jolted out of her thoughts. "What are you talking about?"

He smiled, aware he had been holding this particular card close to his chest. "Miss Seale . . ." he paused. "Libby . . ." An almost imperceptible nod from her and again that fetching blush creeping up her cheeks. "Would you do me the honor of accompanying me to the McKennock ball this Saturday? He sent a few invitations to the *Gazette*, and Mayhew said I could use them."

"I would be honored," replied Libby.

"I believe Walford McKennock is using the ball to launch his bid for Mayor, so the press is being encouraged to attend."

"And what a wonderful cover for us! No one will suspect we are actually there to find out whether he had anything to do with Polly's abduction and murder."

Peter marveled at her businesslike demeanor, despite the fact that he himself had wanted to attend for many of the very same reasons. But he felt a pang that she appeared to blithely assume that the only reason they would attend a party together would be as an offshoot of their detecting work.

"Quite right on all counts," he said with hearty cheer that belied his true emotions. "I believe that, between the two of us, we will be able to find out a great deal about this man and his family in light of what we already know about Polly's short-lived theatrical career."

"Peter . . ." She had just remembered a forgotten question. "If this ring really did belong to Polly, do you think that means Vera knew who killed her?"

Peter saw where she was heading and why it bothered her. "I suppose there are several possible explanations," he answered, rattling off the first few that sprung to mind. "Perhaps they became friends, and Polly asked Vera to hold her ring for safekeeping. Perhaps Vera found it somewhere after Polly was dead and took it because it was valuable. Or . . ." he paused, trying to think of the kindest way to phrase his next sentence. "Or perhaps Vera had something to do with Polly's death, and she took the ring at the time Polly was abducted."

This was what Libby hadn't wanted to face. Although she had to admit the logic of Peter's last scenario, it saddened her to think their investigation might prove Vera was not the sweet soul Libby had assumed. "Of course," she said slowly, "perhaps it's as you said, and Vera simply knew something about Polly's death . . . or rather, figured out something because she found the ring. Yes! If Vera did figure out something after the fact, then that's why the killer was forced to silence her."

Peter interposed gently. "If Vera did see or learn something about Polly's death five months ago and didn't say anything to the police," his logical tone made the inference inescapable, "that would seem to indicate that, at the very least, she was blackmailing the murderer. In which case, perhaps he was the one who gave Vera the ring as part of a blackmail payment."

"She could have gotten the ring for a perfectly innocent reason, from the other person whose initials are on it." Libby had no real reason to defend Vera, but she wanted to try to give her the benefit of the doubt.

"Of course, that's possible, but you must admit it's more likely that Vera's possession of that ring is somehow connected to Polly." Libby nodded resignedly since he was right. Peter went on, "And we don't know yet who else's initials those are on the ring, though we know the ring was inscribed only sometime last year." His brow furrowed. "I'm fairly sure that if Polly was married before she left the boat, Josephine didn't know anything about it."

Libby thought about it. "Which means she got it during those few weeks last June between being hired at the Variety and being killed."

"Which brings us back to McKennock. So I guess we'll just have to see if we can uncover anything at the party on Saturday."

"Yes, you're right." She moved on. "So, before Saturday, you're going to canvass the saloons to see if anyone remembers Vera meeting someone on the night of her death, but what should I do at the theater? If Vera was blackmailing someone, I think Mr. Crowther is the most likely candidate. He is the one who hired Polly, and remember, I once overheard Vera and Crowther arguing in her dressing room."

"I suppose for the moment, he is our main suspect, but I don't think you should make it obvious you suspect him. Besides, if he was being blackmailed for being a white slaver, he's not going to have left incriminating evidence lying around. I think for the moment, the best you can do is keep an eye out for anything suspicious and work hard not to attract his attention." He stood up, reaching for his coat. "I should get back to the *Gazette*."

"Of course," she agreed.

She walked him to the front door, and there was an awkward moment as he took his leave, both of them suddenly unsure what to say. He broke the silence. "Can you be at the *Gazette*'s offices Friday at nine in the morning?"

Libby considered this. "I don't have to be at work until ten." she said. "Why?"

"I thought you might want to be there when I telephone Signor Carlo," he replied, and with a tip of his hat, he was off into the dark

February night. As Libby watched him walk away, she felt unsettled by both the shape of their investigation and by her growing feelings for the handsome reporter. She knew she mustn't let herself get emotionally involved with him, but it felt so natural. She told herself that they were just becoming better friends, and there was no reason to assume he thought of her as anything more than a sister. Why shouldn't two close friends attend a party together? Despite misgivings, she had to admit she was excited at the prospect of a grand party at the McKennocks'. Whatever would she wear?

Mentally reviewing her meager wardrobe, she closed the door and went off to see if Mrs. Pratt needed any help with dinner.

NINE

LIBBY USED THE ORNATE brass knocker on the door and nervously adjusted the basket of sewing supplies at her hip. After a few moments, a frail voice from within called out, "Who's there?" There was the sound of footsteps approaching the door, which opened to reveal a middle-aged woman wearing a simple dress of brown muslin. Simple, but obviously a well-made garment, thought Libby, and the small cameo pendant at her throat appeared to be expensive ivory. Behind her, a large foyer with a wide, handsome staircase was visible.

Clearing her throat, Libby tried to affect a subservient manner. "I'm here to offer my services, ma'am, to do any mending or piecework you might have. I can sew anything quickly and I do quality work." She was wearing her oldest dress and a faded white apron, and—to complete her disguise—she had carefully unpinned her hair and pulled it back in a messy plait down her back, shoving a cloth cap over the unruly mop.

"Oh, I don't know. I'm not sure I need . . ." As the woman faltered, Libby had a sudden fear that after all the careful planning, her ruse to infiltrate the Crowther residence would end with a door shut in her face.

Summoning up her most plaintive tone, she interrupted the woman whom she assumed was Mrs. Crowther. "Pardon me, ma'am, but it's cold and rainy out here and I'm getting soaked to the bone. Might I come in and rest a moment and trouble you for a glass of water?"

Indecision played on the other's face as she surveyed the seamstress. Despite her meek manner, she had the stately bearing of one used to turning away life's beggars. But her kindness won out, and she opened the door wider. "Come in, you poor thing. Here, let me hang your wet coat up." She ushered Libby into an overly furnished room and motioned to the divan closest to the fire. "Sit down, and I'll ask Berthe to make us tea." She left Libby there, and through the house, Libby heard her murmuring to someone she assumed was a household servant.

It was odd, thought Libby, that this house was so luxuriously decorated, and yet no maid had answered the door. She wondered briefly if the Crowthers were economizing, despite the fact that the house was in the wealthier part of Portland's west hills. She supposed owning a theater must be fairly lucrative—the Variety usually sold out both shows on weekends and had respectable houses even during the slower parts of the week.

But, to be sure, she could just as easily have pictured him living in a smaller, more rustic dwelling, all alone. Until that day in his office when she had made a fool of herself, she had not even been sure if Crowther was married. No one at the theater spoke, or seemed to know, about his home life.

But Libby had decided that since she didn't dare investigate Crowther openly at the theater, she might find out something useful at his home. Perhaps she could establish his usual schedule and maybe even find out where he was the Saturday night Vera was killed. When she had noticed him go into a meeting with several booking agents this morning—a meeting which she figured would go on for hours—she knew her opportunity had arrived. She impetuously told Hatty she felt ill and needed the rest of the day off, rushed home to change clothes and gather her sewing basket, and made her way to the Crowther residence.

And her ruse for gaining entry had worked! Perhaps she was getting more proficient at investigating. Here she was, warming herself by the fire and hopefully soon to be extracting useful information from the lady of the house. Feeling somewhat smug, despite not knowing what the afternoon's conversation would yield, Libby pulled herself closer to the fire and basked in its warmth as her damp clothes dried.

Peter was soaking wet. His hat was little protection from the torrential downpour, and he nearly turned around to go back into the warm tavern he had just left. But there were several more names left on his list, and he had to be on his way. He had spent all afternoon canvassing the various restaurants and bars around Crowther's where Vera might have met someone after the show. So far, all he had to show for it was a wet hat.

This early in the day, most of them were empty, save for a bored bartender who was more than willing to take a look at the photo of Vera in her low cut dress. Several of the barkeeps laughed openly at the idea they could identify any of the numerous patrons who crowded their taverns late at night. Ducking his head down as he walked, he headed east on Stark Street.

The Anchor consisted of one dark, low-ceilinged room with wooden tables barely visible in the gray light that came in through the grime-covered windows. A smell of old beer and smoke hung in the air, despite the fact that not a soul was visible. Peter supposed the years of business had imbued the place with a patina of both. Walking over to the bar that ran along the back wall, he leaned in toward a small doorway. "Hello?"

A stout man in an apron came out the door, wiping his hands on a towel. As he had been doing for the last hour, Peter pulled the now-creased photograph from his coat pocket and asked if the woman was familiar. The man winked and immediately said, "Yep, I know her. She was in here a couple times . . . not recently, though."

Peter nodded, trying to hide his elation. "Quite a beauty, isn't she?" Nonchalantly, he added, "Tell me, did she come here alone?"

"No, no. If she had, I would have thought she was, well . . ." He gave Peter a look that indicated they both, as men of the world, knew what a woman alone in a bar was looking for. "But she always was here with the same fellow. She never let any of the other men here chat with her." He looked again at the handbill, ogling her. "She was in that show over at the burlesque house, right?"

What a genius, thought Peter, it said so right on the flyer. Still, he forced himself to smile conspiratorially. "So she always came here with the same man, I see. Can you describe him?" He slipped a half-dollar across the bar. "It may be important." The bartender looked at him, openly curious now.

"You a detective or something? I don't want to get her in any trouble. She's a real good customer."

Peter debated whether or not to tell the man the truth, but he reckoned it was common enough knowledge that the popular magician's assistant had been found in the tunnels. "I'm afraid she will no longer be one. Unfortunately, Miss Carabella died a few weeks ago."

"Wait, now I remember. So she was the one they found down there?" He motioned below ground, and Peter agreed. He didn't want to get sidetracked telling all the details to the man, so he steered the conversation back to his original question. The only problem was, the bartender honestly couldn't remember much about Vera's friend, other than that he was tall ("but not too tall, mind you") with brown hair ("no, not too dark . . . but not light brown either, exactly") and clean shaven. One couldn't ask for a more generic description. "To tell the truth," the bartender said, idly wiping down the bar as he stared off into space, squinting, "I don't think I ever paid the fellow much mind." He put down the rag and winked again at Peter. "You have to admit, when she was in the room, no one looked to see who was standing next to her."

"Was the man old? Young?"

"Well now, I really couldn't say. Not too old, I guess. But not really young, either. The two of them usually got a drink or some food and sat way back in the corner there." He pointed to a table in the shadows of the already dim room. Peter realized he wasn't going to get any more information, and he wearily set off to explore the last few pubs and taverns in the area, but no one else had ever seen them. Apparently the Anchor, with its unobservant barkeep, was their only regular haunt.

Libby stood as the woman entered the room again. "Tea will be just a moment," she said, sitting down on a small chair to Libby's right. She regarded the sewing basket, which overflowed with the ribbons and trim that Libby had scrounged in her haste to look like a credible peddler. "I am sorry, Miss, but although I am happy to offer you a cup of tea and a place out of the rain for a few moments, I don't believe we have any sewing work for you. I checked with Berthe as well, but she tells me the household mending is well under control."

"I understand and thank you, Mrs. . . ." She paused.

"Mrs. Crowther, I'm sorry. I should have thought to say. And what do they call you, dear?"

In her haste, Libby had forgotten to prepare a false name, but she knew that she dare not use her real one. "My name is Maisie Farrington from down Salem way." She pulled the name from her memories of New York. Maisie Farrington had been a fellow seamstress at the

121

Gold Eagle Dressworks back in New York, a blowsy, red-faced woman who never got to work on time. I do hope she doesn't ask me about Salem though, thought Libby.

"Mrs. Crowther, that's such a lovely dress, so elegant and classic. But perhaps I could make it even more special with a bit of velvet trim around the bodice, like so?" As she spoke, Libby had pulled a wide olive ribbon out and held it up to the muslin. Next to the brown, the ribbon shimmered, and the effect was lovely. "No charge at all," she hurriedly added. "This would be my gift to you for being so welcoming."

"Oh, no, no, I couldn't . . ." She was interrupted by the entrance of Berthe, a gray-haired older woman with a businesslike manner, who placed a tea tray down on a table, looked at Libby mistrustfully, then back at her mistress. It was obvious from her protective manner that she questioned her employer's judgment in welcoming a stranger into the house.

In a slight German accent, she said quietly, "Do not tire yourself out, Madam. The doctor said you must rest." Turning on her heel, she left the room.

Libby felt this odd outburst deserved some comment, and she said sympathetically, "I'm sorry, you are not well?"

Mrs. Crowther sighed. "No, no, I am fine. Berthe has been with me for many years, and she worries. You see . . ." She paused. "Oh, but I don't want to burden you with my troubles, Miss Farrington."

Libby paused, then said delicately, "Sometimes it is helpful to share your troubles with a total stranger."

The woman fingered the fine ribbon, hesitating. She held it against her sleeve, and a hint of a smile crossed her face, but almost immediately she pulled it away and handed it back to Libby. "I have no need for finery like this, I rarely leave the house any more." She motioned to the tea tray. "Please, help yourself." For a few moments, the two women sat sipping their tea in silence. Finally, she spoke again. "It is true what Berthe says; I haven't been well."

Haltingly, she began to tell her story. She and her husband had wanted for many years to start a family, and two times God had blessed them with a child, only to cruelly snatch its little life away after less than one month. Then came the third child, Agatha, and although it was a difficult labor, she had been a healthy girl, so full of life. Much to their happiness and joy, she had grown bigger and stronger, seemingly ending the curse that had so long beset the Crowther household.

Alas, two years ago, this sweet daughter, nearly four years old, had died of pneumonia. Dully, Mrs. Crowther told her of the three small gravestones in a row, and how she had never really recovered from the last tragedy. "The doctor says we can't have any more," she said quietly, as she played with the material of her skirt, balling it up in her fists. "I know it must be God's plan, and my husband tells me we must not mourn forever, that life goes on. But oh! If you could have seen Agatha's blue eyes, her beautiful smile when I would sing her a silly song. We had a little game we used to play. I would cover my eyes, and . . ." Unable to finish, she broke down, fighting back tears.

Libby moved in to comfort the woman, but when she laid an arm gently on her shoulder, Mrs. Crowther sat up. "Miss Farrington, I think perhaps Berthe is right, and you should go now. I mustn't get upset like this. The doctor has been here twice in the last two weeks, and he told me I need to rest."

"I'm so sorry," murmured Libby, near tears herself. She was terribly moved by the story, and although she had not found out any useful information about Crowther's whereabouts the night of the murder, she had no choice but to stand up and gather her basket. Suddenly, an idea struck her. "I'm sure Mr. Crowther is a great comfort to you during your illness," she said. "He must feel very worried about your health to send for the doctor so often."

"He is very good to me," the woman agreed. "He works rather late. His job demands it. But, as I said, twice in the last two weeks, he has come home from work to find me ailing and turned right around and rushed out to fetch Doctor Biggs, even though it was nearly midnight."

"But surely your husband could stay here in the evening with you if you are ill!" said Libby, indignantly. "Does his job require that he work such long hours?"

Mrs. Crowther gave a little laugh. "Oh, he must work evenings, very late sometimes. But he is truly devoted to me, please do not misunderstand." She stood up, smoothing her skirt. "He owns a theater, you know, Crowther's Portland Variety."

"Really? I'm afraid I'm not really familiar with Portland's amusements. But I imagine it is rather late when he gets home, then."

"Oh, not so very bad. He usually leaves right away after the show and arrives home well before midnight, which is a blessing. Twice in the last week—no, it was two weeks ago—on Wednesday and then again on Saturday, I was up in bed, feeling really very ill when he got home, and he turned right around and fetched the doctor although it was already eleven o'clock. I said to him, 'No, no, don't bother that poor doctor. I'm sure I'm fine,' but he would have none of it. He rushed out of here and came back with Doctor Biggs." She thought for a moment. "The doctor gave me a tisane and told me to rest more."

Libby couldn't believe it. That was the very night Vera had been killed. It seemed almost too fortuitous that Crowther should have an alibi for just that Saturday night. For a moment, she wondered if Mrs. Crowther was repeating a prepared story, especially concocted to give her husband an alibi, but then she realized that there was no way Mrs. Crowther could know that Libby was investigating Vera's death. "Two weeks ago, you say, on Saturday night?"

Mrs. Crowther looked at her oddly. "Indeed. Is something . . . ?"

Libby interrupted, trying to cover herself. "I was just going to remark that you are lucky to have a doctor who will come see you on the weekend. But if this all happened not so long ago, you really should not overexcite yourself. As you said, it would probably be best for me to go." They were at the front door now, and Libby opened it, noting with satisfaction that the rain had abated somewhat. "I thank you very much for your hospitality. Maybe next time I stop by, you will have some mending work for me."

She walked thoughtfully to the tram stop, reflecting that she had quite a bit of interesting information to share with Peter tomorrow morning.

There was a crackling on the line, and the smooth voice of the Central Exchange girl came on. "Please hold for the operator in San Francisco." For a few moments, nothing happened. Peter stood leaning against the wall by the telephone, holding the earpiece close to his head and listening intently. Across the room, Libby sat, watching with interest.

"Is there a connection yet?" she asked, trying to gauge from his expression what was happening on the line. Of course, she had seen more and more telephones being installed in the years before she left New York—Mr. Fein at the Dressworks had been so proud of his new phone that she could remember him using it constantly and loudly, careful to leave his office door open—but she herself had never used one. She supposed that someday a telephone call would be as commonplace as a letter, but for now, she couldn't contain her wonder that here, standing in the *Gazette*'s offices in Oregon, Peter was going to speak with a man who was 500 miles away.

He waved a hand at her, not wanting to break his concentration. But as the silence continued, he began to feel silly shushing her. "I'm holding the line," he explained. ". . . for the girl in San Francisco."

Libby nodded. He listened for a moment, then said, "She told me it will be a few minutes."

"I wonder what Carlo will tell us," she mused aloud. "He must have some idea of what made Vera act so strangely the last few weeks of her life. And maybe he knows who the gentleman at the Anchor Saloon was . . ." Peter had caught her up on yesterday's labors when she arrived today, and she had told him of her visit with Mrs. Crowther. For some reason, she couldn't get the image of the three small grave plots out of her mind; the sad tale had touched her deeply.

"Hello? *Bon Giorno?*" Carlo's voice shocked him out of his reverie. The Italian was practically screaming, and Peter was forced to hold the earpiece away. Libby leaned in to listen.

"Hello! Hello, Mr. . . . er, Signor Carlo! My name is Peter Eberle!" Peter said loudly and clearly into the mouthpiece mounted on the wall. "Thank you very much for agreeing to talk to me."

"The newspaper man, he tells me to come to his office, that there is an important phone call for me this morning! He says the man in Portland wants to talk to me about Vera Carabella, God rest her soul!" Libby could almost see the expressive magician crossing himself elaborately as he said it. "Did they catch the monster who did that?"

"No, no, I am sorry to report we are still investigating. That's why I called."

"You are a detective, Mr. Eberle?"

Peter hesitated. "Well . . ." he looked at Libby frantically, not sure if he should lie. She shook her head slightly. "I am a journalist, Signor, and I am writing an article about this tragic killing. I wanted to ask you some questions that might shed some light on the case and help the police in their inquiries." There was silence, and for a moment, Peter was worried that Carlo had broken the connection. But after a pause, the magician spoke.

"Of course, of course, we must work together and find out who did this!" he said, indignantly. "But I do not know how I can help. I left the theater that night to . . . spend time with a friend, and I never saw *la mia bella* again. She was in her dressing room when I left."

"I realize that, but I am curious about Miss Carabella's behavior in the weeks before her death. For instance, I understand she paid her boarding house rent in cash when she moved in, in full for the whole four weeks in advance, and there was a great deal of cash among her belongings as well. I wondered if you were aware of any reason why she might have recently come into a large sum of money."

"She was not a pauper, my Vera! I pay her well, you know!"

"I'm sure you did."

"I pay her in cash at the end of every run, so she always have money when she gets to the new town! It is not very mysterious, Mr. Journalist. But you say, she pay for four weeks rent plus there is money with her things as well? Let me think a moment . . ." Carlo mumbled under his breath, and they could hear him reciting numbers as he struggled to reach some conclusion. "No, *non e vero,* it is not possible! She should not have that much cash from me, because of course, we must pay for the train, and to buy new photographs for the advertisements. So she had a large amount of cash? I pay for her funeral, you understand, because I think she has nothing. I see I need not have worried." There was a pause, and Libby expected any second to hear him ask for repayment. "Not that Signor Carlo would ask a dead woman to repay him, but . . . I am just, how you say, surprised."

Peter shot a look at Libby and raised his eyebrows. Now they were getting somewhere. "I see. Do you have any idea if she came into a sum of money recently, either in California or here in Portland? An inheritance, perhaps, or a gift from an admirer? Or was she maybe also working at a second job?"

"A second job? My Vera would not need another job! I pay her well, very well! Signor Carlo is good to his assistants!" Peter felt the conversation was quickly turning confrontational, and he struggled to find a way to change the topic.

"I was wondering if Miss Carabella had a man, a particular man, she had been involved with. Do you know if there might have been?"

"We did not discuss personal matters. We worked together, you understand?" Carlo's accent was rapidly fading as he spoke. "Which is not to say . . . Of course, we did spend much time together in our work. Rehearsing the act, performing two times a day, sometimes three . . . It is a lot of work—you people do not realize." He took a breath and continued, speaking faster now. "Naturally, I knew when she met someone. In San Francisco, you know, before Portland, she saw a man." Dramatically, he added "Oh, if we had only never come to your city of crime and horror!"

Libby couldn't contain herself, and said in a stage whisper, "Maybe she met the Anchor man in San Francisco!"

Peter motioned to her to be quiet. The last thing he wanted was for Carlo to ask if someone else was listening to their call. "Signor, do you know who this man was?"

"I never met him. She could be very . . . how you say . . . secretive about her personal life. But she stopped coming to rehearsals, and she was late two times for our show. Once I even had to trade places on the bill with *un poco soprano* because Vera she did not get to the theater in time! I was very angry, I must tell you. But she promised me to be better in Portland, and she was. She said that . . ." He stopped, and Peter got the feeling he had decided against telling any more. "No, no, it is not important what she said. She is gone now, the poor girl, and it is not right I should be telling you these things. I think I need to go now."

"Wait!" Both Peter and Libby were leaning in so close to the phone that their heads nearly collided. Peter frantically went on, desperate not to alienate the magician. "I know this is hard to talk about, Signor, but this could help us to find her killer. Do you know anything else about the man? Was he in Portland this month?"

In an annoyed tone that made it clear he was tired of the topic, the magician answered. "I do not think he was in Portland. Maybe . . . no, I do not know. I think she did have a man in Portland, but was it the same one? Who can say? I never knew his name. I am sorry. Are you finished with the questions?"

Peter could feel he was losing the man and knew he'd better get to most difficult question. "I also understand that she was considering leaving the show. Is that true?" Even as he asked it, he suspected that Carlo would be less than forthcoming about Vera's possible defection from the magic act, but to his surprise, this line of questioning seemed to raise no rancor. Instead, Carlo sighed deeply.

"Ah, *si, si,* it was something she said she might do, but we were a good team, it is not so easy to find a beautiful woman who can fit in a small wooden box, you understand? She told me when we got to Portland that she had some thinking to do and that she would let me know by the time we got back to San Francisco if she would stay or leave. But of course, she never got a chance to tell me anything." For all his bluff posturing and over emoting, the grief in his voice as he spoke that last sentence sounded genuine. "Will you find out who did this to her, Mr. Eberle? Was it this man?"

"I don't know," replied Peter, and he realized he wasn't sure to which of the two questions he was replying. Perhaps both. "Is there anything else you remember that might help this investigation? You have been most helpful already, of course, and I appreciate your time."

"I will think about it," said the Italian. "I can use this telephone if I need to speak with you again?"

"Of course, of course!" Peter cried, figuring he would certainly owe his friend at the Examiner a steak dinner the next time he went to San Francisco.

"*Bene, bene,* I must go to my rehearsal now!" Carlo yelled. "I am breaking the connection now! Good bye!" They heard him asking someone what he was supposed to do with the little black box, then a series of fumbled clicks, then silence. Peter hung up his own phone and sat down at his desk across from Libby.

"Well," he said. She looked at him unblinkingly. He felt sometimes that she was like a cat, watching him and waiting for him to do something awkward. "What did you think? Could you hear him clearly?"

"I could hear him just fine. In fact, he sounded loud enough to have communicated without the benefit of the telephone." He grinned, as she went on. "I wonder who the man in San Francisco was. Do you think the same man followed her up to Portland?"

He shrugged. "No way to tell. Not much of a description I got: tall, brown hair, clean shaven. That could be half the men in Portland."

"But not, alas, Mr. Crowther, with his handlebar moustache." She bit her lip, thinking. "Jack Reilly and Mr. Maynard are both tall and clean shaven. Not to mention several of those men who gathered in her dressing room." She drew pictures in her mind of the men she was thinking of. "Although, now that I think of it, Jack's hair is dark red."

"I should mention that this establishment hardly has enough light to determine nuances of hair color." He rolled his eyes. "I'm afraid that the bartender's description is little better than useless."

Libby had thought much the same thing when Peter had told her of his conversation at the Anchor. "I wonder . . . Mightn't the man she spent time with in the Anchor have been just a local paramour who had nothing to do with her death?"

"I'm not sure that's true. Think of it this way. If our mystery man was not involved with her death, then he doesn't have information for us anyway. He might say, 'Yes, I met her for a drink, and then she went back to the theater', and we're right back where we started."

Peter thought for a moment. "Yes, of course. But even if that is the case, it could only help us shed light on her murder if we could find him, especially if he saw her on the last night of her life." A thought occurred to him. "You were at her funeral, weren't you?" She allowed as how she was and gave a brief description of it. He went on, excitedly, "Doesn't it seem logical that if she was meeting someone regularly, he would have been at the service?"

Libby tried to recall the faces of the mourners she hadn't known, but her memories were indistinct, and as she recalled it, most of the men were over fifty. The only real possibility from the funeral was Lars Englund, and she told Peter as much. Englund had acted nervous when Libby had show up at Vera's boardinghouse, and his wife had appeared to think something had been going on between her husband and the magician's assistant. But something didn't feel right to Libby. "All right, maybe Englund was having an affair with Vera, but if he was connected to her death, chances are he would have made sure to stay far away from her funeral, not wanting to attract attention."

Peter looked at her with admiration. "Good point."

She smiled shyly. Having him compliment her made her blush. "Unfortunately, that brings us right back to the start. We can't seem to gather any information that actually helps us solve this mystery."

Peter looked at her, surprised. "That's not true. First of all, your talk with Crowther's wife provides him with an alibi. She says he arrived home before eleven on that Saturday and then was taken up with fetching the doctor. We know Vera was alive at eleven because you saw her in her dressing room. So, although Crowther could just possibly have gone home first, seen his wife, run back to the theater and killed Vera, and then gone on to get the doctor, I think it's unlikely enough to take him out of the running."

"Fine. So we have one less suspect." Libby interjected glumly. "Plus, we know about a man she was meeting regularly before she died who might be Lars Englund or any one of a thousand nondescript men in Portland. He might even have been from San Francisco and already returned there."

Peter went on, pushing himself to sound more sure than he was. He honestly felt they were moving closer to a solution, although he couldn't quite figure out the missing piece. "We've also learned a lot from Carlo. We know for sure now that she was thinking of leaving the act. And that she seemed to have a new source of income all of a sudden. You said she made some comments to you about settling here in Portland, coinciding with this new source of income and a ready supply of cash. Suppose . . ." He stopped to gather his thoughts, and then the words tumbled out of him quickly. "What if the man she had been meeting all those nights in the tavern was not a lover, but a business associate?"

"A business associate . . ." she repeated, pondering. "Maybe she was passing information about possible girls to abduct at the theater?"

"Or she heard him say something, or saw him do something, perhaps witnessed him committing some crime, and was meeting with him to collect her blackmail payments."

She suddenly realized that she must have been here for nearly an hour, and she had planned to get to work by ten in the morning, to make up for leaving early yesterday afternoon. Jumping up, she pulled on her coat and hat, apologizing for running out in the middle of their conversation. "What time is the party tomorrow night?" she asked, wondering if she would have time to alter a dress tomorrow during the day. "We can discuss this further then."

"It starts at eight o'clock," he answered. "I'll be at your boarding-house to pick you up at 7:30. Is that all right?"

"Of course." They smiled at each other, and as their eyes met, for a moment Libby knew how Vera must have felt when Carlo sent volts of electricity through her body. With some difficulty, she broke Peter's gaze and walked briskly out of the building, bidding farewell to John Mayhew, hunched over his typesetting table.

She tried to figure out what to do as she walked, wondering if she could take part of tomorrow off to work on a dress. She had missed work yesterday afternoon and had been late several times in the weeks before that, so she worried that Hatty might not take kindly to a request for more time off. As much as her job at the theater seemed less and less important to her life (Peter and their investigating seemed to consume more of her energy and attention), the truth was Libby needed the money. She had only herself for support, and she most certainly could not afford to lose this steady job—especially with the economy in its currently poor state. Why, people were out on the streets starving for lack of work!

There was only one thing to do. She would have to confide in Hatty that Peter and she were going to this grand party, hoping that Hatty's desire to see her settled with a nice young man would mean she could have all the time off she needed—even if it also meant Libby would be forced to endure endless questioning on what this party date meant. Hatty would never believe Libby and Peter were merely friends. Libby wondered if she believed it herself anymore, recalling the look she and Peter had just shared. Her inner voice warned her that she should cancel the date, but she knew she was not going to do that. She needed the afternoon to get herself ready for Portland high society, and she would just have to face Hatty's speculations and insinuations. She picked up her pace and soon was at the Variety.

TEN

LIBBY GLANCED AT THE clock. It was almost six forty-five. She was only just finished with her sewing and had not even begun to think about what to do with her hair. It had taken her longer than she had thought to alter one of the dresses from Vera's suitcase, but as she surveyed it now, she judged the result very successful.

Of the few evening dresses in the case, she had chosen a dark apricot one which she felt would most flatter her pale skin and brown hair and eyes. It was cut along last year's lines, if a little racier (as befitted Vera), and was made from a heavy floral silk moiré. There had been an elaborate chiffon overskirt, draped asymmetrically and gathered in elaborate folds over the small bustle. Libby removed it completely and used this fabric, along with scraps of silk culled from raising the hem (Vera had been a good four inches taller than Libby's own five foot one), to widen the bodice, since Libby was unable to lace her corset tight enough to match the showgirl's narrow silhouette. Finally, she filled in the low décolletage with some silk flowers she had picked up just that afternoon downtown.

Holding the dress up in front of her, she gazed at it critically. Whereas before it could have been described as elegantly racy, now it appeared fresh and just this side of demure. Once she put it on, Libby wasn't sure she recognized herself. The weight of the fabric, and the drag of the sweeping skirt when she moved made her feel a bit like a little girl dressing in her mother's clothes. And there was also a part of her that felt odd about having taken her scissors to a dead woman's prized fashions, even if it was in the cause of solving that woman's murder. But she conquered the fluttering in her stomach and decided that Vera would not only have approved but would have wanted the frock to be enjoyed by someone.

As she sat down at her dressing table, her eyes caught sight of her boots, and she realized she really ought to have some evening slippers. But there was nothing to be done about it now, even supposing money were not so tight. She had used most of her weekly food budget to purchase the silk flowers plus a pair of elbow-length white evening gloves. Libby supposed she would just have to keep her feet hidden in the folds of her heavy skirt if she needed to sit at any time during the evening.

She quickly unwrapped the rags she had rolled in her bangs when she arrived home hours ago and expertly fluffed out the resulting curls. The rest of her hair she tucked up in a narrow S-shaped twist which rested on the top of her head in back and pinned a few of the smaller silk flowers in it for effect. All in all—taking into consideration the dim gas lamplight and the fact that she had to crouch on her bed, skirts in hand, in order to see the upper half of her body in the room's only small mirror—she looked very presentable.

She glanced again at the clock and saw to her horror that it was nearly seven thirty; Peter would be here any moment. She picked up her one evening bag, which had been her grandmother's, a gilt-clasped and tasseled one with floral embroidery picked out in glass beads, and shoved in her handkerchief and gloves plus a little notebook and pencil. As she headed down the two flights of stairs to the parlor, she was suddenly anxious about Peter seeing her like this, dressed up, with her arms and neck bare. Even her respectable décolletage now seemed too risqué, and she had to resist the temptation to run back upstairs and stuff more flowers in her cleavage. Her heart hammered as if she was awaiting the arrival of a courting beau, and she had to remind herself that this was not a romantic evening; this was merely an investigative exercise.

Mrs. Pratt, aware that Libby had been up to something all afternoon although she had not known what, practically gasped when Libby entered the room. "Miss Seale! My faith, look at you! Paddy, Conor . . . look at our Miss Seale." The two cats, being like most males completely uninterested in matters of fashion, paid Libby no attention and continued licking themselves.

"Thank you, Mrs. Pratt. Do I really look all right?" Libby gave a twirl, allowing Mrs. Pratt a full view of the gown's sweeping, un-adorned skirt.

"Pretty as a picture," Mrs. Pratt cooed, "But where can you be off to, dressed as pretty as Cinderella for the ball? And would by any chance our handsome newspaper reporter be going there as well?"

It seemed that the entire older female population of Portland was trying to push Libby towards Peter Eberle, which was no help considering how hard she was finding it to keep her thoughts about him on a businesslike footing. She distracted Mrs. Pratt with a question. "I do have a favor to ask of you. It would be such a help to me if I could borrow your black cape. I'm afraid my day coat would look silly over this dress."

"Of course, dear." She crossed into the hall, then changed her mind and disappeared up the stairs, leaving Libby alone with the cats. When she finally reappeared over three minutes later, she carried not only the black cloak, but a small jewel case which she placed in Libby's hands.

"It was a present from my Brendan," Mrs. Pratt said breathlessly, having winded herself climbing the stairs. When the box was opened, it revealed a delicate gold bracelet from which dangled tiny cut crystal pendants. "It would give me great pleasure if you would wear it tonight."

Libby was overcome by the sweet gesture and was for once at a loss for words. Luckily, her lack of a reply was not missed, as into the silence there came a jaunty knocking on the boardinghouse's front door. Peter had arrived.

The McKennock home was in the northwest part of the city, and the houses became larger and more widely spaced the farther north Libby and Peter went in the carriage he had hired for the evening. Most of the houses out here had been built within the last few years and were larger and more ostentatiously elaborate than any Portland had ever known. Although, thought Libby with a bit of Eastern snobbery, compared to the grand mansions of Fifth Avenue in New York, they looked like no more than comfortable middle-class homes. Their driver turned left on Pettygrove Street and from the corner, Libby could make out the glow of lights and a row of carriages parked up ahead. As they drew closer, she saw that the short path from the street had been lined with gaily colored Chinese paper lanterns, so that walking up to the front door gave one the feeling of floating through an enchanted garden.

Peter took her elbow as they climbed the steps to the wraparound porch and approached the wide oak door, which opened before they had reached it. A maid stood at the door and took Libby's wrap with a slight bow. "Madame," she murmured, handing it to a small boy whose only job, it appeared, was to disappear through a small side door with coats. Peter handed their invitation to her, and she gestured toward an arched opening through which the sound of tinkling glasses and laughter could be heard.

With a pang of fear, Libby suddenly had the horrible feeling that her apricot gown was going to be all wrong for this party, that she was out of her element and would somehow manage to make an absolute fool of herself. So what if she had often walked down Fifth Avenue and gazed at the mansions of the wealthy? That hadn't prepared her to navigate a formal evening such as this. Her personal experience of parties extended no further than family birthdays, block parties, and the occasional wedding. For a moment she felt unequal to the task that faced her. People in Portland were mostly pleasant, but they weren't like the people she had known back East. It wasn't just the fact that she knew no other Jews here, it was something else. Something in the way people out here welcomed change and adventure, and faced adversity with a coarser energy and less tradition-bound attitudes. Vera's death had forced her to meet so many new people—not just meet them, but converse with them, to try to understand them. Suddenly she missed her New York, and her family. Would she ever be able to go back home and be around people she wouldn't have to work to understand? Home . . . where she would be welcomed and enveloped by a community she understood thoroughly and intuitively?

As if he sensed her hesitation, Peter put a hand on her back and gently guided her toward the room beyond, leaning down to whisper in her ear, "You look wonderful tonight."

To be honest, Peter himself was feeling a bit overawed at the surroundings—although he would never have admitted it. This was his own first experience, too, with a fete as lavish as this one. Trying to act as if it were the most natural place in the world for him to be, he looked around, taking in the great expanses of gleaming Oregon pine, the cut glass chandelier, the imported Oriental carpet, and the well-dressed celebrants sipping champagne as laughter and conversation swirled all around them. Discreet red, white, and blue bunting hung from the room's cornices, but there was nothing gaudy or showy about the display.

"Champagne?" A maid balancing an enormous silver tray stopped in front of them, and Peter took two of the delicate glass flutes, handing one to Libby with a smile. "Miss Seale," he said, formally, and she smiled back, making a slight curtsey as she took the proffered glass.

They stood a moment, but before she could reply, an older man with great sideburns and a jovial manner was bearing down upon them. "Hello, hello! Welcome to my humble home!" he boomed. "You're the fellow from the *Gazette*, am I right?" He turned to Libby without waiting for an answer. "And I see you brought a beautiful lady along. You know, running for Mayor has the unexpected side benefit of introducing me to the most beautiful ladies in Portland."

Despite his overbearing and flirtatious manner, Libby found something endearing about the man. And upon reflection, he seemed much younger than she had originally assumed. He might have been over sixty, she calculated, but his demeanor and energy were that of a man in his forties. He took her hand, his gray eyes focused intently on her. "H. Walford McKennock, pleased to meet you."

Peter jumped in. "This is Miss Seale, a friend of mine," he said smoothly. Extending his own hand, he went on, "Peter Eberle, of the *Portland Gazette*. Perhaps later we could talk a bit about your bid for Mayor. I'm sure our readers will want to know your platform."

"Of course, of course," agreed McKennock, reluctantly removing his attention from Libby. "You newsmen are always on duty, eh?" He turned back to Libby. "I never yet met a reporter who could just relax and enjoy a party. They're always looking for that next headline, wouldn't you agree, Miss Seale?"

"Indeed," she said warmly. "And I must say, this party seems far too splendid to be ruined with thoughts of work."

He looked around with an air of satisfaction. "I just want to be a good host; anyone would do the same." He pointed to the far end of the room, where French doors stood open to reveal a long table covered with white linen and laden with serving platters. "Make sure to get yourself some eats, Miss Seale, Mr. Eberle." He seemed about to leave them for more hostly mingling when he spotted a couple approaching and waved his arm to beckon them. "Charlotte, over here, dearest! There are some people I want you to meet!"

The woman he called Charlotte was tall but stocky, and her ornate hairstyle and overabundance of glittering jewelry did little to obscure the fact that her wide face was quite plain. Libby noted that her dress, an elaborate confection of midnight blue trimmed with yards of gilt fringe, was less than flattering, especially given her ruddy complexion. The man beside her was tall and handsome, and Libby found him vaguely familiar. Where had she seen him before?

Walford McKennock put his arm around the woman and drew her into their circle, while her escort stood off to one side, looking vaguely ill at ease. "This is Mr. Eberle from the *Gazette*, and his companion Miss Seale. I'd like you to meet my daughter, Miss Charlotte McKennock," he boomed. "Of course, she won't be wearing the McKennock name much longer! Just three more weeks or so and she'll be marrying this gentleman. Mr. Gerald Williams, my future son-in-law!" Behind his cheer, Libby thought she could detect a note of something unpleasant . . . condescension perhaps?

A deep crimson blush spread over the woman's face. "Oh, Father, really. I'm sure the *Gazette* is not here to write about my wedding." She turned to Peter and Libby. "Pleased to meet you, Mr. Eberle, Miss Seale."

Gerald Williams nodded politely at Peter, but he wouldn't meet Libby's gaze. He was obviously uncomfortable about something. With a flash, Libby remembered where she had seen him before. This was the Gerald that had been in Vera's dressing room the night of her murder! She didn't see how she could possibly mention it at this moment without it being socially awkward, so she simply said her polite hellos to them both, but she was wondering if she could find a way to talk to him alone later.

Lost in thought for a moment, Libby realized Walford McKennock was addressing her, and she turned her attention back to him.

"I hope you'll pardon me if I borrow your Mr. Eberle for a few minutes. I'm sure my daughter and Mr. Williams will take good care of you while I do my damnedest to get the *Gazette*'s endorsement for my campaign." He winked. "Pardon my language, Miss Seale."

Peter caught Libby's eye, and she understood this was exactly what he had been hoping for, a chance to talk to McKennock alone. She watched as the two men crossed the room and disappeared through a small doorway and turned back to Gerald and Charlotte, seeking some topic for party chatter.

"My congratulations to you on your upcoming wedding," she began, addressing herself more to Charlotte than Gerald, since he was still pretending not only that had he never met Libby, but also that she wasn't standing in front of him now.

"Three more weeks. Sometimes it seems like three years," Charlotte enthused. "I wish the wedding were tomorrow, don't you, darling?" She gazed up at Gerald with a rapturous smile, and he quickly murmured his assent, although to Libby it seemed obvious that he didn't share his fiancée's enthusiasm. Of course, it was always possible that Libby was letting her knowledge color her judgment, since she knew it was only a few weeks ago Gerald had been visiting Vera in her dressing room, enjoying his bachelorhood. Perhaps it was just the difference between the way men and women faced the prospect of matrimony. Libby dragged her mind back to the conversation.

141

"There must be so much for you to do to prepare, though. I would think every moment would be filled making happy plans." My god, thought Libby despairingly, this conversation was even duller than she had feared. Surely there was a way she could maneuver a moment alone with Gerald to discuss Vera, but how?

"Oh, no. Father is making all the arrangements." She sounded a little sad. "He pampers me so, I don't need to plan a thing."

Finally Gerald piped up, but it was only to effect a quick escape. "Dearest, don't forget we promised a moment to Mr. and Mrs. Abernathy. I believe they wished to congratulate us as well, and we were only supposed to be gone for a moment to fetch some punch." He began to steer Charlotte toward the dining room archway. "Do forgive our briefness, Miss Seale. It was a pleasure making your acquaintance."

And with that they were gone, leaving Libby alone. She glanced about, in the vain hope there might be somebody at the party she knew, but as she had suspected, all the faces were unfamiliar. She considered getting something to eat, the food smelled delicious, and she had skipped her lunch to finish the dress. But she quickly rejected the idea when she realized that Gerald and Charlotte had disappeared in the direction of the dining room. As unobtrusively as possible, she made a circle round the room, attempting to find somewhere to alight inconspicuously until Peter returned. At the far end of the room, she discovered an open door through which she could see masses of potted plants and hanging flowers, obviously a solarium of some kind, and she decided to wait there.

The room was long and narrow, and the blue moonlight which shone through the thousands of panes of glass which made up the walls and ceiling provided most of the illumination, except for the spill of golden light from the windows of the parlor. The space was surprisingly warm, and even in the half light, Libby could see that the flowers and plants were lush and well-tended. This was clearly a rich man's folly, for she could only guess at the cost of maintaining an indoor greenhouse through the winter. She walked along, enjoying the heady floral perfume for a few moments, then settled herself in a cushioned wrought-iron chair at the far end of the room, gazing out over the wooded grounds.

Suddenly there were voices, and shadowy figures flickered in the lit doorway to the house proper. Before Libby could reveal her presence to the two women, they were in the middle of a conversation, obviously one they had begun indoors and sought the privacy of the solarium to continue.

"But to not even put in an appearance at his own father's ball. Mark my words, Eleanor, the relationship is even more strained than we knew." The first voice was supple, clearly belonging to a woman in the prime of life.

Her companion's reply marked her as an older woman, and she spoke in pronouncements rather than sentences. "The day Will was born he was trouble. Sada McKennock nearly died bringing him into the world and from a start like that, no good can come."

"It wouldn't surprise me if his father is planning to cut him off completely. Despite all the advantages he's given his son . . . and let me tell you, the favoritism shown that boy is shameful, shameful, and a bald-faced insult to the men who actually make that company go . . ."

"Robert is a bulwark of the firm, Annie. If this world were a just place, he would be handed the reins of power at McKennock Enterprises if Walford becomes Mayor."

"Why, thank you, Eleanor. And I trust that you're not saying that just because Robert is my husband." Annie resumed the thought she had dropped earlier, "But as I say, despite all the advantages he's given him, I do believe Walford McKennock is on the verge of placing his son-in-law, or soon to be son-in-law, in Will's place."

"Really!" This was the first genuine excitement Eleanor had shown. Even though she couldn't see their faces, Libby felt she was getting a very clear picture of the two gossips. "I knew there must have been a reason Walford changed his mind about letting Charlotte marry him. He's decided he requires a new son."

"Not that Charlotte isn't a lucky girl to get any man," Annie chimed in, "She is nearly twenty-five, and I don't believe there have been many gentleman callers lately."

These two were truly awful, thought Libby. She had been trying to think of a way to reveal her presence and join the conversation. But as their talk turned completely to petty, mean gossip, she began to doubt she could learn anything really useful from them. She sank further back in the shadows, hoping to stay hidden, and praying for some sort of release from her eavesdropping vantage point.

Annie was still spewing venom, "You would think at least her father's money would attract a few offers. She is homely, no doubt about it, but that necklace she has on tonight looks as if it could support a family of four for a year."

"You never saw a lovelier woman than that girl's mother. It's a shame she takes after her father . . ."

". . . in every way but brains," Annie cut in, and the two shared an uncharitable little laugh.

"But I suppose that's why he dotes on her so," Eleanor concluded. "There were a few suitors early on, you know, dear, years back when Charlotte was eighteen or nineteen. But Walford felt they were courting his fortune, more than courting Charlotte, and he drove them all away."

"I suspect her brother would like to drive this one away . . . with a buggy whip. I'm sure there's no love lost between Will McKennock and Charlotte's Gerald."

"I wouldn't mind riding away in a buggy, if it was with the estimable Mr. Gerald!" Eleanor gave what Libby supposed was a coquettish, girlish giggle, but what came out was more like a predatory cackle.

"Oh, Eleanor, you are being bad tonight! How many glasses of champagne have you had?"

The two moved on to the subject of the catering this evening and from there, to a discussion of what must be every single gown at the party. Libby adjusted her weight slightly in the chair and settled in for what appeared to be a long wait.

McKennock's study was a small room, and Peter noted with interest that the compact writing desk was completely bare. The bookshelves looked pristine, with row after perfect row of books apparently lined up by size and color, giving the impression that they had never actually been read. Walford McKennock opened a drawer in the desk with a key from his watch fob and took out a sheaf of papers. He carefully re-locked the desk before motioning to the two armchairs arranged in front of the small fireplace and sitting down in one of them with a small grunt.

"Sit down, sit down, Mr. Eberle. I look forward to chatting about my agenda with you. I only regret that my guests necessitate this being a brief conversation." He played with the papers on his lap. "At any rate, I can give you some of my campaign literature. It will do a fine job of explaining the McKennock platform for reform and growth. Those are my twin pillars, you see . . . Reform. Growth." He paused, trying to gauge the impression of his rhetoric on the reporter. "Say, are you going to write any of this down?"

Peter pulled his small notebook and pen from his inside jacket pocket and jotted down: Reform. Growth. He looked up and met his host's eyes. "Tell me, Mr. McKennock, are you a big supporter of the arts in Portland? I'm sure our readers would love to hear about your thoughts on the various local theatrical offerings."

The older man looked at him oddly for a moment, caught out by the unexpected topic, but recovered his composure and waved a hand lightly. "Unfortunately, I do not get to the theater as much as I might like."

Peter went on, acting as if he had not heard. "I saw a wonderful bill at the Portland Variety myself, just a few weeks back. The dancers there put on a humdinger of a show."

Now McKennock was noticeably annoyed, and his tone was chilly. "I'm sure there are many fine theaters in the city; however, I would prefer to discuss my platform, Mr. Eberle. As I have already mentioned, my vision for Portland's future is one that both acknowledges the need for reforms in the present day and looks ahead to a time of unparalleled growth for this region of the country."

Peter pretended to check something in his notebook as he debated the best course to take in the conversation. "I'd like to hear about your plans for reforming Portland's shameful traffic in human lives, for the sailors and prostitutes who go missing and are never seen again. Tell me, do you have a plan to clean up the waterfront?"

"I'm glad you asked," McKennock replied. He launched into an obviously prepared speech about his commitment to double the police force, ensuring that all citizens would be protected from thieves and ruffians as well as the sinful crime of prostitution. Peter listened for a few minutes, then jumped in when the man paused for breath.

"Those are fine plans, sir, but I do still have a few questions. Not, you understand, for the *Gazette* necessarily, but merely for my own elucidation."

"Of course, I am always happy to clarify anything about my platform."

"Let me tell you a little story, Mr. McKennock, and see what you think of this. Suppose a high ranking man in this city, let us say he is a respected businessman and politician, is a frequent visitor to one of the bordellos of our fair city. To this man, prostitution is not a crime; it is his privilege to enjoy it when he will. Imagine that this man decides one night that he has become especially fond of one of the girls in the bordello, and he arranges with the madam to buy the girl's freedom. He pulls some strings and gets her a job in a local theater."

He paused. It was a calculated risk, but Peter hoped that by showing enough of his hand to alert McKennock that his role in Polly Pink's hiring at the Variety was known, he would force the man to reveal more in his desire to clear his name. "I wonder," he went on, "how your administration would react if such a crime were to be discovered? And why do you suppose a scion of the community would risk being caught up in such a scandal . . . if it were to be made public?"

As Peter spoke, maintaining an even conversational tone, McKennock's face grew dark, and his fury was palpable. He jumped up from his chair. "That's—" But instead of continuing, he stopped abruptly. Quietly, he composed his features into the avuncular guise of a few minutes earlier and attempted a smile before speaking again.

"That's an interesting story, Mr. Eberle. With an imagination like that, perhaps you should be writing novels. It certainly isn't fit to print in a newspaper."

Peter returned the smile. "Of course not. I was simply stating a hypothetical situation."

McKennock's voice was level but his eyes were icy. "Well, given this fanciful hypothetical situation, I can only repeat that, naturally, my administration would stand for truth and justice." With that, he handed Peter the printed pamphlets he still held and crossed to the office door. "I do regret cutting this interview short, Mr. Eberle, but I'm afraid I simply must return to my guests."

He wrenched open the door and, for a second, Peter had the impression that he would slam it behind him. But instead, the door slowed just before it reached the frame and closed with a soft, final-sounding click.

Peter was annoyed with himself. After this, there was no hope of approaching McKennock again on anything resembling a friendly footing. He dreaded having to go find Libby and tell her how badly he had bungled the interview, not managing to extract a single useful piece of information before totally alienating their host.

His eyes swept the room, coming to rest on the conspicuously locked desk. He would give anything to know the secrets it contained . . . could he possibly . . . ? He rejected the idea almost immediately, since McKennock would know who the culprit had to be and would probably have him thrown in jail before breakfast tomorrow. Still, he hated going to Libby empty handed, and he wondered if there was anything he could learn without actually breaking the law.

He stepped to the nearest bookshelf and began carefully scanning the title on every spine, hoping desperately for some clue to the man behind the politician.

It was over twenty minutes later when Libby, having finally been set free because Eleanor required more liquid refreshment, was able to rejoin the mass of guests inside the house. Immediately, she looked around for Peter, but there was no sign of him or of Walford McKennock, so she assumed they must still be together. Things must be going very well, she thought, and she couldn't wait to hear what Peter had discovered. Still, since she had to wait, she decided to use her time fruitfully in pursuit of Gerald Williams. Perhaps by this time Charlotte was no longer hanging on his arm, although if this was so, Libby guessed it would be Gerald's doing and not Charlotte's.

Her search for Gerald ended before it began, for straightaway she had decided to look for him, he contrived to find her.

"Miss Seale," she heard a voice behind her and turning, found herself face to face with him. This time Gerald's eyes met hers, and they were friendly but intense. He spoke as if in a hurry, "I was hoping I might have a word with you."

At her surprised, "Of course . . ." Gerald gestured for her to follow him and led the way to an ornate door off the arched passage from the parlor to the dining room.

"I believe we won't be disturbed in here," he said tensely, his eyes darting quickly into both rooms, perhaps for any sign of Charlotte. The small room he ushered her into was masculine in character and octagonal in shape, fully paneled in dark carved mahogany except for insets of Turkish tile work. The only furniture, four massive tapestry chairs, stood against the walls. In the center of the room was a large, free-standing brass urn which, from the smell of it, was obviously used for cigar ashes. "Walford's smoking room. Never used for mixed parties."

Libby suddenly realized the social impropriety of an unmarried couple sneaking off together, closeting themselves behind a closed door, and she hoped nobody had seen them. Irrationally, she wondered if Peter would be jealous . . . certainly Charlotte would be.

Gerald relaxed. "I wish to thank you, Miss Seale. It would have been difficult to explain to Charl—Miss McKennock if you had mentioned that you and I had met before and where. I'm grateful for your discretion." The language was flowery and perfectly polite, but Libby sensed Gerald wasn't fully comfortable expressing himself in this formal way.

"Please, Mr. Williams, no thanks are necessary. You haven't done anything you need to be ashamed of." She was surprised at the guilt that leapt into his hazel eyes, as if he thought Libby was obliquely implying just the opposite.

149

"You mustn't misunderstand. My . . . devotion to Miss McKennock is complete. There was nothing illicit about my visit backstage a few weeks ago. It was merely admiration for . . ." Gerald trailed off and sat on one of the tapestry chairs. "Charlotte is a wonderful girl. I'm a very lucky man." His voice told a different story and, once again, his eyes wouldn't meet Libby's.

Libby felt sorry for Gerald, whose unhappiness was obvious. She was more certain than ever that whatever was prompting his marriage to Charlotte McKennock, it was not true love. The thought flickered that perhaps Walford McKennock was somehow forcing the match, but then she recalled that her purpose here tonight was not to uncover the marital machinations of Portland's elite but to discover a murderer. The woman at issue was Vera, not Charlotte.

She sat on a chair opposite Gerald and said gently, "She was admirable, wasn't she? Miss Carabella, I mean. It's perfectly natural that you should have wanted to express your appreciation." He looked up at Libby and smiled wistfully in agreement. "She was lovely," Libby added.

"Very lovely." His gaze moved past Libby into space. "I remember the first time I saw her . . . a vision in emerald green silk, shining like a precious gem herself under the bright lights." There was a weight of emotion in his voice and a sad look in his eyes.

Two thought leaped simultaneously into Libby's mind. First, that—judging by his tone—Gerald's infatuation with the magician's assistant was clearly more than a passing flirtation. And secondly, that without a doubt, Vera's closing night—the night Libby had met him in the dressing room—was not Gerald's first visit to the show. Being a dressmaker, she immediately recognized that the emerald dress Gerald had described was the one Mr. Maynard had spilled ink on during the first week of Vera's run and which Libby had replaced with a new gown of peacock blue. She wondered if Vera had been aware of his repeat viewings, or whether Gerald had merely worshipped her from afar until closing night, when he finally managed to get up the courage to go backstage.

"She was a good friend of mine," Libby said, then amended, "... perhaps not a close friend, but a good one."

"I'm so sorry." He sounded genuinely empathetic, but didn't take her bait and indicate anything about his own relationship with Vera.

"I hadn't known her long, but sometimes acquaintance of shortstanding can be more intense for its brevity, rather than less."

Gerald seemed to come out of his haze and rose. "We should really rejoin the party."

Libby affected not to have heard him and pretended she was lost in grief. "It's inconceivable to me that Miss Carabella died the way she did. And that her death should go unpunished . . ." She left the sentence dangling to see what he might say.

Gerald spoke carefully, as if uncomfortable with Libby's tender emotionalism. "I read about it in the papers. It appears it was a commonplace crime, as awful as that is to acknowledge. I doubt anything more will ever be known."

She let the topic drop and said demurely, "I suppose you're right. And about rejoining the party as well. Shall we go?"

Gerald left the smoking room first and glanced around, then subtly gestured to her that no one was paying attention and she could exit unobserved. He then struck out for the parlor, while she headed into the dining room for the first time that evening, realizing as she saw the food-laden table how hungry she was. Soon she was balancing a porcelain plate piled with delicacies in one hand and trying to restrain herself from allowing hunger to cause her to eat like a dockworker. Her mouth was full with a deliciously crumbly oyster patty when Peter reappeared and indicated rather abruptly that it was time for them to leave.

Once they were settled in the carriage, Peter turned to Libby sheepishly. "I'm sorry, Libby. I made a mess of the interview with McKennock." His tone indicated to her the depth of his disappointment in himself, and she rushed to reassure him.

"Peter, please. I'm sure you have nothing to apologize for." She gave him a smile and unthinkingly placed her hand tenderly on his arm. She could feel the warmth of him even through the multiple layers of fabric, and she withdrew her hand almost immediately, at once realizing the intimacy of the gesture. Now slightly flustered, she pretended to rearrange Mrs. Pratt's cloak over her skirt. "Tell me exactly what happened."

Peter made no comment about her caress, but the slight flush in his cheeks told her he had noticed. With an embarrassed shrug, he told her about confronting McKennock with the story of Polly Pink. "He obviously knew to what I was referring—it was written on his face—but he chose not to answer. The truth is," he sighed deeply, "we have no actual proof he was involved in getting Polly off that boat, and he knows it. Madame Josephine would certainly deny she said anything to me, and I have no doubt all her employees would do the same."

"But surely he told you something of interest! You were closed up in his office with him for almost an hour."

If possible, Peter looked even more embarrassed. "I spent most of the hour searching the room for anything that might tie him to the white slave trade . . . as though he would leave something like that out for his guests to find! I read the spine of every book on the shelves, but unless we can make a case for the fact that a fondness for leather bound classics is a sign of guilt, we'll need to get proof of McKennock's involvement some other way." He looked down at his lap, "Unfortunately, I fear I won't be welcome in his home again."

He looked just like a little boy, frustrated because he couldn't do his long division or translate a passage from the Latin, and it took all of Libby's self-control not to reach out and touch him again. She decided to change the topic to her own party revelations, "Mr. Williams, Charlotte McKennock's fiancé . . . ?" She made it a question, and Peter nodded slightly without looking up, ". . . was most appreciative that I chose not to mention to Charlotte that I had already met him just a few weeks ago—in a certain performer's dressing room, to be specific."

Peter's head shot up, and his eyes met hers. "You met Gerald Williams in Vera's dressing room?" She nodded at him, smiling serenely, and he gazed at her with a look that was equal parts envy and disbelief.

She continued, giving him a complete précis of her private conversation in the smoking room with Gerald, and Peter's look changed to one of complete respect for the way she had managed to make good use of her time at the party. "I should mention" she added, "that Gerald seems to have been quite taken with Vera and obviously cared for her a great deal." She paused, hesitant to pass along information that bordered on gossip, but deciding she had to share her suspicions. "A good deal more, I should say, than he cares for Charlotte McKennock. I'm not sure what is behind the engagement between Mr. Willams and Miss McKennock, but I can tell you that it is certainly not a love match."

Peter closed his eyes, frustrated, and leaned back against the carriage seat. "I don't know. I . . ." His eyes opened again, and the look of frustration and self-censure had returned. "If only there were some way we could get back into that house! There are so many questions, and now because of my bungling, we have no way of seeking the answers."

"Peter, don't castigate yourself so." The warmth in her voice was as close to a caress as she could make it. "We'll just have to be even cleverer than before," her tone grew chipper, "and think of some other way to investigate the McKennock clan and what they might have to do with the murders at the Portland Variety."

Peter gave her a look of pure admiration. "Miss Libby Seale, you are quite an extraordinary woman." Caught by surprise, she blushed.

Peter tried to ignore it. "Do you suppose Walford McKennock is forcing Gerald to marry Charlotte?"

"I don't know. I suppose it's possible." This was an issue Libby didn't care to discuss, especially with Peter. Fathers did want to force people to get married. For the first time in many weeks, her life in New York rose to the surface of her mind.

At that moment, the carriage stopped suddenly as the driver maneuvered the turn onto the bridge roadway. Without the clop, clop of the horse's hooves, the night suddenly seemed very quiet, and Peter lowered his voice as he went on. "I have to say, I would look unhappy too if I was to marry someone as bland and lackluster as Charlotte McKennock." She turned to him and was struck dumb when she found he was gazing at her with a shy sweetness, "Not when there are bright and intelligent girls in the world to marry."

With something approaching horror, she realized he was about to turn this into a romantic conversation. Surely he couldn't be about to propose . . . they barely knew each other! Even as she had that thought, she knew it to be untrue. She knew him better than almost anyone else in her life, but she couldn't let him continue on in this vein. She might lose him completely—lose his help and his friendship, which she couldn't bear to even think about.

"I hope Mrs. Pratt hasn't waited up for me," she said gaily, as they rode over the dark river towards her neighborhood, although she knew Mrs. Pratt would have. Glancing out the window, she saw the lights of the city receding behind them. "It's so very late. But now we're almost there, aren't we?"

If he noticed her attempt to change the topic, Peter didn't take the hint. "Libby, before we reach Mrs. Pratt's, I hope you'll let me speak plainly to you for a moment. I want to tell you that these past few weeks, working so closely with you, I've come to admire you so much."

She gathered her cloak more tightly around her, and when she spoke her voice was cool, "Why thank you, Peter. I don't know what I would have done if you hadn't agreed to help me. Solving the mystery behind Vera's murder is so important to me and . . ." Peter tried to smile, but his eyes showed the hurt. He understood that she was declining to be drawn into a conversation about the future. "I can never repay the debt I owe you for that."

The carriage pulled up at her house. "Oh, here we are," she said, forcing a smile of her own. "And we haven't even decided on what our next steps should be."

Peter's voice sounded hollow, "Shall we meet Monday morning at nine o'clock before you go in to work? At the Chinatown Gate?"

She indicated her agreement. "And I do want to thank you for a lovely evening on top of everything else. The carriage and . . . the chance to get all dressed up," she finished lamely.

"My pleasure," he said lightly. "Good night."

"Good night."

As she mounted the stairs of her boardinghouse, Libby was filled with a flood of self-recrimination. How had she let the situation get so out of control? She should have told Peter long before this that she . . . that she was already married. She forced herself to face the unpleasant fact.

She had no business letting a gentleman court her, knowing all the while that nothing could ever come of it . . . and it was suddenly clear to her that that was exactly what Peter had been doing for the past few weeks. Mrs. Pratt had seen it; Hatty had seen it. Libby was the only one who had been fool enough to think Peter had merely been offering friendship. Now she had hurt him, she knew that, and it was all so unnecessary.

She shut the door behind her as quietly as she could, but as soon as the latch clicked shut, Mrs. Pratt's head, clad in a starched lace bed cap, poked over the banister at the top of the stairs.

"Miss Seale, home from the party." She started down the staircase.

"I hope you weren't waiting up for me."

"Oh, no," Mrs. Pratt lied gaily, "I just wanted to give the kitties some milk before bed." She waved a hand toward the kitchen. "That's the second time I've seen you with that dashing newspaperman." Libby began to climb the stairs. "He's a nice boy—and handsome. Ah, it does my heart good to see you find someone."

She managed to get out a weak "Thank you." Despite knowing how badly she was disappointing her landlady by not sharing tales of the party, she claimed a headache and fled to her room. There was no point in trying to convince Mrs. Pratt that Peter was not a beau. Especially since she hadn't even been able to convince Peter of that fact.

With every footfall her guilt grew. It was her own fault if Mrs. Pratt and Hatty assumed Peter was in love with her. She should never have tried to keep Mr. Greenblatt a secret from them. She saw very clearly now that some part of her had wanted to believe that if she told no one, and refused to even think about her marriage, then it would somehow make it untrue. She had been hiding in a fantasy, and now she was paying the price.

She had to come clean. But how? And when? If she told Peter now, she risked even more hurt feelings and perhaps the loss of her investigative partner. She wondered if she could simply go on as before, pretending, until she left Portland for good. Perhaps Peter would never return to the subject of romance again. Even so, though, didn't she owe him an explanation for her coolness in the carriage tonight?

She reached her room and threw herself onto the bed without undressing. Jumbled images from New York came into her head. She remembered her shock and outrage when her stern father had first impressed upon her the need to marry their old family friend and the chief supplier of fruit for the store. Her father's voice had been hard, even though his words had made it clear he knew this would be no love match. "He's a good man, Libbeleh. I know he's not young, but he will take good care of you."

Suddenly she was reminded of Gerald Williams at the party, looking lost and forlorn as he said, "I'm a very lucky man." What a contrast his attitude made to Charlotte's rapture at the upcoming nuptials. Despite her own despair, Libby was momentarily filled with pity for him. Perhaps better than anybody, Libby understood what he was facing— a life founded on a lie, a vow that meant nothing because it did not come from the heart. Why couldn't Mrs. Pratt and Hatty see that? See that marriage was as often the source of pain and suffering as of joy?

Joy . . . the word called Peter to mind, although try she might to fight the thought. Just for a moment, she allowed herself the luxury of imagining what her life might be like if she could marry him. With Peter, she could imagine the joy. She tried to imagine a married life based on the kind of closeness and intimacy that came from a love that is shared. But Peter's image was followed by the spectre of Mr. Greenblatt . . . of her husband. The word itself brought a bad taste into her mouth and seemed singularly inappropriate when the sum total of their married life had been less than three weeks. How was it she could be lawfully tied to a man she had barely lived with? And such a man! Nothing in her parents' marriage had prepared her for her brief life with Mr. Greenblatt.

For the first few weeks they were married, he had been generally kind to her in an absentminded, dismissive way. Outside of the bedroom, he mostly just ignored her. As for what happened inside the bedroom, her mind shrank even now from the memory of his porcine face, his clammy hands on her skin. But she could have lived with that indignity, no matter how distasteful she found it. It was over quickly enough to be sure, never more than a few minutes each night before he would roll onto his side of the bed and sleep. Then she could lie back on her pillow and dream she was still a little girl, safe in her parents' apartment.

During the day, she had the house to herself, and although Mr. Greenblatt had lectured her on the precise ways in which every household chore ought to be done—the horsehair sofa in the parlor must be brushed clean once a week, the bathtub must be scrubbed clean every single day, and dinner was to be on the table at half past six every evening, as soon as he walked in to door from work—she was more than up to the housework. It was no more than she had been asked to do in her father's home.

A week after they were married, her sister Rebecca stopped by for an afternoon visit. The two of them laughed together over some of the truly awful wedding presents Libby had received, and they lost track of the time. In consequence, Mr. Greenblatt's dinner wasn't ready when he arrived home. That was the first time he hit her. She could still remember her shock as his open palm struck her cheek—the surprise and disbelief lingered long after the pain had passed. It was just a slap after all. She hurried to finish dinner and afterward, his hands draped contentedly across his full belly, Mr. Greenblatt had apologized. It was just that his day at work had left him irritable, he said, and he *had* told her that dinner was to be ready by six-thirty, so at least some of the blame was hers. Still, he promised her it would not happen again.

He kept his promise for all of three days, at which point it was a scorch mark on one of his shirtfronts that provoked his rage. Once again the violence had been followed by an apology and a promise, although this time Libby was left with a livid purple bruise on her face. Too embarrassed to let anyone know what had happened, she had cancelled a visit with her mother and stayed inside her home for two solid days until the bruise had paled.

She vowed she would leave if he ever struck her again, but each time that week he gave her a shove or shook her so violently by the shoulders her ears rang, she told herself that no harm had really been done and broke her self-imposed vow. She knew that to leave her husband might bring financial ruin, not to mention great shame to her parents and siblings as well as herself.

Then one day, with a fresh bruise on her face, she gathered up her courage and, after Mr. Greenblatt left for work, put on her most veiled hat and wrapped a scarf around her face for good measure. She went home to show her family the truth about her marriage. Surely they would help her figure out a way to end this torture!

To her shock and chagrin, her family, while sympathetic, did not encourage her to stay away. Her mother had been properly horrified, and her older brother Seymour had to be talked down from attacking Mr. Greenblatt physically. Her father swore to give her husband a good talking to, but explained to her in a voice that brooked no argument that a wife must stay with her husband no matter what happened. *Libbeleh, always so headstrong, maybe this is God's way of telling you to learn to be a more dutiful wife.* Libby was too shocked to speak at first, and when she regained her voice, she yelled. She pleaded, she wept, but her father remained adamant. And although everyone in her family agreed she had done the right thing by coming home, after tempers had cooled down, she had returned to her new home the next day.

Whatever her father had said, it only seemed to make matters worse. Only two days after returning to her apartment, her husband had stayed out past midnight and arrived home belligerently drunk. This time she had done nothing to set him off, merely asked him where he had been. That had been the worst beating. If it had not been that he passed out from exhaustion a few minutes later, she wondered if she would have lived to see the next morning. As it was, gazing at his massive frame slumped in a chair, his florid face gleaming with sweat that reeked of alcohol, cradling her arm that was black and blue where he had nearly twisted it from its socket, she knew that she could take no more.

The next morning, after he left for work, she had packed all that she could carry with her one good arm and run to Penn Station—this time without telling her family, as she already knew what kind of reception to expect. She took the next train leaving that was going westward. That had been nearly six months ago.

For the first time in a long while, she considered what her running away must have meant to her family. It was as if she had hurled a great boulder into the placid pool that was her parents' world, and the ripples were probably still expanding. Had Mr. Greenblatt ruined her father's business? Could the situation ever be made right? Perhaps. . . . there was one possibility, and the thought gave her momentary warmth. Perhaps even now, Mr. Greenblatt was seeking a divorce on the grounds of desertion. After all, what good to him was a wife who hated him with every fiber of her being? But how would she find out if he had divorced her? She knew she should write her mother, but she was still afraid that if her family knew where she was, they would send one of her brothers to fetch her home. And whatever it meant for her future happiness, she knew she was never going back to New York if it meant a life as Mrs. Greenblatt.

Yet, somehow she also knew that Mr. Greenblatt's pride and reputation would never let him admit that his marriage had been a complete failure. He would prefer the sham to the public exposure, she felt sure, and unfortunately for her, the choice was in his hands. In the Jewish religion, a man could be formally divorced simply by expressing his intent publicly in the synagogue, but a woman had no way to initiate the proceedings. True, Libby could go to a civil judge to end the marriage, but her family and community would not recognize that she was legally divorced unless her husband gave her a *get*, the official Jewish bill of divorcement. And without formal recognition of her divorce, she would become a pariah—cut off from friends and family forever, a possibility she was unwilling to even contemplate. The warmth that had flickered briefly faded, along with any hope.

No, as far as Libby knew, she was still a married woman. And somewhere in Portland, possibly lying in bed awake at this very moment, was a man whom she needed to tell.

ELEVEN

IN THE GRAY LIGHT of Monday morning, Peter walked briskly towards Chinatown, annoyed with himself for oversleeping. He had arranged to meet Libby at nine, and it was nearly ten past the hour already. If he was honest with himself, it was partially dread about seeing Libby that made him late. Ever since their parting after the McKennock soiree, he was unable to hide from the fact that she didn't feel the same way he did. He had made a mess of everything with his declarations of . . . well, if not yet love, at least the possibility of such. And he wasn't sure whether he should apologize or simply act like the conversation had never happened. So it was with a racing mind, half running in his haste, that he approached the multicolored Oriental gate which marked Chinatown's southern boundary.

Most of the men around him now wore simple black trousers and white shirts; many of them had slender braids of shiny dark hair. Some of the women wore trousers as well—who had ever heard of such a thing?—and were dressed in mostly neutral colors, save for the occasional blue or green scarf or a pair of red silk slippers. Only the children, laughing and chattering in Chinese as they ducked in and out of shops' doorways, were dressed in colorful silks, their long braids flapping in the wind.

Peter caught sight of Libby just as she bent down to keep a small ball from rolling into the street. If Libby felt any lingering unease over the strangeness between them in the carriage, she showed no sign of it . . . at least from half a block away. Laughing, she returned the ball to its rightful owner, a round-faced boy of no more than five, who then scurried away to the arms of his mother.

Peter had suggested they meet in Chinatown since he had work to do for the paper in this part of the city, and it was also not far from Libby's job, but it occurred to him that few white women ever ventured into this part of town. Somewhat concerned that he had made a blunder in suggesting this rendezvous point, he was suddenly acutely aware of the strong fishy smell coming from the market on the corner and of the sideways stares and murmured discussions all around. He reached Libby's side, "Good morning." He paused, somewhat tentative. "I'm sorry I was late. Have you been waiting long?"

"Oh no, only a few minutes," she said. She paused now as well, unsure of how or whether to broach the subject of the other evening here in the middle of the street. Just tell him, a voice in her head prodded. Tell him why you cannot return his affections. But her courage failed her, and instead she made an attempt at lighthearted small talk. "You know, I've been to a few of the sewing shops here, but never really spent any time in this area. It's a bit like being in another country."

Peter seemed uncomfortable, too. "I know where we can get some tea and talk," he said, leading the way down a narrow street in the middle of the block.

The sight of so many Asian faces reminded her of Hatty and for the first time, she wondered whether Hatty lived somewhere in Chinatown. Would these people accept Hatty as one of their own, being as she was only half-Chinese? And how would they feel about her having married an Englishman?

Neither she nor Peter made any more attempts at conversation until they were seated in the small tea room. It was nearly empty but for a few elderly gentlemen sipping tea and reading Chinese newspapers. Libby removed her coat and sat down at one of the tiny round tables, enjoying the warmth and the exotic smells of the steaming teas, while Peter went up to the narrow counter and, through a combination of pointing and pantomime, managed to return with two delicate cups filled with green tea and a square plate containing several almond cookies.

"Peter, I need to tell you. . . . that is to say . . ." she faltered. But to her surprise, he got up and walked across the shop to grab a bowl of sugar cubes. Peter had suddenly realized he didn't want to hear her apologies for not being interested in him that way or to listen to her attempt to let him down gently. She didn't owe him any explanations. He was a grown man, wasn't he? Wise in the ways of the world and easily able to move past this.

Returning to the table, he sweetened his cup of tea and took a long appreciative swig. If only he could make her see that the other evening, he had been simply caught up in the romance of their situation, that she meant nothing more to him than a new friend whom he was assisting in an investigative capacity. But no . . . to open the subject would be to invite more stammering explanations from her. He was suddenly struck with the determination to bring their dealings back to a businesslike level.

"Tell me," he said, "what do *you* think our next step should be? As I told you, I'm afraid my behavior with McKennock has closed the door of his household to me for further enquiries."

Libby was taken aback, but in truth felt a bit of relief that she had just been spared the awkward conversation she expected. She knew she still had to tell him about Mr. Greenblatt . . . sometime. But perhaps it could wait for a little bit longer. With difficulty, Libby switched her mind to the matter at hand.

Lying in bed the night before, she had considered the problem of gaining access to the McKennock house, and she now presented her conclusion to Peter. "I will just have to do some sewing work for Miss McKennock, perhaps help her with her trousseau. I'm sure if I were a regular visitor there, I would learn quite a bit about McKennock's life just by observing who comes and goes at the house and keeping my eyes open."

He nodded slowly. "I suppose that's true. It certainly seems the McKennock family is deserving of close scrutiny. But how will you be able to get work there? I suspect your own welcome in the household may be tarnished by your association with that mudslinging reporter, Peter Eberle." He smiled, the first smile she had seen all day.

"Actually," she said, "I have a plan. In fact, I believe someone intimately connected with the McKennock family owes me a favor." She took a bite of one of the cookies and sipped her tea.

He nodded in recognition. "Of course, I had nearly forgotten! Gerald Williams. . . . Yes, I think after you were kind enough to keep his secret, he will have help you." He ate one of the almond cookies in one bite. "Meanwhile, I had an idea we might approach the Polly Pink abduction from a different angle." She looked up at him expectantly, and he continued. "I hardly dare suggest this after my disastrous interview with McKennock, but I think I should go to the theater and interview Crowther, ostensibly for the newspaper. If I play it right, he might open up to me in an effort to prove his own innocence."

"But mightn't it end up like the McKennock interview? I doubt Crowther will tell you anything, since he knows you don't have any proof."

"Ah, but there you're wrong. I believe I can convince the man that we have some crucial evidence linking him to Polly Pink. Since we know he was the one who actually took Polly off the boat, and since we also know he has an alibi for Vera's murder, let us assume for the moment that he is not the white slaver. In that case, he'll be very anxious to make sure someone else is incriminated, and he may be willing to talk."

By now, the tea was growing cold and Peter stood up. "I'll see if I can set up a meeting with Crowther later this week."

"And make sure not to acknowledge me if we meet backstage. I think Crowther would find it noticeably odd if the reporter interviewing him happens to know his wardrobe mistress, who has already been asking questions around the theater."

He looked at her with respect. "Good point."

Outside, the streets were more crowded than they had been only half an hour earlier, and Libby had to jump backwards to avoid being run down by a speeding bicycle. Peter motioned towards the way they had come. "Will you be able find your way to the Variety from here?" he asked. "I would walk along with you, but I need to meet someone inside Chinatown in a few minutes."

Libby assured him that an escort was hardly necessary. "What is the story you're working on?" she asked. "More about the Coxey's mob a few weeks ago?"

He shrugged. "I suppose you could call it a follow-up story, but it's not about Coxey's Army per se. Mayhew wanted me to do a little sniffing around and find out what the employment situation is like for Orientals in this economic climate. This morning, I'm interviewing a man who is organizing a political coalition of Chinamen to fight against unfair labor practices."

Libby considered. "It doesn't seem to me like they're in any danger of taking jobs away from white people, despite the anti-Chinese hysteria."

"True, I haven't met a Chinese newspaper reporter. But some people say that they are being favored for menial jobs, while other people insist you couldn't find Americans to do the kind of jobs they do for so little money. You know it was only last year that the Exclusion Act expired." Seeing her look, he explained, "It was a law banning Chinese immigrants for ten years, but as of last January, they are once again allowed to legally enter the country. Since then, there's been talk of bringing the law back."

Libby was outraged. "But America is a country of immigrants; there's no earthly reason to single out one nationality as wrong!"

"I agree with you," he answered, surprised at her vehemence. "The *Gazette* wants to present as even a picture as possible and inform the public about any Chinese appeal against the rising tide of anti-immigrant sentiment."

She realized she had once again let her emotional nature get the better of her and wondered if Peter would think she was some sort of radical. But this topic struck too close to home for her, as it recalled the stories of her parents and grandparents who had fled Russia for the United States, believing it a haven of religious and ethnic tolerance. Which it was . . . even if it wasn't a perfect country. Taking a deep breath, she tried to explain all this to Peter. "I only feel so strongly about this because it was not that long ago that my own relatives were persecuted for their 'differentness' . . ." She smiled wryly. "The Jews, like the Chinese, have not always had an easy time being adopted by a new country."

He was surprised, and it showed on his face. It took him a moment to respond, "Seale doesn't sound like a Jewish name."

"I changed my name when I moved to Portland . . . for a number of reasons." Now was the moment. She should tell him that her name was Libby Seletzky Greenblatt and that she had a husband back in New York. But in the awkward pause that followed, she saw in his eyes that he was genuinely taken aback. It had not occurred to her that Peter would have any difficulty learning that she was Jewish. She saw now that she had been foolish. Suddenly, the fact that she was a married woman seemed almost incidental . . . Peter would never think of marrying her now, so perhaps it wasn't necessary to ever tell him about Mr. Greenblatt. More to fill the uneasy silence than because she felt he had a right to know, she said, "I was born Libby Seletzky." There was an edge of bitter pride in her voice.

Peter saw that he had upset Libby with his reaction and, to be fair, he had surprised himself with his discomfort. It was not that he had anything against Jews, but he now knew that the vague fantasy of bringing Libby home to meet his parents wouldn't have been the simple happy affair he had dreamed. Shocked at this realization, he suddenly understood that his family had many of the same perverse insular feelings about race and background as did the worst lout in Coxey's Army. But before he could frame a sentence attempting to communicate his feelings, he saw that Libby was biting her lip and with a quick "Good day, then. I hope your meeting goes well," she was striding away down the street.

He felt horrible and considered running after her, but his contact in Chinatown would be expecting him in the next few minutes. He resolved to have a proper discussion with Libby the next time he saw her and to apologize for any hurt he had caused. As he made his way back to the meeting place, a small Chinese library a few blocks away, he admitted to himself that the most important thing at stake was that he must not lose her friendship and respect. He couldn't bear that.

Libby strode along, back past the boarded up shop, down the narrow alley whence they had come. Thoughts of Greenblatt, of her father and mother, and the familiar streets of the Lower East Side swirled in her head. It was a world unto itself which, if she was fair, was a little like Chinatown in the way it shut out strangers and outsiders and clung to its own ways and traditions. Perversely, she tried and failed to imagine Peter meeting her family, Peter sitting down to Shabbas dinner, Peter and her father discussing . . .

She was so lost in thought she almost didn't notice the familiar figure stepping out of a doorway and crossing in front of her, looking neither right nor left but simply rushing off towards Burnside street. It was Horace Maynard, a long way from his cubbyhole of an office at the theater. All thoughts of her conversation with Peter were momentarily forgotten as she instinctively ducked into a doorway and watched him disappear from view. He was obviously rushing to get to work, for he usually was at the theater earlier than anyone else. But, she wondered, what sort of errand would have brought him to Chinatown at this early hour?

Carefully, she picked her way over the cobblestones to the door from which Maynard had rushed. It was a storefront, but the glass window in the front was covered with a gauzy curtain, and there was no sign at all stating its business. The corner of one pane was uncovered, and she peered in curiously. At first, the room appeared to be completely empty, but as she squinted into the dark hazy space, she could just make out a few low shelves containing boxes of some kind and a bookshelf across the far wall. With her heart beating like a drum, she very slowly pushed at the front door, wanting to get a closer look.

The room had a musty smell. Now that she was inside, she could see that the walls were lined with bookshelves with a haphazard collection of faded spines visible, although the titles were all in Chinese characters. She noticed a doorway in the back and, in the shadowy recesses, a long hallway. Turning back to the nearest bookshelf, she was just debating whether to look further when a voice startled her. She looked up, and an old man with a thin white beard was addressing her in Chinese. Without thinking, she turned and fled, nearly tripping in her haste to get away.

As she passed under the great painted Pagoda gate that told her she was leaving Chinatown, she slowed to normal speed and made her way to work. She wasn't sure what it was about the Chinese shopkeeper that had frightened her so, but she was glad to be walking streets she knew. In fact, the entire morning had been a little discomforting, and she looked forward with relief to an afternoon filled with familiar faces and nothing more troubling than a little mending.

The sun was starting to set, and the McKennock building glowed gold in the late-afternoon light. The marble-floored lobby was bustling with men, all wearing black or brown suits and bright celluloid collars. Not one of them paid Libby the slightest attention as she entered from the street. She approached the elevator and asked the uniformed operator where she might find Mr. Gerald Williams.

"Executive offices, top floor. If you'll step fully inside the car, Miss, I'll have you there in two shakes of a lamb's tail." He closed the brass grill, and the elevator rose smoothly up six floors to the top of the building. "Watch your step, Miss," the operator admonished her, then added, "Down the hall on your left." She found the room easily enough and knocked on the frosted pane of glass which formed the door's upper half.

The word "Enter!" issued forth, and Libby did as she was told. She found herself face to face with a fussy little man wearing a pinstriped vest and spectacles. He gave her a slightly quizzical look, clearly uncertain as to what she could possibly want. "Can I help you, Miss? Are you sure you're in the right place?"

"Is this the correct office for Mr. Williams?" Libby queried tentatively. She wished there had been another way of approaching Gerald, but she didn't know his home address or anything about him, except that he worked for McKennock. Everyone in Portland knew where to find McKennock Enterprises. The company's recently completed building occupied an entire block on Columbia Street, and its distinctive red brick and marble facade was visible not only from most of downtown but from across the river as well.

"Oh." The clerk's look of surprise was replaced by one of curiosity, but he didn't ask her why she wanted to see Gerald. "I am his secretary, Mr. Carpenter. If you'll give me your name, I will see if he is available to speak with you."

"Miss Seale. Please tell him I only require a few moments of his time, and I would be most appreciative if he could see me now."

Carpenter disappeared through an inner door, reappearing almost immediately. "Right this way, Miss." His expression was blank, but Libby had the oddest feeling that as soon as the door to Gerald's office closed behind her, this man's ear would be pressed up against it in an attempt to discover what business she had with his boss.

There was a smile on Gerald's handsome face as he rose from behind his desk, but also a look of curiosity. "Miss Seale, I'm delighted to see you again—and so soon. I do hope nothing is the matter?"

"No, nothing is the matter," she began, "but I *can* use your help." Briefly, she told him the story she had concocted about seeking additional income and asked his assistance in securing a commission for some dresses from Charlotte.

He didn't reply at once and, for a moment, Libby feared he was going to tell her he couldn't help. He seemed to be weighing possible answers with a consideration of the debt he owed Libby for her discretion. Finally, he said haltingly, "I'm not sure what sort of power my recommendation will have with Miss McKennock, at least in matters of this sort, but I will do my best."

"Oh, thank you!" Libby cried, pleased at how simply her plan had borne fruit. "You won't regret it. I promise to make your wife look a credit to you."

Possibly it was the wrong thing to say, reminding Gerald that soon, very soon, Charlotte McKennock would share his name. His face clouded over, and he turned away from her and looked the window at the sluggish river six stories below. "No, I won't regret it, I'm sure."

Libby realized that, although her primary objective in visiting him had been achieved, she might as well use her time with Gerald to delve deeper into the mystery of his relationship to the McKennocks—both father and daughter. Judging by his reaction when she alluded to his upcoming wedding, his feelings were mixed to say the least. Libby crossed to a window near him.

"It's quite a view. I suppose you have to be Walford McKennock to own a view like this one." Her words were truer than she had meant them to be. Not only was her vantage point courtesy of Walford's six-story palace of commerce, but the scene that stretched in front of her encompassed the McKennock shipyards and the new swing-span bridge partially funded by him. "How privileged you must feel sharing it." She looked over at him to gauge his response, but his face was turned away. In the shaft of bright sunlight his hair turned from brown to almost coppery gold.

"I am a very lucky man," he replied, unconsciously echoing his exact words from the party. He turned to face her, "I would never have dreamed that one day, I would have all that I do. When my family came out west, they had nothing but what they could fit into a covered wagon."

"America is a wonderful country," Libby concurred, to be polite. Thoughts of her conversation with Peter this morning floated back to her. She had been stung not only by his obvious discomfort at finding she was Jewish, but by his implied criticism of her for keeping it a secret. Why *had* she changed her name when she moved to Portland? Was she ashamed of who she was? As if to prove to herself that she was not, she consciously added to Gerald, "My family came here with nothing as well, from Russia. It was not every country in the world that was willing to take in poverty-stricken Jews."

Surprisingly, he didn't seem to feel it was odd for her to have volunteered this personal information and gave her a warm smile. And unlike Peter there was no look of on his face of shock or dismay. Ever since their first conversation in McKennock's smoking room Saturday night, there had been an ease between them, a sense that they could allow their feelings to show in a way that Libby thought unusual between men and women in polite society.

"Your family is not in Oregon, though?" he asked, and Libby nodded. "You are a brave girl, making your own way alone in a new city."

"No braver than many," she said, "There are others who face greater persecution and prejudice than anything I have encountered in Portland." She attempted to turn the conversation back to him. "Have you worked for Mr. McKennock long?"

"No, actually only a bit over a year." She must have looked surprised because he went on, "I suppose you might say he is . . ." he searched for a phrase, ". . . an old family friend, though I had never met him until the day I was hired here. Now everything I am, everything I have become, I owe to Walford McKennock." He sounded half-grateful and half-resentful.

Luckily for Libby, Gerald was in a reflective, talkative mood, and without too much prompting, his story spilled out. His parents had come west in 1849, meeting Walford McKennock on the journey out.

All three had settled in a Gold Rush town north of San Francisco where they became friends. While Walford had quickly traded prospecting for shopkeeping, rising to wealth and prominence and eventually moving on to Portland, the Williams had never given up the dream of striking gold and consequently remained dirt poor. Gerald had come to Portland seeking a better life and was working on the docks when Walford spotted him, recognizing him because of his resemblance to his father. Walford offered him a job. Just a few weeks later, he had been invited to dinner at the McKennock home and met Charlotte, who was apparently smitten on sight. Now, within a year, he was in line to take over the entire enterprise. The story was positively Dickensian.

"America is truly, as you say, a land of amazing opportunity," Gerald said, drawing the story to a close. "You spoke of intolerance and prejudice. It is odd that if my parents had not felt compelled to flee Boston for just those reasons, I would not be standing here looking out this window with the world at my feet."

For a second, she wondered if Gerald could possibly have changed his name like her. "You aren't Jewish?" she asked disbelievingly.

He laughed heartily, the first time she had seen the grave air of melancholy that lingered around him dissipate completely. "There *are* a few other persecuted peoples in the world," he said, but he said it with a smile. "In Boston forty years ago, it was none too fashionable being Irish. That's what little Mary Fitzgerald of County Kerry, later my mother, found out when she fled the famine hoping for streets paved with gold and found 'No Irish Need Apply' signs instead. Of course, at first she had the support of her countrymen, but she lost that when she married my father. The one thing worse than being Irish was being an Irish Catholic girl who married an English Protestant. And I'm afraid my father's family weren't too pleased with his choice of bride either, so they came west."

One more example, as if she needed one, thought Libby, of marriage bringing trouble. "At least your betrothal to Miss McKennock presents no such obstacles. I assume everyone is well pleased with the match," she said, thinking of his future brother-in-law Will McKennock, who was being thrown over in favor of Gerald as heir presumptive.

"No," he agreed, "Both families are very pleased." It was as if a weight settled back on his shoulders. "My parents are happier than I've ever known them. That alone would make me sure I've made the right choice." Libby thought he sounded as if he meant 'that alone *is all* that makes me sure'. The sun was gone from the sky now, and the room suddenly felt uncomfortably silent.

"I really must be going," Libby filled the silence cheerily. "Let me say thank you again for pleading my case with your fiancée."

"Of course. It is time for me to go as well. I will head downstairs with you." He gathered his overcoat and hat from hooks on the wall. Down on the street a few minutes later he said, "I was headed home now, down by Skidmore Fountain. Which direction are you walking?"

Libby was surprised he lived down by the fountain. While it was a relatively new city landmark, donated to the city only five years previously, its location at the intersection of First and Ankeny placed it amid retail establishments and warehouses—only a block from the river. It was a waterfront neighborhood associated more with sailors' boarding-houses than homes for the city's more respectable citizens . . . certainly a surprising location to find the future son-in-law of the richest man in the city. Clearly, Gerald was marrying up in a big way. And, she thought, it appears McKennock has not yet handed him the keys to the bank.

"May I see you safely to your door?" Gerald finished.

She wondered if he was just being polite or whether there was something more behind the offer. Upon consideration, she decided it was at most a sign of loneliness. Still, she replied, "No, I am just headed around the corner to catch the streetcar, but thank you."

"Good night then," Gerald tipped his hat to her, turned, and walked away. She watched him go for a few seconds, and she wasn't sure what it was that was causing the vague feeling of heaviness in her chest. She instinctively liked this sad young man, but she knew he wasn't telling her everything he knew. She suffered a pang of foreboding as she considered what the next few weeks might bring for him.

Libby stood in the main lobby off to the side of the box office, pretending to read the posted notices of upcoming acts, but she kept turning her attention to the closed door of Crowther's office. It had been almost half an hour ago that she had heard Peter's familiar voice and peeked out just in time to see him laughing with Crowther over a shared joke as they entered the owner's office and shut the door.

Oh, what was going on behind that door? She wondered if she could put her ear to it, just nonchalantly, knowing that, of course, she could not.

She knew she dared not acknowledge Peter when he came out, but she wanted to see if he would at least meet her eyes as he left the building. Yesterday's parting had been so uncomfortable that she wanted to reassure herself they were still friends. She pretended to read the notices and handbills posted on the backstage wall as she loitered, thinking (as she reread the show card for the upcoming Easter Spectacular) of course, we're still friends. We simply need to talk about this and clear the air, that's all. Her thoughts were interrupted by a voice calling her name.

"Libby! Can I ask you a favor? " May came bounding up the aisle through the auditorium, stopping outside the box office where Libby stood. Turning her mind away from Peter, she forced a smile at the girl.

"What is it, May? I'll be glad to help if I can."

"Do you think maybe you . . . well, where you live I mean . . . Do you want a cat?" Before Libby could inquire further, the young dancer went on, rushing to explain her request. "I found a kitten on Sunday and brought it to my boardinghouse over on Vine. He was all alone under the rim of the fountain, wet and shivering . . . just the sweetest kitty you ever saw. It looked like he hadn't eaten for days, so I brought him home, but Mrs. LeClerc—she's the owner of the house where I live—saw me petting Merlin. That's what I named him, Merlin. Anyway, she told me no pets are allowed and I had to get rid of him by the end of the week. Please, please . . ."

She stopped to catch her breath and looked up at Libby beseechingly. "Do you think you might be able to keep him?"

Libby hesitated, not wanting to let May down, but also not wanting to promise anything she was unable to deliver. "I'll tell you what I'll do. My landlady is quite fond of cats. Maybe she would be willing to adopt a new one if I tell her that . . . Merlin, you said? . . . is a sweet kitten who needs a home."

"Oh, will you?" May threw her arms around Libby in an impulsive hug. "I asked some of the other dancers, but no one wants a cat, and I can't bear to think of putting him back out on the streets."

On the other side of the door, Peter and the theater owner sat across the cluttered desk from one another. Crowther was not what he had expected at all; the man bore no relation to the brusque temperamental boss that Libby had so often described, nor did he show any outward sign of the tragedies fate had dealt him and his wife. Instead, he was downright jovial, speaking about his theater and dancers with a hearty camaraderie obviously reserved for those he felt could help him. He wound down an elaborate anecdote about a particular dance number that had called for two extra Whirlwinds to be hired and trained in less than a week, and Peter dutifully scribbled in his notebook.

To his relief, Crowther had not appeared surprised that the *Gazette* had decided on a whim to do a profile of a local theater for their Ladies' Page, detailing for the newspaper's female readership how his dancers were found. "I tell you, Mr. Eberle, I'm tickled that the *Gazette* wants to run a story on my Variety. I do hope that some of your lady readers will be intrigued enough to come see our show."

"I'm sure they will find this inside view of backstage fascinating," Peter lied, knowing that this interview was unlikely ever to see print. Despite this, everything had gone so smoothly that it seemed almost a shame that he wasn't writing a piece for the paper after all. Crowther was speaking now about the inner workings of the audition process, and Peter felt the man had let down his guard enough to be confronted with the true purpose of this interview. He looked up as if a thought had just occurred to him. "I understand from what you've said that most of the dancers are local girls with theatrical aspirations who approach you about a job. But surely there must be occasions when it works the other way around, and you seek out a particular girl and offer her a slot as a dancer?"

"Where'd you hear that?" growled Crowther, suddenly less friendly.

Peter shrugged. "Various sources. Naturally, I cannot reveal them, any more than I would reveal you as my source in a similar situation." He leafed back through his notebook, pretending to check for something, although he simply wanted to pause long enough to let Crowther become uncomfortable. After a long moment, he continued. "Tell me about the dancer who called herself Polly Pink. As I understand it, you appeared at her former job and hired her on the spot. You must have had your eye on her for quite a while."

"Oh, her. She was a special case; that's not important. Most of my girls get hired the way I just told you about." Crowther seemed taken aback, and Peter pushed ahead while he was on the defensive.

"So how did you come to hire her then? From everything else you have told me today, it appears you take great care in selecting only the most qualified dancers. Why offer a job to a gay girl, sight unseen?"

He had struck a nerve, and he watched the theater owner's face as it told the story of his indecision. He was obviously torn over whether to reveal something to the reporter, and Peter could well understand the cause for his hesitation. As a married man in a quasi-respectable position as a business owner (despite said business being a vaudeville theater), the last thing he wanted was to be revealed as one who frequented whorehouses, hiring his dancers from among the ranks of prostitutes. However, it was obvious that Peter had evidence about this particular case, and in order to profess his relative innocence in the matter, he would have to offer up a plausible explanation.

Crowther idly fingered his moustache and started to speak a few times but stopped himself, thinking again. Finally, he spoke. "Do I have your word as a gentleman that this conversation is not to be printed?" he asked.

"You have my word." If only he knew, thought Peter, that this isn't even for the newspaper. "Tell me about Polly Pink."

"Funny about her, that was a real odd case." Again, the man paused, unsure of how to proceed. But when he spoke again, it was with his former friendly tone, as if it were just another amusing theatrical story. "This man came to see me, said he was in the employ of a certain gentleman who is real influential around these parts, asked me for a favor. You'll understand . . ." he said in a stage whisper, "that I cannot mention any names, but he's the kind of man, this gentleman, that when he asks for a favor, you do it."

Peter nodded. "Go on."

"Well, it seems this man had taken a shine to a girl he met in . . . well, you know where he met her. At any rate, he fell for this Polly Pink—I have to admit, she was quite a beauty, Mr. Eberle—and he sent word to me, as I just said, that he wanted a favor. He wanted me to go to the boat where she lived, offer her a large sum of money to quit her profession, and come work at my theater as a dancer. He said he would take care of her salary, so I didn't have to really pay her." He leaned in conspiratorially. "Pretty good deal for me, eh? A new dancer and I don't have to pay her a cent. I figured he must have really liked her a lot to want to get her away from that madam."

Peter grinned back, thrilled that Crowther was revealing so much. "Perhaps this saved him money in the long run. Pretty girls like that at Madame Josephine's don't come cheap." The two men shared a laugh, and Crowther went on with his story.

"Anyhow, I had no idea if she would be any good, but hell, I figured I'd just stick her in the back of the chorus. She'd shake her hips when I told her to; how bad could it turn out?" He sighed. "I'm sure you know how it turned out. For one thing, she wasn't much of a dancer, and she had entirely the wrong personality for the job. None of my other girls liked her. She brought the wrong sort of element into my theater. It just goes to show that you have to take care to get the right sort when putting together a chorus of girls. This one, what happens? She lets in some undesirable character through the stage door after the show one night and look what happened."

Before Peter could make any sort of comment, Crowther abruptly changed the topic. "Enough about her. Like I said before, that was a one time situation. Now . . . did I remember to tell you about our Easter Spectacular? We're planning a resurrection tableau based on one of those old paintings, with all the girls dressed as angels."

"That sounds spectacular all right," Peter agreed, settling back in his seat as he wondered how long he would have to keep taking notes before he could make a graceful exit.

Libby was disappointed that she had not been able to see Peter when he left the theater. He and Crowther had been closeted together so long, she was finally forced back to the sewing room. Therefore, upon arriving home that evening and seeing a light in the parlor, she was pleased to discover Peter sitting on the sofa waiting for her. He stood when she entered the room, and for a moment, she worried that things were still awkward between them. But his crooked smile emerged, and she smiled back. Without a word, she knew that everything was going to be just fine between them.

They both started speaking simultaneously, laughed, stopped, and she motioned to him to continue. "I was just going to say that I . . ." He hesitated. "The interview with Crowther this morning went very well."

She sat down beside him. "I want to hear all about it. Did he mention McKennock by name?"

He proceeded to sketch out all he had learned. "Even though he was coy about naming Polly's benefactor, it was obviously McKennock, though it seems he used a go-between to actually effect the hire. Something tells me if we have any hope of finding the proof that will link him to these deaths, the missing piece of the puzzle will be found in the McKennock home."

Libby realized she still hadn't told him about yesterday's meeting with Gerald, and she was even more pleased to be able to report that her plan had already paid off. "When I left work today, Sam was waiting for me with a note from Mr. Williams. It seems he was successful in convincing Charlotte to take me on as a dressmaker, and I am to report to her home tomorrow evening after work to begin working with her."

As she had described her meeting with Gerald, Peter tried to ignore the growing suspicion that she seemed slightly taken with the young man. At the very least, it appeared that she had gotten the seamstress work on the basis of whatever friendly feelings he held for her, and Peter did not like that thought one bit. But he merely congratulated her on her fine investigative skills and was somewhat reassured when she laughingly replied, "I feel as if the main skill I'm utilizing is a heretofore unknown acting talent. I had no idea before we started investigating Vera's death that I would be so able to slip in and out of various personalities in order to get information."

He looked at her thoughtfully. "Perhaps you're working on the wrong side of the footlights."

She shrugged. "No, thank you. Backstage work suits me better." This reminded her of seeing Mr. Maynard in Chinatown, and she quickly described the odd scene to Peter. For a few moments, they tossed out ideas about what he might have been doing there, but it was clear that the only way to find out was to go back to the mysterious shop.

"I can take care of that," he said, "It shouldn't be too hard to determine what sort of shop it is." She described its location to him, and he jotted it down, and they made plans to meet again in a few days. He stood up, donned his overcoat, and opened the front door. Libby trailed behind him.

"Libby, I . . ." They stood at the open door, and he hesitated, stumbling over what to say. With a soft smile, she interrupted his halting speech to straighten his coat collar.

"You'd better get home before you catch a chill standing on my porch."

TWELVE

For the first time in over two weeks, Libby arrived early for work. She already had her shirtsleeves rolled up and her arms elbow-deep in the laundry sink when Hatty arrived.

"Libby, I'm glad to find you here—and already hard at work I see," Hatty said, removing her overcoat and sniffing the air. "Weak bleach bath?"

"Yes, the whites are almost ready to come out now." Libby dried her dripping hands and pointed to the sorting table, "And I've divided the rest of the laundry. It looks to be another heavy week."

"Yes," Hatty said dryly, "there's been more than usual since Frau Blumentraum arrived. I never knew hitting high notes was such strenuous work. That woman perspires like a work horse." She shared a smile with Libby, then rolled up her own sleeves as she surveyed the large piles. "You have been industrious this morning. I suppose this means you need to leave early again?"

Trust Hatty not to miss a trick. Libby looked sheepish. "Not *very* early . . . just a little before usual."

"Libby, what is going on? You were so reliable and diligent when you started, but these last few weeks, even when you *are* here, your mind is somewhere else." Hatty pulled Libby away from the laundry, sat them both down, and regarded her assistant seriously. "I realize the work is not fascinating, but I do need some help and I would like you to be honest with me and tell me if I'll need to find someone new."

She sounded so genuinely concerned Libby immediately felt guilty. She knew her attention to her work had slipped off lately, but hadn't realized it had been so obvious to Hatty. Now she was planning to take even more time off, and she suddenly realized that Hatty would view her dressmaking for Charlotte McKennock as confirmation she was seeking alternate employment. For a moment, she considered simply lying about the reason for today's early departure, but given the comparatively small community of seamstresses in Portland, Hatty was bound to hear the real reason eventually. The silence was stretching out too long, and Libby impulsively decided she had to tell Hatty at least some of what she was really up to.

"Hatty, please believe me. You have no cause for concern, but I do need to leave a bit early today. I am doing some dressmaking on the side." Hatty started to speak, but Libby pressed on, haltingly, choosing her words with care, "It isn't what you think. I am sewing some dresses for Charlotte McKennock, but only as a way to gather information on her father. You remember Mr. Eberle, the newspaperman?" Silly question, for Hatty had been dropping Peter's name for weeks. "Well, I am helping him investigate a news story regarding the connections between certain prominent men in Portland and the . . . criminal element."

There, thought Libby happily, she hadn't needed to mention the investigation at the theater at all. Not that she'd ever seriously suspected Hatty of being involved, but it might have created a difficult atmosphere if Hatty knew that Libby was scrutinizing everything that happened backstage. And this explanation also ought to stop Hatty from endlessly speculating on Libby's relationship with Peter.

Hatty's reaction was not at all what Libby expected, however. After her first open-mouthed surprise passed, her face clouded. She said, "Libby, I'm surprised at you. I thought you had more common sense than to allow yourself to get involved in a fool's errand like this one. Be very careful. Men like Walford McKennock are ruthless, and he would hardly hesitate to crush you if you got in his path."

Libby was at a loss as to how to respond. "I'm . . . We're being quite careful. I'm sure Mr. Eberle knows what he is doing."

"He isn't the one going into the McKennock house as a spy," Hatty replied crisply. "I think I was wrong about your reporter friend. I'm not sure he's at all the right sort of young man for you."

Libby bristled at the implied insult to Peter. As if he would send her off into a dangerous situation while staying safely on the sidelines. She supposed Hatty would never believe her if she said all of this had been her idea. "I do thank you for your concern, but I still need to know if it will be all right for me to leave this afternoon." The words were formal and almost prim, and Libby hardly recognized the tone as her own. It was certainly a change from her usual friendly conversation with Hatty. "I cannot stop investigating now, not when there are innocent lives at risk from these men. I would think that you would understand that."

Hatty sighed, and when she spoke, her voice carried the weight of experience. "One can't right all the wrongs of the world, child There will always be crime, and there will always be innocent victims. And nothing you do will bring back your friend, Miss Carabella." Libby looked at her in surprise. "That's what all this is about, yes? Surely you don't believe Walford McKennock had anything to do with her death?"

Libby didn't answer. She no longer wanted to continue this conversation, but Hatty went on.

"Take my advice and be sensible. Let Mr. Eberle investigate on his own." One look at Libby's stony face, and Hatty rose from her chair, signaling the end of this conversation. "Of course, you may leave early today, but please be careful." Her voice grew brisk again, "And see that you don't forget your duties here."

"My *duty* is to try and stop evil, if it's at all within my power to try!" The words just slipped out of Libby, intense and self-righteous.

Hatty sighed again. "Just be sure that you aren't seeking the role of savior for the wrong reasons. Are you certain you're not allowing your grief over the death of a friend, or even the charms of a bright young man, to push you into a dangerous course of action you would never otherwise have chosen?"

Libby's only response was to start pulling the whites out of the sink and start laying them out on the draining board.

At about a quarter to twelve, Sam poked his head into the wardrobe room. "Miss Seale, there's . . ." He cut himself off when he noticed Hatty across the room. "Oh, hello Mrs. Matthews, didn't know you were there. So quiet in here, I thought you were alone, Miss Seale."

It had been a quiet morning, Libby reflected, with conversation at a bare minimum and only concerning the job at hand. She wondered what Sam wanted to say, and why he didn't want to say it in front of Hatty.

"Can I help you with something, Sam?" she asked sweetly.

"Is it the lining in your overcoat again?" Hatty interrupted, "Bring it to me and I'll be glad to tack it back. There's no need to bother Miss Seale."

"No, thank you, Mrs. Matthews, the lining's as good as the day you fixed it. Better than new it is now, praise be." Libby didn't know that

Hatty had been doing domestic favors for the widowed doorman. "There's nothing needs mending at all. It's just . . ." Sam looked uncomfortable, screwing up his face as if he were trying to come up with a lie.

"Hatty, would you excuse us for a minute?" Libby jumped up from her seat and led Sam out into the hallway. "Sam, what on earth is it?"

"You've got a message . . . an urgent message. And the man that brought it said to make sure to be discreet in giving it to you." Well, so much for that, thought Libby. If Hatty hadn't known Libby was up to something before, she certainly did now.

Sam pressed a small, folded paper into her hand, and she opened it. It read: "The Anchor, 12:15." It was unsigned.

"Sam, who brought this by?" Libby asked.

"Ordinary looking fellow . . . brown hair, medium build. Kept his hat down over his eyes . . . just sort of ducked into the stage door and back out again."

It had to be Peter, didn't it? But Libby was uncomfortably aware that the description also matched that of Vera's mysterious Anchor companion. "Thank you, Sam," she said distractedly as she headed back to the wardrobe room, already wondering what Hatty would have to say about her early lunch.

"You be careful, Miss," Sam called after her. It was getting to be rather a refrain.

The Anchor's interior was gloomy, except for the shaft of brilliant sunlight that poured from the open doorway in which Libby stood. She entered hesitantly, at first not seeing much of anything as her eyes adjusted. Then she felt a hand on her arm and turned to find Peter's grinning face only inches from her own. "Not very smart of you, coming to meet an unnamed note-leaver. It could have been anybody. It could have been someone dangerous."

To cover her instinctive rush of fear, she forced herself to speak with a bravado she didn't feel. "Oh, you don't look too dangerous. We already know I can outrun you."

He smiled briefly, but then the smile dropped. "I'm serious. You've got to be careful, especially . . ."

She interrupted, exasperated, "I wish everyone would stop telling me to be careful. It's not as if I'm about to jump off a bridge! I can do without all the sage advice."

Peter wondered at the intense response, which was completely out of proportion to his simple comment. He remained silent, hoping Libby's flare-up would pass. He led them to a table in the back, away from the door—probably, thought Peter, the same table around which Vera and her mysterious friend had huddled. "I'm sorry, you're right. It's only that it seems the stakes have risen this morning, which is why I wanted to meet you right away. I apologize for the cloak and dagger routine, but I didn't want to risk seeing Crowther if I paid you a visit at the theater."

Libby accepted the apology and asked without rancor, "Tell me, what's happened this morning?"

Peter took a breath and began his story. He related how he hadn't been at the *Gazette* offices for even five minutes this morning when the vast shadow of John Mayhew had settled across his desk.

"All right, Eberle . . . time to come clean. What's this big story you're working on? The story which you *claim* isn't a story but which seems to be filling up your mornings, afternoons, and every spare minute." John Mayhew's look had been stern. "Either there's a story or there's a woman . . . and a very accommodating woman by the look of your schedule."

"Really, John." It was a rebuke, but mild, and Peter left it vague as to whether it referred to the off-color insinuation about Libby—and they both knew that Libby was the woman of the moment in Peter's life—or the fact that Mayhew no longer believed Peter's repeated denials. "I suppose my word isn't enough?"

"I see you're gonna make me drag it out of you." Mayhew slumped in a chair beside the desk. "Okay, whatever this non-story is about, it is upsetting some people. Important people. The kind of people who have hired thugs with nothing better to do than interrupt a hardworking editor at his breakfast to threaten bodily harm if he doesn't pull his ace reporter off the trail." He scratched his head theatrically, "My only problem is, I haven't a clue what trail that might be, though I have a pretty good idea who the reporter in question is."

Peter realized he would have to tell Mayhew everything, and he did so as quickly and professionally as he could, glossing over the almost complete lack of hard evidence linking McKennock and the dead girls. He knew the evidence so far was scant, but he also knew this story could be a big scoop for the *Gazette*.

Mayhew's face registered a certain amount of shock as Peter told his tale, but once it was through, all he said was, "McKennock. Well, you always did aim high. You realize of course, there's nothing yet we can go to press with?"

Peter looked chagrined, "But there will be. All I need is a little more time."

"Well, I'm not going to tell you what you can and can't investigate, Petey. But I will tell you this . . . if you're seriously going to hunt a man like Walford McKennock, you better kill him with your first shot, because if you only wound him, you won't survive to take aim again. It's up to you." And with that he rose and headed back to the front office.

Peter finished telling all this to Libby, having edited out the crack about an accommodating woman, and looked to see her reaction. Her face betrayed apprehension even before she said, "You say these thugs threatened him, and yet he was still willing to let you . . . let us . . . continue investigating?"

"He's a good man. And he can watch out for himself."

"But if anything should happen to him or to you . . ." She couldn't go on for a moment. Then, without a transition, all in a rush, she told him about her conversation with Hatty that morning and Hatty's repeated urgings to drop the whole investigation. "Maybe we really are in over our heads, Peter. Maybe we *should* stop."

Peter was adamant, "Not on your life! This warning means we can't stop. The men this morning didn't tell Mayhew who sent them, but it's got to be McKennock, doesn't it? No one from the theater commands that kind of power. It means we must be headed in the right direction."

She still wasn't fully convinced it was wise to continue. Somehow it had seemed simpler when she was only worrying about herself, and the biggest risk she faced was the embarrassment of getting thrown out of the McKennock house for snooping. Now it appeared that she and Peter might be putting others at risk, and at risk for far worse things than a bruised ego. She said weakly, "I suppose you're right."

"Libby, if you don't want to work in the McKennock house, you don't have to," Peter's voice was gentle. "There are other ways we can continue."

The calm, almost tender confidence in his voice made her ashamed of her weakness. She squared her shoulders and said firmly, "Of course, I want to. I was just being silly. It's the best chance we have of finding out the truth, and I don't want to stop until we know what that truth is."

Peter looked pleased and, truthfully, excited. Libby suspected he was actually enjoying the whiff of danger that accompanied the morning's threat. "As soon as I leave here, I'm off to the county courthouse to check on McKennock's holdings. That might help us get to the bottom of this."

"What are you looking for?" Libby asked.

"I'm not sure, but I hope they'll be some tangible link between McKennock and the vice trade in Portland. I mean, it stands to reason that if he has a financial stake in the slave trade, he probably owns one or two of the bordellos in town or some of the waterfront saloons. It's all listed in the public record, if you know where to look. Trouble is, most people don't or don't bother to try. They did pass a law a few years back—I guess it was before you arrived in Portland—stating that the owner of a rental property had to state his name on a plaque by the front door. They were hoping to shame some of the influential citizens into evicting prostitutes, but in the end, it came to nothing."

"It sounds like a wonderful idea, but . . ." Libby didn't recall seeing any plaques in her time in Portland, "But then, shouldn't it be simple to find out who owns the bordellos in town?"

A ghost of a smile played on Peter's lips. "Unfortunately, someone's high-priced lawyer, perhaps even McKennock's, discovered a loophole. Nowhere in a the actual wording of the law did it say the signs had to be in English." He couldn't keep the amused grin at bay as he explained the reform movement's ridiculous outcome. "Suddenly, there were plaques in Chinese, Arabic, or Cyrillic scripts all around town. Beautiful-looking brass plates, but useless to those of us looking for information in plain English. Frankly, I'm amazed they were able to find people who could translate into some of those languages." Libby smiled too.

"In any case," Peter went on, "What I'm doing at the courthouse records office likely won't escape notice, and we'll see what Mr. High-and-Mighty makes of that. Maybe it'll force him to do something rash, something we can prove."

Libby's smile faded, "You mean something violent . . . with you as the target."

"Don't be concerned. Now that John knows what I'm up to, it would be risky for them to move against me. And it would look too suspicious if anything happened to me right after publicly checking out the records of McKennock holdings." Peter sounded so confident, it went a little way toward reassuring Libby. "Best of all, John is cognizant of our investigation . . . at least I don't have to continue trying to fit this story into my regular schedule."

At the word "schedule," Libby realized that her brief escape from the theater had gone on too long. With a start, she rose from the table and, with a hurried goodbye, rushed out the door. She didn't meet Peter's eyes the whole time, and as he sat looking after her, he wondered if she was still having second—or third—thoughts.

As she rushed the few short blocks, Libby was uneasy, but it wasn't exactly worry. She didn't know what it was. True, she had been the one to start the investigation what felt like so long ago, but now Peter was willing to put himself at risk, and John Mayhew, too. Was she putting her few friends in Portland in danger? They were making their own choices, she knew, but it had all been at her instigation. There was no turning back now, though; that was also true. One thing was certain, she had never expected that finding out what really happened to her friend Vera would lead so far outside the small confines of Crowther's Portland Variety.

Charlotte McKennock fussed over Libby like an old friend rather than a prospective employee, and Libby got the impression she had few if any close confidantes. Any fears Libby might have had about getting her to open up and talk were put to rest quickly, for once the heiress found herself with a sympathetic listener, she barely stopped talking long enough to breathe. But Libby couldn't rid herself of the vague uneasiness that had hovered around her since lunch with Peter, and she was disconcerted to realize she was having a difficult time concentrating on Charlotte.

". . . and of course, we'll be moving into our new house next door when it's finished. But Father just approved the architect's plans last week, so it will be months and months until it's ready. Gerald will be joining us here, just as soon as we return from our honeymoon in Hot Springs." Charlotte paused for a sip of tea, and Libby interposed as politely as she could.

"Have you given any thought to fabrics and colors? I suppose for two weeks in Hot Springs, you will require at least five afternoon dresses and perhaps two formal gowns as well?" It prudent to at least spend a moment discussing her ostensible reason for being in the McKennock house.

"Well . . . I think . . ." Charlotte seemed at a loss. "My favorite color is—that is to say, Gerald favors me in blue." It was as if nobody had ever asked the girl for an opinion before. "Miss Seale, I'm sure you know best. Why don't you bring some fabric samples with you next time? I much admired the gown you were wearing the night of Father's party, perhaps something like that."

"Thank you," said Libby, somewhat surprised. She hadn't thought Charlotte had noticed anything that night except her fiancé.

"Perhaps we could match the colors to some of my jewels . . . would you like to see my jewelry?" Without waiting for an answer, the ungainly bride jumped to her feet with girlish excitement and hurried out of the parlor and up the stairs. She was obviously having a marvelous time, and her glee was almost contagious.

Sitting here in this pleasant room, Libby wondered why she still felt on edge. Something was nagging at her, but before she could figure it out, Charlotte bustled back into the room with a large leather case and opened it to reveal a wide array of jewelry. Surprisingly, she bypassed the flashier, more valuable contents and reached first for a simple string of colored glass beads. "I'd like to wear these with my going-away dress. They were a present to me from Gerald on our engagement."

Libby took the necklace from Charlotte's outstretched hand, making appropriate complimentary noises as Charlotte went on speaking. "Oh, I know it's not a valuable necklace, but you know Gerald doesn't have much. . . . I mean, it's the thought that counts," she finished breathlessly, realizing it was tactless to allude to her groom's poverty.

"It's lovely. I'm sure we can match the color perfectly. Tell me," Libby asked in a casual manner, "How did you meet Mr. Williams?" Though she already knew the answer (Gerald had told her that day in his office), she wondered if Charlotte's side of the story might prove revealing.

"Oh, Father brought him home one day for dinner. He didn't usually bring home employees from the waterfront, but he said something about Gerald being the son of old friends. Right away I thought he was the most handsome, the most wonderful man I had ever met. We saw each other constantly after that. I'm afraid Father didn't care for that very much, despite the fact that he was the one who introduced us." She leaned in conspiratorially to Libby, "You know, the first time Gerald asked for my hand, Father said no. I'm not sure exactly how he phrased the refusal, but they went alone into Father's study and half an hour later Gerald left upset, left the house, left Portland. He was so distracted with unhappiness, he even forgot to say goodbye to me! And then I didn't see him for two whole months!"

Charlotte paused. Clearly some sort of response was called for. "My goodness!" Libby said, unimaginatively. "Then how . . . ?"

"I wouldn't even speak to Father after that. He tried to reason with me, but I took all my meals in my room until he agreed to let me marry Gerald." She beamed proudly, and Libby wondered if that was the first and only time Charlotte had ever defied her father. She also would love to have been privy to the conversation between Gerald and Walford that led to Gerald's angry exit. Had they argued over Gerald's lack of fortune, or had there been another cause for disagreement? Was there *ever* a case where marriage was a simple affair? She tried and failed to picture the conversation Mr. Greenblatt and her father must have had when they agreed that Libby would become Mrs. Greenblatt.

Why did everything these days remind her of her life back East? For months in Portland, she had managed to suppress these memories, but now all the carefully constructed walls she'd hidden behind were crumbling. Wherever the investigation had led her, wherever she went digging into Vera's (and Polly Pink's) past, it seemed her own past was waiting to meet her. She realized that this was the nagging feeling which had been dogging her all afternoon.

It had begun during her conversation earlier that day with Peter with the realization that, once again, she might be the cause of trauma and uncertainty for people she cared about. Peter, and now John Mayhew, were the closest friends she had in Portland. Now she had placed them at risk, just as she had her friends and family back in New York. And now all this talk of weddings with Charlotte reminded her of her own small ceremony. As Libby considered the events of the past few weeks, she saw clearly that probing into the lives of strangers in Portland was forcing her to face some unpleasant truths about her own past, truths she had been trying to avoid.

There was her instinctive sympathy for the sweet and sad-faced Gerald. Why, when he was about to have his fortune secured, was he so strangely melancholy? She still didn't know for sure that McKennock was forcing Gerald to marry Charlotte, but because of her personal experience, Libby had decided it must be a forced wedding. Now she wasn't certain. Perhaps she was just so focused on her disastrous arranged marriage, she was completely misreading Gerald's true situation.

Whenever she spoke with Peter lately, thoughts of her past kept popping into her mind. She didn't know exactly how or why her association with him raised unpleasant questions about her running away, but it did. The issue of her name change for one. Was it true that she had she had been, intentionally or unintentionally, trying to obscure her religion as well as her marriage when she chose to use the name "Seale"? Suddenly, she wasn't sure. All she did know was this investigation had awakened her conscience. For her first few months in Portland, she had been sleepwalking—she saw that clearly now. She had steered clear of all personal entanglements and done little more that eat, sleep, and work. While outwardly she had seemed to adapt to a new city, inside she was still a New York refugee, waiting for some miracle that would set her life to rights and allow her to return to the predictable comforts of home. Did she even want to slip back into that life now? She didn't have an answer for that question either. Time was swiftly passing, over half a year since she had gotten off the train in a strange city, and she was no closer to a solution for any of her problems.

She tried to drag her mind off these musings. Now was not the time to be having thoughts like these . . . she should concentrate on the reason she was here. Right now, the problem she had to solve was Vera Carabella's murder. Charlotte was still prattling on, "It took days and days for Father to track Gerald down wherever he had gone to and bring him back to Portland. That was six weeks ago, and they have been the happiest weeks of my life!"

"I'm so happy for you," Libby smiled. "I'm sure you deserve every happiness." She couldn't help herself . . . she slipped into her own thoughts again, reminded of the weeks leading up to her own wedding. Certainly, happy was not the word she would have used to describe those. She pushed the thought aside, but with difficulty.

"I know your childhood must have been difficult," Libby ventured, "losing your Mother at such a young age." For many reasons, she wanted to get off the subject of the wedding and onto the subject of Walford McKennock. It meant being socially inept by mentioning a family bereavement, but that couldn't be helped. She tried to cover the subject change with, "I myself lost . . ." but then she trailed off. She had started to say she had also lost a parent, hoping it might excuse her bluntness, but she trailed off because she found she could not quite bring herself to lie. Her grandmother's superstitious admonition that to mention person's death would cause it to happen silenced her tongue. Though, in a way, she thought, she had lost her parents . . . only it was her own doing and not the workings of fate.

If Charlotte noticed the abrupt change of topic, she gave no sign. But she looked sad as she replied, "Yes, she died when I was six, trying to give birth to my sister, Marjorie, who died within a day. They were buried in the same grave." She grew silent and looked so lost, it was easy to see in her the little girl she'd been.

Libby tried to imagine how empty her own life would have been if she'd had to grow up without a mother, and suddenly she missed her mama with the fierce passion of a small child. Mama . . . what pain she must be bringing her. Libby had never even written to say that she was alive, and her mother probably assumed the worst. Libby knew her mother would never believe her daughter would willingly cause her such worry and anguish. What an unnatural daughter she had turned out to be! After all, hadn't her mother had been on her side in that last terrible fight with her father? Perhaps her mother would have understood, even encouraged, her leaving. She pondered how she could let her mother know she was well and happy without revealing her location. Perhaps she could put no return address on the letter? Or maybe get some traveler to postmark it from San Francisco?

"Is everything all right, Miss Seale?" Charlotte seemed nervous about interrupting Libby's train of thought. Good lord! Libby realized she had been sitting in silence, brow furrowed, for at least a full minute. She pulled herself together, reminding herself that she was here to gain information on the McKennocks, not brood about her own family. She vowed she would write her mother tonight, no matter what. Or at least she'd try. With difficulty, Libby turned her attention back to the matter at hand.

"I'm so sorry. I just couldn't help thinking about what you just said—the loss of your mother and baby sister in one day. That must have been hard on all of you—your brother, too, and of course, your father."

"Yes, of course. But I was too young to truly know how Father suffered. All I know is that he was always so good to me, I never lacked for anything. He always made sure I had the best of everything . . . clothes and toys, then later," Charlotte gestured to the open leather jewel case almost apologetically, "jewelry."

Libby gazed at the bright gemstones and gleaming gold, and her mind flashed on the ring they had found in Vera's suitcase, the one with the initials H. M. on it. Even if it was a wedding band from H. Walford McKennock to Fanny Watson, Libby didn't suppose Walford would have let his daughter know about the marriage. Still, it couldn't hurt trying to ascertain his general dealings with the opposite sex. "Did your father ever think of remarrying?"

"Oh, yes, I always hoped he would—not to replace my mother," she hastened to add. "I admit it was lonely sometimes being the only girl. Once I thought Father was on the verge of asking a woman to be his wife, but that was only a few years after Mother passed away and, well, the woman wasn't really suitable . . ." Charlotte trailed off, then hastened to indicate that she wasn't a snob, "Not that she wasn't a wonderful woman. She was so nice, and actually a wonderful seamstress, too, like you. She made all my clothes, and they were just the prettiest things you ever saw. She was a local widow who had been hired to care for my brother and me, but she quickly took Father in hand as well. Why, it hardly seemed to matter that she wasn't . . . well . . ." she trailed off again. Then after a moment of silence, sighed and wrapped up her story quickly. "Anyway, one day, she was just gone, no explanation and no goodbye. And there were no others ever again. Right after she left, though, Father went away too, for a long time, to the East Coast for business. It was like losing Mother all over again. I think it was the loneliest time in my life."

It *was* a sad story, but Libby couldn't imagine it had anything to do with Polly Pink or Vera. She cast about for another avenue for conversation, grasping at straws. "You have a brother . . . Will? . . . to share the losses with. That must have been a comfort. He's older, isn't he? Surely he looked out for you."

"Will? Yes, he is three years older . . . but I'm not sure whether he has ever been called a comfort by anyone. My earliest memories of Will are all of him slamming doors in my face." She looked downcast, "I suppose it's only natural for a little boy not to want to play with his baby sister?" It came out a question, and Libby nodded. "Still, how I used to hate him! When he was thirteen, he burned the hair off my favorite doll, and when I told Father, he whipped Will so hard he couldn't sit down for two days. You can imagine who he blamed for that. Mostly, I guess he just ignored me."

"Well, sometimes brothers can be troublesome," Libby allowed. "But now, I must admit, being so far from home, I miss them terribly."

"Oh, I'm sorry," Charlotte patted Libby's arm ineffectually. "It must be hard to be away from your family."

"Well, I don't want to dwell on it." Libby didn't want to get sidetracked into talking about herself or return to her earlier brooding. She went on brightly, "I only mentioned it because I'm sure you and your brother must get along better now. Is he going to be part of your wedding party?"

"Oh, yes. He's one of the groomsmen. Father wanted him to be Gerald's best man, but you see Gerald has a cousin he is very close to." She looked a little uncomfortable.

"Of course, that's perfectly understandable. Still, Mr. Williams and your brother Will do get along well?"

Charlotte still looked uncomfortable. "I believe Gerald asked Will more to please Father than anything else. Gerald is very considerate of Father, as I guess is natural. But it pleases me that the two men I love best in all the world, my father and my fiancé, get along so well. Certainly better than Father and Will ever did, well . . . do. Oh, the rows they get into! I don't like to hear them going at it, so I try to stay out of the way whenever Will—" She stopped, as if suddenly realizing that Libby was, after all, a comparative stranger, and she was airing all the family dirty laundry.

Libby hastened to reassure her, "There are disagreements in all families."

But Charlotte had decided not to pursue the topic and busied herself rooting through the baubles in her jewel box. "Do you like these?" she asked, holding up a large pair of hideous amethyst and pearl earrings. Libby demurred, reaching for a smaller pair of earrings with delicate garnet drops. Soon they were caught up in a conversation on the relative merits of various gemstones, and matters of fashion dominated the rest of their time together.

Peter's chin dropped onto his cupped hand. For the briefest moment, he let his eyes shut and his other hand stop turning pages in the enormous ledger, one of a great stack, most of which still lay unopened beside him. So far, in two hours, he had discovered nothing. And as for attracting notice, well, there was one clerk in the records office; once he had directed Peter to the correct row of books, he had paid him no mind whatsoever. Peter had the oddest feeling that the dusty, unfrequented office somehow existed out of time and space, as though nothing that happened here could possibly affect the real world.

It felt like forever since he had taken a breath of fresh air or seen the sky, and the afternoon was only half over. The records room in the County Courthouse was surprisingly small for a city that was growing so fast, but then this was only supposed to be a temporary home. Since 1891, plans had been put forward to build a City Hall—a foundation was even laid once, before it was decided that the plans had to be scrapped and done again from scratch. Despite the hiring of architects and over two years of endless planning meetings, the city seemed no closer to actually getting one built. Meanwhile, the town council had to rent meeting space at various buildings around town, and at the moment, all the city records resided in the cramped conditions here.

Not that the County Courthouse, a new building with a dome-shape cupola, wasn't imposing. But at the moment, it housed not only all city records dating back to the 1850s, but all the courtrooms and jury rooms for county trials. The basement even served as the town jail. Everything you need for justice, all under one roof, Peter thought, hoping that this long afternoon might yet serve some purpose and help put another criminal behind bars in the basement.

Only three o'clock, he saw when he glanced at his pocket watch, reluctantly deciding that meant he had plenty of time to continue his search. He opened his eyes, turned to a fresh page, and began scanning down the listings.

Unfortunately, property registrations were listed chronologically by date of purchase rather than by purchaser, so he was forced to look at every page, every entry, for the name McKennock. The name occurred frequently enough, but mostly attached to land and buildings Peter already knew about like the shipyard and the new downtown offices.

He was working his way backward through the ledgers and was midway through 1886 when he began to notice a strange batch of McKennock acquisitions, all in Chinatown. As far as Peter knew, none of the properties housed a brothel, but he had to admit his knowledge of Chinatown was far from complete. He did notice two addresses on the short street where Libby had seen Maynard on Monday morning and wondered if one of them could have been the house from which Maynard had been exiting. He added both street numbers to his list, and made a mental note to check them when he made a visit. It had already been the next item on his list and he momentarily considered stopping the tedious search right away and heading over there. But his willpower reasserted itself. Besides, he felt it would be better to visit the area once darkness fell, and he could observe from the shadows before venturing inside.

A few minutes later, he was very glad indeed he had stayed with the books. The entry looked much like the one above it and below it, and he almost missed the name because this time, it was listed in the column for seller rather than buyer and because the other name in the record wasn't at all what Peter had been looking for. But there, in faded brown ink, was proof that not one but two of the people he had spoken to in the past week had been lying.

THIRTEEN

LIBBY SLIPPED A SHEET of paper onto her small writing desk and took out her pen and ink. She was determined to try and make good on the vow she had made at the McKennock's this afternoon and finally write her mother.

Dear Mama, I . . .

Libby paused to unlace her boots. It had been a long day, filled with too many people from whom she wanted too many different things. If she was going to concentrate, she needed to be comfortable.

Dear Mama, I'm so sorry . . . I know you will find this hard to believe, but . . .

But she wasn't sorry she had run away, was she? It seemed wrong to start with an apology. And she knew they would not believe how horrible things had been with Mr. Greenblatt. They would tell her she was overreacting just like before. Her chair seemed very hard all of a sudden, and she wondered if she should get a pillow to sit on. No, that was silly. She crumpled the page in front of her and took out a fresh sheet of paper.

Dear Mama, I wanted to let you know that I am well. I realize that I should have written you sooner, but for the longest time I could not face

She crossed out that last phrase and reached again for a fresh page, then thought better of it. She could not afford to waste more paper, so she decided to keep writing and make a clean copy later.

but for the longest time I could not face for a long time, it seemed simpler to pretend the past was not real—simpler for me, I know, not for you, and for that I apologize. I am in Oregon, Mama, in Portland, but I will be coming home soon. Before I can leave Portland, I need to

She stopped again. What could she possible tell her mother about what she was currently doing in Portland? She couldn't tell her mother she was investigating a murder in mysterious tunnels that ran underneath the city. And if she mentioned the white slave trade—well that alone, if nothing else, would bring family members west as quickly as trains could carry them. Perhaps she could talk about her term of employment at the Variety, but that sounded weak even to her own ears. Besides, she wasn't sure her mother wouldn't be almost as upset by the idea she worked in a vaudeville theater as by the thought she might be abducted by white slavers.

She feared that Minnie and Josef Seletzky would never understand the views and attitudes that their daughter now took for granted, and she wondered if the woman she had become would appear a stranger to her family. Her recent experience of the wider world had shown her that there were opportunities and possibilities that her parents had never dreamed of, as well as a sea of humanity, both good and bad, outside the confines of the Lower East Side. Her parents, shaped by the political turmoil and religious oppression of the old world, believed the only safe alternative in America was to stay in ghetto neighborhoods that were virtual reproductions of the communities they had left behind.

Her father made halting attempts to master the American tongue, but her mother spoke nothing but Yiddish. The two of them were both amazed and a little baffled by the torrent of English which poured from the lips of their eldest daughter, their first child born in this new country. But still they were proud of her, for in every other way, she had been content to follow her parents' ways up until the moment when she fled her marriage. But that Libby, the quiet, desperate girl who had arrived in Portland six months ago, was gone now. Especially in just the past few weeks, trying to solve Vera Carabella's murder, Libby had changed and grown into someone different. Could she pretend she was still the girl she had been to please her family? In her heart, she knew she had altered too much.

But what would happen when she went home? Her first thought was that it would mean she'd never see Peter again, and that was a painful idea. Maybe if he went back to New Haven, which was only a few hours from New York. And then . . . then what? Even supposing she convinced Mr. Greenblatt to divorce her, how and where back East could two people from such different worlds build a life together?

She tried to remind herself that she didn't know that Peter actually wanted to marry her. All that had happened was that he had tried to broach the topic of romance once or twice. She had never let him get far enough to tell her exactly what was in his mind. Good lord, they had never even held hands! She had never even kissed him . . .

Libby was still imagining kissing Peter when her reverie was interrupted by a soft knock. "Miss Seale?" Mrs. Pratt's breathless voice came through the door, "You have a visitor. I asked him to wait in the parlor." Muffled footsteps faded away.

Libby didn't even bother to put her boots back on or stop to tidy her hair. Lugging herself down the two flights of stairs, she wondered what could be so important that Peter had to see her for the second unscheduled time in one day. She supposed he could have found something truly momentous, but she doubted it. The Peter she had been daydreaming about, she thought, would not be bothering her this late. Just for an instant, Libby resented Peter's easy ways and his assumption of his own importance. She knew she was being unfair because she was frustrated with her letter home, but she also knew without asking that Peter had never had to struggle to define himself as she did. He was what the world thought of when it uttered the word "American"—a good Christian man with ambition and intelligence who used his energies to get ahead in the world. She entered the parlor with a withering comment all prepared, something to the effect that men seemed unable to do anything unassisted, but to her surprise, the figure with his back to her was quite unlike Peter.

The man turned at the sound of her step. With a start, she recognized Lars Englund. He hesitated, standing almost meekly with his hat in his hands, regarding her curiously. She realized she must look a fright with her hair mussed and in her stocking feet.

"Mr. Englund!" she managed, blushing slightly.

"Didn't know if you'd remember me. You've got a good memory, Miss." He made no mention of her odd appearance, and she decided to brazen it out as if nothing was unusual.

"Please, have a seat." He remained standing, unconsciously twisting his hat in his hands. She tried again, "Is there something I can do for you?" Suddenly, she remembered the conversation with Peter where they'd theorized that Englund might have been the man from the Anchor. She should really have followed up on that—now it appeared that maybe their surmise had been correct. "It's about Vera, isn't it? You knew her rather better than you let on when we met before, didn't you?"

He looked uncomfortable, almost alarmed. "I . . . how did you know that? Yes, it's true, I did and . . . I'm sorry to have bothered you at home. I thought about leaving you a message down at the theater, but I just figured you'd probably have it here at home anyway, so it would save time."

Suddenly, it was Libby's turn to look uncomfortable—it hadn't even occurred to her to wonder how he had known where she lived. He must have seen the faint look of alarm cross her face, for he added, "No mystery about finding you. Small world, Portland boardinghouses. Just asked some of the other proprietors. Soon enough, someone knew you were boarding here with Enid." Libby couldn't remember if she had ever heard Mrs. Pratt's first name before.

But he had lost her with his statement about having something at home. "I'm sorry, perhaps you could explain what is it you think I have?"

"I'm sorry . . . It's one of Vera's things . . . a photograph. A particular picture in her belongings which . . . I would very much like to have to remember her by." All of a sudden, he seemed on the edge of tears, and Libby quickly gestured for him to sit down.

Libby wanted to ask to which picture he was referring, but a different question formed itself first. "What makes you believe I still have the photographs? I told your wife I was going to find Miss Carabella's next of kin and deliver her belongings to them."

At the mention of his wife, he looked unhappy and a little guilty. But after a moment, his story began pouring out, if haltingly. "Yes, my wife told me you said that. It's just that . . . you see, well, you seem to know already somehow, but I did know Vera well a long time back. I knew when you took her luggage that none of her kin was left for you to find." So this wasn't about meeting Vera for a tryst at the Anchor—or at least not just that. Englund went on, "Mrs. Englund, she wanted Vera's things out of the house, and I wouldn't let her just toss them out. So when you came looking . . ."

He trailed off, then hung his head and went on, "I let my wife deal with you that day because she had never been happy about Vera lodging with us in the first place. It upset her to hear me talk about . . . the past. By the time you were ready to catch a hansom with her things, it was too late for me to say anything, and anyway, I didn't realize how much it would mean to me." He stopped and raised his head, his eyes meeting Libby's with a look that bespoke grief. "You *do* still have them, don't you? The photographs?"

Libby was so nonplussed that she was unable to muster any reply other than to mumble, "Yes, yes, of course . . ." and head up to her room to gather Vera's photos. As she climbed the stairs, her head began to clear, and all the questions which she should have asked came flooding back to her. Had Lars Englund and Vera been lovers? He was certainly grief-stricken enough. Was it before his marriage, or since? And when was 'a long time back'—and where had they met?

She found the small stack of pictures among Vera's things easily enough and quickly glanced through them. Perhaps Englund knew what had happened to Vera's husband and who some of the other people in the photos were. Could any of this have had something to do with Vera's death?

Libby returned to the parlor determined to get some answers, but it proved unnecessary to ask questions at all. As soon as she seated herself on the sofa next to Lars Englund, he reached for the photographs and began speaking as he looked at them.

"After she . . . that is after the police came to tell us they had found her, I went to her room and just looked at these for hours. The next day, too. That's why Anna packed them all up and wanted to throw them out. You see, Vera stayed with us whenever she was in Portland. She and I had grown up together . . . My wife knew that when she came the first time."

His attention focused on the pictures in his lap, and he appeared to forget Libby was there. She pulled him back to the present, speaking softly but firmly.

"Mr. Englund, I'd very much like to hear about Vera's past." He looked up, and she wondered if she should tell him why she wanted to know, but there was no questioning look in his eyes. "Tell me where the two of you grew up and how you found each other again." He looked down at the photographs again, shuffling them. "Please."

Lars Englund found the picture he was looking for and held it up to Libby. It showed a small group of about ten children, ranging in ages from about six to fourteen posed formally, outdoors, with a clapboard church steeple visible above their heads in the background. He pointed to a boy and girl standing in the back row. "That's me, and this was Helen—Vera, I mean, she was Helen then, but it's hard for me to think of her any other way when I imagine her there. Geneva, Illinois. That's our Sunday School class in . . . must be around 1870."

His voiced warmed with the memory, grief forgotten for the moment. "She was so excited to have her picture taken. Fella came into town with a camera—none of us had ever seen one—been a battlefield photographer during the war so he had portable photographic equipment. Now he was making a living going from town to town shooting church groups and town councils. I remember it clear as yesterday. We almost missed the photo we were so late, but she wouldn't run. Didn't want to muss her hair, all done up in ribbons, see? So she insisted we walk slowly. We lived nearby each other, and in those days, we walked pretty much everywhere together."

He laughed lightly, "It was pretty innocent, but Helen was half a year older than me. I think she was far more knowledgeable about what going out walking could mean. Not that she was fast, you understand." It was clearly important to him to make sure Libby understood that. "But she was beautiful even at fourteen and was already attracting attention from just about everything male in Geneva. I was a little bit in love with her, too, I guess, as much as a thirteen-year-old can be. If my family hadn't moved away a year later, perhaps . . ." He left the sentence unfinished, but Libby could see from the way his jaw tightened and the sad look returned to his eyes the direction his thought ran: perhaps Vera would have been Mrs. Englund—and perhaps she would be alive now.

"Well, the rest I only know secondhand. My ma kept in touch with folks in Geneva, so I heard what happened. Helen never wanted to talk about it, so I only know from what the neighbors said. About three years after we left, her mother died very suddenly, leaving her alone in the world. She lost her Dad when she was just a baby and didn't have any siblings either. At the time her Ma passed on, she was being courted by Jeb Morell, son of the biggest landowner around and a nice enough boy, though I would've thought he wasn't nearly clever or handsome enough for Helen. She married him almost straight off—she was only sixteen or seventeen, but I guess she didn't have much choice. Then he got himself run down by a plow a few years later when his horses bolted. Bled to death in the field before anyone even thought to go look for him. She could've remarried in a heartbeat. From what I heard, she was being courted by more than a few locals, but apparently she worried about her little girl being brought up in another man's house. So she lived with Jeb's parents until . . ."

"I didn't know she had a baby!" Libby couldn't help but interrupt, she was so taken aback. "What happened to her?"

"That's what I was about to say. I'm not sure . . . I never was told exactly. It was probably scarlet fever. All I know is, shortly thereafter, Helen left town, and she left alone."

He paused to take in the incredulous look on Libby's face. "I know, I know—awful run of luck. But it sounds worse told all of a piece like that. We only heard scraps of news a few times a year, and I'm skipping all the parts where it seems like things must've been all right for her." He dug around and pulled out the wedding photo. "She looks very happy. I like to think she was happy, at least for a while."

Libby stared at the photo of Jeb and Vera Morell on their wedding day. No, not Vera . . . Helen. She found it hard to think of her friend as Helen Morell, but gazing down at the young, smiling face and the fresh-faced, white-blond groom at her side, Libby remembered that she really knew very little about this woman, certainly not who she had been at a much earlier time in her life.

"She never went back to Geneva. She didn't have any ties left there, and I imagine the place held bad memories. Rumor always had it she ran off with a troupe of actors, but I never believed it. Not until the day I attended a show at the Portland Variety and saw her there. She was calling herself Vera Carabella by then, but I recognized her right away. When I went backstage, she didn't try to deny it. In fact, she seemed glad to see me. She said it had been a long, long time since someone had called her Helen, and she had missed it. When we were alone, she liked me to call her that, even though I was careful to use her stage name when other people were around. Anyway, I insisted she come board with us at the rooming house, and ever since then . . ." He made a gesture to indicate that brought the story up to date.

"Tell me, did you notice anything different about Vera, her behavior or her attitude, this last time she was in Portland?"

Libby had hoped he wouldn't notice the change of topic, but the telling of his story had released much of the tension in Englund. He was alert enough now to turn to her and ask, "Miss Seale, what is it you're after? I don't understand why you want to know—or what difference it can possibly make now."

211

Libby sighed, not sure how much she wanted to reveal. "Mr. Englund, I believe that there was more to Vera's, that is to say, Helen's murder than . . ."

He interrupted her, suddenly animated. "You're saying it wasn't the white slavers got her after all? I always thought that seemed suspicious. What have you found out?"

"Nothing conclusive, I'm afraid. But I am convinced that her death was more than the simple botched abduction attempt the police believe it was, and I am determined to get to the bottom of it and see the guilty party pay."

He seemed shocked, perhaps as much because a woman was talking like this as anything else, but as they continued their conversation, he warmed to the idea. He seemed almost comforted by the thought that Vera's murder hadn't been just a random act, a case of being in the wrong place at the wrong time. Because if Vera's killer had a motive, he could hopefully be discovered; and if he could be discovered, then Englund could have vengeance.

"If I could just have two minutes alone with that bastard! My hands around his neck . . ." Lars Englund's face was bright red. "Promise me you'll let me help you hunt him down. Anything you need, just ask."

Libby was taken aback by the vehemence of his response, and she tried to restore some calm to the situation. "What I mostly need now is information: anything you can remember about the last weeks of Vera's life. Did she seem different? Did she say *anything* about what was going on in her life?"

He thought about it, and his face returned to its normal color. "I wish I had something concrete I could offer, but truthfully, I saw less of Vera this time than I had during previous stays. If anything, though, she seemed happier than before. Not happy in a manic way, but somehow settled and pleased with the world. In the one real conversation we had, she wanted to talk about the past, our shared past . . . something she usually didn't want to do. I remember her saying something about time taking you on some strange detours but leaving you right where you planned to go in the beginning. And then she laughed and said 'Here I am with you, just like when we were twelve.'"

Libby tried to ask as tactfully as she could, "Mr. Englund, you hadn't become involved with Vera again, had you?"

He wasn't offended; he just looked sad. "No, nothing like that. I think she just meant we had been neighbors as children, and now here we were living in close proximity again . . . at least, whenever she was in Portland."

"Your wife said she paid her rent up front, all in cash, this visit. Did she say anything about money?"

"My wife handles all financial matters, and I certainly never discussed anything like that with Helen . . . uh, Vera when we were alone." He scratched his head. "No, I really can't remember anything out of the ordinary."

Libby accepted defeat, and the long day suddenly seemed to come crashing back down on her shoulders. She felt beyond weary, and it must have shown, for Englund gathered himself and the photographs and said, "Thank you so much for these, Miss Seale. I apologize for having kept you so long."

"No, thank you for being so forthcoming." They were at the front door now, "And you will call again if you remember anything else?"

Englund nodded and headed down the walk, tucking the pictures inside his coat to protect them from the drizzle. Libby stood in the doorway, relishing the feel of the chilly breeze, until the pale figure was swallowed up by the night. Then she went upstairs to try and finish her letter home. But somehow the fire had gone out of her resolve, and she crumpled up all her attempts and put them in the trash. She knew a day of reckoning would have to come sooner or later, but that day would not be tomorrow. Feeling drained of all energy, she turned down the lamp and went to bed.

Sleep hadn't come, at least not easily and not for long last night. Now, riding to the McKennock house, her head dropped to her chest every few seconds until she jerked it up, realizing she had almost fallen asleep. She found the steady rhythm of the horse-drawn streetcar—the lines that led to the outer districts of Portland hadn't all been electrified yet—very calming, as the clip-clop of the horse, combined with the blue and restful late afternoon light, reminded her of childhood rides and simpler times. Yawning again and again, she sat up straighter, trying to shake off her lethargy.

Lying awake the night before, remembering Lars Englund mourning for a lost friend, had reminded Libby that at the center of this investigation into Portland's white slave trade was the death of one particular human being, someone whom she had known and liked. Despite all she had been through, as Libby now knew, Vera had still enjoyed life. And if all the twists and turns of fate that had taken her from the fields of Illinois to the bright stages of the vaudeville circuit had ended only in a dank tunnel under Portland, it was less than she deserved.

Who had Vera Carabella been that she needed to die? In all her nosing around, Libby had never been able to come up with more than hypothetical causes for Vera's murder, nor had Peter. But if Libby was correct in her assumption that Vera's death had been intentional, then there must have been a motive. Why had someone considered it necessary to eliminate her? And why, on that particular night, her last night in Portland?

Or was it? Vera had dropped hints that she was considering staying here, and Libby and Peter had been told by more than one person that Vera seemed different on this visit. So the key to her death *must* lie in this city, and there had to be some trace of it somewhere.

But outside of her contacts at the theater, there were pitifully few traces of Vera's life at all to follow up on. Now that Englund had explained the photographs and given Libby a full report on Vera's past, that avenue had ended in a cul de sac. Or at least Libby could see no motive in anything Englund had revealed. There was the man at the Anchor, but other than crossing Englund off the list of possibilities, they were having no luck in identifying him. Then there was a little gold ring with the initials of a dead prostitute, which shouldn't have been in Vera's possession but was. Libby felt certain if she could only figure out the significance of the ring, the only known link between Polly Pink and Vera Carabella, she would be able to figure out who killed Vera and why.

On the surface, the two had much in common. Both were statuesque beauties, although the raven-haired magician's assistant was a good twenty years older than the blonde dancer. Both were small-town farm girls who had changed their names and ended up as performers, although Vera had clung to the fringes of respectability, peddling only her image instead of her body. For a brief moment, they had shared the stage at the Portland Variety. Libby wondered if Vera had been a little jealous of the beautiful dancer: as fair as Vera was dark, but young enough to remind Vera she was getting old. Or had the two been friendly, brought together by their similar backgrounds? Nobody at the theater recalled ever seeing the two together, but there had to be a connection or she wouldn't have had Polly's ring.

Libby clutched the brown paper on her lap. It contained a selection of rich and elegant fabrics for Charlotte's perusal which Libby had picked up this morning before work. The last time she had shopped for fabrics as lovely had been with Vera, when they went shopping together for Vera's new costume. How Vera had loved the beautiful silk, taffeta and crepe. Judging by Lars Englund's stories, she had enjoyed pretty, feminine frills even as a child. Thinking about little Helen, so proud of the satin ribbons in her hair, Libby's heart grew sad again.

Libby was so caught up in her thoughts, she almost missed her streetcar stop. Just in time, she called out to the conductor, scooped up the parcel which sat beside her, and alighted at the end of Pettygrove Street.

FOURTEEN

PETER SHIVERED AND GLANCED surreptitiously at his pocket watch for the third time in half an hour. Only 11:30 . . . hours to go before he could call it a night. He rubbed his arms vigorously through the threadbare coat, hoping the motion, if not the friction, would provide some warmth. But it was no use; the thin cloth was incapable of keeping out the icy breeze, and the effort only seemed to leave him colder than before.

Most of the clothes he had on did not belong to him. The ink-stained work shirt and ragged set of overalls were borrowed from John Mayhew, who kept them around the offices of the *Gazette* for use when there was a messy job like cleaning the presses. The coat and slouchy hat Peter had purchased for a nickel just this afternoon in a rag shop on the waterfront. He didn't want to think of their provenance.

He was currently wedged in a narrow alleyway between two buildings on Davis, a narrow street which led up from the river into China-town, in a back doorway which offered a clear view of the building that Horace Maynard had visited three days before. The buildings on either side of him cast great shadows, rendering him almost invisible to passersby, as well as blocking, to some extent, the brisk wind that had blown in around sunset, turning a temperate afternoon into an wintry evening. He thought longingly of his warm room at Park House and of the cozy offices of the *Gazette* where John Mayhew was probably still hard at work bundling up tomorrow's edition.

Mayhew had been very attentive this afternoon when Peter pulled him aside to bring him up to date on the state of the investigation, though he hadn't immediately seen the use of tonight's vigil.

"Dirty pictures, you say? Not exactly front page news . . . a store in one of Portland's seedier neighborhoods selling French postcards."

"By itself, that's true." Peter had been insistent. "But taken together with the fact that it's a store in Chinatown, run by a Chinaman, which stocks only pictures of white girls, *and* the fact that one of the key-holding staff of the Variety—which is an entry port for the Oriental slave trade—was seen coming out of there in the middle of the morning . . . Frankly, I think it's worth a little further scrutiny."

John scratched his head, "I guess so. I'm glad it won't be me out there tonight. They say there's a cold front coming in . . . Still, you're welcome to the ratty duds in the storeroom if they're of use to you. So, I guess this means you think that this Maynard fellow is the link from the theater to the slavers? Sounds like he's now your prime suspect for the Carabella killing?"

Peter hemmed and hawed a bit. "Well, one of two. I discovered another interesting fact yesterday at the records office which points in a different direction. On the surface, it doesn't appear to have anything to do with the postcard shop, but maybe there's a bigger picture I can't make out yet." Peter paused to heighten the dramatic value of what he said next. "It turns out that the theater is owned by none other than H. Walford McKennock." Mayhew's eyebrows went up, but Peter rushed on, "Well, not precisely the theater—the land it sits on. Back in '84, McKennock leased the land on a thirty-year lease—at very favorable terms I might add—to one Arvide Crowther. Once again, in and of itself not a damning piece of information, but both Crowther and McKennock claimed they were unacquainted. The fact that they lied means *they* feel it's something to be secretive about."

Mayhew digested this, then asked, "Any chance both Crowther and Maynard are in on the slave trade business?"

"Possibly, perhaps even likely. Which is one of the reasons I feel step one is to watch the Chinatown property. If I spot Crowther going in or coming out, then there's something concrete to confront him with. Or if I see Maynard there again, maybe I can trail him inside and discover what his business is there. This is all assuming the Chinatown store is connected to the slave trade in some way. But I think there's a good chance it is, since Libby described Maynard's exit from it as surreptitious."

"Well, he could just be ashamed of buying pornographic postcards."

"True," Peter allowed, "But why was he there in the middle of the morning? If his visit was provoked by our investigation, it makes more sense, because perhaps whatever he was doing there couldn't wait until after dark. It did follow pretty quickly on the heels of my confrontation with McKennock."

"It's not impossible . . . But there's no proven link between McKennock and *Maynard*, is there? So you're still just making conjectures . . . strings of conjectures. And if even one of them is false, the whole picture could change."

Peter stood firm. "Don't you worry. If there's proof to be found, I'll find it. Maybe tonight. Now, where did you say you keep those work clothes?"

Peter had done his best to sound optimistic and positive for his boss, but now as he slowly froze in the damp, cold alleyway, he admitted to himself that John had been right. There was no hard evidence of wrong-doing that could be tied conclusively to any one person. And even though they had narrowed the suspects at the theater down to two, he still couldn't even say which one was the more likely—or if indeed the two were in it together. Though if both were in on the scheme, that could explain how Crowther had an alibi for the night of Vera's death.

Peter wished he had spoken with Libby before donning his tramp garb and making his way to Chinatown, but the timing hadn't allowed it. He wanted to warn her (gently, of course, so as not to offend her) that it would be wise for her to be even further on her guard around both Crowther and Maynard now, especially given that the last time she and Peter had spoken, it had appeared Crowther was out of the running. But Peter hadn't wanted to appear again backstage at the Variety, since he had been there in his professional guise as newspaperman. He was also aware that Libby was heading straight from work to the McKennock's for another session with Charlotte, so she wouldn't be back at the boardinghouse until after he needed to start his observations. Oh, well, he supposed tomorrow would be soon enough. Maybe he would try to catch her before she left home in the morning.

The traffic in and out of the unmarked door across the street from him had been slow but steady, a few customers every quarter hour. None of the faces had been remotely familiar, and placed as he was, Peter was able to get quite a good look at faces either as customers approached the door or left by it. Most of the men—and the clientele was exclusively male, needless to say—arrived and left alone and were inside the shop for three to five minutes at the most.

Once in a while, a man would go in and not reappear at all, though these tended to be the most disheveled and derelict looking ones. When Peter had been inside the shop yesterday, he had noticed the faint smell of opium smoke coming up from the stairs at the back of the shop. He surmised that there was a flophouse down there for unfortunate addicts. He suddenly wondered if this could have been the part of the establishment Maynard had been patronizing when Libby spotted him. Maynard didn't fit the usual profile of an opium user, but it was just conceivable that he managed to confine his habit to the evening hours and hold down his job. Perhaps he had only recently begun the habit and had not yet begun the long slide down into the gutter which opium invariably caused. If this was true, then Peter was completely wasting his time here, his fingers and toes turning numb to no end. He pushed the thought out of his mind.

As midnight came and went, the stream of customers turned to a trickle and then dried up almost completely, although a light continued to burn, visible under the door and in the margins of the covered windows. Peter couldn't stand outside in the cold any longer, but rather than head home, he took refuge in, well, to call it a saloon was to do it too much credit. It was simply an underlit room with a few tables and a row of barrels at the back from which, for a modest fee, the bored looking proprietor would fill an unwashed pint glass with home-brewed beer or whiskey.

Peter got a whiskey, hoping the alcohol would kill anything on the surface of the glass, and seated himself at a table in the front by the grimy windows. It was colder near the door, but Peter had rationalized deserting his post outside with the notion that he could still keep an eye on the shop's door from in here. Given how few callers there were by this point, he didn't need to be as vigilant. Inside the bar, there were a handful of tired men, and at a table in the back, three bedraggled girls, obviously prostitutes. He took a swig of his drink, and the fiery burn of the moonshine traveled throughout his body, going some way towards warming up his chilled limbs.

Because his gaze was trained out the window, Peter smelled rather than saw the man come and sit down at the table next to his. Turning, he gave a wary smile to the newcomer, wondering if he was about to be accosted. But the man smiled back, revealing a row of crooked, grayish teeth and leaned in conspiratorially.

"Lookin' for a pretty bit to keep you warm, friend? My girls over there might be more than willin' t'offer a fella a few minutes of pleasure, iff'n I tell 'em you're a friend. Maybe even a bed for the night, the price bein' right."

Peter glanced over to take a better look at the girls, two of whom were Chinese, one no more than thirteen years old. The third was a sallow white girl whose face was covered by some sort of rash Peter didn't care to contemplate for long. All three looked beaten down by life, as unkempt and dirty as the room itself. His stomach lurched. This nausea was followed by guilt, despite his complete lack of attraction to the barroom whores, for having even considered them as possible bedmates. It made no sense, but there was an insistent image in his mind of how Libby would react if she knew that made him feel ashamed.

"No thanks, friend." Peter tried keep the education out of his voice and attempted to match the pimp's coarse but friendly manner. The last thing Peter wanted was to get dragged into a confrontation if this man thought he was insulting his flock. But the man didn't take offense, nor did he leave.

"Don't see nothin' you like, huh? That ain't all the fillies in the stable, mind. What you lookin' for?" Apparently the thought that Peter wasn't looking for anything didn't enter his mind.

Afterwards, Peter wasn't sure why he said what he said next, most likely to force the man to admit defeat by demanding a girl he couldn't possible supply. And perhaps because an image of Polly Pink had just popped into his mind, along with the sudden realization that a vast chasm separated these sorry girls from their pampered sisters on Madame Josephine's floating palace—an even wider chasm, he suspected, than that which separated Josephine's call girls from the honest women of Portland. In any case, what he said was, "A blonde. Tall . . ." Peter gave a contemptuous sniff, ". . . and clean. Don't suppose you get many girls like that around here."

The pimp's reaction was fast and furious. "Oh, you're one a them!" he practically spat out, jumping up from his chair, "Get outta here. We don't need no more like you comin' 'round here. And you stay away from my broads, ya hear?" He turned on his heel to go back to his girls, but Peter grabbed him by the arm and stopped him.

"Hey . . . nothin' personal, friend. I think you're mistakin' me for somethin' I'm not." Peter wondered if he was overplaying it, dropping all his final 'g's.

The pimp looked unconvinced, but he stayed where he was, shaking Peter's hand off his arm after a withering glance at Peter's hand. "What d'ya want here? Don't think I ever seen ya before."

Peter looked down at his clean fingernails, realizing that despite his attempt at disguise, he was still the most presentable person in the room. No amount of ratty clothes or "common" speech would convince these people that he was one of them. "Just waiting for a pal, that's all. Don't want him to see me . . . don't think he'll be too happy to see me . . . so I was keeping watch through the window. Honest injun." He thought it best to stick close to the truth. Anyway, he hoped the reason made him sound disreputable and maybe just the slightest bit dangerous. Well, he could always hope.

The pimp assessed him, "So why ya here askin' for tall blonds then? Some other high-toned fella like you, prob'ly one of your 'pals,' been 'round couple months back askin' for the same thing. I sent off m'best girl Annie with him . . . Never seen her again. Hadn't heard how you people were scourin' the city for blondes then. Annie was prob'ly good as gone the minute I let her go off with your friend. Likely she was on a ship out t'China before I even thought t'look for her." The man took a belligerent stance, attempting to intimidate Peter physically, although Peter was twenty years younger and had a good half foot on him. "Well, I ain't fixin' t'lose any more to you lot. Go poach on someone else's territory."

Peter's mind raced. If he was following what this troll-like man was saying, it meant the white slavers in Portland were always on the lookout for statuesque blondes, which could explain the surprising amount of effort someone had put into the Polly Pink abduction. "Wasn't no pal of mine. I swear on my mother." He felt dirty having this conversation, but he knew this was no time to let his finer sensibilities get involved. What else might this man might be able to tell him if only Peter could convince him he wasn't a crimper for the white slavers. "Listen, let me buy you a drink. Whiskey?"

A torn look flitted across the man's face, but in the end the desire for free alcohol won out over his still obvious distrust. "Well, won't make up for Annie goin' missin', but I guess a drink's a drink, no matter who's buyin'," he added under his breath.

Peter got two more whiskeys, and settled back in a chair across the table from the pimp. "So you say they've been pulling in blondes? No wonder there's nothing decent left on the streets for a man to look at. Ugh, no offense meant, friend," Peter inclined his head slightly over to the table with the three girls.

"Nah, none taken. I know they're trash. Ain't easy findin' girls these days, I tell ya." The free drink had really loosened his tongue, and he spoke to Peter in a manner halfway between friendly and defeated.

"Yeah, a man's got to make a living," Peter replied convivially. "Tough in Portland these days, I hear. Down in Sacramento where I'm from, we don't have these big organizations muscling in on the independent businessman."

"I don't know nothin' about big organizations . . ." the weasely fellow looked wary, "but it's been a bad year up here for me. Lately, all I can get my hands on is the scrawniest street birds, and they don't bring in enough to keep a man in boots."

The pimp was already eyeing his empty glass meaningfully and looking longingly back at the barrels lining the rear wall, obviously wanting Peter to spring for a new round of drinks. Peter suddenly felt an urge to get away from this man as fast as possible. He affected to see movement out on the street and, pushing his own almost full glass at the odious man, said, "Here, finish my drink. I see my pal coming down the street."

Peter made it to the door in less than three steps, worried the pimp might notice the street outside was empty, but before he was even outside, his former conversational partner had switched his entire attention to the nearly full glass of moonshine in his hand.

Peter was back in his alleyway before he took the time to notice that the light under the door and around the window of the pornography shop cum opium den had gone out. He kicked himself for having gotten so wrapped up in conversation, he had completely forgotten to keep an eye on the comings and goings across the street. Well, he consoled himself, in all likelihood, nothing important had happened. Even before he had gone in for a drink, the shop's trade had all but ceased. And in truth, he had learned more that might be useful during his twenty minutes inside the watering hole than in the almost three frigid hours loitering in the alley. So he could feel that the long, exhausting evening had been worth the effort. Now it was easily time for a well deserved rest, especially since he wanted to be up early to catch Libby at Mrs. Pratt's before she left for work.

With relief, he turned his feet towards home and began the long walk to Park House. Once he had left the bawdy district behind, the city lay dark and silent around him. He was glad the streets were deserted because now he felt conspicuous in his tattered jacket and stained over-alls. The streets he was now traversing were filled with modest, solidly middle-class homes. If these people had been awake and about, they would have cast baleful glances in his direction, ladies crossing the street so as not to have to brush by him on the sidewalk.

Portland was in many ways still the small, almost provincial town it had been twenty years before. No, that was wrong. Actually the city had changed almost beyond recognition, growing and sprawling at a rate that would have been alarming in a living creature. It was much of the populace that was still the same—hardworking, god-fearing, and early-to-bed. Portland's evolving character lay in the complex ways these two coexisting cities rubbed up against each other. The friction between the old guard and the new, fast crowd, devoted to the hedonistic pleasure that a modern city could offer, is what made this an exciting place to live and work as a reporter.

Peter felt in Portland he could be respected for who he was, rather than his family name. Here men were known for what they them-selves accomplished, and every man had an equal chance to climb. Peter also enjoyed a sense of freedom that came from being beyond the reach of his almost suffocating extended family. As the youngest of seven, he had been doted on and smothered with affection from the day he was born, but he was also hemmed in by his role as "the baby." It wasn't until he came west that Peter discovered he was just as capable as the next man, if not more so. He also discovered, much to his surprise, that he enjoyed solitude—it was a rare commodity in a house with seven children.

He was so lost in his musings that it was with a start that he real-ized he was almost at Park House. Simultaneously, he became aware that he was not alone on the street. There were footsteps coming from behind him, and he wondered how long someone had been dogging his steps without his having been aware of it. He turned, but the street was empty. Suddenly, he wasn't sure if he had heard anything after all. He *was* so tired his progress bordered on sleepwalking. He started walking again, listening carefully, but now the night was completely silent once more.

Two frosted globes glowed warmly at the entrance to his residential hotel halfway up the block ahead, but he decided that he would rather use the unmanned rear entrance since he didn't want to be observed entering the building as he was presently dressed. Consequently, twenty yards before the front door, he turned into the alleyway which ran along the side of the building. It was the shortest way to the back door, much quicker than walking all the way around the block. Its only defect was that the light from the gas streetlamps didn't penetrate back here, so he was lost in velvety blackness along the narrow way. That didn't bother him. Even as a little boy, Peter had never been afraid of the dark.

In his mind, he was already slipping off these threadbare garments and climbing gratefully into his soft and blessedly warm bed, so this time he didn't hear the footsteps breaking the silence until they were less than ten feet behind him and gaining fast. He realized too late that the solid brick walls of the alley muffled the sound of a scream as well as a footstep. But there wasn't much to be heard anyway—only his one, brief, shocked cry. Then the night became silent once more.

Oddly enough, what woke him wasn't a sound but a smell. Peter struggled into consciousness, aware at first only of the stench of the dank watery river clogging his nostrils. This realization was followed by another, more disturbing one: when he tried to move, he found his wrists and ankles tightly bound. Trying not to panic, he took slow careful breaths. As his eyes adjusted to the scant light from the cloudy night sky, he thought he could make out the hulking, silent silhouettes of ships along the river, and he realized he had been brought to one of the piers.

A voice behind him broke the stillness. "Well, looks like he's awake. Sorry, Mr. Newsman, it's not time to get up yet. Someone wants to send you on a special assignment . . . far, far away . . ." Peter wriggled around, trying to see who was talking, but his bonds were too tight, and he was too weak from the beating. Before he could say anything, he felt a wet rag over his face, and everything faded away again.

FIFTEEN

Jack was knocking on dressing room doors, calling "Five minutes!" for the early show, by the time Libby was finally ready to leave the Variety on Friday evening. She rushed around delivering all the mended and pressed costume pieces to the proper performers, wondering if she should spend money on a hansom cab to the McKennock house. She was just putting on her coat when she heard a noise at the door to the costume shop.

May was standing there in her first costume, a blue and white crinoline which made the porcelain-skinned dancer look like a Dresden doll. "Libby, Libby . . . !"

Trying not to sound exasperated, Libby set down her bag. "What is it, May? Have you caught your skirt on a nail *again*?"

"No, it's not about costumes at all."

Libby suddenly realized she had forgotten to ask Mrs. Pratt about adopting the kitten, and she resolved to do that first thing tomorrow morning. "I'm sorry, May, I forgot all about the kitten. Can I let you know next week?"

May seemed unconcerned. "Oh, he ran away. I forgot to tell you." For a moment, she seemed forlorn, but then her whole manner brightened. "But, Libby, it's so exciting . . . I think someone has finally noticed my talent! I'm not supposed to say, but I might . . ." She stopped suddenly, as if trying to decide what she could reveal.

After a moment, Libby realized the girl wasn't continuing and asked gently, "May, can this wait until Monday? I'm late for an appointment, and you are probably due on stage any minute for the opening number."

"The opening number . . ." May repeated, suddenly in a hurry herself. "Oh, Libby, next week I'll tell you everything, and you can help me with gowns like you promised!" She grabbed Libby's arm and propelled her out into the hallway, giving her a quick hug before running off toward the stage.

Libby turned toward the outside door as May headed toward the backstage, and she shook her head as she watched the young dancer disappear into the wings. Her "big news" was likely a solo in the new number or a miniscule pay raise, but true to her show business breed, the smallest details of her career were of the utmost importance.

And now, Libby realized, she really was quite late. Looking at the clock on the wall by the stage door, she saw that it was after seven. Charlotte would have expected here there by now. Sam was at his usual post, and she asked him to find her a hansom.

"Sure thing, Miss. And about that investigating you asked me to do, well . . ." He leaned in and lowered his voice. "I think I might be on the trail of something. Can't say more yet, but there have been a few mighty suspicious things going on here. Oh, nobody else might notice them, but if you happen to be sitting here by the door all day watching, well, then . . ."

Libby was intrigued. She had nearly forgotten Sam's offer to do some sleuthing and had certainly assumed that, since she had heard nothing from the elderly doorman by this point, he had given up trying to unearth information. "What is it?" she asked, all thoughts of her journey momentarily forgotten.

He lowered his voice even further, and she had to strain to hear him. "I don't want to say anything here, you never know who might be listening." He looked around theatrically. "Satan takes many forms, and some of these dancers with their bodies on display . . . Women like that, you never know *who* they might be mixed up with." She nodded, trying to smile but feeling uncomfortable as she always did when Sam went on like this. "Tell me, Miss, have you found anything out on your own?"

She hesitated, not sure what to tell him, and also aware that she did not have time right now anyway. But Sam mistook her hesitation for a negative answer and went on. "That's all right, Miss. I may have some interesting information. Can you meet me Sunday afternoon after church?"

"What about tomorrow, Sam? We could take a stroll during the lunch hour."

"No, no . . . It needs to be Sunday." Sam looked around conspiratorially, "We shouldn't talk around here. We can pick somewhere out of the way, where I can tell you what I know and we won't be bothered by strangers. And we won't be rushed because the theater is closed, and we—"

Libby cut him off. "That would be fine, Sam. Right now, I really do need to get a cab. I'm late to an appointment and besides," she couldn't resist adopting a dramatic tone, "I wouldn't want anyone here to notice us talking and get suspicious at this conversation we're having."

"No, no, Miss," he agreed solemnly.

They stepped outside to the street, and Sam began looking for one of the distinctive black carriages that were cabs for hire. "Can you meet me behind the Baptist Church over on Clay Street? There's a little gazebo out back there where we won't be disturbed. Perhaps at four?"

As Libby recalled it, the Baptist church was in the middle of an empty wooded area that was not yet developed, although it was a short walk from the more populated area near St. Mary's school. "I have a better idea. Do you know where Jake's Crawfish Restaurant is?" she replied, uneasy at the idea of meeting Sam alone in a deserted wooded lot.

But Sam clucked disapprovingly. "No, people might hear us in there. Near the churchyard is more fitting, and the gazebo is quite comfortable, Miss. We've got new benches and everything."

With a flick of his hand, he was guiding an approaching taxi to the curb. A decision had to made right now, so setting aside her reservations, Libby agreed to meet him there two days hence. Tipping his hat as he opened the door for her, he repeated under his breath, "Four o'clock, Sunday . . ."

Settling into the comfortable carriage, she gave the driver her destination and arranged her sewing basket and bag on the seat beside her. Now that she had a few moments to herself, she found herself wondering for the first time today what was keeping Peter so busy. She had not heard from him since their lunch at the Anchor on Wednesday, and here it was already Friday evening. Ah well, she figured, more than likely something had come up at the newspaper office, and he wasn't able to get in touch. She suspected there might be a message waiting for her at Mrs. Pratt's, since Peter was avoiding the theater after his interview with Crowther.

It was funny, she thought, with Peter it was feast or famine. Either he was sending her secret unsigned notes and popping out from behind lamp posts or else he was nowhere to be found for days at a time. Well, there was nothing to do but wait until he made contact with her, since at this point, she had no way to reach him until Monday at his office.

Charlotte McKennock turned around self-consciously as Libby pinned pieces of a dress together around her. "Will you be wearing this corset on your honeymoon, or is there another one you would like to try on with the dress?" asked Libby, all too well aware that sometimes a dress which she pinned perfectly during a fitting looked all wrong when completed if worn with a different set of undergarments.

Charlotte blushed. "I believe this is the one I'll wear . . . Do you think I should make it tighter?" She looked miserable, obviously hating the close attention being paid to her heavy figure. Good Lord, thought Libby, for someone of such wealthy means, she certainly was uncomfortable being waited upon! As if reading her mind, the bride-to-be continued. "Father normally doesn't approve of dressmakers. He has my measurements taken and sent to a tailor in San Francisco for most of my gowns." Libby thought of the ill-fitting blue dress Charlotte had worn at the party, and she could well believe that no extensive fittings had taken place.

"This will look lovely on you when it's finished," she murmured, carefully lifting the partially-constructed garment off over Charlotte's head. As Libby busied herself putting the various pieces of gowns-in-progress away in her basket, Charlotte drew her dressing gown around herself and looked with interest at the neatly folded bolts of sample fabrics piled on the settee beside her, absentmindedly sorting them by hue.

"Ah, hard at work, I see!" Both of the women were so intent on their tasks they had not heard the large door to Charlotte's private parlor. They both looked up at the same time as Walford McKennock strode in and sat down on one of the chairs opposite them. "Are you pleased with your new gowns, my dear?"

"Oh, yes, Father. Miss Seale is doing a splendid job. Look at this beautiful Chinese silk she found!" Charlotte held the material in front of her, glowing. "And this French mousseline is from Paris. Isn't it chic? I just can't decide which one we should use for my second evening gown. One gown is already finished which is a sort of deep azure. I think the second gown should be lighter just for contrast, don't you, Father?" Libby thought that was probably the longest speech she had ever heard Charlotte utter.

McKennock smiled indulgently, "Of course, my pet."

"Which do you like better?" Her father grunted something non-committal, indicating the choice was up to her. "The bronze is pretty, and the fabric is so light. Although . . . I do think I prefer the ivory." She looked at Libby for confirmation, unsure even of her taste in materials.

"The silk does look lovely with your coloring," Libby said after a moment.

McKennock turned his attention to regard the seamstress. "Chinese silk, eh? They do have a way with finery, don't they? . . ." He trailed off, obviously all out of small talk. Libby was sure he had little interest in the particulars of his daughter's trousseau.

Libby agreed, "Yes, it's certainly a finer cloth than anything we produce locally."

He turned back to his daughter, speaking in the same friendly conversational tone. "Charlotte, would you please leave me alone with Miss Seale? We have some matters to discuss."

"Of course, Father." Charlotte sounded a little confused as to what matters those could be.

Libby wondered too, as she set her sewing basket to one side, and felt vaguely nervous for no reason she could put into words. McKennock had never indicated in any way that he associated her with Peter or that he remembered she had been with Peter the night she met him. But she knew that Peter's continuing investigations had drawn McKennock's ire. She wondered if the moment had come when she the subject would rear its ugly head. Well if it did, she would deal with it as best she could.

Suddenly, Hatty's dark warning that Walford was a "ruthless" man leapt to the front of her mind, but she pushed it back and tried to keep her composure. McKennock still had a smile plastered on his face, but his eyes were narrow and focused on his daughter as she made her way to the door. Surely nothing truly awful could happen here . . . McKennock would never accost her, even verbally, in his own home, in the middle of the day, and with his daughter on the other side of the door.

Charlotte hesitated at the threshold. "Thank you for all your work, Miss Seale. I can't wait to see the finished gowns at my next fitting. I think Gerald will be very pleased with them." And then, like a scared rabbit, she was gone.

For a few seconds, Walford McKennock sat staring at the door. It was hard to determine what he was thinking, but he obviously was composing his next words. Libby wished she could see behind his blustery façade and penetrating gaze. When he turned to look at her though, it was with such a warm and friendly smile that she kicked herself for having been worried at all.

"Miss Seale, I would like you to make both the dresses as a surprise for my daughter. Tell her you're making her the silk one, then also make whatever she said that other one was, the Paris one. I will be happy to pay for the both of them, whatever the cost." He rose to leave.

"That's a very nice surprise, Mr. McKennock. I'm sure your daughter will be pleased to have more choices on her honeymoon."

"Yes, yes," he waved a hand dismissively. "I just want her to be happy, that's all."

He left Libby to see herself out, as Charlotte had apparently disappeared to another part of the house. Libby finished packing her things and made her way downstairs. She stood in the large foyer, retrieving her coat from a wrought iron stand by the door, and was about to leave when the sound of angry voices coming from Walford's study caught her attention.

Very quietly, she edged her way along the hallway, hoping to hear better—and hoping no household servant chose this moment to walk through the front part of the house. The thick oak door was closed, and at first all she could hear was the indistinguishable sounds of two male voices—one angry, one placating. She was just deciding this was a useless exercise when the louder of the two voices, obviously Walford McKennock, pierced through the heavy door so that she could hear some of his words clearly.

"I will not have my family name dragged through the mud! Do you know what the press would do if they got hold of some of this evidence? Good god, I'm running for Mayor!"

There was a slam, as if something made contact with the desk, and the noise frightened Libby enough to send her scurrying backwards toward the front door. Without looking back, she slipped outside and practically ran toward the streetcar stop. What on earth would she have done if McKennock had opened his office door and found her skulking in the hallway, obviously eavesdropping?

In the distance, she heard the clop of horses' hooves and looked impatiently down the dark boulevard for the streetcar. She felt like her heart was beating out of her chest and was still having difficulty catching her breath, which she feared had more to do with her nerves than the exertion of running for the tram. For a moment, when Walford McKennock asked to see her alone, she had thought her investigation was about to come to a violent end. While she was glad his comments had proved totally innocuous, there was also disappointment that the case seemed stalled. At that moment, she had no idea what the weekend might hold in store.

SIXTEEN

The shadows deepened around Libby, as Sunday afternoon slid inexorably toward night. Gaunt trees towered over her, so numerous she could just make out the back of the steeple, though the building was less than twenty yards away. The wind through their branches covered all but the occasional sound of passersby on the far side of the church. She sat in the gazebo—Sam was right, it certainly was isolated. It would have made a perfect hidden meeting spot if only she had someone to meet with. Sighing, she reached again for her small pocket watch and noted with annoyance that it was nearly thirty minutes after the appointed hour, and Sam was still nowhere in sight.

The snapping of a twig made her turn her head abruptly, but she could see no source for the noise. It was probably just a small animal making its way through the wood. She felt a prickle of nervousness but decided her nerves were just on edge. She rose from her seat and tapped her foot unconsciously against the railing.

Where *was* Sam? From everything she knew of him, he hardly seemed the sort of man to make an appointment and then miss it. A small worry wormed its way into her consciousness . . . Could something bad have happened to prevent his arrival? No, she was being ridiculous. Maybe he had simply forgotten their plan or had some personal emergency. At any rate, she decided suddenly, whatever he had to tell her would have to wait until tomorrow. She didn't intend to spend her entire Sunday afternoon on a fool's errand. She gave one last look around before stepping out of the small gazebo.

Libby walked slowly through the shadowy grove, dawdling in fading hope that she would hear Sam's voice calling out to her that he had finally arrived. But she reached the street without interruption, then crossed Clay and headed north on Fourth Avenue towards her streetcar stop. She didn't notice the figure running towards her, calling out her name, until John Mayhew was almost upon her.

"Miss Seale!" he repeated breathlessly. "How lucky I am to see you here today! I've been wondering how to get in touch with you!"

"Why Mr. Mayhew, what a pleasant surprise," she replied, only then noticing his almost wild demeanor and flushed face. He looked as if he had been running a race. "What is it? Is there something wrong?"

"It's Petey," he panted, still catching his breath. "Please tell me you've seen him. To be honest, he has me a mite worried. He didn't come into work Friday or yesterday, and the desk clerk at his hotel says he hasn't been there either. Not like him to miss two days of work without sending a message, not like him at all. So . . . have you?" He looked at her hopefully. "Seen him, that is?"

Libby shook her head. "I assumed he was busy at the paper these last few days. Are you sure he's not doing some work and is too busy to check in?"

Mayhew shook his head emphatically. "I know all the stories he's working on. I also know some of them are a little bit dangerous . . ." He stopped himself, obviously not wanting to upset her. "Oh, I'm sure he'll turn up. I just wondered if you had heard from him—"

Her voice shook slightly as she interrupted him. "I didn't think much of it when I didn't hear anything from Pe . . . Mr. Eberle for several days, but now that you say he hasn't been at home or at work, I must confess, you have *me* a bit worried!" She looked up at Mayhew, who was uncomfortably shifting back and forth as if he wanted to run off. "You will let me know as soon as you hear, won't you? You can leave a message for me at the Portland Variety."

"Of course, of course!" he agreed, "But that Eberle can take care of himself. I'm terribly sorry if I've caused you any concern. He's probably just got caught up in some new story and forgot to tell me." He waved his arm lightly as if regretting his earlier show of such gravity. "Well, then, I do have a few more places I wanted to check for him. Tell me, can I walk you to your destination, Miss Seale?"

She suddenly felt anxious to get away from Mayhew so she could think. Nothing was turning out right today; everything seemed to be spinning out of her control. "No, no," she demurred. "You were going the other way. Besides, my streetcar stop is right over there." Libby pointed across the street.

He insisted on walking her across the street and even waited with her until the familiar sound of the approaching trolley interrupted their desultory discussion of the weather, more rainy than usual for February. As her streetcar pulled away, she watched him hunch deeper into his overcoat and stride off in the direction of the *Gazette* offices, looking worried.

Libby let herself into her house and closed the front door quietly, hoping to avoid having to make small talk with her landlady. Unfortunately, Mrs. Pratt swooped immediately into the front hall, almost as if she had been hovering just inside the kitchen waiting for Libby's arrival. "Miss Seale! Oh dear, look at your coat! You are soaked to the bone . . . has the rain started again?"

Carefully hanging her coat on a peg, Libby answered in the affirmative. "It just started while I was walking back from the streetcar stop. It's chilly out, too."

"You go change into something dry, and I'll make us a nice cup of tea, why don't I? Father O'Bannon's sermon this morning was quite fascinating. I would be most interested to hear what you thought of it."

Libby sighed inwardly. If she agreed to a cup of tea, there was no telling when she would be able to excuse herself and get back to her room. Right now, all she could think of was the box of biscuits and bottle of juice weighing down her carpet bag. "Mrs. Pratt, I'm afraid I'm just too tired even for a cup of tea, but thank you for your kind offer."

The older woman's face fell. She had obviously been waiting all afternoon for some company, and Libby felt a pang of guilt as she climbed the flights of stairs up to her room. But instead of opening the door to her bedroom, she rapped softly on the next door over, a room that had been empty ever since the last tenant left six weeks back. Slowly, the door opened a crack.

"Libby?" Peter stuck his head out into the hallway nervously, relaxing when he saw that she was alone. He was still wearing the baggy tramp garments Mayhew had lent him, and it was obvious from his jumpy manner that he was going a little crazy cooped up in this room, hidden away. She thanked the fates once again that Mrs. Pratt hardly ever ventured up to the top floor of the house, so that when Peter had appeared out of the bushes and waylaid her last Friday night, it had been a fairly easy matter to sneak him into the house and up to this unused room.

She only hoped that Mrs. Pratt had not noticed the disappearance of some food from the kitchen, but, Libby reasoned, a few days of sneaking rations upstairs for Peter would hardly make a dent in Mrs. Pratt's overstocked larder. Which reminded her . . . "Just a moment," she said to Peter, gently pushing him back into the room. She reached into her bag for the groceries, and he set upon them with a ravenous hunger as she slipped off her coat and sat down on the windowsill.

He paused between bites to look up at her. "What did Sam say?" he asked. She quickly filled him in on the events of her afternoon or, more to the point, the lack of event. "And when I finally decided to leave, I was on my way home when who should I run into but John Mayhew!" She couldn't keep the note of pride out of her voice as she described her feigned surprise to hear that Peter was missing, but she realized as she spoke that he was looking more and more uncomfortable.

"Libby, John Mayhew is a good friend as well as my employer. I don't feel right hiding here like this while he's running all over town so worried about me. I think I need to go talk to him right away." He paced around the small room, brushing the crumbs off his shirt reflexively even though he knew it was already stained beyond hope of salvation.

"But what will happen if you're seen in public, after you were supposed to have been shanghaied?" she asked, reasonably. "I thought we decided you would stay here until those men stop looking for you."

"I can't stay here forever! We don't know how long those men will continue to look for me—or if they're even looking at all."

She said gently, "But if they *are* looking, then for at least a few days, you need to avoid the places you normally go, like your hotel and most especially the *Gazette* offices."

He grudgingly agreed. "But only for a few days. After that, no matter what, I need to get back to work." He gave a frustrated sigh. "If only there was some way we could force the killer's hand . . . force him to make some move which would reveal him to us. Once we stop the slaver at the theater, I have no doubt that whoever the people are behind the attack on me will back off." He threw himself back on the bed and lay staring at the ceiling, as though if he looked hard enough, the answers to his problems might appear there. "We just need a plan . . ."

As he spoke, she noticed again the wild look in his eyes that Peter had acquired since his brush with violence. In some ways, she hardly recognized the man before her. His normally tailored appearance had been replaced by that of a down-at-heels vagabond. And, although she had washed his clothing yesterday when Mrs. Pratt was out shopping, his face still had the grimy pallor of one who has been too long away from soap and water. They had decided it would be too risky for him to go down to the second floor to bathe where one of the other tenants might see him.

She felt a pang of tenderness when she looked at his haggard face. The vague knowledge that both of them were risking their lives by continuing the investigation had been made real. He could have been killed last Thursday! As she thought about it now, some of the horror she had felt when he had first told her what happened to him that night returned to her.

"There were two of them. Rough fellows, from the sound of their voices, but not too bright. After they put the chloroform in my face, they must have assumed I was out cold for the rest of the night, because when I awoke some time later, they didn't seem to be thinking about me at all. I didn't know where I was and, being bound and gagged, I could barely look around. I knew I was somewhere along the waterfront because I could hear them as they walked to and fro, smoking and talking. The sound of wooden boards underfoot, plus the lapping echo of water, told me we were on a dock." His voice was weak, and as he spoke, Libby had to resist the urge to sit beside him and stroke his forehead. Her eyes lingered on his bedraggled state and noted his sickly pallor. He stared into space for a few moments, as if reliving the scene. "I smelled cigar smoke, or maybe they were smoking opium, I'm not sure. Something pungent . . . I was moving my hands, trying to loosen the ropes, very slowly." He rubbed his wrists, grimacing. "They didn't do a very good job of tying me up. Of course, I tend to think their usual customer is dead drunk, so it didn't occur to them I might try to untie myself."

"Could you hear what they were saying? When did they notice you were awake? Did they chase after you?" She realized she was peppering him with questions, but she wanted to know everything that had happened. He unlaced his shoes, looking at her nervously, as if at any moment, she would chastise him for being overly familiar, but she immediately said, "Oh, I should have thought. You must be terribly uncomfortable. Here, let me get you a blanket and please, make yourself comfortable." She crossed over to the large built-in wardrobe and took a quilt out. Somewhat awkwardly, she set it on the edge of the bed, this new intimacy feeling strange.

Peter crawled under the cover and leaned up on one elbow, resuming his story. "There really isn't much more to tell. After I got my hands loose, I untied the ropes around my ankles. When the men's voices seemed as far away as they were going to get, I slipped off the ropes and ran off into the night. I didn't look back to see if they were following me. I just ran and ran, not even sure where I was going. I kept alongside the river with Front Street to my right because the tall ships in port blocked me from view. I . . . I don't remember exactly what happened next. I heard voices behind me, yelling. I was dizzy, I think from the chloroform, and ducked into an empty flour warehouse. It was cold and damp and smelled like wheat, but it was quiet and there were lots of places to hide among the sacks of flour." He shivered, and stopped talking for a moment.

Libby had been standing by the window as he spoke, but she went over and sat down on the edge of the bed. "You slept there then? Did you stay in the warehouse all day today?"

"No, no, I woke up there this morning—well, not that I got much sleep. It was cold, and my whole body ached. I don't know if they had been planning to kill me or just press me into service on one of those merchant boats headed for the Orient, but I think they must have beaten me while I was out because in the morning light, I could see I was covered in bruises. Or maybe I just got banged up as they carried me to the docks, I don't know. In any case, I'm afraid I was still a little bit delirious when I heard the voices of the workers coming in for the morning shift. I knew that they would soon be moving all the sacks of flour. I was sure the two men would be waiting for me with evil grins on their faces . . . I suddenly imagined they would slice through a sack of flour to get at me, and there would be blood everywhere . . ."

She gasped involuntarily, and Peter suddenly realized he was scaring her. "I know that sounds crazy," he amended, "I think it was the exhaustion and the throbbing in my head that made me think like that, but at any rate, I knew I had to move away from there. The farther from the waterfront, the better off I would be. I slipped out the back door of the building and started walking towards the *Gazette*. Then I figured they would be looking for me there. Same thing with my hotel. I didn't want to head home and fall right into a trap. So I turned around and headed east, crossing over the Madison Bridge, and made my way to this part of town. Of course, I knew you would be at the theater, so I went to Lone Fir to spend the day."

"The cemetery?"

He nodded. "I figured it was as good a place as any to hide away, and I was right. No one bothered me at all. I sat on a bench near the back of the lot, and when it got dark, I came over to your street and waited for you to come home." He looked at her questioningly. "Of course, I didn't expect you to be quite so late. It got pretty wet waiting outside there."

"Oh, I was at the McKennock house tonight. I got there late, so I didn't get away until almost nine." She looked at him worriedly. "Are you shivering? You don't look at all well." Almost as if she were another person, Libby took his cold hand in hers. For several moments, the two regarded each other silently.

She reminded herself that she was a married woman. I should let go of his hand right now, thought Libby, but he is so cold, and he looks so ill . . . Peter squeezed her hand, and much to her dismay, the gesture reminded her of Mr. Greenblatt back in New York. Self-pity and resentment washed over her in equal measure: self-pity that she found herself the bride of a loathsome man 3,000 miles away, and resentment that she should not be able to follow her heart right here and now without it being so complicated. As these thoughts swirled in her head, she could tell Peter was filled with the same sort of nervous confusion. As if in a dream, she leaned down and kissed his forehead gently. He reached up and held her face between his hands, staring intently into her eyes.

"Libby," he murmured softly and pulled her face down to his, kissing her.

She knew in her heart that this was madness, to pretend that they were a young couple in love when all along she knew they could never have a normal courtship. She pulled away, saying, "Peter, we must stop. I have to tell you something important."

"It will wait," he said with honeyed voice, and she let herself be silenced by his lips. Emotion overcame reason and, without considering the consequences, Libby kissed him back.

Monday morning, Libby entered the Variety prepared to upbraid Sam for failing to meet her in the gazebo, but when she came through the stage door, he wasn't at his post. Although the backstage area was filled with people, the usual Monday morning bustle, she didn't see Sam there either. That was odd . . . Sam rarely left his high stool by the door during working hours unless it was to direct a new arrival through the maze of corridors backstage. She paused to hang up her coat in the wardrobe room, intending to resume her search right away, but before she could do so, Jack popped his head through the door and said, "Everybody onstage now. Mr. Crowther's got an announcement."

She looked to Hatty, but the older woman's face showed the same bafflement as Libby's at this unprecedented occurrence. The two costumers headed to the stage with the rest of the staff and performers, about forty people all told, everyone buzzing about what could possibly be the subject of their boss's announcement. Mr. Crowther was standing center stage, his back to the auditorium, looking solemn. Once the murmuring had died down, he began to speak.

"I'm afraid I have some sad news to share with you all. One of our Variety family has been taken from us in a senseless act of violence . . ." Libby knew who it was going to be, who it had to be, before Crowther said the name. "Sam, our faithful stage doorman, was struck down late Saturday evening during what appears to have been a robbery attempt. I was informed today by the police that his lifeless body was found yesterday by some local lads down by the Morrison pier." The murmurs started up again at a higher pitch than before. Shock and consternation intermingled with fear and a certain kind of excitement in the crowd's reaction.

Libby felt as if her stomach had dropped to her toes, as if the wind was knocked out of her. It was with an effort she remained standing. She should have known that only death would have kept Sam from meeting her the day before, not that the knowledge would have made any difference. To think that all the time she had waited in the gazebo, getting more and more cross with him, Sam had been lying in the city morgue with whatever he knew lost with him. Robbery attempt indeed! Libby was positive that the timing of Sam's death could not be unrelated to what was going on at the theater, to the "close watch" he had told her he was planning to keep over the weekend the last time she spoke with him.

Crowther was drawing to a close. "Sam was a dedicated and loyal employee of this theater and was as devoted to the old adage 'the show must go on' as any performer. Thus, as much as in our grief and sorrow we might like to close for the day, let's honor Sam by smiling through our tears and going on."

If she hadn't already felt nauseous, the oily platitudes Crowther was disseminating would have done the trick. Libby, who had perhaps spoken more closely to Sam than most who worked at the Variety, knew that in Sam's view, most theater folk were little better than Jezebels and snake-oil salesmen. "The show must go on," indeed! She was willing to bet that the real reason Crowther wasn't closing the theater was because it had been less than a month since he'd had to cancel two shows the day Vera's body was discovered!

Though he hadn't mentioned Vera's name, Libby was also sure she couldn't be the only one thinking of the other death to touch the theater in recent weeks. There was the same air of unreality about the situation, as if what had happened couldn't possibly be true. She remembered the eerie silence backstage that day and May rushing up to her, eyes wide with fear like a child. Libby wondered how May was coping with this new death, and she gazed around the stage trying to catch sight of the young dancer.

She spied the cluster of Dancing Whirlwinds stage left, but May was not among them. All of a sudden, her queasiness turned to cold fear. Where was May? Surely she should be with the other dancers, or at least somewhere on this stage, but she was nowhere.

And, like a jigsaw puzzle, disparate pieces fell into place in Libby's mind, forming a horrible picture she didn't want to see: May trying to tell her about someone at the theater taking a special interest in her lately; Peter telling her that white slavers usually befriended naïve, younger girls with no family; the man in the sleazy saloon saying the slavers were looking for blondes; May, burbling on about something that was going to happen over the weekend; Sam, on Friday, saying he was going to keep watch over the next few days. If only she had listened more closely, hadn't been so preoccupied making dresses for silly Charlotte McKennock, perhaps she could have prevented not one but two needless . . . Wait. Maybe she was jumping to conclusions. Perhaps May was upstairs in the dressing room this minute or running late on her way to work.

Crowther had just concluded his remarks, something about the unattended stage door remaining locked for the day, that they should all just pitch in and keep an ear out in case anybody knocked. The assembly onstage was breaking up, people slowly heading back to their own areas with heads down and voices hushed (but tongues wagging nonetheless).

Libby caught up with the claque of Whirlwinds as they were starting to climb the stairs to their dressing room. "Excuse me, girls. Have any of you seen May?" A frieze of blank faces stared back at her. "She didn't send a note saying she would be out sick, did she? Or let any of you know she wouldn't be coming in today for any reason?" As one, the girls shook their heads silently.

Tallulah spoke up. "I thought it was odd. She's usually first one here on Mondays. Says she misses the theater on her day off and can't wait to come in every week." She rolled her eyes with all the hauteur of a world-weary twenty-three-year old. "Kids!"

Distractedly thanking them for their help, Libby rushed back to the sewing closet and bent over her hemming with such diligence and industry that Hatty couldn't help but stare at her in disbelief. Libby didn't even notice, so wrapped up was she in trying to ignore the icy dread which gripped her enough to concentrate on her sewing. Only one thought drove her forward. If she finished this whole pile of petticoats, Hatty would *have* to let her take her lunch break, no matter how early it was. Above all else, she needed to talk to Peter—and as soon as possible.

The single block known as Vine Street had been demolished to make way for the Skidmore Fountain five years before, and Peter stood at the intersection of First and Ankeny trying to get his bearings. Libby had told him she was fairly sure she remembered May telling her about finding a cat near her Vine Street boardinghouse. He figured that whoever owned the building must have been close enough to Vine to have retained the name when the street itself had been razed to make way for the fountain.

There were only two large houses on the block where he stood, and he was in luck because one of them had a sign peeping out of its grimy front window: *Rooms to Let.* Patting himself on the back for a detecting job well done, he mounted the stairs to the porch and mentally rehearsed his story.

"Well, what is it?" The woman who opened the door looked none too pleased to see a stranger, and Peter reminded himself that with his stale clothes and unwashed pallor, she had likely sized him up as one of the area transients. "I got two rooms available, but you better be able to pay the first week up front."

He shook his head dismissively. "I don't need a room, ma'am. I'm looking for a girl that lives here, name of May. She owes me some money."

The woman laughed, and it was a sharp bleat. "Get in line, then, why don't you? She ain't been back here since Saturday morning, that one."

Peter felt a chill run down his spine. So Libby's dark suspicions had been right! "She moved out then?"

"If you want to call it that. More like skipped town, if you ask me. Left here Saturday morning for that theater job, same as always. She's some kind of dancer at the burlesque, but I guess you know that, Mister. Never came home that night. Never even packed up her things, not that she had much worth packing. Matter of fact, I was just setting to clean out her room." She paused. "You might want to try over there at the theater. Oh, and if you see her, tell her Missus LeClerc is looking for last week's rent."

"Yes, ma'am," he replied, but the door was already shutting in his face. With heavy heart, Peter made his way back down to the street and headed idly along Front Street, lost in thought. Poor May. And poor Libby, too. Peter knew she was already blaming herself for not predicting that May might become the slavers' next victim. When she had arrived from the theater this afternoon in a frenzy of fear and grief, nothing he said could allay her guilt that if *only* she had been more thoughtful, if *only* she had warned May to be more careful . . . And then there was Sam. She felt personally responsible for drawing him into the web of corruption and murder that eventually led to his demise. He worried that the tumultuous events of the last few days were taking too great an emotional toll on Libby. Although, he reminded himself, she had been a bastion of strength when he most needed her. He could hardly remember anything of the first day after his attack, and it had seemed almost like a hallucination to find himself in the small attic room at Mrs. Pratt's with Libby leaning over him and smoothing his fevered brow.

The memory of their kiss was still fresh in his mind, and he wondered sadly why she had pulled so abruptly away from him. It was obvious to him that she felt uncomfortable getting closer to him, but he couldn't quite understand the cause of the obvious barrier she had mentally erected between them. Was it her religion? Their conversation about her Jewishness still made him squirm with discomfort at his own awkward surprise. But she was being ridiculous, he thought angrily. This was nearly the twentieth century, and they were Americans—they hardly need be slaves to the social mores of the older generation.

His walk had led him toward the Morrison Street pier, site of Sam's supposed "random robbery attempt" and murder. He agreed with Libby that Sam's death had to be related to the slave trade at the theater and May's abduction, but she had had to rush back to work before they could discuss what the repercussions of that assumption were. Peter decided that a little on-site investigation wouldn't be out of order. In fact, he already had an idea of what he was looking for; he just wasn't sure where to start. He knew, by reputation only, that all the waterfront neighborhoods he had seen today were littered with entrances to the Shanghai tunnels. They had been designed to transport goods from the docks to the city, but there was no reason that they couldn't be used to transport something from the city to the waterfront as well . . . something like a dead body. If Sam really had discovered some incriminating evidence or witnessed May being abducted by the slaver, then he had probably been attacked at the theater, even though his body had been discovered here by the Morrison pier. There had to be a fast and safe way someone had gotten his body from Crowther's Variety to the docks.

Now that he was at the foot of the pier itself, he realized with surprise it was just a few yards from the Albers Mill building in which he had hidden just a few days ago. He noticed by the light of day that the mill was actually a new-looking structure, the freshly painted reproductions of flour sack labels on the side of the building proudly proclaiming its purpose. On the next dock over, two men called instructions to a third as they worked together to hoist large sacks of flour up to a waiting ship. A fourth man appeared and yelled something at them, but Peter was too far away to hear what he said. With a jolt, he realized this man in the red shirt looked familiar—could it be one of his mysterious assailants? He certainly resembled the image Peter had in his head, and fragmentary images from that horrible night were burned into his consciousness. Well, even if his mind was playing tricks on him, Peter wasn't about to stick around and find out for sure. His head swirled around seeking a quick place to hide from view.

The warehouse at his back showed no signs of occupancy, so with quiet movements designed not to catch the eye, he climbed the short flight of cement stairs and ducked under the overhanging roof. As he hunched back into the shadows, he berated himself for being so skittish, but the fear of being caught again was too strong, he found himself wishing longingly that he was back at Mrs. Pratt's house in his cramped but safe third-floor hideout. He felt exposed here, even with the overhang above him. Looking around, he saw the set of wide, shed-like doors was gaping open a little, and without pausing to think, he slipped inside.

As his eyes adjusted to the light, Peter could see that he was in a large damp warehouse, probably a holding point for many of the goods that came in and out of the port every day. Currently, the room was nearly empty, and a propped-open door in the far corner revealed a staircase heading down. He knew at once that this must be an entrance to the Shanghai tunnels, and laughed to himself, thinking how his would-be abductor had just done him a favor, helping him locate an entrance to the tunnels on his first try.

Holding on to the wall as he made his way down the narrow staircase, Peter was seized with equal parts curiosity and fear. As much as Peter knew about the existence of the underground network of tunnels beneath the city, he had never actually been inside them. Down here beneath street level, the cold air smelled of clay, and as he looked down the dark corridor ahead, all he could make out were wooden beams holding up a makeshift tunnel. He stood still, listening for the sound of people nearby. It was a weekday afternoon; certainly some legitimate cargo deliveries might be taking place here underneath the city—but all was quiet.

Setting off in the direction he judged was west, he soon became disoriented. At first, it had seemed so simple to envision the streets up above him, but the winding curves of the underground warren bore no relation to the even grid of the streets above. Peter soon realized he was hopelessly lost. His thought had been to see if he could determine how far it was from the Variety to the waterfront exit of the tunnel, but as he passed by shadowy doorways leading into what looked like saloon basements, he realized the chances of even recognizing the theater from this vantage point were slim. Above him, the ceiling dripped the remnants of last night's rain, below him, his feet encountered shallow muddy puddles and assorted debris every few yards.

The passageway he was in ended suddenly as it met another, and painted in whitewash on the dirt wall was a faded set of arrows: the one pointing left said "Taylor," the one to the right, "Yamhill." Since he knew that the Variety was on Taylor Street, he thanked his luck and turned left, ducking to get through since the ceiling was lower here. Spread before him was a rather orderly wide passage, drier and mustier than the other. Instead of arched openings leading to basement subsections of the buildings above, a series of ramps and small staircases led up to large wooden doorways, each painted with the scrawled name of the business it led to. He saw the name Frank's Chop House, which meant that Crowther's should be just a few storefronts away. Sure enough, with very little difficulty, he found himself in front of the door marked with the name of the theater.

He looked up at the name "Crowther" written in yellow letters on the door. Despite his disoriented wandering, he estimated that he had been in the tunnels no more than five minutes. For someone familiar with the labyrinth, the journey might have taken even less time. The close proximity of Sam's body to the Morrison Pier tunnel exit was looking more and more suspicious. Most likely, he thought, Sam's life-less body had been carried along the very same path he had just tra-versed, and the thought made him shiver. Not to mention was likely the path May—and who knew how many other unfortunate young women—had probably been shepherded along on the first stage of their infamous journeys.

Glancing around, he realized he was standing on the very spot where Vera's body had been discovered a few weeks before. Not really expecting to find any evidence of Vera's final moments, or Sam's, Peter lit a match and gazed around. Surprisingly, right away his eye fell on something on the ground in front of him which glittered red in the faint light of his match. Brushing aside the fanciful notion which popped into his head that it was some sort of enchanted blood, linger-ing here to point the finger of guilt at the murderer—the eerie other-worldliness of the tunnels was getting to him, he supposed—he bent down to pick it up and realized it was a sequin of some sort.

No doubt Libby would know the exact term and derivation for this metallic bauble that looked like part of a costume, and he slipped it into his pocket, eyes now glued to the dirt floor in front of him. He squatted close to the foot of the stairs leading to the door marked Portland Variety, and he made out distinct footprints in the muddy tunnel floor made by a shoe that had half a heel missing. Not that he was an expert, but the marks looked fresh to him. Certainly, among the jumble of marks on the tunnel's floor, he was still able to make out at least four of the distinctive left shoe, which meant nobody else had walked on top of them since they had been made.

Suddenly, he was aware that he could hear the sounds of activity dimly from behind the door to the theater, and remembering that it was the middle of a workday, he decided he had better not linger there. Despite all logic, the cellar door into the Variety was not secured, though there was a rusty padlock and chain hanging to one side that he suspected was fastened at night. However, if someone were to come into the tunnel at this moment, there would be no warning, and Peter would be discovered.

So he headed back the way he had come, moving as quickly as possible while still keeping a careful lookout to see if he could follow the tracks made by the half-heeled shoe. Holding lit matches close to the ground in front of him, he managed to make one out every few feet or so. He was also rewarded every once in a while with another sequin sometimes red, sometimes yellow. It was easier to navigate now that he was following a predetermined path back the way he came past all the saloon basements and out toward the empty warehouse. As he passed back into the first tunnel, which was noticeably more damp and muddy, he noticed something else along with the footprints.

Just after he bypassed a large puddle, he noticed two parallel lines of thinly caked mud extending from it, each about three-quarters of an inch across and spaced about two feet apart. The footprints right after passing through the puddle were more clearly defined too and seemed to always fall between the two thin lines.

Although this pattern sometimes disappeared for yards at a time, he would eventually see evidence of the parallel lines and those distinctive boot marks again, and the path would continue. As he walked, he tried to figure out what the pattern represented. From somewhere deep in the recesses of his mind, he recalled a day many years before when, accompanying his father to Yale on a day when a new ornamental garden was being laid out, he had seen much the same sort of tracks. So, he realized, half-heel man had been pushing a wheelbarrow. Or perhaps not a wheelbarrow but something like it . . . judging by the narrow wheel gauge, it was not a gardener's or construction worker's wheelbarrow. It was something more delicate. But whatever the conveyance was exactly, it confirmed Peter's suspicion that the tracks he was following had been made by Sam's murderer as he transported Sam's body to the pier.

Lost in thought as he was, and concentrating on the floor, the mud and loose rocks he encountered made it easy to lose his balance as he went. A few times, he almost stumbled and had to catch himself, but eventually he was back where he started, blinking at the suddenly bright daylight out by Morrison pier.

Carefully, he looked around, willing the man with the red shirt to be gone, and sure enough, he was. The ship with its new cargo of flour was pulling out of port, and the dock was empty. It had started to rain in that peculiar Portland way, with a bright sun overhead while cold pellets of rain came down. Peter pulled his collar up against the wet and made his way back to Mrs. Pratt's boardinghouse as fast as he could.

While Peter had been examining footprints underneath the theater, ten feet above him Libby had been rushing around in a frenzy of over-work. Ever since she had arrived back from her lunch break, the theater had been buzzing. Sam's death had only served to re-open discussion of both Vera's and Polly Pink's relatively recent deaths. Two of the dancers had already quit suddenly, saying this was not a safe place to work any more, while several others were loudly debating whether or not to defect to one of the other vaudeville houses in town . . . if not leave the theatrical profession entirely.

Hatty was in a foul mood, the most unfriendly Libby had ever seen her. With pursed lips, she led two Whirlwind alternates to Libby and, practically throwing several ill-fitting costumes at her, muttered that these needed to be altered and right away, thank you very much. The two girls, despite being a good deal taller than the aging wardrobe mistress, seemed cowed by Hatty and were relieved when she left them alone with Libby. As Libby measured and sewed, they chattered nervously about the evening's show.

"When my Pa hears about all the goings-on here, I don't think I'll be staying on much longer," said Sue-Ann, the more talkative of the two. She prodded her quieter friend, "It figures, don't it—we finally get ourselves into the first act closer, and I just know Pa'll yank me out of here so fast my head will be spinning."

"Maybe he's right." Her voice was so quiet Libby had to strain to hear the girl as she chided her friend. "I don't want to end up like that dead girl in the tunnel." Libby wasn't sure if she meant Vera or Polly, but before she could ask, Sue-Ann was already talking again.

"Oh, I'm not worried! The way I figure it, I'm only here at Crowther's 'til I get noticed by one of those circuit men who book all the big theaters. Then I'll set up my own act—maybe something like Ida Fuller—and become a famous vaudeville star!" She raised her arms up in an exotic pose, and Libby was forced to interrupt.

"Please keep your arms still while I'm measuring, dear."

"Sorry, Libby," said Sue-Ann, suddenly contrite. "Say, is this costume going to look right on me? It used to be Tallulah's, and she's *much* bigger around the middle than I am!" She winked at her friend. "That Tallulah was always putting on airs, don't you think, Millie?"

"It will be just fine, if I can finish pinning it," answered Libby, resisting the urge to "accidentally" poke a pin into the stuck-up dancer. "There . . . now if you'll step out of it carefully, I'll finish up those seams and bring it to you as soon as it's done." She turned to Millie with a smile. "Now let's see what we can do for you . . ."

By the end of the afternoon, Libby's fingers were raw. Hatty had eventually returned to help her with the sewing, but there had been a strain between the two women, and Libby was at a loss to understand its cause. Perhaps her habitual lateness and long lunch hours had finally caught up with her, and the costume manager was choosing today of all days to show her disapproval.

The two women sewed silently, until at last Libby put down the final costume piece for Millie and sighed. "I'll just bring the girls their new costumes then," she said, grabbing the bundle of completed outfits and heading toward the chorines' dressing area. The stack of clothes she was holding was so high that she nearly bumped into Jack as she made her way backstage. He was holding a shoe and looking at it strangely.

"Miss Seale! Just the woman I was hoping to see . . . I have a bit of a costume-related favor to ask you."

"I'll be happy to help. Just let me give the dancers these new costumes, and I'll be right back." She did so and found Jack still standing in the hallway, turning the boot in his hands over and over.

"Tell me," he said, "do you or Miss Matthews have any experience fixing shoes for the actors?"

She nodded. "I think so . . . We have some cobbling materials in the costume shop. Can I get it back to you tomorrow, or did you need it right now?"

"No, no, tomorrow would be fine." He held out the boot to her. "These are just the spare boots I keep backstage for when I need to go into the tunnels for deliveries. It gets awful muddy back there." Anticipating her question, he went on, "I don't know how it happened. Mr. Crowther must have needed them this weekend, because he just brought them back to me. Only he didn't mention the left one was broken. Fact is, I didn't notice 'til I tried to put them on right now and practically fell on my backside." He smiled a friendly smile.

Libby took the boot from him and turned it over. No wonder Jack hadn't been able to stand straight . . . Half the heel was missing.

SEVENTEEN

ARVIDE CROWTHER SAT AT his desk, listening intently to the flurry of sounds out in the lobby that signified the last of the cast and crew leaving after the final curtain. He glanced down again at the block-printed note in front of him, but he did not read it again. He knew exactly what it said, as he had been turning the well-creased paper over and over again in his hands ever since he had returned to his office earlier tonight and found it slipped underneath the door.

Pushing away from his desk, he slid open the bottom drawer and pulled out his gun. He stroked it idly while trying to decide if he should carry it.

After a while, he heard the familiar sound of the wide front door click shut and the turn of a key as someone, probably Jack, locked the place up for the night. Despite being practically able to recite it from memory, he looked one last time at the letter, carefully unfolding it and straining to read by the dim gaslight.

It must have been hard fitting Sam's body into that rickshaw.
Is that how you broke the boot heel?

Meet me on the stage tonight after the last show.

With a sudden burst of anger, he crumpled the paper and threw it across the room, mouthing a profanity silently under his breath. His wife had trained him well, he thought, grimacing. Once he would have thought nothing of cursing the damned bastard who was trying to blackmail him, but nowadays such words never escaped his lips, at least not audibly.

He was not a stupid man. He knew there were those who would say he deserved whatever he had coming to him, but even he had never stooped to blackmail. It was a coward's crime, and he wasn't a coward. To his way of thinking, profiting secondhand from someone else's crime while not even getting one's hands dirty was truly despicable.

He listened intently and decided the theater was empty at last. Well, almost empty. Presumably, one person besides himself was waiting here now, somewhere in this dark silent building, waiting for him to show. The irony didn't escape him. A midnight assignation on the stage was a scene he had taken part in many times with many girls, over the years. But this time, he was not the one in control of the situation.

When he had first read the note, he had wondered how its writer could possibly have known this exact routine, the carefully arranged meetings on an empty stage after the final show of the night. He concluded finally that it was impossible; the naming of this particular time and place was sheer coincidence. The only people in the world who knew this particular gambit of his were either halfway around the world or dead.

With a sigh, he stood up and crossed to the office door. Dimming the light, he took one last look at his office before shutting the door behind him and heading down toward the front of the house. The gun in his pocket was heavy, and he hoped it would not be necessary to use it, but if he must, well then, that was just the way of it. The main thing was, he had to be sure to contain the damage. Before doing anything to silence the blackmailer, he had to find out if this man had told anyone else of his suspicions.

As he made his way up the small stairs at the side of the stage, he felt an unfamiliar pang of fear. Dammit, when he had found Sam, that old fool, lingering behind the curtains Saturday night, spying on him, he had assumed the old man was simply curious about a noise late at night in his precious theater. Now it was clear Sam had been acting upon orders from someone else—someone who had sent him in as a spy—and that meant who knew how many people might be involved in this web of deceit?

He heard a noise from the opposite side of the dark stage and looked up to see who his enemy was. Impulsively, he put his hand in his pocket and ran it over the smooth, substantial gun, which relaxed him slightly.

Libby Seale stepped out from behind the curtain. Crowther smiled . . . this might not be as bad as he had feared. It was just that pushy little costume girl. She was always asking questions and must have stumbled onto the Sam thing by accident. Too damn nosy for her own good, that's what she was. But at least he knew he could buy her off, so the gun wouldn't be necessary. He knew exactly how little the Variety paid her and was certain she must need the money. After all, if it wasn't money she wanted, she would have gone straight to the police, wouldn't she?

Libby felt her knees shaking as she stood facing Sam's murderer. She was thankful for her heavy skirts, which hopefully hid her trembling legs. She had been right to sense an undercurrent of violence in Crowther. He had always reminded her of Mr. Greenblatt, the same instinct to bully those who were weaker than he was. This time, she vowed, she wouldn't flee. She would stand her ground and fight . . . Didn't they

261

say bullies usually backed down when faced with real opposition? Of course, Crowther wasn't a bully who merely beat his wife like Mr. Greenblatt, he was a ruthless career criminal. She summoned her bravery and confidence, mentally reviewing her goal: she must get Crowther to confess to the killings so that there would at last be definitive proof of his crimes. The footprints in the tunnel would probably not have lasted out the day yesterday, and without whatever proof Sam had uncovered, it would just be her word against Crowther's.

"Mr. Crowther," she said slowly, with as much civility as she could muster. "Thank you for meeting me here tonight."

"What do you want?" he growled. "How much?"

Right to the point, she thought. He is not a man who takes his time skirting around an issue. "Are you alone?"

He nodded tersely. "You think I have help around here? How much do you think one girl every few months brings in?" He threw his arms wide, as if to say search the theater if you want to, "Just me. And I'm not making a mint. So how much do you want?"

"Why Sam?" Her voice cracked slightly, but she looked straight into his eyes defiantly, and the air between them crackled with an almost electric energy. "Is there suddenly a demand for elderly male geishas?"

"Found him spying on me Saturday night while I was . . . having a private chat. That wasn't like Sam . . . He worked for me for eight years, a damn good stage doorman. Thought I could trust him. A little cracked in the head with all that religion, but at least that way I knew he'd never mess with any of my girls."

"And no one's supposed to mess around with 'your girls' except you, right?"

"You put him up to it, didn't you? Sam wasn't the type to go snooping around . . . Too bad it had to end the way it did . . ." He actually did sound a little sad, which made Libby queasy. Clearly, Crowther placed the death of a man, a valued employee, in a completely different category than sending innocent girls off to a life of misery. "Happy, Miss Seale? If you'd sent me your note a couple of days ago, that old man would still be alive."

The accusation stung, even though she knew that a few days back, she wouldn't have known where to send the note. She tried to ignore the image which popped into her mind: Sam's eager face offering to help her investigate. "Sam was as eager to find out the truth as I was about . . ."

"So you two cooked up this scheme all by yourselves?" Crowther cut her off, his index finger sliding in his pocket to wrap around the trigger.

She saw the trap. "We're not the only ones . . . a disturbing number of girls seem to quit the Variety without giving notice. How many girls did you think could vanish before someone would notice? Marie, Lily Belle, May . . ." She felt a lump rise in her throat at the mention of May's name, and emotion threatened to overwhelm her. "Not to mention the ones who turn up dead in the tunnels—"

"That was an accident. So what . . . why do you care so much? They were all a bunch of whores anyway . . . do anything to further their precious careers. If they were stupid enough not to see the risks, well . . . they deserved what happened to them." Besides, he finished the thought to himself, life isn't fair. What had he done to deserve three dead daughters and a wife who was now so convinced she was dying, she didn't have any room in her life for any man but Jesus? No, he didn't waste any time worrying about those girls. When had any of them ever worried about him or his unhappy life?

He glared at Libby with undisguised scorn. What gave her the right to sit in judgment upon him, standing there waiting for him to buy her silence? God, he wanted to shoot that smug look of superiority off her face, even though it seemed likely now that she wasn't acting alone.

Perhaps he should just shoot her and then shoot himself. Save his superiors the trouble, once they discovered he'd been found out, which they were bound to eventually.

Self-preservation won out. He'd pay her off for now and find some way to eliminate her later, before the higher-ups discovered what had happened. He strode across the stage and did his best to loom over her menacingly. "Okay, enough chit-chat. Tell me what you want."

She seemed to answer without moving her lips, and it took him a second to realize that it was a new voice he was hearing, calling out, "Crowther, you're under arrest."

He whirled around and saw three men standing in the stage left box, three guns trained directly on him. In one fluid motion, without consciously planning it, Crowther swung his left arm around Libby's neck and pulled her in front of his own body, meanwhile drawing his revolver with his right and pressing it to her temple.

"Drop the guns, or I'm taking her with me."

The younger of the two plain clothes men dropped his pistol immediately and turned to the police officer and the bigger, burlier man, obviously trying to get them to drop their weapons as well. With their focus momentarily on each other, Crowther took his chance. A dim, half-plan had formed in his mind . . . if he could only move fast enough before they had time to regroup. It would take them at least half a minute to clamber down from the theater box and get backstage. After that, they wouldn't be familiar with the maze of corridors back there, so he might gain even more time.

Out of the corner of his eye, Peter saw Crowther make his move, dragging Libby backwards into the wings. Things were happening too fast, and Peter, overwhelmed, could barely keep up with the changing situation. Crowther, on the other hand, seemed to him to able to act without thinking, with the unruffled calm of a man for whom violence was not noteworthy.

Officer Branson raised his gun, attempting to get one shot off before Crowther and Libby disappeared in the shadows. "No!" Peter lunged for Branson's arm. It was bad enough Branson and Mayhew hadn't dropped their weapons when Crowther had first grabbed Libby. He couldn't actually be serious about firing his gun when Libby's body shielded all but Crowther's head from view. Let Crowther escape. That didn't matter at all, not compared with making sure Libby wasn't hurt.

He knew he would never forgive himself if something happened to her. This entire setup had been his plan. It had been his belief that Crowther would be less confrontational if he thought his adversary was a woman, that he'd be more cocky and more likely to confess. He knew now he should never have let Libby be the one up there on that stage.

Branson and Mayhew were heading for the private stairs that linked the box seats to the side aisle of the auditorium, which actually meant they were heading away from the stage. That way would take too long, he thought. "Can't we jump to the stage?" he called out. "It doesn't look that far."

Mayhew called back over his shoulder, "It's over fifteen feet, Petey. Don't risk it. We'll get her back, don't worry." And then he ran on, not wanting to spare breath to talk.

Peter stopped to retrieve his gun and followed unhappily, bringing up the rear as they made their way down the stairs, up the aisle, and through the door leading backstage. They paused, stymied.

"Which way now?" Branson said, perplexed, looking to Peter since of the three of them, he was the only one who had ever been there.

"We'd better split up. Libby said the dressing areas are upstairs," he pointed, looking at John Mayhew who rushed off. He turned to the policeman, "Why don't you look in the wings and behind all the curtains. I'll . . . I think the costume and scenery shops are back that way."

Alone now, his gun raised in front of him, Peter made his way slowly down the unlit corridor, peering through each doorway he came to. He passed a cleaning closet, filled with buckets and mops, and what he knew must be the costume room, where racks of clothing stood silent and still. He could almost picture Libby sitting in the chair there, head bent over her sewing.

A faint sound reached his ears. Something metallic, a sort of clanging. He ran out of the costume room, listening intently, trying to determine where the sound was coming from. He thought it came from the end of the hallway, so he headed there to an open doorway he hadn't yet crossed.

He found himself in a cavernous, drafty space, glowing dimly blue in the light from a row of dirty windows high up on what must be the back wall of the theater. Various scenic pieces and props were carefully set out against the walls and in neat rows down the center of the room. A design of yellow and red sequins along the edge of a cart caught the moonlight, and he recognized immediately that his was one of the rickshaws Libby had told him about. Looking at the ornamental conveyance, he couldn't believe that something so delicate and gay had managed to do the nefarious work of transporting a dead man just days before.

He pricked up his ears, hoping to catch another sound. There were no more metallic clangs, but he thought he could just detect the sound of feet scuffling. Then he head a muffled cry. All at once, he realized where the sounds must be coming from.

"He's got her in the tunnels!" he cried at the top of his lungs, lunging for the doorway. "John! Branson!"

It took him only seconds to find the doorway, once he knew what he was looking for. Down a few steps, at the back of the room, he saw the inside of the same double doors he had seen yesterday while searching in the tunnels. But now the rusty chain, which had been hanging loose the last time he saw it, was holding the doors together. He grabbed it with both hands and pulled, but he knew even as he did so that it wouldn't give. The sounds he heard had been Crowther looping the chain through and fastening it on the other side with the padlock.

Crowther had had to let her go in order to fasten the padlock and chain. He'd shoved her to the ground with such force that the wind was knocked out of her, but Libby had still struggled to her feet as soon as her breath had returned and done her best to stop him. Unfortunately, he was over a foot taller than she was, a mass of muscle, and she might as well have been a kitten for all the energy it took him to fend off her arms. Besides, there was still his gun to consider, even if it was no longer pointed at her.

Finishing up with the doors, he grabbed her roughly by one arm and started pulling her along beside him through the heavy darkness. Libby could make out only the blur of dirt walls and wooden beams as she struggled to keep up with his long stride. She tried to pull away from him, but he only grabbed more tightly around her arm and kept racing down the dark passageway.

Abruptly turning, he yanked her arm, and she nearly slammed into a wall. As they emerged into a new branch of the tunnel, Libby had to duck suddenly to avoid hitting her head on a low archway. From his labored breathing, she could tell that Crowther was losing his momentum, and she squinted into the darkness ahead, trying to determine how far they were from the Morrison pier exit Peter had described to her. She hoped Crowther was taking the same route out this time. Peter had said it was only a few minutes walk, and they were moving at a fairly brisk pace.

She was scared, but she told herself that if she could just keep up with Crowther and not upset him, if she could just make it a little further until they were outside, it would all be fine. Lars Englund was waiting there at the pier—an extra precaution they had decided on, just in case Crowther had tried to make a run for it through the tunnels. The possibility that she might be with Crowther as a hostage hadn't occurred to any of them.

Suddenly, she remembered with a jolt that Hatty had told her the tunnels went all the way from the river to northwest 23rd. Suppose Crowther was taking her somewhere entirely new—in the opposite direction from the pier, to some underground prison, perhaps? Or to an exit from the tunnels in a different part of town? Despite her forced bravado, she let out an involuntary cry at the thought.

It occurred to her that this might really be the end. She was in the grip of a man who would not hesitate to hurt her if he thought it would help him to get away. And the comforting sounds of her ostensible rescuers banging on the other side of the theater door had long since receded into the distance.

Trying to run while holding on to his hostage was taxing his strength, and Crowther felt his energy flagging. She kept squirming, and it seemed like he had to yank her forward every step of the way. He considered just casting her aside so he could continue more easily. But what if that damned policeman and his friends broke through the doors and into the tunnels? Those creaky old wood doors wouldn't hold forever, and his pursuers might already be racing their way towards him, in which case it would be best to have Libby with him, in case he should need to shield himself from their bullets.

He ran along without even looking where he was going, this section of the tunnels as familiar to him as his own home. At last, he reached the stairs leading up to the outside world and relative safety.

Once he was out of the tunnels, there was no way he could be cornered . . . the girl was just a useless encumbrance now. With a savage shove, he did what he had been aching to do ever since he had first run from the stage and savagely pushed that interfering bitch to the ground, kicking her for good measure.

With a whoop, he ran up the stairs and towards the embrace of the waterfront district, knowing all he needed to do was lay low for a day or so and retrieve the money he had thoughtfully hidden away for just such an eventuality. Soon he would be on a boat to Seattle or San Francisco or maybe . . . well, to a new city, at any rate. This might be the best thing that had happened to him lately. At last, here was a chance to leave behind the misery of his life in Portland and start fresh somewhere else.

Libby groaned as she pulled herself to her feet. Looking back the way she had come, she thought she could hear voices, and hoped it was Peter, John Mayhew, and Officer Branson on the way at last. Gingerly, she made her way up the stairs after Crowther, not wanting him to hear her, but figuring she wanted to be able to tell the policeman which way he had gone when they caught up with her.

At the top of the staircase, she found herself in what seemed to be a large empty room, but as her eyes adjusted to the light, she saw it was not empty after all. Two figures grappled in the darkness, and as they made their way over to the open back door, a sliver of moonlight revealed Crowther and Englund, locked in combat.

She was sure they had not noticed her, and she watched transfixed as the fight moved outside. It looked to her like the door led to a small loading dock, and she thought she remembered Peter mentioning a stone staircase there that led down to the level of the piers. Keeping to the shadows, she made her way around the perimeter of the room and reached the door just in time to see a body tumbling down the stairs.

She gasped and rushed to the edge of the platform. Crowther's body lay ten feet below in an awkward position that instantly telegraphed that he was wounded, if not dead.

Lars Englund stood looking down at his fallen adversary. So Crowther had taken her to the correct exit after all, where Englund had been told to wait. It was good they had planned ahead, but this was not the way things were supposed to have turned out.

"That's for Helen," Englund said quietly, and it was only then that he noticed Libby standing beside him. "Miss Seale, are you all right?"

Through her tears, she was unable to form an answer. Pushing him aside, she ran down the stairs toward Crowther. A pool of red spread from beneath his head, and all she could think was don't die, not yet. She wanted to hear how Vera had died. Had it been an accident? The rest she understood, but she was no closer to understanding why the magician's assistant had been murdered than she had been the day she discovered Vera's straw suitcase.

Reaching Crowther's inert form, she squatted down beside him. His eyes registered her presence, then flickered and closed. "No!" she screamed, shaking his shoulders. "I want you to tell me about Vera! Why did you kill her? Why did Vera die?"

Crowther's eyes opened, and a look of puzzlement crossed his face. He started to speak, but was unable to. Soon enough, the light left his eyes. He lay there unmoving, his chest no longer rising and falling. Libby sat over him, sobbing. She had not cared for this man, and he had tried to kill her, but he was a human being, and now he was dead. She cursed the day she had ever gotten involved in this business.

She was so upset, she didn't even hear the voices of the other men finally arriving on the scene. When Peter held his coat around her and gently led her away from the body, all she could do was cry.

EIGHTEEN

LIBBY WANTED CROWTHER'S DEATH to be the end of it, but it wasn't. Somehow she hadn't realized how much explaining she would need to do, starting with the police surgeon's arrival at the pier and continuing all the way up to the inquest, which was a few days later and at which she was to be a principal witness.

Mrs. Pratt, of course, had demanded a full account, to say nothing of the constant interrogations she received at the theater. Nobody there knew what the future would hold. For the moment, Maynard was running the theater, but there was an uneasiness in the air. Two more dancers had quit, claiming the theater was cursed.

She had seen little of Peter since crying in his arms down by the pier. The moment Crowther's body had been shipped to the city morgue, he and John Mayhew had rushed back to the *Gazette* offices to get the story into print, barely pausing on the way to find her a hansom cab and pay the driver. The story, which appeared in Thursday's paper, had caused a sensation, despite not telling the whole story.

Crowther was presented not as a cog in the city's crime machine but as a lone thug, an opportunist who took advantage of his position as the employer of young, beautiful, and often naïve girls. While it was acknowledged that some girls were sold into bondage overseas, the paper regretted to inform its readers that, owing to the criminal's death during an attempt to flee the police, it would be impossible to pursue any of his confederates—or allies or trace any of the missing girls.

Much was made of the three deaths attributed to Crowther. Peter outdid himself with a description of the dank stretch of tunnel where Polly and Vera had met their end, and many a young lady's handkerchief was dampened with tears shed for the gallant, elderly stage doorman, who (after Peter was through eulogizing him) sounded like a candidate for sainthood.

Libby and Peter's unofficial investigation was not mentioned, and Libby's name appeared only as an innocent bystander who had been caught up in the final chase as a hostage. Neither of them wanted the notoriety or craved the limelight; that was not why they had become involved in the case. The police, on the other hand, were more than happy to claim credit for collaring such a dangerous man, and the Mayor himself was using the case as proof of his commitment to ridding the city of vice.

Both Libby and Peter had been less pleased that Crowther's links to McKennock, at least regarding Polly Pink, were not being aired. But Mayhew had rightly pointed out that since Madame Josephine wouldn't testify, there was only Peter's word to go on. Likewise, though logic indicated that Peter had been shanghaied as a result of asking questions about McKennock, logic was not support enough for a slanderous accusation against such a prominent man.

The mayor had personally congratulated Peter on helping bring Crowther to justice and had assured him that by making it appear

Crowther acted alone, Peter was merely lulling the slave traders into a false sense of security, making it easier for the police to entrap them later. But as Peter had confided to Libby, when he stopped briefly at Mrs. Pratt's Wednesday night to give Libby an advance copy of the following day's *Gazette*, there was every reason to think that the slavers' sense of security would not be false at all.

Libby had spent much of the afternoon at the local shipping offices of Pacific Mail, the company whose ships were the likeliest candidates for Crowther's successful abductions. She had started at the harbor master, hoping to identify the boat on which May might have been sent away, but every man she spoke to swore up and down that the cargo and mail ships contained nothing but legitimate cargo, and that she must be looking in the wrong place for her friend.

As she told Peter about it, tears of frustration in her eyes, he sadly added that even if she were able to name the ship she thought was the one, there would be no record of May or any other girls on the official paperwork. Furthermore, once this highly illegal "cargo" was unloaded in Japan or China—or even earlier in Vancouver, Canada, for all they knew—there would be no trail to follow.

"So, that's it then? May is just gone, and all of the men growing rich selling innocent girls will go on just as before?" Libby asked, not wanting to believe it, but knowing it was true. She sighed heavily. "Despite all that we know, Walford McKennock will probably be Portland's next mayor."

Peter didn't reply and didn't even turn to her from his place staring out the window at the dark street. She could see his face reflected in the glass, however, and he looked disgusted with the way of the world and with himself for not fighting it harder.

They were almost uncomfortable being alone with each other without the investigation to discuss, and Peter left just a few minutes after that exchange without making any excuses. He left behind a distraught Libby. She wondered if it would ever be possible for them to build a friendship without a shared goal and without any hope of a real romance.

But it was not thoughts of her relationship with Peter that filled her head now. She sat up late sewing, unable to sleep for the second night in a row, with the nagging sense they had failed. She reminded herself that their original goal had not been to wipe out the slave trade in Portland, but to discover who had killed Vera, and that they had done. Or so she tried to tell herself. But all day, little unexplained facts and unanswered questions had continued to pop into her mind.

Crowther had had an alibi for the night Vera died, and Libby could still come up with no satisfactory explanations for how he could have faked it. He had died before she could ask him about it, and she couldn't erase from her mind the last look that had crossed his face, when she finally had asked him directly about Vera's death. The confusion in his eyes as his life ebbed away, as if he didn't understand why she was asking him about Vera, had been all too genuine. At a moment like that, having already admitted to a host of other crimes, she couldn't believe he would have bothered to pretend he knew nothing about Vera's murder.

She reviewed their last conversation on the stage of the Variety over and over, but everything Crowther had said had related to Sam or the slave trade abductions. When she had started to ask him about Vera's body in the tunnel, he had just cut her off and said it had been an accident. The more she thought about it, the more convinced she became that when he said that about "an accident," he believed she was asking about Polly Pink. His answer made more sense that way. After all, Polly was the one who had died from an overdose of chloroform.

She tried to weave what she knew about Vera and Crowther into a whole cloth, but no matter how she tried, she could never make it come together. There were too many loose threads, and as soon as she started to pull on them, the whole fabric began to unravel. Finally, she admitted to herself what she had been trying to deny for two days: she didn't believe Crowther had killed Vera. Which left her exactly where she was when she had started a lifetime ago on that afternoon she had shared her suspicions with Peter over a cup of coffee and an apple fritter.

But even as she sighed, she knew that couldn't be true. They had learned so much . . . surely something they already knew could lead her to the truth. One of those loose threads was the crucial one which led to an answer. If only she knew which one.

Rain pelted against her window, and she knew that sleep would not come easily. She set aside the dress she was working on for Charlotte McKennock and reached over to her dresser, and picked up a dainty lace handkerchief that had belonged to Vera. Libby turned it over and over again in her hands, wringing the cloth as she tried to decide what, if anything, she should do now.

Peter, too, had spent these last two days with a feeling of unfinished business. Libby's comment about McKennock's ability to keep his name away from any hint of scandal kept a perpetual frown on Peter's face. It galled him at least as much as it did Libby that this powerful man would not only emerge unscathed from this web of slavery and murder, but would likely win the next mayoral election. He had to do something.

So it was with a sense of moral purpose that Peter pushed through the brass-trimmed doors of Erickson's Saloon late Thursday night. Erickson's was just opened, the latest in a long line of new bars and restaurants in the growing city which, unlike the small corner saloons of yesteryear, were larger than life. Everything about it was grand and impressive, from the wide expanse of polished oak that served as its bar to the cavernous main dining area the size of a city block. Around the entire perimeter of this room ran a balcony wreathed in curtains. As Peter looked up curiously, one of the curtains pulled aside, and a large florid-faced man stepped out, stopping to help guide his companion from the booth revealed within. So the balcony was lined with private dining booths, each complete with drapery to shield it from view! Peter suspected that given the average crowd at a Portland watering hole, these "private booths" would prove a popular innovation.

"You looking for the fundraiser?" A short man wearing a waiter's uniform approached Peter. "It's in the back, upstairs." He gestured toward the corner of the bar, where a small sign had been placed next to the staircase leading up to private banquet rooms. "Better hurry if you want dinner. They been up there for hours . . ."

Peter smiled his thanks and made his way up to the second floor, where he could hear male laughter and the clinking of glasses and cutlery. He pushed open the door in time to see Walford McKennock stepping down from the dais, ducking his head modestly as the roomful of men exploded into cheers and applause.

McKennock had sat down at the head table, but he stood again and quieted the crowd with a small wave of his hands. "Gentleman—oh, and you too, Charlie—" (Huge gales of laughter as a sheepish-looking man, who Peter presumed was part of McKennock's inner circle, reddened) "Thank you all for your obvious and very vocal support . . . Let me just say once more that together, with that sort of enthusiasm, we will bring Portland into the modern age!" He motioned for people to hold their applause. "Now lets have no more of that cheering, fellows, save some energy for eatin' some of these fine steaks!"

He sat down and demonstrated by tearing into the food in front of him. Soon all attention in the room was focused on the waiters bustling around refilling pint glasses with ale and plates with second and third helpings of the hearty food.

Peter found a seat at the end of a table of fellow newsmen, none of them from the *Gazette* but a few writers for *The Oregonian* whom he knew vaguely. They chatted companionably about the state of city politics and, more importantly, debated the question of which candidates provided the best spreads of food for their supporters. The general consensus was that Walford McKennock, whatever his politics, was no slouch in the "entertaining the press" department.

Peter sipped his beer, casting sidelong glances at McKennock's table, where the great man seemed lost in conversation. At one point, McKennock looked away from his friends to survey the room. As his eyes swept over the sea of tables, they locked on to Peter. The candidate gave an almost imperceptible nod of recognition.

Rising from his seat, McKennock deliberately wended his way through the tables of his supporters, shaking hands and sharing small talk until he stood in front of Peter, reaching out to shake his hand. Under his breath, he said, "Meet me on the balcony in five minutes."

Before Peter had a chance to react, McKennock had moved on, and after whispering something to the man he called Charlie, he ducked out a side doorway. A few minutes later, Peter followed and found himself on the far end of the balcony he had admired earlier from below. The row of perfectly drawn burgundy velvet curtains was broken by an opening, and he made his way to that booth. Walford McKennock motioned him to sit down, then carefully drew the drapes shut before turning to regard the reporter. Between them, the highly polished dark wood table glowed by the light of a single oil lamp.

"Mr. Eberle," he said and paused. Peter's mind was racing, but he willed himself to wait silently for the man to continue. "I understand you had a run in with some thugs. I'm very glad to see you looking so well."

"Thank you," replied Peter, wondering what the man's game was. "A risk of the trade, I suppose." He stopped, trying to figure out the best way to broach the subject of McKennock's criminal connections.

"I wonder what they hoped to accomplish by going after me, a simple newspaper reporter. Though I did have this crazy idea it might have had some connection to the goings-on at the Portland Variety . . ."

It was clear that McKennock knew what Peter was talking about, but he was steering clear of making any statement to confirm that knowledge. The older man regarded Peter expectantly, as if daring him to make a direct accusation. Unfortunately, Peter had no real proof to throw at him, only a lot of circumstantial evidence that McKennock had been league with Arvide Crowther. Would it be enough to convince McKennock to drop out of the race for mayor?

He imagined Libby sitting beside him in the booth as he drew a deep breath and looked McKennock square in the eyes. "What a shame for you that your business partner, excuse me . . . your tenant . . . should have turned out to be involved in such nasty crimes. People might start to talk. Perhaps it would be unwise for you to continue your bid for office."

What came next was completely unexpected. McKennock laughed, a deep hearty chuckle that spoke volumes about the level of risk he felt Peter posed. "Ah, Mr. Eberle, I'll give you this. You're no coward." He leaned in conspiratorially. "Between you and me, and I trust this is off the record . . ." Peter nodded. " . . . I have already decided to withdraw from the mayoral race. I'm simply waiting for a convenient time to make an announcement to that effect."

Peter tried to hide his shock. "Indeed? Well, sir . . . I . . ." He forced his voice to return to its normal low register. "I think that's a wise decision. It would hardly have done your reputation good if it had been whispered that Portland's Businessman of the Year trafficked in prostitution and slave labor on the side . . ."

By the flickering light, Peter saw McKennock's face harden, and the smile on his face was replaced with a steely determined look. Sitting completely still, he gave the impression of a coiled spring about to snap, and he cut Peter off mid-sentence.

"Let me tell you something, Mr. Eberle . . ." He made Peter's name an epithet. "The fact is, Portland today is a second-rate city. It's growing with every passing month, but if you're smart, you'll know that it's not lumber and wheat alone that will bring us into the twentieth century. There's a price for economic growth, and sometimes it's an ugly price, but I guarantee this: this city needs someone like me at the helm to help it grow into the next century."

As much as he wanted to emulate the older man's cool demeanor, Peter couldn't contain himself. "Help Portland grow? You call luring innocent young girls into a life of slavery helpful? Because of this 'ugly price' as you call it, at least two women are dead, not to mention an innocent man who never harmed anyone. And you have the audacity to sit here and tell me this is some sort of economic necessity?"

McKennock's dark eyes shone angrily, but his voice was steady. "You can't hold me responsible for the fact that there's a demand for men to work on ships or for women to work as call girls, for that matter. And if I'm not mistaken, Mr. Eberle, you have been known to patronize some of our town's finer 'gentlemen's establishments' yourself." Peter felt his face redden. "It's certainly unfortunate that matters of late have not always gone according to plan. Perhaps I made the mistake of trusting certain parties to discharge their duties in a professional manner when they were not always up to the task. I won't deny that, at this point, it makes tactical sense for me to remove myself from the mayoral race, but if you think that will rid Portland of crime, you're a far stupider man than I gave you credit for."

With that, McKennock pushed himself up from the table. With a tug on the curtain, he was gone. From far away, Peter heard the tinkling of female laughter, and some men in the barroom below started singing a drinking song off key. He sat there, staring at the small lamp and trying to decide if he had scored any sort of victory at all. At least he would have the pleasure of telling Libby that McKennock would not be the next mayor.

The inquest had been short, but surprisingly well-attended. Besides the police surgeon and Officer Branson, the only witnesses were Lars Englund and Libby. It hadn't really occurred to Libby, but since there would be no criminal charges against Crowther, owing to his untimely death, no evidence was entered relating to his purported crimes. The only issue to be settled was how he met his death, and without retiring to deliberate, the judge declared that Crowther had met his end accidentally and as a result of his own actions. Therefore, there would be no charges brought against Englund. The courtroom emptied swiftly following the verdict, all the spectators pouring out into the courthouse's marble lobby.

There were two people in the crowd Libby didn't want to see, but she knew seeing both of them was unavoidable. She decided to speak to Lars Englund first, since she figured he would be the easier of the two.

"Miss Seale!" There was a broad smile on Englund's face as he caught sight of her coming towards him through the crowd. His wife Anna was standing next to him, still looking long-suffering and obviously wanting to get back to the boardinghouse as soon as possible. She gave Libby only the barest hint of a polite nod, and her sliver of a smile couldn't compare with her husband's grin. "That went well, I thought."

Libby was unsure how to answer him. Despite her testimony, she knew in her heart that Crowther hadn't "accidentally" fallen down that flight of steps, and however much she felt he had deserved to die, she found Englund's ebullience at this time and place in poor taste. "Yes, I suppose." She purposely kept her voice somber. "But it wasn't pleasant, having to relive that night . . . and I can't help feeling a little sad that this was an inquest, rather than the first day of a criminal trial."

He looked at her strangely, unable to figure out why she didn't share his good mood. "If there was ever a man who deserved to die . . ."

She wondered how he would respond if she told him that he had killed the wrong man . . . not an innocent man, to be sure, but not the murderer of his childhood friend either. She took the easy path and decided not to find out. "His death doesn't heal the past, Mr. Englund."

Anna Englund spoke up, "Lars, we really must be getting back to the house." Her tone left no room for disagreement on his part.

"Well, then, Miss Seale, I guess this is—" He stopped. "You can stop by the house any time, if you'd like to talk." He looked so hurt at what he took to be Libby's coldness, for a moment, she pitied him. She knew that, from his perspective, he had for once in his life done something heroic, and he wanted to revel in it. His wife was clearly not a sympathetic listener on the topic, especially when the underlying issue was his loyalty to Vera. She felt bad that she couldn't be the friendly ear he needed, but under the circumstances, that was impossible.

"Goodbye, Mr. Englund, Mrs. Englund."

They started to turn away, but at the last moment Libby's sympathy got the better of her. "Wait, Mr. Englund . . ." she gave him a small but genuine smile, "We all owe you great thanks. Your actions the other night probably saved many a young woman from a horrible fate. You should be proud."

A smile lit up his eyes once more, but instead of answering her praise, he merely nodded and continued on his way. Libby stared at the Englunds' retreating backs until they vanished from sight, then turned to seek out the other person she needed to speak to.

Elise Crowther stood pale but ramrod straight beside her housekeeper Berthe in a small knot of people. Her companions were all jabbering away at her, but she herself was saying very little, only murmuring a reply when absolutely necessary. Libby approached her from behind and gingerly tapped her on the shoulder.

"Mrs. Crowther? I'm Libby Seale . . ." She knew it was unnecessary to introduce herself, since she had stated her name on the stand before giving her testimony. As she had done so, she caught sight of Mrs. Crowther in the front row, looking shocked. Elise Crowther turned and looked at her now without emotion. "I . . . wanted to say I'm sorry. Sorry for your loss and . . . I just wanted to apologize for pretending to be someone else when I came to your house a few weeks ago. I didn't like having to lie to you, but . . ." Libby tried to ignore Berthe's eyes boring holes into her skull, but they were making it difficult for her to compose her thoughts. "I don't want you to think it was a trap . . . that I was trying to set your husband up for . . ."

Mrs. Crowther put Libby out of her misery. "Miss Seale, I'm sure you did what you thought proper at the time. And if you had a hand in bringing my husband to justice, I believe you are to be congratulated, not censured. I don't approve of lying, true, but it is a minor sin compared with the sins of which I am now told my husband was guilty." She cast her eyes skyward. "Perhaps it is for being blind to those sins happening right under my nose that I have been . . ." she amended, " . . . *am being* punished."

"Mrs. Crowther!" Berthe began to remonstrate her employer, but Elise Crowther was not be stopped.

"All that you saw, Miss Seale—the fine house, the expensive furnishings—were purchased with the proceeds of sin. It was a home built with blood money, and I allowed my babies to be brought there, to be raised there, to sicken, and so die there." Her eyes seemed to shift to some place far away, as if she was seeing the row of graves: three small ones for her dead babies and now a new one for her disgraced husband.

Libby thought the conversation was over, but after a few seconds Mrs. Crowther drew herself up and refocused on Libby. "I am going back to my people in Nebraska. I should let you know that I am closing the theater. I am sorry; this means that you will be out of a job."

Libby was upset, not so much for herself—for she had already wondered whether she could stay on at the Variety now in any case—but for all the dancers, stagehands, and other employees who would be hard pressed to find work if the theater closed. "Do you mean you are selling it? Perhaps a new owner will keep it open under a new name."

"No, I have spoken to Bishop Brouillet, and the building is being donated to the Archdiocese in the hope that, perhaps in some small way, that can redeem it in the eyes of the Lord." She saw Libby's face fall and added evenly, "I'm sorry, Miss Seale."

There was a strange peace about Mrs. Crowther now, thought Libby. Almost as if, in facing this final horror, she had finally found some sort of meaning in her suffering, some sort of purpose in her life. Libby tried to be glad for her, but instead found that Elise Crowther's newfound strength just made her less sympathetic. Still, she was deserving of pity, if nothing else. "Once again," Libby said formally, "please accept my condolences. And may you have a peaceful journey back to Nebraska."

"Thank you. And I wish you peace as well." Mrs. Crowther allowed Berthe to lead her through the crowd and out into the misty rain.

"What a cold woman," a voice over her shoulder said, echoing Libby's own thoughts, "Her husband hasn't been dead three days, and all she can do is spout platitudes about sin and redemption. I wanted to feel sorry for her, but . . ."

Libby turned to find Peter gazing quizzically down at her. "Peter, you shouldn't say things like that." Even if we're both thinking it, she added silently. "Her life hasn't been easy."

"But you know it's the truth. Other people have suffered too—and at the hands of *her* husband. Somehow she has managed to turn all of their suffering into a mere sideshow in the great pageant of her own testing by God."

Despite her frown, Peter thought, Libby looked very fetching today. She was wearing something dark green, which made her eyes look almost hazel. Their glow reminded him what he wanted to talk to her about. He tried to find a way to raise a new topic. "Do you think she ever really loved her husband?"

Libby didn't reply immediately, apparently thinking over the question seriously. "I'm sure at the beginning, she thought she did. She couldn't have known how their life together would turn out. I think it's very possible to marry someone and not know he's a monster." It was not the sort of a response Peter had wanted, and he was stymied as to how to continue.

For her part, Libby hoped he would drop the subject of Mrs. Crowther. She, too, had other things she wanted to discuss with him today and took advantage of his silence to broach the subject on her mind. "Peter, I have been thinking and . . ." She looked around to make sure they couldn't be overheard, but the lobby had all but emptied. " . . . I don't believe Crowther murdered Vera."

He stared at her incredulously, his own train of thought broken. She rushed on, "I know he abducted Polly and May and Lord knows who else, and I know he killed Sam, but . . ."

Peter found his voice, "So you believe there are two murderers at one small theater in Portland? Working independently? Or don't you believe Crowther was telling the truth when he said he was the only one involved in the abductions?"

"No . . . I mean, yes, I believed him, but . . . Oh, I don't know." In the light of day, her belief that Crowther hadn't murdered Vera seemed more far-fetched. "He never confessed to killing Vera, just Sam and the abductions, and . . . Just because he was the only white slaver doesn't mean he killed Vera, too. Maybe her death had nothing to do with the white slave trade."

"Then why did she have Polly Pink's wedding band?" Peter shot back.

"The ring! I didn't even think of that last night." She realized excitedly that it was one piece of evidence they could still follow up on. "But it doesn't point to Crowther."

"It doesn't exactly point away from him either. We just don't know what it means, and we probably never will now."

"But that's exactly it, Peter," Libby was so frustrated that this time Peter didn't seem to see what was so obvious to her. "We've never uncovered any sort of evidence linking Crowther and Vera. Crowther had an alibi for the night of her death, and right before he died, when I asked him why he killed her, he just looked at me, puzzled."

Peter took Libby by the arm, gently propelled her to a bench, and sat her down. "The man was dying. You don't know whether he was even able to understand the question by that point. I know we don't know why Vera died, but Crowther must have had some reason for killing her which will remain unknown. That's not easy to accept, but you have to accept it."

"Even if it means Vera's real murderer is walking free?"

"Do you really believe that?" Peter shook his head. "Libby, I know this isn't how we wanted this to end, but it's over. You're the smartest woman I've ever met, but sometimes you're so determined to know everything that you can't face the fact that some things are unknowable."

Despite her displeasure with him, Libby noticed the compliment and had to try to hide her smile. "Some things, yes . . . but not this."

Peter stared at her. She was so determined. He had the oddest feeling that the last few weeks had all been a dream, and this was still their first real conversation, the night at the coffeehouse when she had first corralled him into helping her find her friend's killer. Why couldn't she face the obvious truth, despite the unanswered questions? Could this be about him? Could she be afraid that without their shared investigation, he would desert her? And she had just found out she was going to lose her job, too! It was no wonder if she was anxious about the future.

He stopped feeling annoyed and was instead filled with tenderness. "My dear Miss Seale," he began in his best front parlor manner, "I want you to know that meeting you and working side-by-side with you has been the best thing to happen to me since I came to Portland. If you're afraid that—"

"I'm not afraid," she cut in, "I'm disappointed in you. And if you won't help me find out who really murdered Vera, then I'll just have to continue alone." Without further ado, she got up and walked out of the courthouse into the rain.

Peter couldn't fathom what had just happened. What had gotten into Libby today? One minute they were sharing their contempt for Elise Crowther, then they were arguing over a crackpot new theory, and the next moment, she had walked out on him. He didn't think he would ever understand Libby Seale, so perhaps it was just as well she had gone without hearing him out. To think he had come today prepared to ask her to be his wife.

NINETEEN

It had taken until almost ten the previous evening to finish the third, and unplanned for, Charlotte McKennock gown. Libby didn't want to think how late she might have had to work if she hadn't gone straight home from the inquest, skipping work at the theater entirely. She knew Hatty would probably have some sharp words on the subject of her absence, but that didn't seem important since she no longer had to worry about keeping her job. Best of all, keeping her hands busy all day had made it easier to avoid thinking about Peter and about the fact that she was now on her own as far as uncovering the truth about Vera's death.

The McKennock house was bustling when she arrived in the middle of the morning. Extra servants had been hired for the evening's wedding reception, and many of them were busy laying out tables with starched white linen and gleaming silver or decorating every available surface with masses of hothouse flowers. Upstairs in Charlotte's suite, it was a little more peaceful, though there was still excitement in the air. The hairdresser was just finishing with Charlotte when

Libby staggered through the doorway with the three large dress boxes. While the final touches were made to the elaborate coiffure, one of the two maids hovering in the room helped Libby lay out the finished dresses on the divan.

The smile on Charlotte's plain face when she came over to examine the gowns made all the late nights worthwhile. "Oh, Miss Seale, they're so lovely! But," a shadow crossed her face, "you made both the ivory and the bronze . . . you were only supposed to make one. I don't know if Father will—"

Libby laughed to dispel the sudden tension in the room and said soothingly, "Charlotte, it was your father's idea. He told me to make the third dress as an extra wedding present for you." The worry disappeared from Charlotte's face, and she went back to scrutinizing the new additions to her wardrobe. "Since we had only discussed two dress patterns I took the liberty of creating a new design which I think will suit you."

"Miss Seale, thank you." Charlotte's eyes transmitted her gratitude eloquently. "Do you think . . . Could I try one on now?"

One of the maids stepped forward, "Miss, I don't think it would be wise. It's almost time to get into your wedding gown." Charlotte's face fell.

Libby briskly humped in, "Don't be silly. The wedding doesn't begin for hours yet. Here, try on the bronze one, Miss McKennock . . . Oh, it won't be Miss McKennock for much longer, will it?" Charlotte giggled delightedly with Libby, took the proffered dress, and disappeared behind a dressing screen with the disapproving maid.

In less than three minutes she reappeared, looking lovelier than Libby had ever seen her. Libby had created a simple, almost severe gown, with a gently draped skirt and full train of shimmering mousseline over a base of dark brown raw silk. The gown's only extravagance, which made it seem youthful instead of matronly, was a cloud of sheer brown tulle gathered about the shoulders and across the bosom. The color made Charlotte's eyes shine, and the narrow skirt and wide square neckline helped make her figure come across as solidly graceful rather than heavy.

Charlotte gazed at herself in the mirror rapturously. "Oh, Miss Seale. I think it's the prettiest dress I've ever seen. No . . . pretty isn't the word for it . . . it's lovely. I look almost . . . sophisticated."

"You look beautiful, Miss McKennock."

"Please . . . will you call me Charlotte? I would like that very much." She spoke hesitantly, "And may I call you Libby?" Libby smiled in agreement. "Gerald will be so pleased, I know. The dress will be perfect if we move down to San Francisco. They're so much fancier down there, and I want to be a credit to him."

"San Francisco?"

"Yes, we . . . well . . ." Charlotte motioned uncertainly to the two maids, indicating they should leave the room. "I'm not supposed to say anything, but now that we're real friends . . . if you promise not to tell anyone?"

"You may depend on my discretion, Charlotte."

Charlotte smiled to hear her Christian name on Libby's lips, then leaned her head forward in a secret-telling pose. "My father is dropping out of the mayoral race."

Libby had to work hard to keep her jaw from dropping. She wondered if Peter knew about this. Could it possibly have anything to do with Crowther's recent death and the revelations about the slave trade at the Variety? She wanted to rush off right away to tell Peter and then remembered that yesterday, he hadn't wanted to have anything further to do with the investigation. She realized Charlotte was still talking.

". . . and because of all his friends and contacts there, Gerald is the ideal man to head the new branch office. Or so Father feels. Besides,

San Francisco is closer to where Gerald's family lives, so he'll be glad to be down there again."

"Yes, of course," Libby said mechanically, only half listening.

There was a polite knock on the door before one of the maids came in, "Would you like to change out of the evening gown now, Miss, and into your wedding dress?" Her tone made it more an order than a question.

Perhaps it was the confidence gained by having Libby by her side, or perhaps Charlotte was actually beginning to develop some self-confidence, but she replied evenly, in a fair attempt at an imperious tone, "No, thank you, Maggie. Miss Seale and I are not through talking. I will ring for you when I am ready." She turned to Libby and giggled, "I've been wanting to say that to her all day! Everybody is pushing me and prodding me today, ordering me about and telling me where to stand and what to do. Well, it's my wedding day. I think I should get to do what I want to do."

"Of course, you should." Libby was pleased that Charlotte was showing some spirit, but she wondered how long this conversation would go on. She glanced at gilt clock on the mantelpiece. It showed the hour to be close to noon, and she really needed to be getting to the theater. "But it is getting late. Perhaps you should get dressed. The service begins at two, doesn't it?"

"No, three o'clock. But they can't start without me, can they?" Libby had never seen Charlotte so giddy or so talkative. She rose from beside Libby and regarded herself in the full-length pier glass. "I don't want to change out of this dress yet. You know, I think it's the nicest dress I've had since . . . I feel like I did when I was a little girl, and Mrs. Matthews made up all my dresses. She always tailored them just for me, and they made me feel so pretty and special." Charlotte suddenly grew wistful. "I know it's silly, but I still miss her sometimes. And today especially."

"Mrs. Matthews was the seamstress you told me about, the one who almost married your father?" A horrible suspicion was forming in Libby's mind.

"Yes." Charlotte paused. "How wonderful it would be if she were here. Then I would have someone like a mother to help me get ready for the wedding and to hold my hand as we rode to the church. I remember Hatty so much more clearly than I do my own mother, since she died when I was such a little girl. I suppose that's why I'm thinking about her." She turned to Libby, who had frozen at the mention of the name Hatty. "You don't think that's wrong of me, to be thinking of Hatty rather than my real mother?"

"No, no . . . not at all." Libby managed to get out. "Miss McK . . . Charlotte, I'm afraid I really must go now."

"I was hoping you could ride with me to the chapel," Charlotte implored, then blushed and looked embarrassed. "I'm sorry I can't invite you to the reception, since Father handled all of the arrangements, but . . ." Libby hadn't expected to be invited to the grand ball being held for Gerald and Charlotte, so she wasn't offended, and she was touched by the shy girl's plea. "I have to go right now, Charlotte, but I will try to be there at the church . . . I can't promise. You said the service is at three? And . . . I don't even know which church."

Charlotte reached for a thick, cream-colored card on her desk and handed it to Libby, who was struggling quickly into her coat. "All of the information is on the invitation. Oh, please do try to be there!"

Libby pocketed the invitation, reiterating her promise to try. Flying down the stairs and out into the street, where solid sheets of rain had begun to fall. She ran for the streetcar pulling up to the corner that would take her to the theater—and to Hatty.

Libby was soaking wet by the time she got to the theater, her coat and hat having offered scant protection against the torrential downpour outside. As she clambered through the unmanned stage door, Libby remembered with a pang the many happy times she had spent at this job talking to Hatty as they shared the duties of a busy theater, before everything had gotten so violent and complicated. Hatty and Walford McKennock? What did it mean? Was this the final connection she needed to piece together the puzzle of Vera's death?

When she entered the costume shop, Hatty barely looked up at her before continuing with her work, packing up all the sewing notions and threads into several large boxes. As she sorted through a rainbow of spools, she spoke without looking at Libby. "I could have used your help yesterday packing up the dance costumes."

"I'm . . . I'm sorry, Hatty . . ." Libby was momentarily thrown by Hatty's stern demeanor. This wasn't how she had imagined starting this conversation. "You did get my note that I wouldn't be in?" She sloughed off her coat and almost unconsciously began emptying out the far row of cubbyholes.

"I did get your note, Libby, but I don't think you realized what a difficult day it would be for us all when the announcement was made that the Variety would be closing immediately." Hatty's voice softened, and she turned to face Libby. "I know this hasn't been the easiest job for you. But life is never easy, is it? If only you had confided in me more about your suspicions, about your other activities at the theater, perhaps . . . Oh, well, I guess it doesn't matter anymore. I'm pleased you're here now." Hatty smiled.

"Hatty . . . did you know what Crowther was doing?" Libby was shocked to hear these words coming out of her mouth. This wasn't at all what she had intended to ask Hatty.

Hatty seemed genuinely shocked. "Of course not!" she sputtered, setting down an armload of sewing supplies. "Of course, I knew some of the girls disappeared over the years. We all knew that. But I would never have continued to work here if I had known that Mr. Crowther was the man responsible for it. How can you ask such a thing, Libby?"

Despite Hatty's obvious discomfort, Libby felt compelled to continue. "You told me several weeks ago that I should beware of Walford McKennock. I believe you called him 'a ruthless man' and—" Undecided as to how to continue, she blurted out, "Hatty, Charlotte McKennock told me the whole story about how Walford wanted to marry you, and you jilted him, and . . ."

Hatty's eyes blazed. "That's what she told you?" Her voice rose. "That foolish girl! That's not what happened at all." As if suddenly realizing that her impassioned speech might be heard by someone in the hall, Hatty lowered her voice as she went on. "Charlotte was a sweet child, but she was just a child, Libby. This was fourteen, no, fifteen years ago, after all. But I admit, I was concerned when you told me you were doing some piece work for the McKennocks."

"Concerned because of Walford's ruthlessness or concerned that Charlotte would reveal your secret to me? Why didn't you tell me that you knew him personally? Why rely on veiled insinuations about his character?"

Hatty didn't meet Libby's eyes. "I didn't want to have to tell you— one relives things in the telling of them. And I've always believed that when your life takes an unfortunate turn, it's best to set it aside and move on. My problems with Walford McKennock all happened so long ago, I didn't see what good could possibly come of reopening that can of worms."

Libby looked up intently. "Hatty, what happened all those years ago?"

"What possible purpose could revealing it serve now?"

When Libby didn't answer, Hatty sat down beside her and sighed again. "Perhaps I should have told you all this earlier, although I can't for the life of me imagine how it would have helped you to know." She paused and stared off into space, collecting her thoughts. "I was a young widow at that time . . . this was fourteen or fifteen years ago, and Ralph Matthews, the man I had come to this country for, had been gone for less than a year. I didn't know what to do. I didn't see how I could go back to my mother after leaving as I did. She had never understood how I could marry a 'white devil,' as she called him, how I could change even my given name for him." Hatty looked at Libby, "You realize, of course, that Hatty is not the name I was born with. But my darling Ralph . . . was a gentle man, a kind man, but I'm afraid he was never able to pronounce my real name properly. So he called me Hatty, after someone back home in England of whom he said I reminded him."

Hatty paused, as if realizing she was losing the thread of her story. "In any case, I loved that man more than life, but he left me with very little. He had never really adjusted, I think, to being in America, to no longer being a soldier. Certainly, he was not a success here. I took in sewing to help make ends meet even when he was alive, and so I had a few friends among the seamstresses in Portland who helped me find odd jobs in the year after he died, mostly making clothes for the children of some of Portland's wealthier families. That's how I came to work for Mr. McKennock, who was looking for someone to not only sew clothing for his children but to watch them in the afternoons when the governess had a day off. I ended up becoming quite close to the entire family . . . this was only a few years after their mother had died. Perhaps our grief brought us all closer together.

"Poor Charlotte, she was a quiet slip of a thing. She must have been, oh, eight or nine years old, but not at all adventurous like her brother. No, Charlotte was happiest spending the day sitting in the nursery playing quietly with her dolls. She wouldn't even talk to anyone sometimes, just looked up at you with those big eyes wide with fear. I know Walford worried about her. She never got any fresh air and would just hide away in her room for weeks at a time."

Libby could well imagine that silent girl growing up into the Charlotte McKennock she had come to know over these last few weeks. "What about Will?"

"Oh, Will could take care of himself. He missed his mama, of course, what boy wouldn't? But it was Charlotte who took it the hardest. She confessed to me one day in tears that she had asked her mama for a little brother or sister. She thought that because she had wished so hard for a new baby, it was her fault that her Mama died trying." Hatty shook her head wonderingly, and her voice was tinged with sadness. "All that time, she thought it was her fault."

Libby waited as Hatty composed herself. After several moments, she gently urged the woman to continue. "Tell me about Walford."

Hatty smiled. "At first, I thought he was the kindest man. His sadness made him gentle, and he was so considerate around the children and around me. He was still mourning for his lost wife, and he doted on those children . . . it was a sight to see him laughing and playing with them, trying to keep the household full of good cheer. Oh, Libby, he had me sew lovely new clothes for them. He spared no expense: dresses in the latest fashion for little Charlotte, and Will must have been the best turned-out little boy this side of the Rockies . . . at least until he went out to play in the mud."

She smiled at a memory, then her voice grew cold. "All that charm and friendliness . . . I suppose I was naive. There I was, far older than you are now, I suppose, and I thought I knew all there was to know about the world, but it hadn't even occurred to me that perhaps this man had other needs he was hoping I could fulfill." She stopped, clearly not liking to go on.

Libby tried to picture Hatty as a young innocent, but the Hatty of today was so very competent and experienced that the picture wouldn't form in her mind. "Something happened," Libby prompted.

"Of course," said Hatty crisply. "He invited me to stay late and dine with him one evening after the children were both in bed. And he made certain proposals to me of an indelicate nature, which I won't elaborate upon. I believe he assumed, because I had married a white man, that I was some sort of concubine, to be sold to the highest bidder." She looked angry, even all these years later. "I was offended and told him so, in so many words. He got very angry—he was more than a little drunk by that time, I think—and lurched rather threateningly toward me. And so I fled." She gazed into Libby's eyes, "I like to think he would not actually have attacked me, but at that moment, I wasn't sure. But it's what happened next that made me warn you against him, Libby, not that night in the dining room. If it had just been a drunken pass, I might have been able to forgive it as the misjudgment of a lonely and frustrated man."

Before Hatty could go on, there was a knock at the door, and Jack poked his head in. "I just wanted to make sure the packing was going smoothly, ladies. Shall I send one of my crew in here to help crate up the sewing machines?"

At that point, Libby would have been happy to carry the sewing machines on her back for a mile just to hear the rest of Hatty's tale. She practically said as much in her haste to assure Jack that no, she and Hatty had matters well under their control, but thanks ever so much for the kind offer. As the door swung shut behind him, she pounced on Hatty, desperate for her to continue. "What did Mr. McKennock do?" she asked, breathlessly.

Hatty shook her head sadly. "I came to the house later that week to drop off the last of my work and say a proper goodbye to the children.

He had given instructions to the staff not to let me in at all. There was nothing I could do, but I felt horrible, knowing that dear little girl would think I abandoned her without an explanation . . ." Her voice broke for a moment, and Libby realized how painful this was for Hatty. She wasn't sure what she had expected Hatty to reveal, but she hadn't been prepared for this sorrow.

"Go on," she said gently, laying her hand on Hatty's arm. After a moment, the older woman resumed her narrative.

She leaned in, and the quiet anger in her in her voice was as fresh as if this had all happened yesterday. "Walford saw to it that none of the families for whom I had been making play clothes would hire me after that. I was nearly destitute. You've seen how people in this city can be about the Chinese—and to them it makes no difference Chinese or half-Chinese. If I had not found a place at the theater, one of the few places with little or no reputation to lose by hiring a Chinese seamstress, I don't know how I would have survived."

Hatty sat looking at her hands folded in her lap, while Libby waited for her to continue. Surely there had to be more to the story. Everything Hatty had said made sense and fit with what she knew, but no matter how she looked at it, Libby couldn't imagine how it could have anything to do with Vera Carabella.

"Did you ever see him again? McKennock, I mean?" Libby asked.

With a sigh, Hatty got up and returned to her packing. "My friend Elise, who had recommended me to McKennock in the first place, was still one of the parlor maids. She told me that Charlotte was crying herself to sleep every night, screaming for me and for her father, who had gone East on an extended business trip. I went by the McKennock house again to try and see the little girl, but even weeks later, the staff still said they were under orders not to admit me. So I swallowed my pride and went to see Walford at his office when he returned to Portland. He wouldn't see me either. He just sent out a note with his secretary saying that I had obviously found his company uncongenial once, and nobody gets a second chance with Walford McKennock.

"Now you see why I called him ruthless and cold. He can be very charming when he wants to be, but when he doesn't get his way with someone, he'll stop at nothing to exact vengeance on them. He doesn't seem to care who else gets hurt in the process. When I think of the trauma he put his own daughter through!"

"Thank you for telling me, Hatty." Libby considered the possibility that there was more to the story, but for the life of her, she couldn't figure out what. Hatty had seemed genuinely upset as she told her tale, and there was nothing to do but accept it at face value and move on.

Hatty became her no-nonsense self once more, signaling the end of her confession. "Now, Libby, help me get this sewing table into the crate . . ."

While they finished packing the remaining contents of the costume shop, Libby was warm enough, but as soon as they finished, she began shivering and realized it was freezing in the theater. She slipped on her coat and went in search of Jack to ask why the boiler was off, but as she traversed the forlorn theater, she saw she wasn't the only one feeling the cold. In the cavernous scenery shop, she saw several of the stagehands wearing their coats and gloves as they pulled apart large set pieces and dismantled canvas flats. She deduced that Mrs. Crowther had decided heating the building was an extravagance now that it was no longer a working theater.

A sense of sadness and weariness overcame her, which was derived only partly from the exertions of packing. She had been so sure her conversation with Hatty would lead to the solution to the murder, but it had ended in another dead end. At least she could bring Charlotte some happiness by telling her that Hatty had not abandoned her by choice. Perhaps she could even bring the two women together, as long Walford wasn't told about the meeting.

She paused by the stage door and gazed out at he rain. What an awful day for a wedding, she thought, hoping Charlotte had made it to the church without becoming drenched en route. That reminded her of her promise to Charlotte. Her watch told her it was only quarter to three, her coat couldn't get much wetter if she ventured out into the rain again, and even Hatty couldn't object because the packing was completed. She pulled out the invitation Charlotte had given her from the pocket of her coat to check the address of the church.

H. Walford McKennock invites you share in his joy
as his daughter Charlotte Amelia
is joined in bonds of holy matrimony with
Mr. Fitzgerald Williams
Saturday the 19th of February,
St. James Church . . .

Libby stared at the invitation in her hand, disbelieving her eyes. Dimly, she recalled his melancholy-tinged voice saying, ". . . little Mary Fitzgerald of County Kerry, later my mother . . ." Of course! She should have made the connection to his real first name right away. Even as she struggled to make sense of this new piece of information, her mind raced, filling in gaps. Suddenly, things which had seemed incidental in the course of the investigation assumed a new importance. She saw for the first time a full and startlingly clear picture not only of who killed Vera, but why she had died.

She ran out the door without pausing to button her coat, wondering if she would be too late to stop the wedding.

TWENTY

THE ELABORATE STONE FAÇADE of St. James Cathedral towered over the tree-lined block, but Libby didn't notice its architectural beauty as she rushed through the front doors of the church. Inside, the pews were filled with Portland's most worthy citizens, all turned out in their finest clothes, but she only gave the chamber a cursory glance before accosting an usher standing at the head of the center aisle.

"I'm looking for the groom," she gasped. Numerous heads in the rear rows turned to see if something interesting was happening, and Libby lowered her voice to repeat her request more politely. "That is, I was hoping you could direct me to Mr. Williams."

If the usher found anything strange about a disheveled, soaking wet woman asking for the man of the moment, he gave no sign of it. "Try down that way, Madam," he said, pointing along the far aisle and down in front. "There are several small rooms in the back where the family usually waits before the ceremony."

"Thank you," said Libby over her shoulder, as she practically ran past the statues of saints under stained glass windows, looking frantically for some sign of Gerald. To the left of an ornate pipe organ, a dark wooden door stood slightly ajar, and with no time to think of what she was going to say, she pushed it open.

Gerald Williams stood by a small cross-hatched window, looking uncomfortable. Beside him, another man in a dark suit was straightening Gerald's tie and murmuring something to him. Both men looked up in surprise at her entrance, and the stranger asked, "Is it time to begin?"

Ignoring the question, Libby focused her gaze on Gerald. He met her eyes, and it was obvious without a word that he knew why she was there. After a moment, she spoke. "I need to speak with you about your wife." She emphasized the final word.

The other man in the suit laughed. "Well there, Miss, my cousin isn't a married man yet! Are you one of Miss McKennock's bridesmaids?" He stopped, suddenly appearing to notice she was not dressed in a formal gown, and looked at his cousin with confusion on his broad features.

Gerald spoke for the first time. "Dominic, would you please give us a moment alone?" The confused look never quite leaving his face, the cousin headed for the door. "It's all right. This will just be a few moments . . . please don't let anyone disturb us." Gerald closed the door behind his cousin and slid the bolt into place before turning to face Libby. "How did you know?" he asked.

"I found your wedding ring. I found it quite a while ago, but it was only when I saw your name on the invitation that I realized what the inscription meant: F. W. and H. M. Eternal Love 1893 . . . Fitzgerald Williams and Helen Morell!" She stood facing him, daring him to disagree, but instead he looked away, as if trying to remember something. Finally he spoke.

"Ah, the ring. I couldn't find it that night, but I had hoped that if I couldn't, no one else would either." He looked at her, "Where . . . ?"

"It was in a hidden compartment in her jewelry box, along with her first wedding ring."

He looked surprised and then gave the slightest hint of a shrug. "I didn't even know she had been married before. I suppose there was a lot I didn't know about her. But when I met her, I thought . . . of course, she was beautiful, but it was more than that. She was so . . ." he searched for a moment. "Adoring. When she looked at me, I felt like the most important man in the world. And at the time, I needed that." He stopped again, lost in thought.

Libby filled in the details as she put together the story in her mind. "Walford had just turned down your proposal to Charlotte. You must have thought nothing in Portland would work out for you, so you went home to San Francisco. Charlotte never knew where it was you had gone."

"I thought it was best that way. I never dreamed Walford would change his mind and come looking for me, and by then . . ." He trailed off.

Libby finished his sentence. "You had already married Vera." She regarded him quizzically. "When I spoke to Carlo, he told me Vera had met someone in San Francisco . . . but even he never guessed she had gotten married. Why didn't she tell him?"

"She was going to tell him, of course. But when McKennock sent for me, well, Helen and I had only been married two days. To be honest, I knew even then that I had made a mistake. Oh, Helen was wonderful, but I think she expected too much of me."

"What I can't figure out is . . . what did you tell her when you left to come back to Portland? She can't have sent you back here to marry Charlotte!"

"Of course not!" He seemed shocked at the thought. "I didn't know yet that that was why I was being summoned. I thought Walford had simply reconsidered our disagreement and was offering me my job back. So, naturally, I returned here, and Helen agreed she would stay with Carlo and the act for the time being. After all, we knew we would be reunited soon enough when they got up here to play at the Portland Variety." He leaned in to Libby, beseeching her to understand. "Once I got up here, Walford told me what he expected of me, and he made it clear that everything was contingent upon my marrying his daughter. I didn't know what to do! I intended to tell him I was already married, but somehow it was easier to say I was only engaged to a woman in San Francisco, and then easier still to tell him I would break it off and marry Charlotte after all. You must understand, Miss Seale, he was offering me the life I had always dreamed of—a prestigious job, an entrance into society . . ." He looked at her, embarrassed. "I must sound terribly shallow to you. Try to understand how much this all meant to someone like me. You don't know how it was when I was growing up."

She almost felt sorry for him, then remembered why she was there. "No one at the theater even suspected! She never told anyone she was married, even after she got here."

"Believe it or not, that was Helen's idea at first, keeping it secret. Oh, don't misunderstand, she was very excited about settling down. Back in San Francisco, she had withdrawn all her savings and was having a grand time planning our dream house." Well, that explained all the cash with Vera's things, thought Libby. "But she felt it was for the best not to announce our marriage until her run here was over and she left the stage. You work in the theater. You know that people never want to see a married woman up there on the stage. It would ruin the glamorous image! Besides, if she had told Carlo she was going, he would have made her life miserable.

"When she arrived in Portland, I told her it would be better for me as well to get this business deal straightened out before I announced my marriage." It seemed somehow important to Gerald that Libby see his side of things, and he continued passionately, "I knew I should have told her right away about Charlotte. Every time we met secretly, I started to try, but somehow I finally convinced myself that it would be easier on her if I told her when her run was finished. That way, she wouldn't have to be in the same city with me once she knew what a heel she had married."

"You met her in the evenings." Libby wondered how she could have been so blind as another piece of the puzzle fell into place. "You were regulars at the Anchor. You sat there night after night, listening to your new wife plan your future life together, all the while wondering how to get out of the mess you were in."

He looked at her with respect. "So you found out about the Anchor, too." Suddenly he sat and gave a defeated little chuckle. "I should have simply confessed everything to you that night at Charlotte's and my engagement party. As soon as you started asking me questions, I feared this day was inevitable. That's why you came to my office, isn't it? You suspected me from the beginning."

The look on his face was one almost of betrayal, and Libby felt the need to explain herself. "I didn't suspect you at all then. I really did want to work for the McKennocks because I was hoping to . . . well, it's not important. The truth is . . ." she trailed off. What she had been going to say was that she had liked him that day, quite a lot, but in light of what she knew now, she wasn't sure she wanted to admit it.

He gazed at her with real curiosity, "The police were satisfied that her death was a botched abduction attempt. No one else was suspicious . . . why did you keep on asking questions?"

"I was horrified at the lack of initiative taken by the police department!" Libby paused a moment before adding, "I still am."

"I didn't think anyone would care enough to look closely." He no longer sounded curious, just resigned. "You must have cared for her a great deal to continue investigating her death after everyone else closed the book on it."

"Yes, I did care about her. Ver—Helen—was a friend of mine. But you cared about her a great deal too. That night at the party when we first spoke, what struck me most about you was that you were the first person I had met who actually seemed to be grieving for her. You loved her. How could you have killed her?"

"I didn't mean for her to die! That last night, after her closing performance, I told her I wanted to annul the marriage. She got so upset, she . . . she attacked me." He saw the disbelief in Libby's eyes. "No, truly she did! It was horrible. She was screaming and hitting me and saying she would never go away, she would never leave me, and I . . . I pushed her away, just pushed her, but when she fell she hit her head on the mantel . . ." He stopped, seeming near tears. Libby wondered if he was going to start crying.

When he didn't go on, she prompted him. "I don't understand; was this still at the theater?"

"No, no, we were at my boarding house. I tried to wake her up, but she was . . . dead. I didn't know what to do. I swear to you, it was all a mistake. If only she hadn't fallen so hard and . . ." His next words came out all in a burst, as if he couldn't get them out fast enough. "She was dead, and all I felt was relief that now I could go ahead and marry Charlotte, and everything would work out. But I knew I had to get rid of the body.

"Then I realized . . . no one had seen her come into my boarding house with me. If I could get her back to the theater, they would never connect her death with me. I remembered that some girl had been found dead at the theater a few months before, and I got the idea to make Helen's death look like the same thing."

A light dawned as Libby burst out, "You brought her in through the tunnels!" So Vera *had* left the theater that night, as reliable old Sam had said. It had never occurred to Libby that Vera's body could've reached the tunnel beneath Crowther's through any entrance but the one in the theater's scene shop.

He nodded, almost proudly. "I told you I was working on the docks when Walford found me last year, so I know my way around under the city. And I live down by the waterfront, right near one of the tunnel entrances. I waited until it was the darkest part of the night . . . that was the hardest part, the waiting. I went through her little basket and burned her diary and anything else that looked incriminating. I thought about her wedding ring then, but figured it must be with the other belongings at her lodgings."

"Why didn't you just burn everything?"

"I don't know. I suppose it's because her bag was too big to fit in my fireplace. But I knew I had to get all traces of her away from my room, so I put her bag on my shoulder as I carried her outside through the back door, careful that no one saw me. It was dark that night, and I had waited until nearly three, so the streets were empty. Even so, I was mighty afraid someone would happen along while I was carrying her body in my arms. I was never so relieved as when I finally got her into the tunnel. Once we were inside, it was easy to get to the Variety. I know my way through those tunnels like I know my own hand. I got to the theater and laid her down there on the floor, about where I figured that other one was found. Then I noticed the door to the scene shop was open. They hadn't even locked the back door, can you imagine? I suddenly had this idea that if I put her little bag of things inside in her dressing room, it would look like she never left the theater that night. I think that's really what I wanted to believe, too . . . that she had never left the theater and none of the things that had happened since were real."

He paused, spent. Libby watched him, hardly registering what he was doing until he had pulled the gun out of his pocket. Too late, she realized he was standing between her and the door, which was of course locked. As if reading her mind, he said quietly, "Don't scream. I won't hurt you."

Now that he didn't have to juggle his reporting with the demands of the investigation, time seemed to lay heavy on Peter's hands. That was why he was simply hanging around the *Gazette* offices in the middle of the afternoon, moping as he thought about Libby.

So, even though it wasn't one of his favorite tasks, when John Mayhew asked him to proof the next day's paper, he acquiesced almost eagerly. At least it would take his mind off yesterday's scene at the courthouse. Then he realized that in the coverage of the inquest, which of course dominated the front page, Libby's name would certainly appear. So he flipped the paper over and began with the back page, the Ladies' Page, and its features on fashion, housekeeping, and society.

The McKennock-Williams wedding announcement caught his eye immediately. He breezed through the brief paragraph, but his eye kept returning to the name Fitzgerald Williams. At first, he couldn't figure out why. Then in one instant of clarity, he saw how completely he and Libby had been led astray because of one ridiculous coincidence: that Fanny Watson and Fitzgerald Williams shared a set of initials.

He grabbed his hat and raced for the door, not bothering to explain to Mayhew why he was leaving. The announcement had placed the wedding at three o'clock, in just a few minutes, and though he had no particular love for the McKennock family, Charlotte was the most blameless among them. He felt it was his duty to stop her from marrying a murderer if he could. As his feet ran the several blocks to St. James Church through the downpour, his mind raced as well, continuing to make connections.

So Gerald had been the man at the Anchor; her marriage was the reason Vera was going to leave the act and settle in Portland; and . . . Damn it all, so there had never been *any* link between Polly Pink's death and Vera's! And that meant . . . Could Libby ever forgive him for not hearing what she was trying to tell him after the inquest? She had been right: Crowther hadn't murdered Vera, and Peter had belittled her intelligence and dismissed her intuition.

He was composing his apology in his head when the church reared up in front of him. Sprinting up the steps, he flew through the door soaking wet and gasping for breath. He rushed up to the nearest usher, "The groom . . . can you tell me where he is?" Surprisingly, the unruffled usher seemed to find this question somewhat amusing, but, shrugging and rolling his eyes, he pointed to a side door at the front of the chapel. Peter tried to compose himself as he made his way down the aisle, ignoring the looks he received from Portland's elite.

He reached the door, but as his hand went for the doorknob, a voice to his left stopped him. "Are you looking for the groom?"

"Yes, I . . ."

The well-dressed man with an orchid in his buttonhole pulled him aside. "He's in there with a young lady, and he asked not to be disturbed." The man looked puzzled at this behavior, but was clearly determined not to let anybody pass.

Peter was unsure what to do, then it finally dawned on him what he'd just heard. The man had said a young lady was in there with Gerald. Libby? He was suddenly certain it had to be. After all, Gerald would hardly be having a private conference minutes before his own wedding for any other reason than—but there was no way she could have figured it out! Except the same way you did yourself, he realized belatedly. Why did it seem like she was always one step ahead of him?

He was distracted by the beginnings of a commotion in the church. The pitch and volume of the murmuring crowd went up a few notches, and above it he could hear the unmistakable voice of H. Walford McKennock whispering fiercely, "Where the hell is he?" Peter spotted

McKennock heading down the side aisle with a clergyman dogging his steps a few feet behind him. Seconds later, McKennock spotted Peter.

"What are you doing here?" he asked Peter incredulously, "And what's this about Gerald not being ready to begin the ceremony?" Walford was having a hard time keeping his voice below a roar.

The minister had caught up to them. "No, it was the other young man who told me that Mr. Williams wasn't . . ."

Walford swiveled to the other man, "Well?"

"You must be the bride's father. I'm Dominic Williams, Gerald's cousin, and he . . ."

"Never mind," Walford hissed and marched to the door behind which presumably Gerald still waited. "Gerald! If you value your job, your future, and your hide, show yourself this minute!" The murmuring in the church slowly stopped, as row by row the assembled guests became aware of the unfolding drama.

Into the silence, from behind the door, there was a woman's scream quickly followed by a gunshot. Peter threw himself up against the door, "Libby!"

Nothing moved in the church. Everyone had heard the sharp crack of the gun, and no one breathed as they waited to find out the source of the shot. The door swung open slowly to reveal Libby Seale. Her eyes darted frantically from Peter to Walford to the minister and back to Peter. She tried to speak, failed, and then fainted into Peter's waiting arms.

The police had come and gone, and the guests had left for home. Libby assumed Charlotte had been whisked away as well. The chapel was almost empty now, except for the men from the morgue clearing away all signs of Gerald's body, and Libby and Peter sitting to the side in a front pew. Her hand rested gently in his, and though she was still pale and drained, her composure had returned.

"I begged him not to do it. I thought I had almost convinced him, but when he heard Walford's voice through the door, he just put the gun in his mouth and pulled the trigger, as casually as if he was straightening his tie." Peter waited for the tears to well up, but for the moment, she appeared to be cried out. "To tell you the truth, he looked almost relieved."

"I'm just relieved he didn't decide to take you with him. He had nothing more to lose, after all."

Libby turned in her seat, "He wasn't like that Peter. I always thought that when I found Vera's killer he would be pure evil, and it would be easy to hate him. Instead, all I feel is sad."

He squeezed her hand, and they were silent for a moment. Peter remembered how jealous he had been of Libby's fondness for Gerald. Now it seemed foolish. He searched for a new subject, and realized he had news for Libby. "I didn't even tell you. Walford McKennock is dropping out of the race for mayor."

"I know," she said, "Charlotte told me." She squeezed his hand back.

He should have known. "You always seem to know what I'm going to say before I say it," he tried to keep his tone perfectly casual, "so I suppose you know that now I'm going to ask you to marry me." He was gratified to see complete surprise reflected in her eyes.

"Libby, please say yes." He slipped off the pew and kneeled in front of her, still holding her hand. "I know I was a fool not to listen to you the other day, and I'm not nearly good enough for you, but . . . when I heard that shot and thought for a second you might be gone . . ." He grinned crookedly at her, "From the moment I first saw you, racing down the street, skirts flying, I knew that you were the only woman for me. I love you, Libby Seale. Say you'll be my wife."

She gazed down at him and, unable to help herself, she smiled. Looking at his lopsided smile, his unruly hair, and his eager eyes, she knew beyond a shadow of a doubt that what she felt for him was love. There was no denying it. And the knowledge that he loved her in return made her feel that perhaps the world was not the lonely, painful place she had thought. The word "yes" hovered on her lips, and for a moment, the joy and happiness which might have been hers had she been able to utter it coursed through her.

Then a sharp stab of guilt followed which was worse than pain. She should have told Peter long ago that she was already married. She should have told him long ago that they could never be more than friends. Then she would have spared them both the heartbreak of this moment, with him kneeling here waiting for an answer she couldn't give. Now she would stand revealed as thoughtless, unfaithful, and duplicitous—and would probably lose his respect and friendship as well. It occurred to her she had done exactly what Gerald had done, convincing herself that she could keep her marriage a secret—that somehow there would never come a reckoning.

Peter was standing up, and she realized that he had noted her long pause and lack of an answer. Without stopping to think of the words to use, Libby blurted out all that she had hidden for so long. "I . . . I'm a married woman, Peter. I'm so sorry I never told you, but at first when we met, it didn't occur to me that we would be anything more than friends. By the time I realized my own feelings about you, I was, well, I was ashamed. So much time had gone by, and I didn't know how on earth to raise the subject after I had let you think for so long that I was Miss Libby Seale, unmarried seamstress." She saw the hurt flash in his expression but, was unwilling to stop until she had said everything. "Oh, Peter, I was afraid you would think less of me if you knew that I had run away from my husband . . ." She faltered, but went on, "Yes, my husband, Mr. Greenblatt, whose name I should by rights be using!" She paused yet again, not knowing how to begin to explain what she had done or why. He deserved so much more than any answer she had to offer him. "I'm so sorry . . ."

Peter looked at her for a moment. When he spoke, his tone was lightly barbed, "I take it, then, that your answer is 'no'?"

Libby cringed. He wasn't going to make this easy, but she knew she deserved every bit of mockery he might throw at her. "I know . . . I should have found some way of telling you before . . . before now." He stood looking at her for a long while, unspeaking. She saw a range of emotions in his eyes: sadness, incomprehension, anger. She couldn't stand the silence, so she went on, trying to fight back tears. "Oh, Peter, please understand. I knew it would hurt you if you knew, and I never wanted to hurt you. But I guess I always knew eventually I would have to, and now . . . now I've hurt you worse than if I'd just told you right away, that night after the McKennock ball in the carriage when . . . Oh, I've made such a mess of things . . ." She lost her battle against the tears, and they rolled down her cheeks silently as she waited for him to talk.

When he finally did, he seemed to be carefully trying to remain composed. "Miss Seale. Or I suppose I should say Mrs. Greenblatt? I suppose I do understand, at least in some way. At least now I understand why you always seemed to pull away whenever I . . ." Suddenly, anger burst through his shock and reserve, "No, dammit, Libby, I don't understand. I don't understand why you didn't trust me enough as a friend, if nothing else, to tell me the truth. And I don't understand why you came here to Portland at all if you have a home and a husband in New York. Was this all some sort of game? Why did you get married in the first place, if . . ."

Libby broke in, "Peter . . . Peter. It wasn't like that at all. I never wanted to be married. Or, what I mean is it wasn't *my* choice to marry Mr. Greenblatt. If there was anyone I've ever wanted to marry it's you!"

At that Peter stopped short and gazed at her dumbly. He tried to be pleased, but all he felt was confusion. What sort of woman fell in love with one man already having married another? "I don't understand," he said. But he was no longer shouting.

"Mr. Greenblatt was . . . rather, is a business partner of my father's . . ." she began, and the whole story poured out of her: the pressure from her family to marry, the mounting horror of her three disastrous weeks as Mrs. Harold Greenblatt, her hurried flight (arm in a homemade sling) from the only home she had ever known. She stumbled and halted as she made her way through the story, but Peter remained silent, offering her no support. When she finally finished her narrative though, her eyes were red-rimmed but dry, and the look on Peter's face no longer held any anger, but sadness.

"Libby, I'm sorry." He looked up at her and amended, "Not sorry for mistaking your intentions or for falling in love with you—but sorry that something like that should ever have been allowed to happen to you." His voice became wistful, "You deserve better. Much better." He took one of her hands, bent down, and kissed it gently. She gazed down at the top of his head, and her heart broke.

"I do love you, Peter. You must know that. I . . . I've known it for a long time, though I didn't want to admit to myself that that's what it was." She leaned in and rested her cheek on the top of his tousled hair. They remained curled into each other that way as the minutes passed, breathing as one in the empty church. To any outside eye, thought Libby, they might be an artist's idealized depiction of young love. But still they lingered, silent, since they both knew that when this moment passed, when they finally left the sanctuary of this pew, they would have to face reality.

Finally, Peter sat up slowly and turned to her. "I should go before John Mayhew sends out a search party looking for me. I did leave the office rather abruptly." He tried to keep his voice steady, with only partial success.

"Can I . . . will I still . . . see you?" Libby asked hesitantly, afraid to catch his eye. She knew she must sound pathetic, so she tried to brighten her voice, tried to mimic that breezy tone of Peter's that she loved so well, "Is there any chance the St. James Choral Society might be planning a musical evening sometime soon?"

He stood and answered slowly, "I don't think so, Libby." He paused and said with a ghost of a smile, "They felt that the singers should devote some time to learning a few new tunes."

She took his meaning and felt cold thinking of the empty days and weeks ahead of her. Still, she had to admire his way with a metaphor, and so she tried (for what might be one of the last times) to meet his sally with a matching wit. "Well, I suppose it would be unfair to expect more of a little city like Portland. It's really just a town compared to New York." Why had she brought up New York? She didn't want to think about New York. "Do you have any idea how long their . . . hiatus might be?" She tried to smile, but all the joy had gone out of their banter.

Suddenly, he was serious again. "I'm sorry, Libby. I shouldn't have tried to make a joke out of the situation. It isn't funny. I honestly don't know if I can be your friend. Or be *just* your friend. Not when I was hoping for so much more." He turned away from her, "But . . . is there any reason for me to hope the situation might change? I can't say I'll wait forever, but if I only knew there was an end in sight . . ."

She didn't answer at once, but glanced up, and the large cross over the altar caught her eye. What was she doing here? Little Libby Seletzky from Rivington Street . . . in an Anglican church three thousand miles from her family and her faith, in a city where nobody knew the first thing about her, where she didn't even have a job anymore. All she had was Peter. In a moment, he would walk out the door, and she might never see him again. She considered explaining to him about the Jewish divorce, how she was powerless unless her husband agreed to provide the necessary *get*. But the thought of explaining Talmudic law to Peter was more than she could face at the moment. Instead, she said dully, "I should go home." And for a moment she didn't know whether she meant New York or Mrs. Pratt's boarding house.

"You don't mean back to Mr. Greenblatt?" Suddenly, he sounded like a little boy.

Hearing his barely concealed despair, Libby sensed a sudden change in his attitude. Peter had assumed she meant home as in New York. And, despite what he had just been saying, she could tell he didn't want her to leave—not to leave Portland, not to leave forever. He didn't want to be apart from her any more than she did from him. It didn't mean he was ready yet to forgive her—perhaps for a while there would be an awkwardness between them, perhaps they would even avoid each other for a few weeks—but she felt certain that this was not the end. "Actually, I meant Mrs. Pratt's," she said, and her voice was warmer.

Of course, she thought to herself, of course, she had meant Mrs. Pratt's. How could she even consider going back East? She wasn't the same girl she had been in New York, and she knew she didn't belong there anymore. No matter how low she was feeling at this moment, even if it was sometimes a struggle to fit in, she knew coming to Portland had been the right thing for her to do. For a moment, her spirit swelled as she thought about Portland's damp, green beauty, the masses of roses in the summer, and the sense of space and freedom sweetened by the fresh Oregon breeze. Even the thought of the near endless rain, which had depressed her when she first arrived, caused her to smile. It wasn't so bad, really. Mostly the rain was no more than a light drizzle, and like most locals, she just ignored it and went about her business as usual. Like most locals . . .

She wondered when this miraculous change had overcome her. Looking back, she couldn't pinpoint the moment. But she realized that when she said the word home now, it was only Portland that she meant. Suddenly, she knew she would be able to finish the letter she had been trying to write her mother, because for the first time, she knew what it was she wanted to say. She was anxious to get back to her room to begin. "I'm ready to go now, too," she said.

Side by side, she and Peter went up the aisle and out onto the stone porch. At the bottom of the steps, Peter turned to her and kissed her lightly on the forehead. "You'll be all right getting home?" he asked. She replied firmly, "Yes. I'm fine," and she meant it. And with that, Peter squared his shoulders and walked off toward the *Gazette*'s offices without looking back.

She watched him go for a moment, without despair and without pain. Too many waves of emotion had crested and broken over her this afternoon and she found that now all she was longing for was her own warm, dry bed. She would curl up in her sweet little room under the eaves and finally write her mother. As she walked through the chilly, rainy afternoon, she began to compose the letter.

Dear Mama,

I am across the country in Portland, Oregon. I know that I must have caused you great pain by leaving, and I am sorry for that. But I am not coming back. Mr. Greenblatt did something terrible, and you must believe I had no choice but to go. I am happy here, Mama. And I am going to stay . . .

Yes, I am going to stay, she thought. Peter would get over his hurt eventually and be her friend. John Mayhew, too. Perhaps she would take the Englunds up on their invitation to pay them a visit. And Mrs. Pratt would make her a cup of hot tea when she got back to the boarding house, and they could sit beside the stove and stroke the cats as they talked about silly, inconsequential things. Tomorrow would be soon enough to look for another job. Just picturing the scene, she felt warmer.

Gathering her damp coat tightly around her, Libby Seale smiled and headed home.

Read on for an excerpt from the
next Libby Seale Mystery by M. J. Zellnik

Murder at the Rose Paperworks

COMING SOON FROM MIDNIGHT INK

PROLOGUE

THE SUN HAD BEEN up less than two hours, and already Andrew Matson knew it was going to be a lousy day. One of the two revolving boilers was coughing, and it looked like he'd have to take the damn thing out of commission for at least thirty-six hours, until it cooled down enough to get inside and check it out.

Striding across the cement floor of the Rose Paperworks, Matson gazed out over the sea of glossy black hair, and once more cursed his boss's decision to replace real Americans with this cheap-as-dirt foreign labor. At least, he was glad to see the main boiler had sputtered and come to life. As he passed, two men tossed the first rags of the day into its steaming confines. He was on his way to deal with the third, and by far, the most serious of the just-beginning day. Something was wrong with the hollander, the heart of the mill. It was a giant steel cylinder, lined with rotating knife blades, which in less than three minutes could turn stripped rags into a thick paste suitable for boiling. Usually it whirred and hummed all day, providing a background drone to everything else that happened in the mill, but this morning, just after the whistle marking the start of the workday had sounded, it had rasped a few times and stopped with a grinding metallic groan. He thought there was probably a dead bird or a rat (hardly a novelty in a paper mill) gumming up the inside works. Wouldn't be the first time, but today of all days he didn't need this. By the time the poor creature, or what was left of it, was fished out, and the machine was all cleaned, it'd be lunchtime. One dead bird meant missed quotas for the day, and Mr. Rose would have his hide. He was hoping against hope the problem was electrical.

He reached the foot of the staircase leading up to the catwalks. In front of him a couple dozen chattering Chinese girls were bent over their laps, ripping buttons and hooks and whalebone from the scraps of material before throwing them into bins. Who knew, thought Matson with annoyance, what in the hell they were saying. "Enough chitchat! Back to work!" he yelled to no one in particular and, in spite of the language barrier, his order was clear enough. The incomprehensible babble subsided as he ascended the network of catwalks that connected the various sections of the factory, allowing the foreman and management to supervise what went on below, and to move from one end of the vast space to the other without having to skirt the massive vats and presses.

Matson had climbed the staircase nearest to the hollander. As soon as he reached the top, he could see down into its red-slicked interior. Two things entered his consciousness at almost the same moment. The first was that there was far too much blood for this to have been a bird or a rat, and the second was that, on the far side of the great cauldron, a section of the catwalks which led to the executive offices had collapsed and was partially sunk into the hollander itself. A horrible possibility entered his mind—who else ever used that section of catwalk?—just as he noticed what could only be the remains of a human leg, still encased in a chewed-up leather boot. All thought of missed quotas fled his mind as, almost silently, Andrew Matson fainted.

ONE

Libby Seale had been thinking about husbands. Two husbands in particular—the husband she wanted but couldn't marry, and the husband she already had but wished she could lose. So perhaps it was inevitable that her first thought, upon hearing about Hiram Rose's untimely death, was how lucky his wife was now to be a widow. One look, however, at the tears tracking down Adele Rose's plump cheeks made Libby realize that this particular wife did not share her view. She quickly arranged her own features into something resembling more conventional sympathy, and hoped none of the others in the room had noticed her initial look of, well, one could only call it envy.

For Libby had been trying in vain for three weeks now to think of some way she could be rid of the man she was forced to call her husband. Her marriage to Harold Greenblatt had been an arranged one. Although she felt it was a travesty to have to call her marriage just that, it had culminated in one particularly violent episode which left her with her arm in a sling and a determination to take no more. The next day she had run away, taking the train from New York's Penn Station to the furthest destination she could find—Portland, Oregon.

It was here in Portland that she had met Peter Eberle, a young reporter for the *Portland Gazette*, and over the months she had known him she had, quite simply, fallen in love with him. Just over three weeks before, Peter—who at that point was still unaware of the existence of Mr. Greenblatt—had asked her to marry him. She had been forced then to tell him everything: that she was a married woman, that she had run away from her legal husband and family, and that she had even changed her name so no one in Portland would know she was married. She explained how in Jewish law a wife couldn't get a religious divorce without the husband's consent, and if she chose to ignore her faith and get a civil divorce she would become an outcast, ostracized by her entire family and community.

Peter had claimed to understand, and had forgiven her the deception, but Libby hadn't clapped eyes on him or spoken even a syllable to him since that awkward day. She missed him dreadfully. She suspected he missed her too, but she hadn't had the nerve to call on him at the offices of the *Portland Gazette*, and he had made no attempt to see her. She feared Peter might be lost to her forever. As lost to her as Hiram Rose was to the woman crying in front of her.

She was still wearing her hat and coat, having arrived at the Rose home moments before only to be told the shocking news that there had been a tragic accident at the paper mill. Libby wondered if she should simply turn around and head home, leaving the somber family in front of her to grieve in peace. But her offer was brushed aside immediately by Miss Baylis, the Rose's pale-faced governess who had drawn her aside to explain the situation.

"Oh, no, Miss Seale, please stay and wait with us. I can't bear to be on my own with them . . ." she gestured toward the sofa, where Adele

Rose's hand was being held by an equally distraught Eva Fowler, her sister-in-law and Hiram Rose's sister. Mrs. Fowler and her husband lived next door, and Libby had been hired to do some dressmaking work for both ladies, though the work was always conducted here at the Rose's much larger and more accommodating home. "Mr. Fowler has gone off to the mill to find out exactly what has happened. All we know is that Mr. Rose fell into some sort of machine or other, and . . ." Miss Baylis paused, not wanting to get more graphic than necessary, "and Mrs. Rose keeps asking how this could have happened, and I don't have any answers to give her. Besides, I really ought to look after the boys, and make sure they are . . . well, as well as can be expected."

Miss Baylis cast a worried glanced toward the Rose's two younger sons, a set of seven-year-old twins named Isadore and Adolphus (but called Izzy and Fussy by everyone but their governess), who were over by the fire playing with the cast-iron pokers. Izzy already had a smudge of ash over one eye, and Libby could tell Miss Baylis was growing anxious as to what might be coming next. The twins were holy terrors, fascinated by fire, and required constant supervision to keep them from burning down the entire house. There was no sign in the room of Elliot, the oldest son, a moody boy of sixteen, and Libby wondered if he had preferred school to the gloom at home. However, she didn't see how she could escape. "Of course," she said. "I'm happy to stay. At least, of course, until Mr. Fowler returns with more news. I'm sure then the family will want to be left alone."

Divesting herself of her damp outerwear, Libby made her way to the sofa and tried her best to console to the two weeping women ensconced there. Although she would not have said she was close to either woman, of the two she liked Mrs. Fowler better. Adele Rose was a rather haughty woman, with the look of a pampered lapdog. She was soft and pink and rounded at every extremity. It took all of Libby's ingenuity, not to mention the sturdiest whalebone corset available from Sears & Roebuck, to bring Mrs. Rose anywhere near to the ideal of a fashionably dressed lady. Mrs. Fowler, on the other hand, presented a different set of problems from a dressmaker's perspective. She was now three months pregnant, and just beginning to show. Even in the two weeks she had been working for her, Libby had been forced to let out her bodices twice, in one case having to resew one of the brand-new gowns which she had made and which had not even been worn out of the house yet.

This was frustrating, but Libby couldn't afford to complain since it was precisely this need for constant alterations that was responsible for the household hiring Libby on a more or less regular part-time basis. And Libby needed the work. Her previous employment at Portland's Variety Theater (as a wardrobe mistress) had been abruptly terminated when the theater closed almost a month before, and now she was hoping to make ends meet until she found a new permanent position by doing piecemeal work for Portland's elite. Her friend Charlotte McKennock, daughter of one of the city's richest men, had provided her with introductions to a dozen or so wealthy and influential matrons, but other than a few small one-day jobs, the work she was doing for Mrs. Rose and Mrs. Fowler was her only regular source of income.

Although there were many available seamstresses in Portland, two factors had tipped the balance in Libby's favor when Mrs. Rose had been choosing whom to hire. The first was that Adele was an Easterner, like Libby, and it pleased her to have a dressmaker who had worked in New York's Gold Eagle Dressworks, and who had firsthand knowledge of high-society fashions which were only now, a year later, reaching the smaller cities on America's West Coast. The second factor, much as Libby disliked to admit it to herself, was her religion. Even though she herself had made no mention of it, Adele had ended their initial interview by asking point blank if Libby were Jewish. When she had, stammering, answered in the affirmative, fearing that an anti-Semitic Mrs. Rose would then ask her to leave by the back exit, she was surprised when Adele had only smiled and said, "Good." It transpired that the Rose family were also Jewish, although like Libby herself they had altered their name (Rosenberg to Rose in their case, Seletzky to Seale in hers) in order to sound less Hebraic. The admission shocked Libby, for she would never have guessed. Even now, after two weeks working in the house, she had seen no visible signs of a household run along traditional Jewish lines. There was no menorah, no mezuzah by the door, and she knew for a fact that the cook had prepared a pork roast for supper one night the previous week. But, surprised and a bit discomfited as she was, Libby could not afford to hold their assimilated ways against the Roses, since they were her employers. And she had to admit that as a woman who had abandoned her husband and fled her family, she had no right to sit in judgment on anybody.

Libby sat on the sofa beside Adele, and patted her ineffectually on the hand. "Oh, Miss Seale . . . how could this have happened?" Adele wailed. "I don't understand."

"Adele, please try to control yourself," Eva Fowler said gently, but with a hint of disapproval. Although more conventionally feminine than her sister-in-law, Mrs. Fowler was in more control of her emotions, despite the fact that it was her brother who had been killed. "Augustus will be home soon, and we will find out what happened. You must be strong for the children. Hiram would want . . ." she faltered, and for a moment it seemed she would cry. "He would have *wanted* you to be brave."

The two women leaned into each other and cried softly. Libby sat uncomfortably wondering how long it would be before Mr. Fowler would return. She tried to feel sad that Mr. Rose was dead, but she had barely known him. She had only met him once, a week before, when he had paid her for the work she had done thus far, and she had not even liked him on that occasion. He had insisted on paying her himself, since he did not allow his wife to handle money, and he had queried her closely on the invoice she had written up for him carefully detailing the hours she had worked and fabrics she had purchased. It appeared Hiram had kept an iron grip on the accounts, and she wondered who would be responsible for paying her for the new work that was bound to come her way, now that the entire household would need to be fitted with proper mourning attire.

The crumpled ball of paper flew across the newsroom and hit its intended target smack in the middle of his forehead. Peter Eberle looked up, annoyed. Across the large room, filled with inky presses and overflowing trays of type, a grinning John Mayhew raised his empty hands in a gesture of innocence.

"Sorry, Petey. I just wanted to see if you'd even notice." The lanky editor crossed the room in two strides, and perched on the edge of his star reporter's desk. His face showed both amusement and concern as he leaned in to talk to Peter. "I have to tell you, you haven't seemed all here lately." He paused for a moment, regarding the man before him. Peter's face was pale and there were deep circles under his eyes.

"I'm fine, John, really I am." Peter didn't meet Mayhew's eyes as he picked up the paper ball and lobbed it into the trash can.

Mayhew pressed on. "I have noticed we've been seeing a good deal less of your friend Miss Seale for the past few weeks . . ."

"I might have known I couldn't hide anything from a newsman of your perspicacity." Peter tried to smile, but it wasn't very convincing.

"Don't waste your five-dollar words on me, Eberle. You can't intimidate me into backing off. Truth is, I'm wondering if I should be worried about you." Wary of seeming too overbearing, Mayhew went back to his desk and sat facing Peter.

Peter knew he owed his boss the truth. "I'm sorry, John. I haven't much wanted to speak about it, but you are right. Lib—Miss Seale and I have parted ways . . . but it was on completely amicable terms.

Believe me." He rubbed his face, "Besides, a man like me needs his freedom. And maybe I'm just tired. You've been working me too hard, that's all."

"Working you too hard?" The older man laughed. "I'd say things have been pretty quiet around here since Miss Seale—" he cut himself off. "Since the fuss over at the Variety was finished up. Fact is, I'm about getting ready to send you out to cover the church choir beat, or to ask you to write a scathing exposé on the latest hemlines from Paris. Of course," he paused, "that might require getting a quote from a local seamstress."

Not meeting Mayhew's eyes, Peter rearranged the blotter on his desk. "The last time I checked, there was more than one seamstress in Portland." After a brief pause, he looked up, and there was a little more of the old fire in his eyes. "Say, John, do you suppose there might be a story in that? I mean, something about the rise of new tradesmen and business people setting up shop here in town. I noticed when Jack Harkness dropped off the latest Portland Business Listings, the damn thing was twice as many pages as last year's edition, even though the national economy is still doing so poorly."

Before Mayhew could form a reply, the bell at the front counter rang. Both men looked up to see a dark-haired youth, too impatient to wait for a response, come bounding into the back past the main counter. "Half-Cent, I didn't expect to see you until Friday to clean the presses," said Mayhew. Billy, or Half-Cent as he was affectionately known by all the newsmen at the *Gazette*, had been hanging around the newspaper offices since he was in knee-pants, though now he was now fourteen and an aspiring newsman of nearly six feet. The nickname had begun as a comment on the fact that he was smaller even than the so-called "penny boys" who sold the *Portland Gazette* for that price on the city's street corners and though now he was almost as tall as Mayhew, the nickname remained. Half-Cent did regular odd jobs around the *Gazette* in exchange for training on the mechanical business of running a newspaper, and John Mayhew, with no family of his own, had come to regard the boy as something of a surrogate son. He was teaching him everything from how to set type to how to write an eye-catching headline.

"I just saw the police heading out of town," Billy panted, out of breath from running. "I found out they're heading to the mill . . . I heard one of them say the body is too mangled to even move . . . if you hurry you can get this into the afternoon edition, right? I came to tell you as soon as I heard about it!"

"Slow down, Billy. What mill?" asked Peter, already pulling on his jacket and stuffing his notepad in the pocket.

"That's what I'm trying to tell you! There's been some kind of accident down at the Rose Paperworks! Hiram Rose himself, all messed up something awful in the machinery. When the workday started, some of those coolies they got working there found him!"

"Hiram Rose, eh?" Peter reviewed what he knew about Rose: wealthy Jewish industrialist . . . family in Portland for two generations . . . paper mill one of the most venerable of Portland's businesses, but one of the last to use the old rag-paper manufacturing methods . . . at the center of the recent labor disputes that had flared up right around New Year's, if he remembered it correctly. Rose had fired all the white workers, replacing them with Chinese who would work for much less. There had been quite a large workmen's demonstration too . . . he would have to remember to look up the specifics later, when he had a chance. But now he needed to head out.

"Here you go, Half-Cent," he said, slipping a quarter into Billy's grateful hand as he ran out the door. He called over his shoulder, "Save me some room on the front page below the fold, John! I'll be back here in time to write up what I have before we go to press!"

ABOUT THE AUTHOR

Seduced by Portland, Oregon's beauty and colorful history, **M. J. Zellnik** enjoyed learning more about her adopted home while writing *Murder at the Portland Variety*, her first novel. A New York City native, she divides her time between New York and Portland, and is working on a second Libby Seale adventure.